Praise for
Gardens of Water

"Sensitive and thought-provoking, *Gardens of Water* is set in a perfectly realized Istanbul, a city where tradition and modernity grind together like the fragments of a collapsing building."

—*The New York Times Book Review*

"A fascinating, heartbreaking book." —*USA Today*

"Drew tells a story mostly related to aftermaths, to the consequences of choices that can shake the ground of one's life." —*Chicago Tribune*

"Solid and persuasive . . . [A] novel about lovers crossed not by the stars but by the clash of cultures." —*Kirkus Reviews*

"Effortlessly transports readers to a wrecked Istanbul and finds shards of hope in the mountains of rubble." —*Publishers Weekly*

Gardens
of Water

RANDOM HOUSE

TRADE PAPERBACKS

NEW YORK

Gardens
of Water

A Novel

Alan Drew

2009 Random House Trade Paperback Edition

Copyright © 2008 by Alan Drew

RANDOM HOUSE TRADE PAPERBACKS and colophon are trademarks of Random House, Inc.
READER'S CIRCLE and colophon are trademarks of Random House, Inc.

Published in the United States by Random House Trade Paperbacks an imprint of The Random House Publishing Group, a division of Random House, Inc., New York.

Originally published in hardcover in the United States by Random House, an imprint of The Random House Publishing Group, a division of Random House, Inc., in 2008.

ISBN 978-0-8129-7844-5

LIBRARY OF CONGRESS CATALOGING-IN-PUBLICATION DATA

Drew, Alan

Gardens of water: a novel / Alan Drew.

p. cm.

1. Families—Fiction. 2. Muslim families—Fiction.
3. Americans—Turkey—Fiction. 4. Earthquakes—Turkey—Fiction. 5. Turkey—Fiction. 6. Domestic fiction. I. Title.

PS3604.R48G37 2008

813'.6—dc22   2007019959

Printed in the United States of America

www.randomhousereaderscircle.com

9 8 7 6 5 4 3 2 1

Book design by Barbara M. Bachman

For Miriam

When the earth with her quaking will quake,
And her burden the earth will cast forth, And
man will say: "What is the matter with her?"
On that Day she will tell forth her news, Because
thy lord will have inspired her. On that Day the
people will go forward individually, that they
may be shown their works. Whosoever has done
an atom's weight of good will see it, And whoso
has done an atom's weight of evil will see it.

—*The Qur'an, Sura 99*

The enemy of the father will never be the
friend of his son.

—*Kurdish proverb*

TURKISH PRONUNCIATION GUIDE

While the reader does not need to know all the subtle sound and accent differences between Turkish and English, it is important to recognize the differences in the following consonants.

c is pronounced like the *j* in *James.*

j is pronounced like the *s* in *leisure.*

ç is pronounced like the *ch* in *child.*

ş is pronounced like the *sh* in *show.*

ğ has no sound, and simply lengthens the vowel sound that comes before it. For example, Başioğlu is pronounced *Bash-ee-oh-loo.*

Part One

Chapter 1

IN THE RUSH OF BODIES TO BOARD THE FERRY LEAVING İSTANBUL for Gölcük, Sinan lost his son.

Five minutes earlier İsmail had been tugging Sinan in the opposite direction, back toward the city, deep into the labyrinth of arcades and electronics stores of the Sirkeci neighborhood. Sinan suspected it was for the exact purpose of missing the ferry home and delaying the pain of the circumcision ceremony that evening. The boy stomped across the bricks in his white circumcision costume, one hand squeezing Sinan's fingers and the other hoisting his tasseled staff in the air like a pasha leading a parade. Sinan let himself be pulled for a while, but the horn had already sounded, and, even though he, too, wanted to delay the ceremony, they couldn't miss that ferry.

When they had reached Reşadiye Avenue, Sinan pulled İsmail into the street just as the traffic broke, Sinan's shoulders rocking back and forth in an awkward dance on his bad foot. He finally pushed İsmail through the metal gate to the ferry dock just in time for them to join the throng of men and women leaving work for the day. They ran from the shade of the dock back out into the searing summer sun, Sinan leading İsmail this time through a sea of elbows, shoulders, and damp backs. They climbed the thin plank of wood used as a bridge from dock to boat, the green water beneath them churning with translucent jellyfish, and they entered the smoky cabin, where İsmail dropped his staff. He let go of Sinan's hand, and before Sinan could grab his son's arm, the boy disappeared, swallowed by the wave of bodies.

Now Sinan shoved through the crowd to get to the boy, but his foot made it difficult. He pushed against the stomachs of men smoking cigarettes, turning sideways to make himself thinner. "*Affedersiniz,*" he said to each person he touched, in a voice barely concealing his rising panic. "Excuse me." But the more he struggled forward, the more he was shoved backward by the jostling mob, and soon he was forced all the way to the other side of the ferry, his back leaning against a rusty chain that kept him from tumbling into the Bosporus.

"Allah, Allah," he said out loud. A man standing next to him glanced in his direction.

"Too many men," the man said. He lit a cigarette, the smoke flying away from his face. "Too many men, not enough city."

"My boy's lost," Sinan said.

The man turned around. He was taller than Sinan and he was able to see over the heads of the crowd.

"Where?" the man said.

"At the entrance."

The man stood on his toes and yelled across the cabin in a voice so powerful it silenced the crowd.

"*Erkek çocuk nerede?*"

That started a chorus of echoes. "Where's the boy?" strangers called, their voices rising above the sound of the engine straining to pull away from the dock. "Where's the boy? Where's the boy?" they yelled into the wind, as the ferry nosed its white hull out into the blue water. "İsmail!" Sinan called, joining his voice to the chorus. The men yelled "İsmail" too, and a pandemonium of concern radiated out through the cabin.

Then thirty feet away, rising above the heads of hundreds of people, came his son. At first İsmail seemed to be floating under his own power, a princely ghost taken flight in the sea-whipped wind, but as he drew nearer, Sinan saw the shoulders on which İsmail rested. The man elbowed through the parting crowd, a cigarette burning in his mouth, his large, hairy hands wrapped around the boy's stomach. İsmail's white teeth gleamed against his skin and his black eyes shone in the afternoon light. The staff was clasped in his fist, and for a moment he seemed to be a king raised high above the people of İstanbul.

"*Teşekkür ederim,*" Sinan said when the stranger handed him his son.

"*Bir şey değil.*"

WHEN THE FERRY DOCKED in their suburb of Gölcük three hours later, İsmail wouldn't let go of the railing. Sinan touched the top of İsmail's head, and reminded him of the gifts he would receive after the ceremony. He tickled İsmail's armpits and tugged on his earlobe, which didn't earn him the usual dimpled smile, much less a loosening of the boy's white-knuckled grip. A few women, shuffling toward the exit, smiled in sympathy. The man who had carried İsmail on his shoulders slid a one-million-lira note into the pocket of the boy's white satin vest.

"What's your name?" the man said.

"İsmail."

"İsmail what?" the man said.

"İsmail Başioğlu."

"That's a fine name. A strong man's name." The man winked at Sinan. "Can't stay a boy forever," he said.

Sinan thought the man was scolding him for İsmail's age—nine, at least a year too old for the *sünnet*—but the man's smile betrayed nothing but generosity.

When the deck was cleared of people, Sinan touched his son's hand and felt the boy's fingers stiffen. "We have to go," he said.

Behind İsmail, the sun collapsed in red bands along the horizon.

Sinan knelt beside İsmail and put his hands on the boy's shoulders. "It *will* hurt, but that pain will pass and God will know you're willing to endure pain for him. A man has to endure pain, İsmail. But it will pass."

İsmail looked at the ground, his long eyelashes pressed against his cheeks.

"Baklava soaked in honey afterward? Two, maybe?"

Finally, the boy smiled.

THEY HAD LEFT HOME that morning, just as sunlight broke above the bay, and took the three ferries the length of the Gulf of İzmit into İstanbul. Sinan hadn't been to İstanbul since they had first arrived in the city from Yeşilli, their village in the Southeast, seven years ago, but it had been İsmail's special request to be paraded around the city on the day of his circumcision. Sinan hated İstanbul—too many people, too much cement, too little sky—but İsmail was fascinated by it. Even after a full day of stomping around the city that caused Sinan's foot to ache, his son's fascination rubbed off on Sinan.

People had been kinder than he had expected. A woman in a pastry shop had offered the boy a slice of chocolate cake laced with pistachio nuts, a bite of which İsmail promptly dropped on the white satin of his pasha's costume, soiling the garment that had cost Sinan a week's earnings. A taxi driver gave them a free ride up to Topkapı Palace, where, like sultans of another age, they gazed out over the shimmering waters of the Bosporus. They marveled at Boğaziçi Bridge, standing like a huge metal suture between the hills of Asia and Europe. They counted the boats crisscrossing the Sea of Marmara— massive tankers that shoved the water aside, lumbering car ferries leaning into the current, driftwood-sized fishing spits—and settled on the number forty-six. As they passed the fish houses in Kumkapı neighborhood, the musicians at one of the tourist restaurants left their table and followed İsmail down the street, blowing their reed flutes to announce his passing.

Nilüfer and İrem had stayed home to cook the food for the party tonight. If they had still lived in Yeşilli, Sinan's aunts and uncles and cousins would have helped, and the whole family would have paraded İsmail through the unpaved streets. Sinan kept the memories of his own *sünnet* celebration to himself; he didn't want his son to know what he was missing. But the images had flashed in his mind throughout the day—his father hoisting him onto their best horse, his mother walking beside him, one hand resting on his knee, and the horse's belly swaying against her own pregnant bulge. It was one of his last memories of her, and even though her face had been white and she wouldn't smile, he hadn't thought to tell his father to get her home. Three days later, his father would leave Sinan with his aunt while he drove his mother to the good hospital in Diyarbakır. She was bleeding, his aunt told Sinan. The doctors would make her better and he would have a little sister or brother when they came home. Only his father came back.

Now the call to sunset prayer echoed from dozens of speakers, the amplified voices ricocheting off the cement walls of apartment buildings. Sinan was nervous, too, and a knot the size of an apricot had hardened inside his stomach. The walk home took them past the fishmonger's, and Sinan gave İsmail money to buy the fish heads and severed tails for the street cats. Eren Bey, the fish seller, wrapped the remains in paper and handed them to İsmail.

"Wait," Eren Bey said, holding up one bloody finger. From a fern-lined basket filled with his best *palamut*, he grabbed the largest fish, wrapped it up with a sprig of oregano, and dropped it into İsmail's hands. "Fish will make you a strong man." He flexed his bicep and slapped the bump of muscle. "All the women in the world will kiss your feet."

Eren winked and İsmail smiled.

"Please," Sinan said, "he's just a boy."

"*Efendim*," the fish seller said, his hands held out as if he were mildly insulted, "just a joke."

They stopped at the rotting wooden *konak* where the street cats lived, but the cats were not there. İsmail threw the fish parts through the broken window anyway, a gift for their return. They took *maghrib* prayer at mosque, and Sinan listened as İsmail stumbled through the Arabic. Afterward, they climbed the hill that led to their apartment, and the bright lights of the amusement park below spun against the darkening sky. Sinan promised, as always, to take İsmail there some-day for a ride on the Ferris wheel.

By the time they reached their apartment, the knot in Sinan's stomach had grown to the size of a small apple. He massaged the spot with his fingertips and it rolled around inside his stomach. He won-dered, briefly, if he could delay the ceremony one more year. But people were already coming, the *sünnetci* was already scheduled, and he would have to make his son suffer the pain tonight.

"Go on and see Ahmet," Sinan said to İsmail. He knew his brother-in-law would spoil the boy, treat him like a child one last time before İsmail had to bear the burden of trying to be a man. "I'll come and get you at the grocery later."

Sinan climbed the curving staircase of his apartment building. American music blasted down the stairwell and rattled the metal rail-ing. He hated their apartment. From the outside it looked nice: the cement walls were painted yellow and the stairway to the front door was made of mediocre marble that shined when the apartment man-ager bothered to polish it. But inside you could hear a man whisper through the plywood doors, the plaster walls were chipped, and on stormy afternoons, when the rain rolled across the bay as though the sea had stood up and formed a wall, the wind slipped through the cracks in the mortar and deposited saltwater and cement dust in the corners of the living room.

In the kitchen, Nilüfer was covered in sweat and a dusting of flour. Little balls of dough stuck to her fingertips.

"Sinan." She smiled. "*Canım,*" she said, and purposely pressed her doughy hands to his face.

"Stop that, Nilüfer," he said, but he let her smear the dough across his cheeks.

She kissed him once on each doughy cheek. Sinan tucked a stray strand of hair beneath her head scarf.

"How long has this been going on?" he asked, motioning with his head toward the music blasting through the ceiling.

She shrugged. "Forty-five minutes?" She looked behind Sinan. "Where's İsmail?"

"With Ahmet."

"Well, go get him. I need to get him ready." She squeezed loaves of bread he had brought from the grocery that morning. "This bread is too hard. You need a new bread man," she said. She walked into the kitchen. "The yogurt is runny. This heat is ruining it all. The *börek* won't rise, the peppers are like rubber."

"Nilüfer, it will be fine," he said. "I'll go to the store and get more bread. Stop worrying."

She leaned a fist on a hip and blew air through her teeth. "As though you don't worry."

He touched his stomach and made a face.

She waved her hand at him. "See."

He laughed. "All right, all right."

He looked around the corner to where his daughter sat watching television and made sure İrem could not see them before touching Nilüfer's hips and kissing her on the lips—a long kiss, the kind he usually gave her only in their bedroom.

"Quit with that," she said, but her hands rested on his chest. She slapped him on the shoulder and whispered, "We don't need any more children."

"What's this?" Sinan said. Some sort of pastry sat in a circular tray on the kitchen table. It wasn't a Turkish dish.

"Pecan pie," Nilüfer said with an astonished lifting of her eyebrows. "Sarah Hanım brought it down for the party." She glanced toward the ceiling.

"The American's wife?" he said. "Pecans?"

An American family occupied the sixth floor, the one directly above them. They spent only the summers here, just sitting around, drinking wine on the terrace, and listening to jazz music, as far as Sinan could tell.

"Her name's Sarah," Nilüfer said, glaring at him. "Sarah Roberts, and she's nice."

"Maybe, then, she could teach her son some manners." He pointed to the throbbing ceiling.

"We should have invited them. I feel bad."

"You should be helping your mother," Sinan said to his daughter, sticking his head around the corner into the living room.

"Baba, I've been working all day." She didn't look at him when she spoke. He didn't know what it was about fifteen-year-old girls, but he had never known a child so rude to her parents.

He glanced at the television. It was an American show dubbed in Turkish, and the actors' mouths stopped moving before the lines were finished being said. A scantily dressed blond girl killed monsters with a stake.

He watched the show for a minute, enough to determine that it dealt with the devil and sex.

"I don't want you watching this. It's not moral."

"Baba, Buffy kills the vampires, the evil ones. What's more moral than that?"

He snapped off the television.

"Baba!"

"Get yourself ready for tonight," he said. "It's your brother's special night."

İrem ran down the hallway. "İsmail, İsmail, İsmail," she said, "always İsmail." She slammed the door to the room she shared with her brother and the music upstairs stopped.

Sinan let out a frustrated breath of air. "How are we raising our children?" he called toward the kitchen.

"You could say hello to her first," Nilüfer said, popping her head around the corner of the kitchen.

"So she could ignore me and stare at this stupid box?"

"Sinan, it's only a television show." He heard the oven door squeak open. "She's been working hard since this morning. Be nice."

He switched on the television again and watched for a minute, turning his head to the side to consider it. There was killing and there was kissing, enough for him. He shut it off.

"I'm going to invite them," Nilüfer said, standing in the hallway now.

"No." It was bad enough they lived above him, but he didn't want the Americans inside his house, especially on this day.

"Sinan," Nilüfer said. "It's wrong. They're our neighbors."

He shook his head, but she was already coming toward him with a smile on her face.

Chapter 2

Irem slammed the door and the music stopped. His room
was directly above hers, just a few feet away. If she stood on her bed,
she could touch the ceiling and feel the beat of his music running
through her fingers and down her arm. It was wrong, she knew, but
she did so sometimes when İsmail wasn't around, and she discovered
that she only felt guilty for a few minutes afterward. Once, when she
heard the muffled strains of his voice talking on the phone, she stood
on her dresser and pressed her ear against the ceiling. She imagined
he was talking to someone in New York City or Los Angeles. She
couldn't understand what he said, but she imagined he was whispering in her ear, and that night she had dreams about him, embarrass-
ing dreams she would never tell anyone, not even her friend Dilek.

She heard his footsteps creaking across the ceiling, the squeaking
of his window opening, and she knew he was waiting for her. She had
been cleaning all day, though, and she smelled of disinfectant. Her
face was smeared with flour and she didn't want him to see her like
this.

A cloud of smoke blew across her windowpane, followed by a tapping on the outside wall of the apartment.

She was wearing rags, her blouse was frayed at the cuffs, and her head scarf was the worst thing you could imagine—green-and-orange-paisley swirls with bleach spots in places. She only wore it inside, when no one but her family would see her. She pressed her nose to her armpits and was embarrassed by her own smell.

Another cloud of smoke blew across the windowpane, followed by a cluster of bubbles floating in the air like orbs of oil-swirled color.

She laughed, forgot her appearance, and scrambled across her bed toward the window.

"What are you doing?" she whispered, sticking her head out the window.

A stream of bubbles splattered in her face, stinging her eyes.

"Stop," she said. "Allah, Allah." She ducked back inside to rub the soap out of her eyes and remembered that she was unpresentable. She leaned against the windowsill but wouldn't put her head outside again. "I've been cleaning all day. I look terrible."

"I won't look," he said. "Here."

His hand suddenly appeared at the top of the window frame, a cigarette burning between his long fingers.

When she leaned out the window to grab the cigarette, his chest hung over the ledge but his head was turned away. She laughed, took the cigarette from his fingers, and admired the tattoos etched over the veins of his forearms. She put the cigarette to her lips and tasted the wetness on the filter. She didn't inhale—she didn't really like to smoke, even after a month of these window-to-window visits—but she simply held it there, her tongue picking up the flavor of nicotine and boy.

More bubbles floated down, lazy, breeze-blown.

"What are you doing?"

"I'm bored," he said. "There's nothing to do out here. Shit, how can you stand it?"

She cringed at the curse word, but he was American, and it wasn't as rude for them as it was for a Turk.

I can't stand it, she wanted to say, but instead she held the cigarette to her mouth and inhaled this time.

She sometimes passed him in the stairwell or watched him walking on the street, his legs moving to the beat of a song on his headphones, but in those places she had to ignore him. There were too many neighbors watching, eyes looking through peepholes, faces behind lacy curtains.

"I miss İstanbul," he said. "Beyoğlu, especially. The action's there."

She listened to him and tried to imagine Beyoğlu. She had seen it on television—the three-story clubs, the women dressed in tank tops with their bra straps showing, the men with their black hair slicked back and shining. It was only three hours by ferry to İstanbul, but it seemed as far away as America.

"I miss my friends from school," he said.

She stared at his hand and forearm, but the rest of him was cut off from her vision by the metal window frame and the cinder-block walls. She stared at the ceiling and imagined his feet, his legs, his whole body just on the other side of that cement and wood.

"Hey," he said. "Don't get greedy." His hand dangled outside the window again.

She took one last drag, leaned out to hand it to him, and was startled when she found him staring down at her.

"Gotcha," he said.

She dove back through the window, embarrassed and shocked, but she could never get really mad at him.

"You don't look so bad," he said.

"Shut up."

"No, no," he said. "I mean it." He laughed. "I'm sorry. It's kind of nice seeing you, like, normal, you know? When I see you outside it's like you're not you."

"Not me?"

"I don't know," he said. "It's like you're too formal or something, too perfect and proper. Right now you seem like—you seem like *you*." She heard him blow out a breath. "I don't know," he said. "Forget it. You just look nice is what I'm trying to say."

She stuck her head out the window and tried to watch him without being seen. His hand disappeared, followed by a puff of smoke, and then it returned. There were long blue veins running up his forearms and they made the muscles look strong.

"I saw your brother this afternoon," he said.

She looked away, up toward the square of blue sky between apartment rooftops. A flock of birds, a large gray cloud of them, flew out toward the hills.

"He gets treated like a sultan," she said, biting her thumbnail now and looking at the floor. "Money, clothes, this dinner."

"Guy deserves a few gifts if they're going to do *that*," he said. "That's gotta hurt."

She felt her face go red. She had thought about that part of a man's body before, but it was never talked about, and her excitement suddenly mixed with a strange distaste.

"Aren't they supposed to do that in a hospital now?" he said.

"It's expensive."

"Man, you can put metal rods through my ears, stab bamboo shoots under my nails, but don't mess around with—wait." He flicked the cigarette butt into the air and disappeared.

She jumped back from the window and sat down on her bed, her heart thumping against her ribs. She heard his footsteps above mix with other footsteps, heard a quiet voice and his louder reply. It was silent then for a few moments, and she waited, holding her breath as long as she could before becoming dizzy.

The ceiling creaked softly.

"İrem," he whispered down.

She sat still and listened to the hallway outside her own door, suddenly aware that her parents, too, could walk in and discover them.

"İrem," he said, louder this time.

"Shh," she said, her head out the window now. "Quiet. My father would kill you if he discovered this."

He smiled his crooked smile.

"No. I mean it."

"We've been invited down to your apartment," he said.

"What? Tonight?"

"Uh-huh."

"Allah, Allah!" she whispered to herself.

"Hah," he laughed sarcastically. "I can't wait to meet you."

Chapter 3

SINAN HEADED DOWN THE STAIRS TO COLLECT İSMAIL AND
to borrow more groceries from his own store's inventory. Nilüfer
needed fresh bread, not the day-old stuff he had brought this morning, bulgur wheat, and dried mint. Not only did he have the pain in
his stomach, but his chest hurt now. The cost of the food would break
him. It was too hot out. People wouldn't come and the night would be
a failure. Nilüfer would cry about her baby becoming a man.

He passed the Gypsy camp on the way to his *bakkal,* where a filthy
boy and his little sister unloaded a donkey cart of cardboard they had
scavenged from the trash that morning. Sinan and his family were
lucky, he reminded himself. As hard as life was for a Kurd, it was
harder on a Roma. If he didn't say anything, no one bothered him
about being Kurdish. But everyone hated the Gypsies. They were
rootless people—from Romania or Egypt or India; no one knew. Even
Sinan, who had good reason to identify with their itinerant life, fought
his disdain for people who made homes out of his garbage.

On Flower Street, a woman lowered a basket from the fifth-floor
window of her kitchen, and left it dangling a few inches above the
street. A boy from Sunrise Grocery, one of Sinan's competitors, took
the money out of the basket and filled it with *pide,* cheese, and a con-

tainer of honey. The woman tugged on the rope and the container rose like a spider on a single thread. This apartment was closer to Sinan's *bakkal* than it was to Sunrise, and he made a mental note to have a sale next week to keep the street's business.

He found İsmail and Ahmet sitting on wooden crates in front of the grocery, both of them chewing on large chunks of sweet *helva*. When they saw him coming, İsmail and Ahmet pretended to hide the candy behind their backs. Sinan laughed, and immediately the tightness in his chest eased.

"Sweets before dinner?" Sinan said. "Your mother won't be happy."

"Don't tell your mother," Ahmet said, winking at İsmail.

İsmail laughed and took another bite of the candy.

Sinan hugged his brother-in-law and kissed him on each cheek, and he could smell the alcohol on Ahmet's breath.

"Just a little *rakı*," he would say on the days Sinan reproached him for it. "If I'm going to spend my life in this grocery, I'm going to live a little doing it. God understands."

"God is disappointed," Sinan would say, and leave it at that because, despite himself, he loved the man.

Sinan owed Ahmet his life. When things got bad in the village, when men were being taken away by the Turkish paramilitaries and it seemed only a matter of time before he, too, disappeared, it was Ahmet who sent them the bus tickets to Gölcük, Ahmet who gave them money for the first month's rent on the apartment. He also made Sinan a partner in the grocery, changing the *bakkal*'s name from Ahmet's Grocery to Brothers' Grocery. There was, he knew, room enough in God's Paradise for such goodness.

"*Teşekkürler*, Ahmet," Sinan said.

"No problem, my brother." Ahmet took Sinan by the arm. "You're limping. You need ice on that foot."

"I'm fine."

"You'll be dancing tonight."

Sinan just looked at him and raised an eyebrow. Ahmet put one hand in the air and rolled around on his ankles. He laughed and slapped Sinan on the back.

"Your wife says to bring bread with you."

"I know."

"She called earlier," Ahmet said. "She wasn't happy. Better do what my sister says, my brother."

"I will," Sinan laughed. "But the house is filled with food."

"I've seen it!" Ahmet said. "*Börek* to the ceiling. A river of olive oil down your hallway."

With a pat on the rear end, Sinan sent İsmail home to get cleaned up. "Finish that *helva* before you get there."

Together he and Ahmet entered the grocery, a one-room, concrete-floor shop lined with shelves of canned tomato puree, canned fruit, canned beans, and canned soda. Ahmet reached behind the counter and held up the front page of the *Milliyet*.

"They locked Öcalan up on Dog Island today," he said.

"I saw," Sinan said. If all the buildings were gone, and they had a clear sight to the sea, they would be able to see the island on which the prison was built. In Ottoman times, the island was where they took the rabid street dogs to let them rip one another to pieces. That's what Öcalan was to the nationalist Turks, a Kurdish separatist dog. "He'll rot there until everyone forgets and then they'll hang him."

Ahmet lit a cigarette. "They say the war is over."

"That's what they say."

Ahmet looked at Sinan, blew smoke to the ceiling, and picked a strand of tobacco from between his teeth. Sinan said nothing and avoided his eyes while he gathered Nilüfer's groceries. He always said he'd return to Kurdistan if the civil war was finished, but now he didn't know. He always thought they'd win and the Kurds would have their own country. A man can accept a life of poverty if it's in his own country, if it's his own doing, but not if it's caused by others.

Ahmet folded up the newspaper and tossed it aside. "Check the receipts," he said. "I can't do the math. Without you I'd run this place into the ground."

"Slow day?" Sinan asked, sorting through the strips of paper.

"You're our best customer," Ahmet said, taking a sip from his coffee cup. "Too hot to shop," he said. "Tomorrow will be better."

The motor to the cooler hummed loudly and Sinan slapped the casing to quiet it. Behind the fogged glass, the goat's cheese and garlic sausage lay sweating in the heat.

"*İnşallah,*" Sinan said, fingering the few bills in the drawer beneath the calculator.

"God willing, they'll shut down the Carrefour," Ahmet said. The French superstore had been built on the other side of the highway in what used to be an empty lot dotted with grazing goats. Their grocery had been losing business ever since. "Fatmah Hanım told me they sell Florida oranges there," he said, turning up his lips in disgust. "They make them without seeds."

"Must taste like piss," Sinan said. "Fruit without seeds!"

It was as close to cursing as Sinan got, and the stunned look on Ahmet's face gave way to laughter.

"Like a man without testicles," Ahmet said. "Fruit without seeds! Allah, Allah." He reached beneath the counter and took a very large drink from the coffee cup.

"You're the *kirve*, Ahmet. Remember that. You have a duty tonight."

"Yes, yes," Ahmet said, and threw the rest of the *rakı* into the sink.

Chapter 4

IREM GRABBED A SMALL BAG HIDDEN BENEATH HER BED AND tucked it under her blouse before running down the hallway to lock herself in the washroom. There she pulled out a small vial of olive oil and colorless lip gloss.

Dilek had taught her a few tricks.

Pinch your cheeks until the red comes out, smooth the oil into your skin to make it glow, roll the lip gloss on but then dab it with toilet paper so it isn't obvious.

She found the tweezers in the bag and yanked stray hairs from between her eyebrows and one growing in a mole on her jaw near her earlobe. She untied her head scarf, pulled the pins from her hair, and let it fall across her shoulders. Her hair was curly and thick and it twisted like vines around her neck. She loved her hair, perhaps partly because she had to hide it away each day — before she was thirteen she hadn't really thought much about it — and she ran her fingers through it now and imagined they were his fingers. She would have to pin it back in place and coil it again beneath the scarf, but she combed all the tangles out of it anyway, and watched as each strand shone in the overhead light. She did this for ten minutes, hoping, dreaming even, that he would recognize its beauty through the cheap silk fabric and want to touch it.

And when she was done, when she had tied her hair up in her best scarf, she dabbed two fingers of rosewater on the back of her neck, right beneath the point in the fabric, just for good luck.

Chapter 5

IT WAS AFTER SEVEN WHEN THE GUESTS BEGAN TO ARRIVE, and İrem was still in the washroom.

"İrem!" Sinan yelled down the hallway. Silence. "İrem! The guests are coming." No response. He walked down the hallway, his feet slapping against the cheap marble flooring. "İrem." A girl who ignores her father!

Before he could knock on the door, İrem opened it, and he found his daughter wearing her best head scarf, the one with the gold leaf, which he had bought her for her last birthday. He noticed the color in her face and the way her lips shone and he was glad to see her looking so beautiful for her brother's party.

"I called you three times."

"I'm sorry, Baba," she said, a smile on her face. "I wanted to look nice."

He wanted to tell her how beautiful she looked, but he didn't want her to start acting pretty. Beauty attracts the wrong type of attention.

"Your mother needs help."

She walked quickly toward the kitchen, and he watched her go, her hips straining her skirt with that womanly walk that had stolen his child away.

Ahmet, Gülfem, and their daughter, Zeynep, arrived first. They lived on the bottom floor of the apartment building, and Ahmet sang a popular Tarkan song as they climbed the stairs. Sinan stood in the corner of the room, the apple in his stomach expanding into an orange, watching as the neighbors joined the party, bringing with them coins and paper money for İsmail, bunches of roses clipped from backyard gardens, and even plates of desserts to add to the table already filled with food. Dressed in the white *sünnet* gown that made him look like a girl, İsmail sat on a raised bed near the open window of the main room, the city behind him sparkling in the heat. The bed was padded with blankets and ribbons, and when people passed to congratulate him, they threw silver tinsel in his hair. İsmail tried to act like a man, tried not to smile, but when ten-year-old Zeynep, on whom İsmail had a boy's crush, kissed him on the cheek, he giggled.

Ahmet and Sinan pushed the couches out of the way, and the guests danced in a circle on the soft-pile rug in the center of the living room. Ahmet turned up the music on the radio, and the hum of oud strings and the twirling notes of a lute crackled out from the old speakers. Sinan turned the music down, but Ahmet turned it up again, grabbed Sinan by the hand, and pulled him into the circle. Everyone linked pinkies, raised their arms in the air, leaned forward with the music, kicked up their feet, and then stepped to the right to begin the dance again.

Sinan's wife and daughter, both dressed in their only silk scarves, served plates of food to the people who were not dancing. Sinan tried to help, once he escaped the dancing, but Nilüfer refused him, telling him it would not be proper. She was right, but he was nervous and he needed to do something to keep calm.

The tables overflowed with *mezeler*, but there was more in the refrigerator, keeping fresh out of the heat. On one table, rice and pine nuts spilled out of stuffed peppers, *dolmalar* sat stacked on tea saucers like a pyramid of grape-leaf cigars, Circassian chicken floated in walnut sauce and pools of olive oil. On a wobbly card table sat fava and green-bean salad, spinach in yogurt sauce, and numerous other plates filled with vegetables and fruit and warm loaves of bread. Minced lamb baked in the oven, and cubed mutton with carrots, onions, and broth stewed in pastry bowls. There were eggplants stuffed with ground beef and nuts and rice and cinnamon, meatballs with hot peppers, *börek* layered with goat's-milk cheese and spinach, and even little bowls of warmed almonds and hazelnuts. Sinan couldn't help counting the lira in his head.

People broke away from the dancing, filled their plates, and ate without missing a note of the singing. Ahmet, true to form, stuffed his mouth with a dolma while spinning in the center of the room with the rest of the dancers, and Sinan wondered if he had had more to drink before coming to the party. There were small cups of *Rize* tea, many of them, and Nilüfer had to keep the tea brewing constantly. İrem made coffee the traditional way, bringing it to a boil three times before adding the sugar. Mehmet Türkoğlu read people's fortunes in turned-over coffee cups, analyzing the bumps and smears of coffee grounds in the little white saucers. "You will marry young and have six boys," he told a girl who lived down the street. The girl blushed. "You will have to choose between three beautiful girls," he told her brother, a boy of only seven. The boy stuck out his tongue at the prospect. Mehmet laughed out loud and reached across the table to hug him to his chest.

The Americans arrived late. After descending the stairs from their apartment, they stood in the open doorway looking lost. Sinan waited a while before greeting them, hoping they might give up and leave, but people started gossiping about them—he was a director at one of the expensive private missionary schools in İstanbul, they were from California and knew famous actors personally, they only summered in Gölcük and owned a fancy apartment in the rich İstanbul neighborhood of Nişantaşı—and etiquette finally forced Sinan to be gracious.

The wife handed Sinan a red package wrapped with a white bow.

"Just something little," she said. Her eyes were green, and when she smiled they became very small, as though she were squinting in the sun.

"Thank you," he said. "Please come in."

If his father knew he was letting Americans into his home! Americans who helped the Turkish government destroy Kurdish villages! Why did he let Nilüfer talk him into these things?

"Can I take your coats?" he heard İrem say before he saw her standing next to him.

The American boy smiled. It was terribly hot, and they weren't wearing any coats.

İrem laughed, her forehead growing red.

"What's wrong with you?" Sinan said quietly.

"I mean, tea." She glanced at him and then smiled to the guests. "Can I get you some tea?"

"Yes," the woman said, taking İrem's hand. "Yes, darling, that would be wonderful."

The party continued, and soon Sinan forgot about the Americans. His son watched from the raised bed, looking upon the scene as though he could not be bothered with such a spectacle. Sinan was happy, but it was time for the *sünnetci* to arrive, and he was nervous for İsmail. Would he cry out with the pain? Would the *sünnetci* slip with the knife and permanently ruin his child? It did happen, although very rarely. There was a story about one boy bleeding to death in his sleep, the parents waking the next morning to find him cold and white as stone in his circumcision bed.

The *sünnetci* arrived, carrying a black bag in his hands. He stood in the doorway, took off his shoes, and waited to be invited in. When the dancers saw him, they stopped, and stood fixing their untucked clothes and ruffled hair. Men snuffed out their cigarettes and women took last sips of tea. Ahmet turned down the music and Sinan welcomed the man.

"*Hoş geldiniz, efendim,*" he said, and kissed the man on each cheek.

"*Hoş bulduk.*"

He was an old man, dressed in black, his cheeks gaunt and sunken, his teeth yellow where the enamel had been stripped from a lifetime of tea drinking. He pulled at his thin white beard with his left hand as he nodded hello to the guests.

From his bag he produced a white sheet, a bottle of antiseptic, a few cotton balls, a bottle of anesthetic, and a battery-powered knife. Ahmet took İsmail's arm in his hand, and whispered something in his ear. Ahmet was the *kirve*, and from this day forward would be like a second father to the boy. If something terrible happened and Sinan should die, Ahmet would raise İsmail as though the boy were his own. Sinan couldn't hear what Ahmet said, but in his own mind he was saying to his son, "It will hurt, but it will pass, it will hurt, but it will pass."

The women stood on the other side of the room, away from the men who gathered around the bed. Mehmet and Yiğit Akay held the sheet in the air like a screen for a *karagöz* puppet show so that the operation was hidden from the rest of the guests.

Sinan stood away, as the father should, but watched his son's face during the operation. İsmail held his jaw tight and looked at the ceiling. The sound of the knife made Sinan's stomach turn. He and the rest of the men said, "Allahu Akbar." İsmail's face turned white and his lips quivered and his eyes filled with water, but he didn't let out a sound, and the water did not spill down his cheeks.

The *sünnetci* dressed the wound and said, "May it pass quickly." İsmail lay there staring up at the ceiling, his face still pale, as ashen as if flour had been sifted over his skin.

Chapter 6

SHE WAS ACTING LIKE A FOOL. "CAN I TAKE YOUR COATS?"!
Aptal! It was burning hot out! İrem spilled a plate of rice in the potted fern and poured tea into Mehmet Bey's coffee, and she was so scared, so entirely out of breath with panic, that she couldn't even bring herself to go over to where Dylan and his parents sat. She thought a month of secret meetings could be read in her face, and even though she could see that they were out of tea and that they needed dessert, she let them wait until her mother made it to that side of the room.

"Don't forget about the Americans," her mother scolded.

"They make me nervous," she said, relieved to reveal part of the truth.

"Oh, you sound like your father!" Her mother left the kitchen bearing yet another pot of tea.

When the time had come for the circumcision, İrem had been genuinely scared for her brother. He was babied by her parents and allowed to do whatever he wanted, but she had held him as an infant and fed him at night when her mother was exhausted and he was crying. She listened to him in the darkness of early morning when he spoke funny gibberish in his sleep. So when she heard the knife, she held her breath until it was done, and she forgot, at least momentarily, about the American boy, Dylan.

Afterward, though, her mother and father went to İsmail and held his hand and kissed his cheeks, and she was left alone to pick up the dishes. She delivered a stack of plates and cups to the kitchen and returned to the living room for another stack. Everyone crowded around İsmail now—his white bed and clothes shining in the lamplight—and showered him with tinsel.

For her there had been no big party, no money or fancy clothes. She simply woke up one morning two years ago with blood on her legs and stains on the sheets. When she told her mother, her mother quietly stripped the bed so as not to wake the still-sleeping İsmail, wadded up the sheets, and stuffed them at the bottom of the clothes hamper.

"You surprised me," she said. "So early."

She had whisked İrem into the washroom and showed her what to do to contain the bleeding while her father waited outside the door, knocking occasionally, and complaining about being late to the *bakkal*.

"İrem. You're a woman," her mother had said, smiling, whispering as though it were a conspiracy. "You must stay away from the boys now."

She had gone to bed a child and awoken a woman, and she had had to stand there in the locked bathroom—the glaring white light shining down, the pad bunched uncomfortably between her legs—and listen to her mother deliver new rules in hushed tones that made her feel ashamed

And for a week afterward her father hadn't said more than three words to her, and that was only after she finally resorted to sitting on his lap one night after dinner. "No, please, İrem," he said, brushing her off his lap. It was like she was suddenly contagious.

Now she dropped a stack of dessert trays in the sink, the shredded remnants of baklava sliding off into the dirty water. She returned to the living room and pictures were being taken: her father with his arm around İsmail, smiling as though the boy had just been born, smiling in a way she rarely saw anymore. She wanted that smile showered upon her.

She balanced dirty teacups in her arms and went to the kitchen and dropped those in the sink, hoping they would break, wishing she wouldn't have to wash them, wanting everyone to stop smiling and notice her for once, even if it meant being yelled at. She dipped her hand in the water and washed the rim of a teacup with the sponge while she listened to the laughter in the other room.

After her father had gone to the *bakkal* that morning, her mother had sat her down in this kitchen, pinned back her hair, and wrapped it away in a scarf. She wasn't trying to hurt her, İrem knew that, but she scraped her scalp with the pins, and pulled her hair back so tightly her eyelids turned up at the corners. She remembered the smile on her mother's face—not quite happy, but satisfied in some strange way. When she was done, her mother kissed her and held her and İrem watched the morning light filter through the dirty plastic skylight. A pot of burning rice steamed on the stove.

And she realized now—as she scraped the gooey cake crumbs of "ladies' navels" into the trash—that she had spent more time since that day in the gray light of this kitchen than she had outside in the sun.

She slapped the plate against the trash can to loosen the pastry from the globs of honey and thought about taking each and every one of the tea saucers and smashing them to the floor.

But then Dylan arrived, carrying an armful of plates.

"Circumcision and food," he said, setting the plates on the counter. "You Turks have got interesting ways of having fun."

"It's not supposed to be fun," she said, scraping harder at the plates.

"Joke," he said. "A joke?"

She stopped, blew air through her teeth, and leaned a fist on her hip.

"They really make you work, huh?" he said. "I'll help."

"No. You don't have to."

"It's too much for one person."

He took the first plate off the top of the stack, scooted closer to her, and ran it under the hot water. She could smell his cologne—not cologne exactly, not like the sharp scents the Turkish boys wore, but something that smelled like sweet burning, an oil maybe. She watched his hands circle the rim of the plate, looked at the back of his neck, admired the place where his earlobe met the curve of his jaw. Something about his posture, the way he concentrated on the washing, perhaps, made him seem so much older than she, though they were only two years apart. There was nothing separating them now, no glass, no metal, no cement, yet now she almost wished there were.

She left him there and returned to the living room. She wanted to get some air. Her mother and father were still sitting beside İsmail, and she thought her brother looked very tired, as though all he wanted was for them all to go away and let him sleep. She stacked as many plates in her arms as possible, all the way up to her chin, and returned to the kitchen.

Dylan was still there, working now on a stack of utensils. She wanted him to stay and she wanted him to leave. She wanted him to be a man and stop washing the dishes, but she loved him for the help.

She placed the new stack of plates beside him.

"Slave driver," he said.

She didn't get the joke, but she smiled and laughed timidly just to make him happy.

He washed and she dried and she wondered if this was what it was like to be married to an American man. She wasn't sure she liked it. What did a woman get in this world if she didn't get the kitchen? But his company electrified her and she leaned in a little more and felt the steam from the sink touching her face and her heart started jumping all around and she had a difficult time getting her breath and suddenly his hand was on hers and she dropped the plate in the water.

"No," she said, pulling away.

They both looked toward the doorway to see if anyone was coming.

He smiled and moved closer again, pressing her against the wall of the kitchen, taking both of her wet hands in his.

"No," she said again, throwing away his hands and squirming free. She leaned against the doorway and adjusted her blouse and straightened her skirt. "Not in this house."

Chapter 7

SINAN STARTLED AWAKE FROM A DREAM IN WHICH HIS FATHER scolded him for abandoning their village. "My grandson will never know Yeşilli, his home," his father had said in the dream, his black eyes staring holes into Sinan. The house behind his father was on fire and it was very hot and Sinan wanted to tell him this but he couldn't make his mouth work.

The clock next to the bed said 2:45. He kissed Nilüfer on the cheek before getting up in the dark and walking into the front room.

In the glow from the streetlights, he saw İsmail there sleeping. A slight breeze blew through the open window, and the few strands of tinsel still stuck in his son's hair sparkled in the wind. He stood next to the bed and listened to the steady rise and fall of the boy's breath. He thought about closing the window—something about the wind touching his son's sleeping face disturbed him—but it was too hot and he decided to leave it open. As he pulled the remaining strands of tinsel from his son's hair, İsmail stirred and swatted at the annoyance. His hand stuck there next to his ear, a loose fist with the palm open to the sky. There was an air of the sleeping infant in the pose, and it seemed to Sinan that only days before he had held the baby İsmail in his arms, the small, pudgy body, the toothless gums of his mouth, that fresh powdery smell of his skin.

He climbed the staircase to the roof of the apartment building, and his left foot, deformed since birth, and sore from the day's walking in İstanbul, throbbed with each step. It looked like Berker Bey, the owner of the apartment, was going to build another level—there was exposed rebar, bags of cement, and loosely stacked cinder blocks—but Sinan knew that he was really just avoiding paying taxes; the government couldn't assess taxes until construction was finished. Life was full of these little immoralities.

From the rooftop he could see over the Americans' terrace, past the other apartment rooftops and their cluttered satellite dishes, and out over the Gulf of İzmit toward the forested hillsides across the water. He stood on the edge of the roof, his shins pressing against the raised edge, and was surprised to see the American wife below him, sitting alone on a wicker chair. Her back was to him, her face turned toward the black water. She was still except for the rise and fall of her right hand, which held a lit cigarette.

For some reason he felt sorry for her, this woman he knew nothing about. She seemed the picture of loneliness at that moment—her stillness in the dark, the curve of her thick, motherly back, her bare white legs dully shining in the light of the waterfront. A lot of things were said about these Americans, but if they were so rich, he wondered, why didn't they have their summer home in Yalova with all the other rich people? Gölcük, though by the sea, was a poor town, a working-man's town. If they were so rich, why did the wife seem so sad? Maybe he should have been kinder to them at the party. He thought briefly about breaking her silence with a "Good evening," but decided against it and retreated out of sight to sit on a plastic chair on the rooftop.

There he took off his left shoe and rubbed the inflamed stump that should have been a foot. He would have to run the register at the grocery for a few days so he could stay off the foot until the swelling went down.

He often sat on the roof when he couldn't sleep. Since Öcalan had been caught by the government and the civil war in the South seemed over, his father had been visiting him more often in his dreams. His father would have been devastated to hear that the Turks had captured the PKK leader. Without Apo, as Öcalan was called by his father and all separatist-leaning Kurds, the Kurdistan Workers' Party was effectively dead, and so was the movement to carve a Kurdistan out of a corner of Turkey. No one else could kill the Turkish paramilitaries the way Apo did; no one else could inspire such fear in the government buildings in Ankara.

Perhaps it was safe to return home to Yeşilli, but it was difficult to imagine it so. He touched the shard of bullet hanging from a chain around his neck—it was all he had left of his father, God bless him. He remembered the night his father was killed, the popping of the M-16 rifle shots, the screaming, the men and boys gathered for the new-year celebration diving away from the bonfires. His father had sent him home when the paramilitary jeeps arrived, and he was already past Emre Bey's butcher shop when his father's friends and the other men began yelling *Long live Kurdistan,* or else he might have been killed, too.

He felt a sting of guilt about having the Americans in his home. If his father had been here tonight, he wouldn't have stepped into the apartment with them there. "The Americans let the Turks do this to us," he would have said. "And now you feed them, invite them to your son's most important day?" He had dishonored his father's memory, and he would have to suffer the pangs of remorse for giving in to his wife's hospitality.

He watched the streak of black water beyond the rooftops, and the city lights strewn around the bay like a necklace. The tea-black sky floated above him, punctured with only three stars, just three tiny pinpricks. At night in the village there were more stars than night sky, more worlds out there staring back than there were people in the whole of this city, probably more than there were people in all of the world's cities. He wanted to return to Yeşilli, he wanted his children to grow up in the shadow of the mountains, but where would he get the money for the trip? How could he leave the business? How would he make a living there? He wanted to explain this to his father, tell him that it was best to stay here, for his children. There was nothing in the South—no jobs, no schools, no future. But even as he built his argument in his head, his father's angry face appeared, and doubt clouded his logic.

The breeze felt like air blowing off an open fire. He heard the metal droning of cranes at the docks, a place that never stopped moving. You could hear its machinery grinding away at all hours of the day, during prayers, waking before sunrise in the morning—it didn't matter, the sound was always there, like the scrape of gnashing your own teeth together. He could see a party boat floating close to shore, the white lights strung from its bow reflecting against the black water. As it got nearer to shore Sinan heard the thumping of music from loudspeakers and watched dozens of people dancing on its flat rooftop. The sound was distant and sad, like the echo of some lost pleasure. But as the boat drew closer to the dock, he heard individual voices, the laughter of women, a deejay announcing a raffle, and the clapping of hands. The deejay played another song, and it was so loud that Sinan got angry because he thought it might disturb his family's sleep.

Then there was another sound, an odd low rumbling like the shuddering of a tank coming down the street. And at first that's what he thought it was, one of the police tanks on patrol, but the rumbling grew louder and it seemed to be rolling across the water toward him, toward the town.

He sat up, looked for a ship leaving the docks, searched the sky for a plane, but the sound wasn't right for anything man-made. Then, in the distance, out of the black water, flashed a brilliant spark of green. The flash was so bright that when he blinked there were little bursts of green blindness in his vision. The rumble had separated itself from the sound of the boat and had become something wholly distinct, a horrible growl. He looked at the party boat, hoping the sound was some new type of music. The shining hull bobbed out there silently, reflecting itself back on the water, but all the dancing people had turned their faces toward the growing sound.

Sinan had an instinct to get back to his family, he tried to run for the stairs, tried to get back to them, but his feet skipped out from beneath him and he found himself facedown on the cement rooftop. He rolled onto his back and lifted himself up, but above him the sky shifted, sending the stars falling across the sky, their pinpoints streaking in his vision.

He got to his feet and wrapped a fist around a piece of rebar, and when he did he looked toward the bay where the boat lifted on a wave of water, rose into the air like a toy ship, tipped sideways, listed, and spilled its passengers into the surging sea. There was nothing to think about it because it was something unbelievable, something in a terrible dream, and as soon as he did think, They won't make it, the building directly next to his own dropped from his vision. The crash was so loud that it was like the silence of blood in his ears.

He heard screams, explosions of gas lines rupturing, the bursting of water pipes thrusting up pieces of road, even the sirens of car alarms, but none of these sounds could be isolated; they were simply the cacophonous rush of destruction. Then Sinan's stomach lifted into his throat and he was dropped through the air. For a moment he felt as though he were flying; he looked beneath his feet to find the rooftop falling. It dropped ten feet and tilted sideways as if the whole building was tumbling into the street. Then his body was thrown over the side of the rooftop. He closed his eyes, sure that this was the end, and fell for what seemed like minutes until he slammed into the tiled floor of the terrace beneath. He was rolled to his left, and got wedged against the railings of the terrace, his arms tangled in the wrought iron and his head dangling over the edge.

As he opened his eyes he saw the white circumcision bed come through the open window below, and on that white bed was his son. İsmail lay on his back with his arms thrown behind him like he was doing the backstroke. Their eyes briefly met. İsmail had a questioning look on his face—he didn't seem scared at all—just a question mark in his cyes, as if to say, "Look, what a strange thing to happen, Baba."

In his white circumcision dress, İsmail floated out above the crumbling building, as if on a pillow of air. Sinan reached a hand out toward his son, stretching his fingers as far as he could. Cement blocks tumbled beneath the boy, crashed together, crushed and disintegrated, and the bed, too, spun around in the air. İsmail did a somersault, his tiny feet rolling above his head, his back coming briefly into view, his whole body flipping gracefully through the sky, before it disappeared in the dust and crumble below.

Chapter 8

SINAN HEARD SCREAMING, A SHRILL SOUND IN THE DISTANCE, like a throng of women standing outside and beating themselves. The screaming pierced his ears, slicing a sharp pain into his temple, and light grew at the corners of his vision. "Sinan," a voice cried. "Sinan!" The sound seemed to move through his body, out into a world that surrounded him with heavier sounds—crashing cement, car alarms, screams, and moans—and when he heard the voice a third time, he knew it was his wife's.

He came to finally and found himself wrapped around the twisted mess of wrought iron. His shirt had caught on the metal, and it was pulled up over his head so that when he opened his eyes he faced the darkness of the material. For a moment he thought he was dead, then the pain at his temple shocked him into consciousness. His legs dangled over the edge of the rooftop. He should have fallen, but the shoulder of his shirt, hooked on the rebar, had saved him. When he touched his head his fingers smeared with blood.

"Sinan!" he heard Nilüfer scream.

He kicked his feet and wrenched himself back onto the terrace. Everything that had happened came back to him, and in the darkness he scrambled across the collapsed rooftop and stumbled in the direction of the stairs. The stairwell was intact. He climbed down into the passageway where the early-morning darkness grew darker. He groped his way down the circling staircase until he heard his daughter crying. He tried shoving open the door, but it was stuck and he had to smash his shoulder against the wood. Inside, the floor slanted steeply and he slipped on the cheap marble tiles where they had become wet from a severed kitchen pipe. He already knew the answer, but he ran into the front room to check the window anyway, hoping that the vision of İsmail falling had been a dream. The bed, the window, his son, the whole front wall of his apartment were gone. The couch and coffee table dangled off the edge of the room, the back feet of the couch suspended in air, balanced delicately against falling. Beyond the missing front wall a cloud of dust hovered in the air like coal smoke. What had once been geometric planes of square walls and straight streets and a traffic circle, was now a jumble of broken buildings.

Sinan, then, began to shake uncontrollably; İsmail was buried out there.

From one of the bedrooms he heard İrem sobbing. He found her and his wife crouching on the floor, the rest of the bedroom stripped empty. Nilüfer clutched İrem to her chest and rocked her like she was a child.

"İsmail?" Nilüfer cried, panicked, her eyes pleading.

"He's safe," he said.

"Where, Sinan?"

"He's safe," he repeated.

"Where? Where is he?"

"We have to get out of here."

Sinan took Nilüfer by the shoulders and helped her stand. She wouldn't let go of İrem's hand, and he had to gently prize his wife's fingers loose before lifting his shaking daughter to his chest. İrem was too heavy for him, but it didn't matter. She clung to his neck and cried huge sobs that convulsed her body and made her harder to carry.

"İrem, *canım,*" he said, whispering in her ear. "You're okay. Calm down. You're okay." He repeated this through the leaning hallway, into the stairwell, and down the cracked steps until the passageway came to a dead end of fallen concrete slabs. He set İrem down and in the darkness ran his hands over the rough cement, trying to find a way out, but there was none. They should have been on the second floor, but the second floor was gone.

"Ahmet?" Nilüfer said. "My brother!"

"I know," he said, and he reached behind to touch her on the wrist.

"Oh, God," she said. "Gülfem, Ahmet, Zeynep." She yelled into the wall, but the sound was stifled. "Oh, God!"

Sinan took her in his arms and held her.

"Nilüfer," he said, "you have to be calm now."

She stopped yelling and breathed deeply, and when she grew calmer he began to panic. He didn't know what to do. His chest constricted and his mind wouldn't work. His head pounded as though his brain were bashing up against his skull.

"Upstairs," Nilüfer said. "The Türkoğlus'."

She took his hand and he grabbed İrem's, and Nilüfer led them back up the stairwell. When they reached the neighbor's threshold, Sinan didn't even think of knocking, but simply threw open the unlocked door and entered their neighbors' apartment.

"Mehmet!" he yelled, but there was no response.

They ran together down the leaning hallway, past the kitchen and into the front room; the wall was gone. This apartment had been on the third floor, but now it sat on the ground, the two floors beneath it a crush of cinder blocks and broken glass.

They teetered out into the darkness of the destroyed town, down nearly thirty meters of rubble. They scrambled over ledges of concrete, stepped over kitchen sinks, jumped across crevasses of rooftops, and the whole time, with each step, Sinan was afraid he might be stepping on his son. He tried to place his feet lightly, but he had to walk, had to lead the rest of his family down, and there was no way to be weightless.

"Forgive me, İsmail," he said to himself.

A water main broke beneath the street, and a rush of water burst into the air. The alarm of a crushed car bleated out a call and headlights flashed on and off, and in each strobe-light flash Sinan glimpsed the outlines of the destroyed town. People were scaling walls, hugging in the street, scrambling out of broken windows. Strafed by the light, their gestures looked mechanical, the clipped preciseness of limbs moving by degrees, and he hoped this might be a terrible dream. But it was real—he felt the dust landing on his skin, the grainy scratch of it in his lungs, the fingernails of his daughter scraping his palm.

Finally they reached the street, and he led Nilüfer and İrem to a little space of green that used to be the center of the traffic circle.

"Don't move from here," he said.

The light from the car alarm caught Nilüfer's face and the look scared him; her eyes were distant, as though a film had clouded over her pupils. He shook her lightly to make sure she understood him. She nodded her head, but it was the movement of someone who could no longer hear, someone who wasn't there anymore.

"İrem," he said, "do not let go of your mother. Do you understand me?"

"Don't leave me," İrem said.

"Do not let go of her, and stay here."

She nodded, but pleaded, "Don't leave me, Baba."

But he was already running back to the pile in front of his apartment.

Now sprinkles of water fell through the air, mixed with the floating dust, and dropped to the ground as mud. The strobe light illuminated the front of the now-teetering apartment building; it looked like a great hulking monster, the ripped innards of insulation hanging from the walls, the sockets of empty rooms, the limbs of electrical wires. Beneath the looming building, he saw people digging in the debris, but his vision was blurry at the edges, prismed through the pain in his head, and he didn't recognize anybody.

He didn't know where to begin, so he started at his feet, digging his hands into a space between slabs and pulling at the first chunk of concrete he could wrap his hands around. He dislodged it and it tumbled onto his foot. Kicking the chunk away, he slipped his fingers down into the rubble again, throwing pieces aside, between his legs. His palms ripped on metal sheeting and shards of glass stabbed his wrists. The cement crumbled under his nails and turned to sand in his fists.

His heart slammed against his ribs and his lungs seemed to shred. His hands worked faster than he thought possible, his arms lifting impossibly large blocks of cement. Digging in again, deeper this time, all the way to his shoulder: he felt something soft. His fingertips met fingertips. Then he felt a ring on the finger, and he knew it was not İsmail. Pulling himself up to where the body lay, he saw the caved-in face of a man. His scalp was cleaved open and it might have been Ahmet, but in the flashing light he couldn't tell.

"*Allah rahmet eylesin,*" he said to the body, and he kept going.

He dug for what seemed like hours before coming to a long slab of unbroken cement he couldn't break through. He climbed out of the hole and tried digging in another area, but he met the same impenetrable wall.

He ran around the corner to Ali Sünbay's hardware store, with the idea that he would get a metal pick and break the slab into smaller pieces, then he could move them with his hands, but the whole street was gone. Three buildings had toppled sideways, the floors strewn across the road like extended accordion bags. Another building had simply jumped fifteen feet to the side, completely intact save the first floor, which was left broken on its foundation. A woman stumbled down the street with a young man in her arms, his head tilted back, his feet scraping the ground. He was too old to be carried, and the woman's legs buckled beneath her. She stood again, holding the man to her breast, carrying him away from the collapsed buildings. Sinan should have helped her, but he was shocked by the vision, and as she got closer he ran the other way.

He was panicked now, running on his twisted foot, the reality of it all expanding in his chest. He was helpless. Everyone was helpless. There wasn't one thing he could do to help his son. When that thought exploded in his head, he dropped to his knees in the dirt, turned his palms toward the sky, and prayed.

Chapter 9

ONLY THE PRAYER AND THE TERRIBLE VISION OF HIS SON falling filled his mind. He had a vague memory of sunlight and darkness followed by sunlight again. Perhaps another night passed, but he didn't know. His head hurt, a throbbing pain as though a hot balloon had expanded inside his skull, and the world outside his head sounded muffled and fluid, like screams drowned underwater. And within this muffled space, he heard his daughter's voice.

"Baba," he heard İrem say, as if from across some great flooded cavern. "Baba, I need your help. Anne is saying crazy things."

But he had to pray; he couldn't break this prayer.

"She's pulling out her hair. I can't make her stop."

His words of prayer were the most fragile strands of a thread pulling İsmail toward life. One skipped phrase, one misplaced recitation, and he knew that thread would snap, severing him from his son.

"He's dead, Baba." İrem seemed to be crying from the bottom of the sea, her voice barely rising through fathoms of water. "İsmail is dead."

He wanted to slap her for giving İsmail up so quickly, but she was too far away.

"I need you," he heard her say again. There was distant sobbing, but after a while it stopped and he didn't hear her voice again.

After that there were only the words of supplication and the space in his head, the space in which he tried to lift his soul closer to God so God could see that he couldn't live if İsmail should die. He might have slept; he had a vague memory of someone making him lie down, tree limbs swaying above his head, but he wasn't sure, and when he was most lucid he found himself prostrated in the very same spot in the dirt. In his mind he offered his own life for the life of his son, he offered his wife's and his daughter's, he even bartered away their time in Heaven. He swore if God should be merciful that İsmail's life would be the picture of Muslim humility; he would see to it, make it his personal mission in life.

Then sometime later, hours, days, when he began to weaken and the sounds of bulldozers rattled his skull and the shouts of men filled his head, he realized he was demanding God to bend to his will. He was not offering God anything; he was fighting him, throwing up his fists and spitting into the sky. And then a calm suddenly came over him, a calm like the moment before he drifted off to sleep, when breathing becomes steady and the brain feels submerged in warm water, and he said clearly in his mind:

"Take my son if it's your will. If it is your will, then it's his fate."

He repeated this in his head, until the words began to lose their meaning, until his voice became nothing and he felt as though every bone in his body was as insubstantial and weightless as a bird's. He whispered it to himself until he no longer felt the muscles in his mouth, and his tongue seemed to have been cut out, until even his heart ceased beating in his ears and he was no longer a father, a husband, or a man. He was dust, simply the grains of God's making.

He heard the voice cry out, "There's someone here." The words pierced the fog and emptiness and shocked him into consciousness. He didn't know how long he had been collapsed in the dirt, but he could no longer feel his legs and he was bent to the side, half-lying in the street. A tractor with a scoop attached to the front lumbered by him, the wheels spinning up dust just in front of his face. The sun beat down and his brain pounded as though someone had hit him in the forehead with a hammer. He was thirsty, starving. He looked toward the voice and found a dozen men pulling at a pile of debris. He tried to stand, but his legs wouldn't work.

"Help me!" he screamed.

The man who had just parked the tractor jumped from the driver's seat and pulled Sinan to his feet.

"I can't walk," Sinan said.

The man carried him to the pile of rubble and set him down. There Sinan began to shove his bare hands back into the shards of broken buildings. As he dug, his legs tingled back to life. He plunged into a hole in the pile and pulled at every torn thing in front of him, searching for something round, something soft—skin, the curve of a skull, the length of an arm, the tender underside of bare feet.

"Stop, stop," a man yelled in accented Turkish. It was the American from upstairs and he stood in a hole just next to Sinan's. Dried blood caked his right eye and his silver-rimmed glasses sat askew across the bridge of his nose. He was covered in white dust. Everyone stopped digging, and the American dropped to his chest, placing an ear to a television with a hole clear through the middle. Thick dust swirled in the air and in the silence Sinan could hear the grains settle on the debris, as though the sky were raining pebbles. Thrushes sang in still-standing trees, an outboard motor whined offshore—sounds of normal life that angered him now. Then an unsteady ping, ping of tapped metal rose from the rubble. A few men cheered, but the American threw his hand in the air and they quieted.

"We're coming," the American said. And then he yelled something in English Sinan couldn't understand.

Sinan climbed into the hole with the man and together they scraped away disintegrated cinder blocks, piling the coarse stuff behind them. He shoved his torn knuckles into the pile, and then the American filled the space with his own bloody hands. One of the American's fingers was snapped sideways, but he kept jabbing his hands into the debris. They pulled and twisted and threw and tugged for what seemed like hours until they finally came to something soft: a white thigh.

The leg poked through a section of broken wood, and exposed wires wrapped around the blue knee like tendrils of seaweed. For a few seconds Sinan and the American froze at the sight, unsure what to do next, and Sinan had the grotesque thought that this leg was no longer a part of a whole body, that it was just the severed meat of what had once been a person. He was sure, though, it wasn't İsmail's leg. It was a woman's leg—the blue spider veins, the delicate kneecap, and the dark stubble of shaved hair left little doubt. The thigh was the American's wife. You didn't need to see her face to know that—few other women in the neighborhood would have left their legs uncovered, even to sleep at night.

The American whimpered something in English and softly ran his hands over the thigh, dug his nails between skin and debris to jostle it loose. The color of the skin and the way it moved under the man's touch left little doubt that the woman was dead. The American repeated a phrase, air escaping from his mouth as if he were hyperventilating.

"I'm sorry," Sinan said.

The man did not look up, but he bent the knee out of the destruction to reveal a broken foot, the ankle blue and swollen the size of a fist. He hugged the knee, pulled it to his chest, and kept repeating a single phrase in English while he rocked back and forth.

"I'm sorry," Sinan said again, resting his hand on the man's back. "But we've got to dig her out."

The American stopped and nodded. Sinan pulled at a piece of sheet metal that shook the leg.

"Gently, gently!" the American screamed. "Gently, please."

Together they lifted the twisted metal from her body. Then they brushed away cement dust that had buried her thigh. Her shorts were pulled high to expose her underwear and a little of what was hidden beneath. Sinan choked with pain for the man, and worked her shorts

down over the smooth edge of her thighs. They removed ropes of rebar and lifted the wet cloth of a rug that clung around her stomach.
They did it so softly, with such slow, deliberate care, that Sinan remembered the night he cleaned his father's body for burial—the way
he scrubbed between the cold fingers, and washed his penis and the
soft skin of his testicles. He remembered squeezing the water from
the wet cloth over a bullet wound where his eye should have been,
the black blood turning red and trickling across the mottled skin of
his cheek and down over his white lips.

A tent of wooden slats leaned above the woman's chest, and they
tried to dislodge them gently so as not to cause damage to her face.
Each one they pulled revealed more of the woman—an arm with a
silver bracelet looping around the wrist, the blade of a shoulder, her
sunburned neck pushing through a shirt. The other side of the
woman's body and her face was covered by a wet shower curtain and
one heavy block of broken cinder. The shower curtain was painted
like a coral reef and colorful fish with smiles on their faces swam in
the imaginary water. They removed the cinder block and suddenly
the shower curtain jerked.

"She's alive," the American said. He spoke frantically in English,
and they both reached to tug loose the waterlogged curtain.

Then a miracle! "Oh God most merciful," Sinan said when he saw
it. Beneath the woman, caught in her embrace, lay İsmail, his face
white with cement dust, his body convulsed in a coughing fit.

"İsmail!"

The boy's eyes flashed open as if he were taking in the world for
the first time, his pupils filling with the angry spark of life.

Sinan didn't wait for them to remove the American wife's body.
He tugged at his son's shoulders and dislodged him from beneath the
woman's weight, but he couldn't pull him free. He turned to see what
was holding him still, and found the woman's hand clamped around
İsmail's forearm. He had to wait for the American to uncurl each stiffened finger before he had his son in his arms, safe, and free from
death.

Chapter 10

WHEN THEY REACHED THE PANDEMONIUM OF THE GERMAN hospital Sinan was told his son had been buried alive for nearly three days.

"Unbelievable," the doctor said when he checked the boy in an examination room filled with dead bodies. Each body was laid out on a gurney, covered in a blue sheet, only the feet sticking out—men's polished black shoes shining like mirrors, pink shaggy house slippers, bare toes red with enamel. "We haven't gotten someone alive all day."

İsmail had a cut above his left eye, swelling around the wound where his foreskin had been cut away in the circumcision, and a mild case of dehydration. They would have to watch for internal bleeding, the doctor said.

"His body should be completely dried out." The doctor shook his head in awed disbelief. "Unbelievable."

"Why won't he wake up?" Sinan asked.

"Exhaustion."

"But he'll wake?"

"Yes."

The doctor turned to Sinan.

"Let me look at you. Your left eye is dilated." The doctor shined a light in Sinan's eyes and the pain flashed in his head. "You have a mild concussion," he said. "We'll have to run some tests later." Then outside the room a door slammed, people yelled, and a man ran by with a woman hoisted over his shoulders. The doctor left and never came back, to run the tests or to do anything else.

Sinan spent the night sitting upright in a metal chair beside İsmail's bed in an icy room surrounded by seven dead bodies. He could hear the hospital's generators laboring beyond the cold walls. He checked the walls for cracks and found one etched from ceiling to floor, marking the edges of bricks hidden beneath egg-colored paint. The other rooms of the hospital were full, the nurse told him when he asked to move the bed, and the hallways were filling up with corpses. The air conditioners had been turned up until there was space in the morgues. She darkened the room to save them the burden of seeing the bodies, and switched on a bedside lamp that threw a weak yellow glow across the bed. The darkness eased the throbbing at Sinan's temples and for a while he could pretend that the rest of the world did not exist, that there was only his son breathing on this bed.

The boy's face seemed sunken, diminished of muscle and fat. Sinan held İsmail's hand and felt the bone of the knuckles, ran his fingers over the soft pads of his son's palm. An IV punctured a vein in İsmail's forearm, and Sinan noticed how tiny İsmail's arms really were. Before this he had felt his son was growing too fast, his body too quickly thickening into a young man's, but now he recognized how truly fragile he was. Life had barely taken root in him and the boy's body seemed ready to give it up.

Sinan tucked the blanket underneath İsmail's shoulders, back, and legs. He rested his head on his hands and watched the rise and fall of İsmail's breath, counting the seconds between each one. Sometime in the night the nurse draped a blanket over his shoulders, and, as if being given permission, he fell asleep . . .

"Oh, Baba, it hurts."

Sinan snapped awake, lifting his head from İsmail's lap where it had fallen.

"It hurts, Baba."

Electrified with panic, Sinan shoved the blankets aside and tried to see if he was bleeding internally. He looked for red streaks, or a rash creeping across the skin. He tried to see something moving beneath the surface. What would it look like? He should have asked the doctor.

"Where?" Sinan said. "Where does it hurt?"

But İsmail just moaned.

"Tell me, İsmail. Where?"

With both hands, İsmail grabbed his crotch. "Here," he said. "It burns."

Sinan tried not to, but he burst out laughing.

"It's not funny, Baba. It hurts! Bad!"

"I know," Sinan said, trying to control his relief. "I remember. But in a couple of days it will all be over."

At that moment the nurse wheeled in another body and pushed it against the wall. After she left, a blue arm slipped from beneath the sheet and hung in the air.

"I'm sorry," Sinan said. "You shouldn't see this. You're too young."

"It's all right, Baba," İsmail said. "Sarah Hanım died and it wasn't bad."

Sinan flashed on an image of the American's wife's fingers clutching on to his son. The rest of her body had been limp, lifeless.

"She just went to sleep," İsmail said. "Then she got heavy. It wasn't bad. Just quiet."

The boy's eyebrows furrowed and his lips downturned in what seemed to be the beginnings of a shuddering cry. Sinan walked over to the body and hesitated before lifting the arm by the wrist. The skin was cold, stiff, and rough-feeling, like the fibrous paper bags he wrapped produce in at the grocery.

"Is that her?" İsmail said.

"No, my son. I don't know where she is."

He tucked the arm away again and held it there a moment to be sure it wouldn't spring back to life.

"It's nothing to be scared of, İsmail," Sinan said. "They're at peace now."

"I'm not scared," İsmail said. "I thought I was going to die and it was okay, just like getting too tired."

Hearing his son speak like this sent a shiver along Sinan's spine.

"Sarah Hanım kissed me before she died," İsmail said. His eyes had not left the body.

"It's okay, İsmail," Sinan said. "Rest now."

"When I woke up after falling," İsmail continued as though the words were spilling out, "she was holding me. She told me Mother loved me and that it would be okay. She said I would see *Anne* again, but I didn't believe her. Her voice was so sad." He rubbed his eyes with the back of his hands, and then stared at the ground.

Sinan touched İsmail's back and felt the boy's heart beating through his ribs.

"Water sprayed on us and made me cold but then it stopped and it got really quiet. She kept reaching behind me and then she'd drip water into my mouth. It tasted real bad, but I was thirsty."

This is what saved him, Sinan thought. May God, His mercifulness, bless her soul.

"She kept talking about a dog in the snow, but her voice was quiet and it was hard to hear her. The dog ran through the trees and pushed his nose into the snow, but then she started speaking English and I couldn't understand her. Her breath tickled my ear and I couldn't scratch it because she was on my arm. It tickled for a long time and I wanted to scratch it so bad, Baba."

"Shh, İsmail." He wanted to cry with thankfulness.

"It made me want to scream. Then it didn't tickle anymore."

Sinan remembered how alone he had felt after his father was killed, how empty and separate from the world, and it pained him to know his son had experienced such loss. If there was one thing he wanted in life, it was to keep his children from such pain.

"I feel bad because I was happy she wasn't tickling me anymore."

"It's okay." He kissed the top of İsmail's head.

"Are mother and İrem dead?" he said, screeching it out.

"No. They're fine."

But he couldn't be sure. My God, he had left them alone all these days. Anything could have happened to them by now.

"Because I thought they might be dead like Sarah Hanım."

"No, no, İsmailcan. They *are* fine." He tried to pull İsmail close, but the boy tugged away, his eyes bulging with fear. "Shh, now. It's okay to be scared."

"I'm not scared," İsmail said. "It was so dark, Baba."

"I know. I know." The boy wouldn't be held and this scared Sinan more than anything. What could happen to a child that would make him refuse to be held by his father?

"It's okay, İsmail."

"It was so quiet." He tried to control himself. "I'm sorry for crying."

"It's okay, *canım*. Cry."

The nurse gave İsmail a couple of pills for the pain and near sunrise they both nodded off to sleep. Sinan woke to yelling and the sound of wheels squeaking down the hall. The noise didn't wake İsmail, and Sinan sat and watched his son's face until sunlight filtered through the single window in the examination room. He woke İsmail with a kiss on the forehead.

"I'll be back," he said.

It nearly killed him to do so, but he left his son alone in a room full of death so he could find his wife and daughter, and as he walked out the door, İsmail called after him in his bravest voice.

"Don't worry, Baba," İsmail said, sitting straight up in bed. "I'm fine."

Chapter 11

NILÜFER WAS GOING CRAZY AND İREM COULDN'T CALM HER. The first two days after the earthquake, while her father sat in the dirt and prayed for İsmail, İrem had followed her mother through the streets, the buildings leaning like card houses above their heads. She followed her into half-collapsed buildings where bodies were being pulled from the rubble. Once, when a young boy was lifted from a pile, his head crumpled like a popped balloon, Nilüfer nearly stripped the boy out of the man's arms before İrem could yank her away. Nilüfer spun around and slapped İrem on the cheek.

"It's not him," İrem said.

Her mother glared at her, her bloodied hand lifted for another strike.

"Mother, it's not İsmail."

She lunged as if to strike İrem, but then slapped her palms to her head and ripped fistfuls of her own hair from her scalp. İrem followed behind, snatching strands of hair from the ground as though she were picking oregano at the stem. She wrapped the hair in her mother's head scarf and clutched the nest to her chest because she was terrified to leave those pieces of her mother on the ground. They spent that night on the cement slabs of the waterfront, her mother finally passing out on her lap as İrem tried to smooth the hair over the raw spots.

They awoke in the morning to an aftershock, waves of water sloshing against the cement and wetting İrem's skirt. One of the leaning buildings spilled over, and even though it was two blocks away, glass and metal clattered at their feet.

"Oh, God. Oh, God," Nilüfer said, as she jumped up and ran down the broken sidewalk, holding her head. İrem caught her, calmed her, and took her mother by the arm so that it seemed they were simply out for an early morning stroll. She sang a lullaby to her mother, one her father used to sing when she was a child, as she led them down the waterfront and out through the fields where yellow chamomile swayed in the breeze and back through the alleys near the slaughterhouses and by the time they wandered into town, the police wouldn't let them back in. Too dangerous, they said. Possibility of disease. Did they know about İsmail? No, the police said. Did they know where Sinan was? No.

Now, on the fourth day, she and her mother sat on a square of cement beneath the leaning sign of a BP gas station, the fetor of gasoline burning her nostrils. The metal pole that held the BP sign was bent and the metal squeaked loose in the wind, but it was too hot to sit in the sun and there was no water to drink and she didn't know what else to do. Earlier that day, she had picked up a shard of blue glass from the ground, a shattered piece of an "evil eye" pendant, and she had placed it in the pocket of her skirt in hopes it still held some power. Now she pressed her thumb against the sharp edge of the glass, and she found that this little prick of pain helped her to stay calm.

"My son," Nilüfer kept saying under her breath, followed by intervals of deathly silence.

"He's okay, *Anne*," İrem said, patting her mother's rounded shoulders. She tried to sound like she believed it, but she heard the lie in her voice.

She wanted to cry for her brother, even though she was, strangely, jealous of him. If he were dead, she wondered if he was looking down now and smiling, satisfied that his parents were sufficiently devastated.

She didn't know if Dylan had survived, or her friend Dilek. She watched every man that passed, hoping to recognize Dylan's gait or the funny way he dropped his hand after puffing on a cigarette. She thought she saw Dilek once, a figure picking rotten tomatoes from a spilled refrigerator. From behind the girl had the same dark hair, the slight, sloping shoulders. She left her mother and started to run to her friend, but the woman turned around and the weight of dashed hope dropped into İrem's stomach. She wanted someone to hold her and tell her it would be okay, but now she knew the limits of her parents' strength, and she was terrified to realize that her strength surpassed theirs.

When she saw her father coming down the hill from the highway she wanted to run to him, but she couldn't. Instead, she waited.

"Here he comes," İrem said.

The tall buildings in the distance, though fallen, towered over him. He looked tiny to her and weak as he limped on his twisted leg, and for the first time in her life he seemed more an ordinary man than her father.

"İsmail?" Nilüfer said, running toward Sinan. "İsmail?"

İrem stayed sitting on the cement, thankful to let her mother stumble away from her, and watched as they held each other. They seemed completely separate from her, their arms like a little fortress.

"He's okay," her father whispered in her mother's ear. "He's all right, thank God, His mercifulness."

Sinan looked at her over her mother's shoulder. His eyes were red-rimmed and sunken and she wished she hadn't noticed because she felt a pang of sorrow for him. He looked more exhausted than she had ever seen him, and this was a man who was always tired.

"He's alive?" Nilüfer said, pushing his shoulders away from her to look into his eyes.

"Yes. Yes, Nilüfer."

Her mother shook uncontrollably and let out a half cry, half laugh. It sounded to İrem as though she had finally broken apart and she wouldn't have been surprised if her mother had fallen to the ground in pieces.

"He's at the German hospital," Sinan said. "A miracle of God's graciousness."

İrem started to cry then, too, but mixed with the relief she felt something ugly rise inside of her, something that made her want to bite off her tongue. Her father took her in his arms. He reeked of sweat and blood and antiseptic and she struggled in his arms, as though her body was trying to shake loose everything she'd had to bear in the last four days. She hit him once in the stomach, and a pop of air escaped from his mouth. And then she let herself be held, just fell into his arms, and he held her up, even after her legs gave out.

Chapter 12

I T WAS THE NINTH MORNING AFTER THE QUAKE, AND ONCE again Sinan had not slept. The sun had not yet struck the sea and the water lay in the distance like a pool of oil. In the early morning blue light, he could see the police boats, assisted by fishermen, working the shoreline, pulling the remaining bodies from the water. After leaving the hospital, he had been told to keep his family away from the water for fear of disease. Ruptured gas lines spewed invisible clouds and it smelled as if the sky would explode. The buildings that remained in town teetered on the edges of their broken foundations, and a scientist from Bosporus University kept speaking on the radio, warning about another quake coming, one larger than the aftershocks that kept splintering the ground. So the safest place was here, up the hill from the sea, in the small grassy center of the highway on-ramp. The buildings up here—the huge Carrefour store, a Fiat car dealership, a couple of gas stations—had not collapsed, and nothing but empty sky towered above them.

He sat beneath the makeshift tent he had constructed three nights before, his hand wrapped in gauze, and watched with amazement— because he wouldn't have been shocked if the sun never rose again— as blue spilled across the sky until, like a hole punched through a screen, the sun struck the world. The peaks of the hills sparked like matchsticks set aflame and soon the whole coastal range was saturated with color, etching ridges and valleys out of shadow. Deer grazed in those hills, wild cats hunted alone, and endangered African birds roosted in the trees until the end of summer. Lakes lay hidden behind the ridges, and meadows of grass fed grazing sheep. There was a whole wilderness just meters away, and the beauty of it this morning felt like a mocking.

Three other families were camped at this spot, along with a man who sat in the burned grass drinking bottles of beer he had looted from a destroyed liquor store. They were camped embarrassingly close to one another, and it was difficult not to notice the intimate routines of life—a woman brushing her teeth, a man relieving himself behind a tree trunk, a husband's arm wrapped around his wife's waist in sleep. He tried to shield Nilüfer and İrem from the others, tried to help them retain their modesty, but the cardboard he had tied together flapped in the wind and in the afternoon light it was easy to see through the white bedsheets he had hung as walls. Last night, İrem had tried to use a washcloth to clean herself, exposing her arms for a few moments, revealing the calves of her legs, and the man with the beer had stared at her skin—sleepy, drunken eyes enjoying the opportunity. Sinan lost his temper and knocked the beer out of the man's hands. The other families watched the scene and he could only hope they understood what he was trying to protect.

He was so exhausted last night that he thought he might sleep, but then the drunken man returned with another bottle of Efes, ensconcing himself in the place he had been before. A car exited the freeway, apparently arriving from a place not destroyed in the quake. Its headlights swept across Sinan's face, and he felt as though he had been caught in some illegal act, and then, when it got quiet and his family and the others were asleep, the questions about what to do assailed him. They had not eaten more than a few pieces of bread and some rotten apples in three days. He had five million lira in his back pocket and that wouldn't even get them to İstanbul. Since returning from the German hospital, he had watched for ambulances or military trucks bringing supplies, but none came. Yesterday when he returned to the apartment to scavenge whatever possessions he could, he stopped with others to listen to a man's battery-powered radio. The government report said the roads between Gölcük and İstanbul had collapsed. Cars still passed on the freeway, though, admittedly, there were far fewer than on a normal morning. People in town said the government would take care of them and when the government didn't they said the military would and now that the military hadn't arrived no one spoke anymore about being cared for.

In the distance now, in some other town where the mosque had not been destroyed, he heard the remaining notes of the call to prayer echo across the water like a forgotten memory. He still prayed—even though he could not wash—on the hillside, prostrating himself. Nilüfer coughed in her sleep and he stopped praying to watch her. She lay with her arms wrapped around İsmail's chest. Her right hand grasped İrem's blouse, the girl having pulled away from her mother's embrace sometime in the night.

Theirs was an arranged marriage. Nilüfer was practically a sister to him. Having been raised just two homes away in Yeşilli, she and Sinan played together as children. He knew from the day he was eleven years old that he would marry her, and she did, too. It could have been resignation to a fate out of your control or the comfort that comes with the securing of your future, but he was prepared to love her years before they were married at sixteen. Even so, this is not what he had promised her. Nothing in their life together was what he'd promised her—the escape from the only home they'd known, the stuffy apartment surrounded by cement, two children instead of the half-dozen they talked about when they were young, and he couldn't help feeling responsible in some way for the earthquake, for the fact that they were homeless.

He watched the sun glance across his wife's face—the wrinkles around her eyes, the wisps of black hair showing at her temples, the mole caught in the fold of her bottom lip. He softly pulled her head scarf back to see splotches of scalp where she had ripped her hair out, and he replaced the scarf to cover up that pain. He could still see the child in her face, lost there behind a layer of concern that remained even in sleep. He wanted to lie in her arms, feel the softness of her chest pushing against his back, feel her breath along the ridge of his neck. He was tired and he wanted to give up, and he thought Nilüfer would understand; he thought she would allow him that weakness if he would allow it himself.

He glanced around the circle of grass. The man who had been drinking beer was splayed out on his back. Two other families had not stirred, and the loose fabric of their tents flapped lonely in the morning breeze. A woman poked at a fire in the third camp, and he smelled boiling tea, but her back was turned to him. Satisfied that there were no prying eyes, he laid his hand on his wife's cheek and kissed her lips.

But a man yelling in the distance interrupted the kiss. When Sinan stood he saw a flock of sheep coming across the highway. A few cars stopped to let the animals pass, something that would never have happened in the normal morning rush. The animals huddled together, a mass of dirty woolen shoulders pushing against one another, their black hooves clicking against the pavement, the tin bell on the leading sheep flatly tinkling. Some of the sheep balked at crossing the road, others bent their heads to the pavement in hopes of finding grass, but the shepherd quickly tapped these animals on the rear end with his staff and herded them back into the flock. Sinan thought he recognized the man, but couldn't remember his name. A wool cap hung low over his eyes and he wore a dark vest over a white long-sleeve shirt. Each Kurban Bayram, the man brought his sheep out of the hills and into town to be sold into slaughter for the holiday feasts, but Sinan had never seen him at any other time of the year. The sheep should be high in the hills now, pasturing the summer away to fatness.

As the flock passed between the tents, Sinan smelled the pungent mildew of wool, and his stomach twisted with hunger. He watched the eyes of the passing animals—big, black, stupid eyes—and could only think of the meat clinging to their bones. The shepherd tipped his hat as he passed. His face was an intersection of bones, the sun-burned skin pulled taut across their ridges—the face of a man subject to nature, rather than the stagnant air of the city. It was a calm face, despite the wear, a face that accepted the role of killer of the animals under his protection.

In a bag full of the things he brought back from their apartment, Sinan found a knife. He stood and followed the last of the sheep through the grass, across the on-ramp, and down the hill into the destroyed flatlands of town. He kept the blade of the knife cupped in his palm. He didn't join the man—there was a solitary nature about the shepherd that was important not to disturb—but rather Sinan followed close behind and a little to his left so that he could see the man's face. The shepherd didn't acknowledge him or seem disturbed by the sight of collapsed buildings, and he whistled as he walked—an old song, a *türkü* about the love for a village girl. The sheep clambered over broken bricks and debris as if climbing the rocky slopes of mountaintops, oblivious to the consequences of the world. Women washing clothes in a bucket turned to watch the flock pass. A few men smoking cigarettes at a card table snuffed out their butts, got up, and followed.

The shepherd reached a field just off Atatürk Street that was surrounded by hothouses for tomatoes, and here he stopped to let the animals graze in the dry grass. What tomatoes were left beneath the plastic domes were rotten and smelled of organic decay, yet there was enough of a hint to the fresh fruit, ripe and full of juice and seed, that it touched the hunger in Sinan. He and the other men stopped in the middle of the field, surrounded by the soft mastications of grazing sheep.

"They're not fattened," the shepherd said to the men. "But they're yours to take."

"Thank you, brother," Sinan said.

He was embarrassed to take advantage of the man's offer, but he had little other choice. He tried to find the weakest animal—a generous offer requires generosity in the taking. Near the edge of a hot-house where the weeds were high, he discovered an old ewe, her movements slow and weak as though her joints were stiffened with arthritis.

He pulled out his knife and took her by the chin. She raised her head as though expecting to be petted. He straddled the ewe's haunches, turned her body toward Mecca, lifted her throat, and made a quick incision that severed the ligaments and windpipe. She kicked her rear hooves, stepping on his toes and cutting his shins through his pants. He held her head to his chest to keep her still and watched her black eye, bulged and blaming, grow soft and flat until it was nothing but a stone.

"God is great," he whispered.

That's when he heard the trucks, their heavy gears downshifting, the engines revving and winding down to a crawl. With the dead sheep's head in his lap, he paused to watch the line of produce trucks bounce violently over potholes and pavement cracks. They were painted red with hand-stenciled flowers and gaudy calligraphy, and their brightness was shocking against the cement gray and burned-out yellow summer landscape.

Every Tuesday in the center of town, an open market was held. At five A.M., men wedged metal poles into the pavement, fastened canvas sheets atop the poles, and hung the fabric across the street to shade rows of wooden tables. For ten whole blocks, fruits and vegetables, fresh spices, nuts, even cheeses and olives overflowed the tables. Sinan's stomach constricted with the memory, and he was filled with a momentary hope that produce was the cargo of this caravan.

But as the trucks approached, he saw that the truck beds were not filled with fresh produce but instead with stacked canvas bags. The first truck passed, blowing an exhaust-filled wind into his face. Imprinted on the canvas bags were American flags and next to that in black spray paint were little crosses and a name in English that he could not read. Three more trucks passed, all of them loaded with food and other supplies. The last vehicle wasn't a produce truck, but a water truck, the valve in the rear leaking a trail of wet on the cement.

Following the trucks was a line of white minibuses filled with Europeans or Americans—he couldn't tell which. Elbows out the windows, their T-shirt sleeves blowing in the wind. Fancy black sunglasses, the bill of a sports cap. A few of the people smiled as they passed, as though on vacation—tourists come down to see the damage. He had heard about this. Some entrepreneurial travel agents from İstanbul had arranged tours to see the towns destroyed by the earthquake, for which "adventure" tourists were said to be paying incredible prices.

He was about to curse them, when through the windshield of the last bus he saw the American director in the passenger seat waving an arm at the driver. The truck downshifted—the sound like metal shearing metal—but did not stop. The American smiled and held his hand out the window in a prolonged wave. As they passed, Sinan caught a glimpse of the man's son, his earphones stuck in his ears, his face grave and drawn looking.

Sinan was ashamed. He had never thanked the American. As soon as he had İsmail in his arms, nothing else had mattered and he had left the director alone with his dead wife—the woman who had saved İsmail's life. Shameful.

Because his hands were full, he nodded and hoped it would be interpreted as thanks, but the bus had already passed.

Chapter 13

İREM COULDN'T STAND IT ANYMORE. FOR FOUR DAYS NOW SHE had sat inside this tent wondering if Dylan was alive. Every hour, it seemed, of each of those four days her mother checked for strange marks on İsmail's skin, watched for enlarged pupils, pressed her palm against his forehead, which was always too hot, too cold, or too sweaty. She tugged on his tongue. "That bump wasn't there this morning. İrem, was that bump there this morning?" İsmail was fine, at least as fine as anyone could be after the quake, but he willingly endured his ears being folded back, his eyelids tugged open, his lips yanked apart, and a prodding finger sliding around his gums.

So when she woke this morning, after yet another dream of her teeth falling out—each one *plunk, plunk, plunk*ing onto the tiled floor of their now-nonexistent bathroom—and found her father gone for the first time since they left the hospital, and her mother and İsmail still asleep, she sneaked out of the tent and ran down the hill into town.

İrem found her best friend, Dilek, and her mother, Yasemin Hanım, camped on the retaining wall that ran from the port along the sea to the destroyed amusement park. They were huddled together beneath a sagging blanket tied to two sticks wedged in cracks in the pavement.

"Both your mother and father are alive?" Dilek's mother asked İrem.

"Yes," İrem said.

"Good," Yasemin Hanım said. She had been a well-kept woman who favored Vakko blouses and tailored pants, her hair always pinned back with a gold broach, but now she wore a shirt ripped at the shoulder and her curly hair was wild and hung in her face. "Good," she said again. "Your mother is lucky."

Dilek stroked her mother's shoulder, and told İrem with amazing calm that her father had been killed in the quake, one of thirty men crushed in the *kıraathane* down Atatürk Street. Behind them, the cars hovering above the water of the half-submerged Ferris wheel rocked in the morning wind, the metal joints creaking.

"I'm sorry for your loss, Yasemin Hanım," İrem said. "May your pain pass quickly."

"Always spending his time at the *kıraathane* playing cards with the men," she said. "What's wrong with me?"

Dilek removed her hand from her mother's shoulder, and placed her arms across her chest as though hugging herself.

"Your father's a good man," Yasemin said to İrem. "He's always home with his family."

"Anne," Dilek said to her mother. "Please don't speak poorly of father."

"Do you know what it's like?" she said, snapping her head toward Dilek. "Always gone to play cards, always gone on business, always gone into town." She pushed her palms against her eye sockets. "He had a woman, I tell you."

"He didn't," Dilek said. "Now stop it."

"He did," she said. "I know it. Always gone playing cards. Humph! If he'd been home," she said, her face in her hands now. "He'd be here now."

"I know, Anne," Dilek said, stroking her shoulder again. "I know."

They sat for a while, Dilek trying to calm her mother, and İrem staring at the Ferris wheel cars still hanging above the water. The sub-

merged cars, mirror images of the ones above, floated beneath the surface like huge, brightly colored beetles.

"İrem and I are going for a walk."

"Yes," Dilek's mother said. "Leave me here alone."

"I'll be back."

"Yes, yes."

Dilek took İrem's hand and held it to her cheek as they walked
along the broken waterfront. The sun was up now and the morning
breeze stirred the smell of rot and gasoline.

"She's driving me crazy," Dilek said. "She won't even let me cry
for him. She just says, 'You wouldn't be crying if he had been
home.'"

Then Dilek cried and İrem held her and pulled her head to her
shoulder and watched buckets of ice cream float out from a half-
submerged ice-cream shop. Some of the buckets had burst open and
green swirls of pistachio glistened on the surface of the water. A moment later a bloated body floated through the swirls, its clothes bursting at the seams, its skin as white and pasty as bread dough.

Dilek tried to pull away from İrem, but İrem held her a few moments longer until the body bobbed past.

"No one can protect us," Dilek said, as they continued down the
sea walk, the cement striated with cracks. "No one."

İrem blinked, and across the black screen of her closed eyelids the
white skin of the floating body appeared. She tried to ignore it, but
she was suddenly scared it was Dylan and she tried to remember, tried
to see the body clearly to be sure it wasn't him.

"I realize that now," Dilek continued. "I used to think my father
could keep me safe."

They stopped at a four-foot fissure in the walkway. Three chickens
clucked past and flapped themselves into the air just long enough to
reach the other side.

"How's Ayşe?" İrem asked. She had seen her friend alive just after
the quake, but she hadn't seen her since.

"She's fine; her family is fine. Her parrot died."

"Well, at least we won't have to listen to that horrible squawking anymore."

Ayşe used to hang the caged bird from a hook outside her bedroom window. From that perch two stories above the street, the bird let out the most horrible noise that was like listening to a child's colicky tantrum. The water boys hated it because the parrot had a habit of aiming its droppings at the part in their slicked-back hair.

Dilek laughed out loud. "Allah, Allah," she said. "That was a terrible bird."

They sat down together on a slab of concrete that overlooked the water. From here, if İrem looked directly away from shore, it was almost possible to forget the chaos that was behind them. The water lulled İrem, calmed her, and she wanted to dive in and stay underwater where nothing could be broken, where nothing could crush her.

"Have you seen Dylan?" she finally asked.

"No, İrem. I heard he went back to America."

"He's alive?"

"Yes."

Relief and disappointment, both, rose inside her simultaneously.

"Back to America?"

"That's what I heard," Dilek said. "He and his father."

İrem picked at her fingernails and watched two jellyfish push up against each other in the murky water.

"Wouldn't you leave, too, if you could?" Dilek said.

"Of course. It's not that. The night of the quake he tried to touch me, but I pulled away."

"Where were you?" Dilek said, and suddenly it was just like it was before the quake. Where were you? What happened? How did it feel?"

"The kitchen."

"The kitchen?!"

"Yes, and my parents in the next room with the guests."

Dilek put her hand to her face, her eyebrows narrowing into a devilish grin.

"Oh, I would have let him, İrem," Dilek said. "He's so handsome."

"Yes, well, your parents are different." Dilek's father had been a school inspector, and, being the good Western-leaning government official he was, had hated anything that even resembled a hijab, and he despised anyone in an *abaya*. He would rather see a woman walk naked down the street, Dilek had once quoted him as saying, than see her wrapped in those fundamentalist robes. He shaved three times a day, according to Dilek, so he wouldn't be mistaken for growing a beard.

"I'll never see him again," İrem said.

Dilek's smile left her face.

"Oh, Dilek," İrem said, remembering her friend's father. "I'm sorry."

"No, no," she said. "It's okay. I understand. This is different. Fathers and lovers are different things."

"He's not my lover."

Dilek didn't know anything about a lover—at least İrem thought she didn't—but she liked to say such things.

"I know, I know," Dilek said. "But it's nice to think about, isn't it?"

İrem just smiled and the smile grew into a laugh until they were both laughing and then the laughing fell back into silence.

"Everything's changed," İrem said. "I've changed. Even before the earthquake."

"I was mad at my dad the night it happened," Dilek said. "Usually I kiss him good night, but I caught him on his cell phone on the terrace. I think my mother is right. He had a woman. But I still wish I'd kissed him good night."

They sat silently for a minute, watching the transparent water become opaque as the sun rose and shone down flatly on the sea. Behind them, coming down the broken road, İrem heard a rumbling. With no electricity, no open stores, with nothing to do but sit around and wait, the silence in town had become deafening, and at first she thought it was the rumbling of another aftershock. In panic, they both spun around, relieved to see a line of trucks coming down the broken road.

"I thought it was happening again," İrem said.

"A professor on the radio keeps saying a bigger quake is coming," Dilek said.

İrem couldn't imagine a bigger quake.

There were five produce trucks at first, and then a line of white buses, like those used to bus rich students to their rich private schools. The first bus passed, and İrem and Dilek could see they were not Turks. The fourth bus passed, and through the window İrem caught a glimpse of Dylan, his head bowed, his earphones stuck in his ears. She waved, but he didn't look out the window.

İrem grabbed Dilek's shoulder. "It's him!" she said.

Dilek hugged İrem and whispered into her ear. "Just remember," she said. "You both might be dead before morning comes."

Chapter 14

THE TRUCKS DROVE OUT OF SIGHT AND SINAN FOLLOWED the sound of their engines until they turned the corner, toward an empty field that used to be the recreation grounds to the old Ottoman prison. Watching the back of the buses throwing up dust from the road, Sinan was reminded of the jeeps the Turkish paramilitaries had driven through the center of Yeşilli. Once he watched a driver speed up to run over a chicken, Emre Bey's family's only rooster, the breast of the bird popping open like a crushed melon. Another time, three jeeps parked in the center of the village on market day, keeping the produce sellers from setting up their tables.

The jeeps were built in America, his father had said.

In the South everyone knew America supported the Turkish paramilitary, the Special Teams, as they were called, giving them training and weapons and shelter from the U.N. while they destroyed whole villages in search of Öcalan and the PKK. All the Turks knew this, all the U.N. knew this, but it was kept quiet as if it didn't happen. "Because America wants to spy on Russia," his father told him once, "we get murdered." Now the Americans were here to help. It was confusing, what to believe about America.

Using twine from the tomato vines, Sinan hung the ewe from a nearby tree, gutted it, and let it bleed. He sat on his haunches and watched the blood drip and soak into the ground.

He was so sick of death. There were people in the world that never had to face death, except in old age, when death is almost comforting. But they never had to face the violence of a young death. They never had to bury their father with tissue paper stuffed and sewn into his collapsed skull. They were mean, stupid people, he imagined, sitting in their homes in America or England, staring vacantly at their televisions, falling asleep in a bored stupor on their couches. He hated and wanted to be one of those vacant people.

Yesterday, at the ice-skating rink, he had identified the bodies of Ahmet and his family. Their faces had been calm, their bodies bloodless, but he could see where their ribs had been broken, where their chests lay as flat as their stomachs. Overwhelmed, he had embraced Ahmet before they wrapped his brother-in-law's body in a bag, tied it together at his ankles and shoulders, and carried him away.

Because officials were afraid of the spread of disease, all the dead, including Ahmet and his family, were tossed into a common grave. The mayor was there, standing at the edge of the open pit, alternately trying to comfort family members who were praying over the burlap bags and loudly criticizing the government.

"I'm sorry," he said, pressing a handkerchief to his nose. "I'm sorry, but we must bury them now." He poured lemon *kolonya* over his already soaked handkerchief and pressed it again to his nose "Where's the government? Where's the Red Crescent?" Touching a mourner's shoulder, he said, "I'm so sorry, but we must do this."

Before the mourners' prayers were finished, bulldozers covered the bags with earth, and still people remained, speaking to the bumps and curves of the torn-up ground.

For a moment now, staring at the swollen flap of the sheep's distended tongue, Sinan imagined death as a one-way mirror, like the glass it was said the Special Teams unit sat behind while watching the interrogations and torture of suspected PKK rebels. Some men—the ones who survived and came back to Yeşilli to tell their story—said it was the being watched, the knowledge that men drank tea just on the other side of the glass while they were being beaten, that made the torture so unbearable. Most of the men who were tortured didn't even care about a "Kurdistan"; they simply wanted to live their lives—speak *their* language instead of Turkish, farm their fields, tend to their sheep, feed their families. Once you were behind that glass, though, Kurdistan Workers' Party or not, separatist or Turkish nationalist, you might as well have been dead, because your body no longer belonged to you; it belonged to the brutality or mercy of a man and that man belonged to the Turkish state and his fists were the fists of the Turkish Republic and his boot was the boot of the Turkish Republic and the electricity that convulsed your body was provided by the Turkish Republic and the blood that was spilled, even if it was Kurdish blood, was the color of the Turkish Republic's flag.

It seemed to Sinan that the living and the dead were separated by a thin membrane through which the living could not see, a membrane punctured only briefly at the moment of death, and he wondered if Ahmet, Gülfem, and Zeynep stood just on the other side now, so close but out of sight and out of reach. He wondered if Sarah Hanım stood there, too—looking in and regretting her sacrifice. His father, even, although he had been dead all these years. He imagined that if he looked closely enough at the dead sheep he would see some reflection of death, some living element in it, but all he saw was an eye, black and empty, and pooled blood as useless as spilled water.

By the time the animal was ready, the shepherd and his flock were gone—where to, Sinan did not know. It struck Sinan that God had sent the shepherd, and if he sent the shepherd then perhaps he had sent the Americans as well. He felt a sudden jolt of hope that this was part of some plan, some reminder from Him not to get too attached to his brief time on earth, because to be with your Father is the greatest—the only real existence. And that's how the dead finally won over all living people, torturer or loving family member. No matter who you were, no matter how weak and helpless, once you were dead you knew what it meant to be with God and the living did not know and the not knowing haunted the living and the haunting was the doubt that God existed at all.

He skinned the animal, untied the twine, and slung the carcass over his shoulders. There was still a little blood coming from the gash and it trickled warm across his shoulders and chest. It was an unclean thing to carry an animal in such a way, and the burden of it made him a little sick to his stomach—he had never liked killing; it always made him brood with guilt. Two of the other men waited near their animals and smoked. Sinan nodded to them as he passed and they nodded back.

"May it go easily," Sinan said.

"For you, too," the older of the two men replied.

CARRYING THE SHEEP ON his shoulders now, he remembered lifting the American's wife from the rubble.

Just like her, the ewe's body felt light and insubstantial.

Just like the American's wife, the animal's skin was still warm, though stiff and lifeless.

It embarrassed Sinan to carry the sheep through the streets where people were forced to watch, their eyes hungry, their memories filled with dead bodies, but he needed something in which to place the meat so it would not spoil. He checked what remained of the grocery, walked two blocks to where the hardware store had once stood, and then down near the ruined port where the men used to sell their fish, but he couldn't find anything, nothing was as it had been. He discovered a blanket, hanging from the edge of a leaning wall, and he pulled it loose with one hand and laid the sheep's body in it.

He carried the carcass up the road through the rubble of town, past the old *kıraathane* where thirty men had been crushed while playing the men's club's late-night card game. He kicked unbroken tea glasses out of his path, and saw the terrible pictures on a loose front page of the newspaper *Milliyet*. Four men were hauling a couch down the street, hurrying their feet as if they were being chased. Coming through the broken front window of an electronics store, a woman carried an intact color television. Where she would watch it, Sinan couldn't imagine.

"Much shame on you," Sinan said to her through his teeth.

She stared back, her eyes flashing with anger, but she said nothing.

He stopped at the spot where İsmail had been buried nine days before. He remembered Sarah Hanım's arms wrapped around his son, the beams of wood and chunks of cement that crushed her ribs instead of İsmail's.

He started back to the tent, but changed his mind. He would have to thank the American director personally; it was, unfortunately, the right thing to do.

His foot was beginning to ache, but he walked in the direction of the trucks, through the settling dust in their wake. The sun was brutally hot and his hunger and lack of sleep made him feel as though he were wading through water. In the field that used to be the prison yard, Mustard grass rose knee-high and poked through metal carcasses of fifties-era Chevrolets once used as taxis. A rusted chain-link fence surrounded the field and still bore government signs warning against trespassing. There had been too many riots here, Sinan had heard, and the government finally had closed the prison down, and moved it to a deserted part of Anatolia where the guards could better deal with uprisings without being bothered by human rights activists. On the far end of the grounds the remnants of masonry stood crumbled atop a cracked foundation—the last of the prison itself.

By the time Sinan reached the Americans, they were already at work. They were unloading bags of rice and stacking them in the grass, unwrapping rolls of canvas, and hammering poles into the ground. Their energy was amazing to see—there was hope in it, a sense that they had things under control, and Sinan stood on the edge of the field, watching. Townspeople surrounded him, watching with awe, but unwilling or unsure about entering the field to help. The

American director yelled instructions, waved his hands, and directed the traffic of young people all dressed in light blue T-shirts emblazoned with white fish designs. Like a blue army, they unfolded canvas to be stretched atop the poles, and soon a large tent began to take shape, casting a house-sized shadow across the ground.

Sinan laid the sheep on the ground and walked into the field toward the American man. No one seemed to notice at first, but as he reached the group a few of the relief workers turned to stare at him. The frightened look on their faces reminded him that he was covered with blood. He wiped his hands on his pants, but the blood was dry, and before he could change his mind the American had already seen him.

"Please," Sinan said. "I'm sorry. A moment, please."

"You're welcome here," the man said in clear Turkish.

"Please, a moment."

Sinan found the water truck and ran his hands beneath the leaky valve. The blood ran off into the grass but little crescents remained beneath his nails. When he finished, the man was already at his side. Some of the young Americans went on working, but many of them were watching and Sinan became self-conscious. The American held out his hand, but Sinan politely refused. His hands were still unclean.

"Forgive my appearance," Sinan said.

"There's nothing to forgive," the man said.

"I must thank you for my son, Marcus Bey."

"Just Marcus, please. Is he all right?"

"Tired, the boy is tired."

"Where is your family?"

Sinan didn't answer. He looked around the camp. Some of the young people had begun working again, but others still stood and stared. Marcus gestured with his hand to a place behind one of the trucks.

"It's a terrible time for us all," Marcus said.

"I'm very sorry about your wife," Sinan said. "I owe you much gratitude." He should have told him the details of his wife's sacrifice; he wanted to, but he couldn't bring himself to do it. He was ashamed because of it, but this shame would be better than the shame of betraying his father. "She was a good woman."

"Yes, she was. Better than I." Marcus clenched his jaw and looked to the sky for a moment, just long enough, it seemed, to keep himself under control. He sniffed and ran his hand over his goateed mouth. The American was a good husband; Sinan could see that. At least he was good at mourning his wife, and that alone was to be admired. Sinan knew men who wouldn't mourn the death of their wife any more than that of the family goat.

"You owe me nothing," Marcus said, shaking his head. "That was God's work. But if you want to thank me, you can bring your family here."

"Thank you, we're fine."

"There's food, tents, and people who'll take care of you."

"Marcus Bey," Sinan said. "You have tents here, we have a tent there. We're fine. I'll care for my family."

" 'A man's pride shall bring him low,' Sinan, 'but honor shall uphold the humble in spirit.' "

" 'No one eats better food than that earned by his own hands,' " Sinan said.

Marcus nodded and smiled.

"You'll have to forgive me, Sinan Bey," Marcus said, enclosing Sinan's hand in both of his despite the blood that remained, "but I will come tomorrow and the next day and the day after that until you reconsider."

Chapter 15

IREM LEFT DILEK AND RAN TOWARD THE MINIBUSES, WHICH
had disappeared behind the remains of the town mosque. She took a
shortcut past the police barricade and ran toward the open field that
used to be the prison. When she got there, she found the field packed
with foreigners pitching tents and unloading bags from produce
trucks. She stopped, a bit shocked by the scene, and watched them
raise one canvas tent after another in perfect white rows. She started
through the field until she saw her father carrying a goat on his shoulders, the whole left side of his body slathered in blood. Instinctively,
she crouched among the weeds and watched him lay the animal in
the dirt. Then she saw Dylan's father coming toward her father, and
her heart jumped, not because she was about to be caught, but because she knew she wasn't going to let them stop her from finding
Dylan. She scanned the crowd of workers, looking for his shape, until
she found him sitting in one of the white buses, gazing out the window.

He seemed to be staring directly at her, but his face was empty, his
eyes glazed, as though he were looking into some deep emptiness encased in the glass window. She watched her father be led into the
shadow between two trucks, and when his back was turned, she ran
across the field toward the bus.

Dylan threw open the window as soon as he saw her, and hung his torso out of the frame. She jumped into his arms, and she dangled there awkwardly against the hot metal of the bus, her feet two inches above ground. She laughed and couldn't stop laughing, and he began laughing too until he lost his grip and she fell back to the ground.

"I was afraid you were dead," she said. "Or in America and never coming back."

"I couldn't find you." He grabbed her hand and kissed it and electricity shot all the way down to her toes.

"Hold on," she said. "My father." She crouched down, sneaked over to the front of the bus, and peered around the bumper; she could see her father shaking Marcus Bey's hand. "My father's over there." She motioned with her head in their direction. "Talking to your father."

"Shit," he said, glancing over his shoulder. "You've got guts." He pointed to the back of the bus. "Come here."

He ran down the aisle of the bus, and she followed him on the ground to where he tugged open another window.

"There," he said, gesturing to the tires at her feet. "They won't see your legs now."

"My dad thinks I'm going to kill myself or something," he said. "Because of my mother. So he keeps looking over here to make sure I haven't slit my wrists."

"Are you?" For some reason she thought he could do such a thing. He was dangerous enough.

"Not now."

She smiled and she could feel her face flush.

"But I miss her," he said, his voice breaking a little.

She took his hand, and let her fingers stroke his knuckles.

"I'm sorry," she said. There was a gash beneath his right eye and the socket was bruised. She briefly imagined dressing the wound, his face pressed against her blouse, the intimacy of a wife caring for her husband.

"You're hurt," İrem said.

"Just a bruise," he said.

"I've been going crazy."

"Me, too," he said.

"Dilek said you went back to America."

"We did," he said, looking at the ground now. "We buried her and got back on a plane. Right after the wake."

She watched the bump in his neck rise and fall as he swallowed down gathering tears.

"You're staying?" she asked.

"We're staying."

He looked at her now, his eyes soft but lit with excitement, and she felt herself getting lost in them.

"Even at the funeral I kept thinking about you," he said.

"No," she said, letting go of his hand. He shouldn't have been thinking about her on a day of mourning; it was disrespectful toward his mother.

"I swear," he said. "Thinking of you kept me from losing it."

He stared at her and she stared back until his blue eyes embarrassed her and she looked away.

"Damn," he said. "Here comes my dad."

She fell to her knees and looked around the tires beneath the chassis of the bus. She saw the bare legs of Dylan's father striding toward them, and beyond him she could see that her father was already gone.

SHE KNEW HER FATHER would take Atatürk Street back to the tent, so she had to cut through what was left of the Gypsy camp. It reeked of feces and rot, and three filthy children sitting in the dirt watched her as she passed. Somebody screamed behind her and a child cried, but she didn't dare look to see what was happening. A street dog followed beside her, his nose low to the ground, his body swaying from side to side, and as she got closer to their tent, she ran through a field to the street even though she knew she'd be caught and have to suffer her father's anger. He had told her not to leave the tent. He wouldn't

even let her walk around outside, unless she and her mother were going to the toilet of a restaurant half-collapsed and stinking of backed-
up waste, just because some stupid drunk supposedly tried to watch
her wash her legs.

But her father wasn't on the road. She knew, then, that he was already at the tent, and she resigned herself to at least a verbal lashing.

When she arrived, she found her mother and father leaning over
İsmail. He was curled pathetically in a blanket, despite the fact that
the day was already so hot she could feel the scorched dirt through
the soles of her shoes.

"Look at that!" her mother said, stroking near the raised, pink skin
of the cut above İsmail's right eye. Her father turned İsmail's face
toward a streak of sunlight filtering through the rips in the blanketed
rooftop.

"İrem," her mother said, grabbing her hand. "Look at that."

"That cut's been there since the quake," İrem said, frustrated, but
she knew what her mother was scared about. The skin was black in
the middle and blossomed in folds of pink.

"It's infected," her father said.

İsmail's eyes were big and sad and İrem wanted to tell him to stop
playing.

"You need to wash it," her father said.

"What do I wash it with?" Nilüfer said. "We have no soap."

"Use the water, Nilüfer."

"Get a rag," Nilüfer said to İrem.

İrem found a rag hanging on the edge of a bucket they had used to
wash tea glasses earlier that day. The water was murky and the rag
smelled of mildew, but she dipped it and handed it to her mother,
who immediately dabbed at the edge of the cut.

"Oh, my baby," her mother said to İsmail. "Oh, my baby. I'm so
sorry."

Her father pulled back İsmail's eyelids. He turned İsmail's hands
over and looked at his palms.

"Do you feel sick?"

"A little," İsmail said.

İrem sat down on the blankets spread across the floor of the tent and watched them, still out of breath from her run back.

"Oh, *canım*," her mother continued.

"A street dog followed me home," İrem said. "He was foaming at the mouth."

"Does anything else hurt?" her father asked.

"I had to run to get away from it." She rubbed her heel and made a face, hoping her father would notice. "I think I twisted my ankle."

"I thought I lost you," her mother said to İsmail.

"I met a boy," she whispered to herself, watching now the unfurling of the tents in the field below. "An American boy," she thought.

"Oh, I thought I lost you," her mother said again, completely lost now in the festering wound on İsmail's head.

İrem briefly imagined being buried herself beneath the rubble, and the faces of her father and mother glowing with happiness and relief as they pulled her back into the world. They hugged her. They kissed her. They wouldn't let her go.

Chapter 16

"WE NEED A DOCTOR," NILÜFER SAID, DABBING AT İSMAIL'S cut.

"I know," Sinan said.

"Sinan—"

"I know, Nilüfer." He pulled the knife from his pocket and stabbed it into the tendon between the ewe's hindquarters and belly. "Stop washing it. It's as clean as it's going to get with that water."

Nilüfer stopped, but she stood there holding the cloth as though ready to strike at the wound as soon as he turned his back.

"What are we going to do?"

The knife was dull, but he was able to separate the joints, carve through muscle, and peel away fat until he had quartered the animal. As he worked he felt their neighbors' eyes on him.

"Eat," he said.

Nilüfer lit a small fire made of gathered wood and dried weeds, and began to cut the quartered pieces into smaller sections for cooking.

"Cook it all," he said. "It won't last."

She overfilled the pot, but still the pot was not big enough. At best the food she was able to cook would last for two days. He carried what remained of the animal to each of the three other families; it wasn't much—the hide of the hooves, a chunk of the hindquarters, the white fat strips—but he was thanked profusely, an elderly grandfather kissing Sinan's knuckles before raising the hand to his forehead. The drunk was watching now, a desperation in his eyes having returned with sobriety. Sinan remembered the way Ahmet's hands sometimes shook in the morning before he took his first sip of *rakı*, and he felt an intruding pity for this man. He cut away the head of the ewe, stripped the remaining skin from around the eyes, and gave it to the drunk, who stood to receive it.

"I am not a beggar," the man said.

"I know," Sinan said. The pleading in the drunkard's eyes forced Sinan to touch his shoulders. "It's a gift. To help my soul get to Heaven."

Sinan sat down in the evening shade of the tent. He was exhausted. His foot ached in rhythm with his heart, but he was anxious and it was difficult for him to be here, sitting idle, waiting for an answer to what to do next. From the hill he could just barely make out the movements at the camp, and the flashing of white material being raised in the midday light. He had no oil or butter, and the meat burned on the stove, sending up a trail of gray smoke. Still, the smell was intoxicating.

İsmail had gotten up and gone to play. Sinan watched as İsmail kicked a ball in the air, chased it down the hill, ran back up, and repeated the process. İrem fussed with her head scarf, scratching at it, pulling and tugging until her hair broke loose from the fabric.

"Where's the government?" Nilüfer said. "This boy's sick."

İsmail threw the ball into the air and headed it when it came down. "He seems fine now," Sinan said.

"You saw the cut," she said. "You felt his temperature."

He had, and he knew a boy could recover and fall sick again soon; he saw it happen in Yeşilli, a sick child survives a fever in winter only to suddenly die feverish in spring.

"The food is done, Nilüfer?"

Nilüfer closed her mouth and spooned the meat onto chipped plates.

The mutton was tough and burned and they ate in silence. The flies were up in the evening heat and they circled around their heads, lit on the corners of their mouths.

"Is there more, Anne?" İsmail said when it was done.

"Not tonight," Sinan said. "Tomorrow."

"We should go to the American camp," İrem said.

He looked at his daughter. Hair poked out from her scarf and he could see the whole of her hairline above her forehead.

"Americans?" Nilüfer said.

"They're building a camp," İrem said. "I bet they'll have doctors."

A wave of anger rose in him, and he let it show in his face.

İrem looked at the ground and fingered the fringe of a blanket. "Don't you think so, Baba?"

Nilüfer looked at him, a question in her eyes that was working its way down to her lips.

"Yes," he said. "I saw it today." He pushed the plate of bones away toward his daughter. She stood and carried it to the stinking bucket they were using as a sink. "It's not done yet."

"We should go," Nilüfer said.

"It's not finished," he said, his voice beginning to crack with frustration.

Nilüfer dropped her head and bit at her nails.

"İrem," he said. "Come here."

She knelt in front of him. He took her head in his hands and began to adjust the scarf. She would not look at him, but instead turned her eyes away and watched the cars on the freeway. She had his eyes; they were dark and furious and he knew he was going to have real trouble with her.

"I know this is difficult, but what's demanded of us doesn't change."

She blew air out of her nose and her shoulders slumped. He

folded the curls of her hair beneath the fabric; even he was a little sad to cover it up—it was so beautiful, black and rich with streaks of red.

"We must still be who we are," he said.

She looked at him, water in her eyes. "Are you finished?" She said it softly enough to hide the challenge.

"Yes," he said.

In the growing darkness he sat and drank cold tea, but Nilüfer's eyes shamed him and he spun away from their tent and walked into the field, looking at the grass at his feet and trying to calm himself. A blast of light lit the field below and he watched the Americans crisscross the dirt, bathed in the bleaching white of floodlights. They looked like shadows walking on scissor legs. From this distance they seemed to have the efficiency of a machine, a hundred moving parts setting tent after tent in rows, each one casting a triangle across the ground. Just a few meters away from the camp, separated by a low hill, Gölcük was lost in darkness, like a bombed-out village—all collapsed roofs and walls that sheltered nothing except the haunting reminder that life once attached itself to this plot of land.

Sinan needed to do something, he knew—everything was gone, everything had changed—but he couldn't bring himself to take his family into that camp.

At his feet, ants moved among the dried blades of grass like black rivulets of water. Some turned circles in the ground, some climbed over the slow-moving bodies of others, and still others climbed upon his shoes and up over his ankles. He walked over to the ewe's carcass and lifted the blanket. The ants were already upon it.

Chapter 17

"YES, YES, MY BROTHER," KEMAL BEY SAID. "I HAVE A COUSIN who can help you out."

For two days Sinan had been searching for a job—at the open market in Gebze, in the clothing bazaar in Yalova, even at the hot springs in the hills—but there were none to be had; at least none to be had by a Kurdish "terrorist dog," as one butcher near Baghdad Street called him, pulling from his wallet—as Sinan backed out of the shop—an army portrait of a son killed fighting the PKK. He had even tried to sell tissues along with the barefoot boys at the Yalova ferry landing, but there were few cars and fewer buyers and he found himself stuck with a pocketful of tissues he did not need and would not sell. On the third day, today, he ran into Kemal in front of the bull-dozed ground that used to be Kemal's shop.

Kemal produced a cell phone from his pants pocket.

"Can you believe this?" he said, pointing with one hand at the flattened spot that used to be his store as he dialed a number with the other. While he held the phone to his ear, he said, "Life is an angry mistress. You want her, but she'll rip your balls off."

Sinan knew Kemal Aras from the grocery. Before the quake Kemal owned a small electronics shop, but he always came in to the grocery to buy lightbulbs for his store. Ahmet teased him about it, but it had been a good business arrangement: Kemal regularly bought their bulbs—a slow-moving commodity—and sold them, just two blocks away in the light-store district, at inflated prices for a small profit. Although Sinan was not particularly fond of the man—his conversation was always interrupted by cell phone calls and they had to listen to him yell at suppliers in front of their customers—he admired the man's business savvy; he had his own truck with the name of his store painted on the side; a summer before he had installed at his store a beautiful red awning that could be seen from a block away.

"*Merhaba, abi!*"

And now even, while Kemal spoke to his cousin, he yelled into the phone.

"No, *abi!*"

He paced in front of Sinan, the phone to his ear, his head bowed to the dirt. His right cheek was covered in a large bandage, and streaks of blood stained the gauze.

"Good man, yes." He spun a circle in the dirt and threw his hand in the air. "No! He's a friend. At least two hundred."

He nodded and smiled at Sinan.

"No." He nodded again. "Of course, of course."

Then he took the phone from his ear and hung up.

"Okay, my friend." He slapped Sinan on the back. "You have a job. I'd take it myself if my back wasn't so bad." He shook his head. "Allah, Allah, one day a businessman, the next day a mule."

The next morning, Sinan took the two-and-a-half-hour ferry ride to İstanbul, and by nine found himself descending the stairs into a Byzantine cistern in the Bazaar Quarter of the city. He was amazed that the cistern had not collapsed in the quake, but nothing in the center of the city seemed to have been damaged. Above him a small exposed bulb dangled from the brick ceiling and cast the only light on the steps. The cavern was eight hundred years old, musty, with green moss clinging to the cracks in the mortar, but where water was once stored, Sony televisions now stood stacked ten high from floor to arches. A leather harness tugged against his shoulders, and a kind of saddle, with a twelve-inch shelf nailed to the base, lay across his back. His job was to strap two televisions onto his back—three, if he could manage it—and carry them from the back streets of the Bazaar Quarter down to the electronic stores of Sirkeci—a good kilometer walk downhill. Then, do it over and over again until the end of the business day.

When he met the owner of the operation, a man known as Aslan, Sinan hid his foot behind a table so the man wouldn't notice. With a cigarette burning in the corner of his mouth, Aslan Bey felt the muscles in Sinan's arms, slapped his back, and even rubbed his hands along his spine, but he never checked Sinan's legs. Sinan would work on commission, one hundred fifty thousand lira per television.

"I was told two hundred," Sinan said.

Aslan sucked on his cigarette, pulled it from his lips, and exhaled before answering. "One hundred fifty."

Sinan thought of accusing the man of cheating him, but thought better of it out of respect for Kemal.

"One-fifty," he said, nodding.

Now at the bottom of the stairs, Sinan spun around and a man positioned the first television on his back. One television was no problem, just a little pinch in his kidneys, two was heavy, but three sent a sharp pain down his left side that exploded in his foot. The man tried to convince Sinan to take only two, but Sinan insisted. The three boxes were fastened together with bungee cords, and he struggled up the stairs, out into the alleyway, and down the hill toward the ferry landings. He dodged shoppers—women lugging bags full of lingerie, men being fitted for Levi's jeans, tourists carrying neatly wrapped boxes of dried-out spices. He sidestepped carts of shaving razors and others full of pirated American DVDs. Once he got hung up on clotheslines from which cheap sweatpants dangled for sale. He leaned for a moment like a tower slowly toppling, before two men working a kebab stand jumped behind him and righted the teetering boxes. It was the steepest part of the hill, cracked brick stairs and splashing gutters, and one of the men helped him down to the flats, offering his hand as he descended the stairs. Even so, he kept twisting his ankles in the sunken mortar between bricks.

"You're better off than the people who buy these televisions," his helper joked.

"Why's that?" Sinan said.

"You get strong, while they sit on their asses getting fat."

"Would you mind getting fat?" Sinan said.

"Truthfully," he laughed, "not at all, *abi.*"

He wasn't able to stop for midmorning prayer, but when the call went out in the afternoon, he was near the Rüstem Paşa Camii. The mosque rose above the street, and a small passageway led from street level into a raised courtyard of marble stone and tiled walls. His televisions bumped the arched entrance to the passageway, so with the help of the knife seller next door, who was standing outside his shop smoking a cigarette, he left the televisions sitting on the street.

He washed his swollen foot in the ablutions fountain, the cool water soothing the cracked and burning skin. It was the most peace he had felt in days—the walls of the mosque glowing with delicate tiles, the sunlit stained-glass windows a rainbow of color, and the sound of men whispering suras from the Qur'an. He wanted to stay; the city just beyond the walls seemed so far away, the destruction of Gölcük even farther, but a temporary reprieve was all the world—and God, it seemed—allowed. When he was done, the knife seller helped him again with the televisions. The weight felt unbearable, but he knew it wasn't if he kept his mind strong, and he bore that load and six more just like it before the day was over.

He earned 3,300,000 lira for the day. It seemed a fortune.

"Come back tomorrow," Aslan said. "Seven-thirty."

Chapter 18

IN THE EVENING RUSH, IT TOOK HIM NEARLY THREE HOURS by ferry to get back to Gölcük. By the time he arrived at the tent his foot was swollen inside his shoe, but he stopped limping when he saw the American there.

"I wanted to speak to your son," Marcus said.

There were purple bags underneath the American's eyes, as though he hadn't slept in weeks. Sinan didn't know what to say to the man. It would have been easier if he'd never had to see him again.

The American boy stood behind his father. Those earphones were wrapped around his neck, the wires running down his chest and into the pocket of his pants, as though the boy was plugged into a hidden battery. He stared at the ground, a length of blond hair falling over his eyes.

"Yes, yes," Sinan said. "Of course. A moment, please."

Sinan ducked inside to make sure his family was decent. Nilüfer immediately grabbed him by the sleeve and whispered in his ear.

"I offered him tea, but he refused," she said. "He's been standing out there for twenty minutes."

"Good," he said.

Nilüfer set out a few pillows they had scavenged from the house, and Sinan invited the Americans in. Once inside, Sinan told İrem to bring tea. İsmail joined Sinan on one of the pillows, sitting on his lap and rubbing his palms over Sinan's knees. Nilüfer and İrem worked silently at the propane stove while he and Marcus spoke idly of weighty things—the university professor who was forecasting bigger quakes, the bridge that collapsed near Adapazarı, the shortage of water, the possibility of spreading disease, the recent rash of people jumping off the Bosporus Bridge—until the tea arrived in plastic cups and without saucers.

"I apologize, Marcus Bey," he said, gesturing toward the cups. "The glass is broken."

"Please," Marcus said. "Don't apologize."

"Could I get some sugar?" the American's son said.

The American gave his son a disappointed look, a small admonishment for being rude, Sinan thought.

"Yes, no problem," Sinan said.

Nilüfer took the boy's cup, but İrem returned it, after she dropped two cubes of sugar inside. Her fingers brushed against the boy's as he took the cup from her hands. Sinan decided it was an accident.

"I'm sorry. This is my son—Dylan."

Sinan shook Dylan's hand. The boy's grip was solid, but he didn't look Sinan in the eye.

"Nice to meet you," Sinan said.

"Yeah," the boy said, and brushed a wave of hair out of his eyes, only to have it fall back in place. "Nice to meet you, Sinan Bey." His Turkish was perfect, but his tone was rude.

The American looked at his son for a moment, the muscles of his jaw working, his brow narrowed.

"Forgive him," he said to Sinan while he still looked at his son. "It's a hard time for Dylan." Marcus patted his son's knee as though he were afraid to touch him but obligated to do so.

"The tea is wonderful, Nilüfer Hanım," Dylan said, his politeness interrupted by the sideways glance he shot his father. The boy took one more sip and set the tea aside.

"Sinan Bey," Marcus said, ignoring his son. "I wanted to ask İsmail what happened after the quake."

"No. I'm sorry, but it's painful for the boy."

"I understand," Marcus said. "But it's painful for us also."

"Please, Marcus Bey. I have much to thank you for, and I'm sorry for your loss, but you need to understand—"

"Sinan Bey," Marcus said. His voice remained polite but forceful. His head shook a little. "I don't mean to disrespect your wishes, especially in front of your family, and I don't mean to hurt your son—believe me about that—but you must understand what it means to us."

Dylan turned his head away and looked at the blanketed wall flapping in the wind.

Marcus massaged his eyes with his thumb and index fingers. "You see—as a man I'm sure you'll understand this—there are things I didn't say, things I hadn't said for a long time."

Sinan did understand. The night of the quake, Nilüfer had been so tired she went straight to bed and he hadn't said that he loved her or that she had done a good job with the party or even given her a glancing smile before she slept. If Nilüfer had died in the quake, he would have known that they loved each other, but some confirmation, some last note of love spoken between them would have settled his heart in her absence.

"I need to know what she said, what was on her mind those last few hours. If she was in pain."

"She wasn't hurting, sir," İsmail said.

"You don't have to talk about it, İsmail."

"It's okay, Baba."

Sinan didn't want the man to know about the water, that İsmail was alive only because of his wife's sacrifice, but how could he stop the boy if he was willing?

İsmail told the story, about falling and waking in Sarah Hanım's arms, about the darkness beneath the rubble and the sounds of heavy wheels above. He told the American about the water she placed on his lips, about the dog and the kiss and finally about the silence.

The American watched with intense eyes, crescents beneath his brows as blue as the tip of a propane flame.

"I don't think she drank any of the water," İsmail said.

Sinan felt sick to his stomach.

"I think she gave it all to me."

They were indebted now. Silence wouldn't have made it less so, but at least the American wouldn't have known and Sinan could have suffered his shame alone.

The blood seemed to drain from Marcus's face, the muscles grew slack as though his skin hung on ridges of bone. He seemed to be frozen, but then he gently grabbed İsmail's hand. Sinan wanted to stop him, but the American was so careful, so calm and caring with his touch, that he couldn't think of any good reason to protest. He turned İsmail's hand palm up to reveal the bruises on his forearm— four finger-sized blue marks stretching across the tendons of his arms. He considered them a moment; then, with his other hand, he ran his fingers over the marks as if they were welts he could touch.

Dylan picked at a piece of loose rubber on his shoe, his long hair covering his face.

"I don't understand the dog," İsmail said.

Marcus laughed and looked up at the ceiling of the tent. "She was remembering the dog she had as a child in New Hampshire. Claudia," he laughed as if it were the silliest thing in the world. "The dog's name was Claudia." He shook his head.

Dylan ripped the piece of rubber off his shoe and dropped it on the floor.

"She stayed here this year because I promised her we'd move back to Plymouth when I finished my twentieth at the school. Just two years more," he said, nodding his head. "She missed the snow. And the maple trees."

Sinan thought he saw a drop of water fall from the tip of Dylan's nose, but the boy made no other movement to betray that he was crying.

"I'm sorry about your mother," İsmail said, and Sinan could hear the guilt in his voice.

Dylan didn't look up.

Marcus took İsmail's hand in his. "I'm very glad you're alive, İsmail," he said. "I miss my wife, but she did the right thing to save you."

As soon as he said it the American boy looked up at İsmail, his blue eyes burning despite the water, and Sinan could see all the anger pooling there. These were not tears of sadness, but tears of frustration, tears of a boy wanting to strike someone but unable to do so. Sinan pulled İsmail closer. Dylan looked away, over Sinan's shoulder, and the boy suddenly seemed embarrassed. He jumped up, accidentally knocking over his teacup. He ripped back the flap of canvas used as a door, and disappeared into the darkness.

Marcus turned his head in his son's direction, but he didn't even seem to consider calling out to him.

Then Sinan said it—the words that acknowledged his debt to the American—in an awkward moment of silence that he wanted to reclaim for normalcy: "We are like brothers, you and I."

Marcus smiled. "That's kind of you to say."

Chapter 19

"A NNE," İREM SAID. "I HAVE TO GO TO THE W.C."

It almost killed her to stand in that stupid tent and serve tea and not be able to talk to him.

"İrem," her mother said. "Wait until our guests leave."

Allah, Allah! She would explode if she had to stay here!

"*Anne,* it's an emergency." She bent over to indicate the seriousness of the situation.

"More tea, İrem," her father said.

Nilüfer looked at her as if to say, What can I do?

"*Anne,*" she said. "You saw all the tea I drank this afternoon!" She squeezed her knees together.

"All right, all right," Nilüfer said. "Go quietly. I'll serve them."

İrem ducked under the fabric at the back of the tent, thankful to have a rear escape. At the apartment, the only way out had been through the front door, past her father and his inquiries.

She saw Dylan walking down the hill toward town. She looked back at the tent to make sure no one was watching. The wind was down today, so the fabric was still. She couldn't see in, so she figured they couldn't see out. She ran down the hill and caught up with him near the old, crumbled walls of the town.

"Dylan."

He stopped and wiped his eyes with his shirtsleeve before turning around.

"That asshole," he said. His eyes narrowed to arrow points.

She touched his forearm.

"Shh," she said. "It's okay." But she knew it wasn't. Why was she out here comforting him while his father was inside comforting her brother?

"We should have been in New Hampshire, but *he* wanted to stay." He threw an angry hand in the direction of the tent. "How can he be glad she's dead?"

She knew that he wished it was her brother that had died. As for her, if one of them had to die, she preferred it was his mother. That was natural, but still, it felt dangerous.

"Shh," she said. He paced back and forth, occasionally looking back at the tent. "Shh, shh." She took his right hand and pulled him toward her. She felt the round muscles in his palms, the warm blood pulsing through his fingers. "Your mother did a brave thing."

He was looking at her now, rage in his eyes.

"She honors your name," İrem said.

He laughed sarcastically and she let go of his hand, hurt by his disdain.

"I don't care about that," he said. "I just *want her back.*"

His eyes were as wide as a child's and she felt something snap inside her chest. She took both of his hands and pulled him toward her, wrapping her arms around his waist. He dropped his head on her shoulder and cried. The heat of his breath pushed the fabric of her scarf against her neck. She felt his rib cage expand and contract. The tips of her fingers brushed the muscles on either side of his spine and she wanted to stay here, wanted to feel each muscle and tendon heave against his bones; she wanted to feel the whole composition of his frame, but then he stopped and lifted his head.

"There they are," he said.

She let go of him immediately and brushed her hands across the fabric of her blouse, trying to smooth away the wrinkles pressed in the shape of his body.

"WHAT WERE YOU DOING with that boy?" her father said as Dylan and his father walked away, down the hill.

"He was upset," she said.

"I thought you went to the W.C."

She self-consciously tucked a strand of hair beneath her head scarf.

"I did," she said, "and when I came back I saw him there."

"Everyone can see you touching him," Sinan said.

She looked around, briefly embarrassed, until she realized that there were a half-dozen people here, huddled under handmade tents, wondering how they were going to get their next meal. How could they care?

"His father doesn't love him," she said.

"A father always loves his son."

"He leaves crying over his mother and his father just stays inside sipping tea; just leaves him alone." She hesitated before saying it. "A father should care more."

"Go inside," he said quietly. He sounded hurt.

She waited a few moments, even a moment or two longer than she should have, before entering the tent. Inside, she joined her mother in the makeshift kitchen and washed the teapots and cups in buckets of gray water. Her father didn't come in for a few minutes and she started washing the cups she had just washed, rubbing the edges with the mildewy rag over and over again. What would he say to her mother? Had he gone to get Dylan to do something horrible? When he did come inside, she watched him sit down on the pillows and finish his tea.

"İrem," he said. "Please get this cup, too."

He almost never said please, and she came to him silently and took the cup, expecting something else, some retribution.

"Thank you," he said, and stared out the door of the tent.

Chapter 20

AFTER THE CHILDREN HAD FALLEN ASLEEP, SINAN AND NILÜFER argued in whispers.

"I don't like these people," he told her. "They're going to want something."

He bent over his foot and untied the laces. As he did, the swollen skin expanded and pushed open the tongue of leather.

"The only thing he seems to want is to help," Nilüfer said, washing the tea glasses for the third time.

"He could bring doctors here if he wants to help," Sinan said. It felt like shards of glass were embedded in the foot, so he cupped the sole of the shoe in the palm of his hand and pulled it off the stump by centimeters. "Why do we need to move down there?"

"What do we have here?" Nilüfer said. "All day we breathe this brown air, all day we listen to car horns. We hide from the sun under a sheet of fabric, while you go off . . ." She stopped herself.

"While I go off and what?"

"Nothing," she said. "I—"

"You think I go spend the day in the *kıraathane* drinking tea and playing games?" he said, his voice rising now.

"No," Nilüfer said. "No, *canım*, that's not what I meant."

"All day I'm carrying televisions on my back like a donkey!" He pulled the sock off his foot. The foot was marbled, like rotten mutton. "Look."

She put her hands to her mouth. "I'm sorry," she said. "Please quiet your voice."

"Don't tell me to be quiet," he said, but he was already whispering again. "I'll make things better," he said, rubbing his eyes with his thumb and forefinger.

"I know you will," Nilüfer said. Her voice was tinged with doubt, but she filled a bucket with fresh water from one of the jugs.

"No," he said. "We need the water to drink."

She ignored him and he was glad for it because the water cooled the pain.

"Haven't I been a good man?"

"Yes, *canım*."

"Haven't I taken care of you?"

"Yes."

He clutched at the necklace around his neck and held the bullet out for her to see, as if she would forget such a thing. "You remember what happened to my father, don't you? You remember the other men, the boys?"

Looking at the shard of metal in his hand, she wearily sighed.

"Simply celebrating Nowruz," he said. "Just a new-year celebration, and they shoot them!"

"I remember," she said, nodding her head. "They were yelling slogans, too."

He almost screamed at her, but he knew she was right. With the guns pointed, he had often wondered, why would the men provoke the Turkish soldiers? He knew, also, that his father had joined the yelling, and his participation in that mass suicidal gesture infuriated Sinan.

"You don't kill over slogans," Sinan finally said, though he recognized the naïveté of his statement.

"What if İsmail is bleeding inside?" Nilüfer said.

He didn't have an answer to that. The boy looked fine, but some harmful things, he knew, could not be seen.

"You are no less a man if you accept help," she said. "Especially at a time like this. Marcus Bey and the American government are not the same thing. Remember what Sarah Hanım did, Sinan."

He knew she was right, but going into that camp felt like giving up. A man gives up and anything can happen to him.

Chapter 21

"PULL UP YOUR PANT LEG," ASLAN BEY SAID.

Sinan stood just in front of the table in the man's tiny shop. Aslan rested his burning cigarette in a tin ashtray, took a last sip of his morning tea, and came around the table to inspect.

"Is there a problem?" Sinan said. He knew there was no use, but he stalled anyway.

"Let me see that leg of yours."

Sinan rolled the bottom of his pants to just above the ankle. Aslan was unsatisfied and he tugged the pant leg up to Sinan's knee. He blew air out of his mouth when he saw.

"You lied to me," he said.

"I didn't lie. You did not ask, sir."

Aslan smiled without revealing his teeth. He was an older man, with strings of gray hair he stretched across a balding head. "I had to find out from my warehouse boy." He let go of the pant leg. "Cover that up," he said, waving his hand at the offending leg.

"He's good to look after you," Sinan said. "But it seems unnecessary. I moved thirty-three televisions yesterday and thirty-five the day before."

"I have boys moving forty-three, forty-eight even."

"It shouldn't concern you," Sinan said. "I earn what I move. You're not out anything."

A young boy appeared with a fresh glass of tea balanced on a silver tray. He set the glass on the table in front of the boss and disappeared.

"Do not make the mistake," Aslan said, "that you can tell me how to run my business."

He was a soft man, his belly stretching the fabric at the buttons of his shirt, his arms like two slabs of fatty goat meat. Even with Sinan's bad foot, he knew he could beat this man down, knock him to the floor with his fists.

"Of course, you're right," Sinan said.

Aslan touched his hand to his hair, pulling in place a strand that had fallen over his forehead. He then rolled the ashes loose from his cigarette before lifting it to his lips.

"Aslan Bey," Sinan said. "I have a family. We lost our home."

The boss held up his hand and nodded. Blowing smoke, he crushed the butt in the ashtray.

"Thirty-eight today," he said, apparently feeling charitable now. "At least."

Sinan's foot throbbed even before he carried the first load. It was market day. The streets of Sirkeci were packed with street sellers, some illegal and others legitimate, and Sinan had to force his way through the crowd. He had never seen anything like this street market until he came to İstanbul. The legal sellers sold clothes from wooden tables that, when unused, sat stacked against the walls of nearby buildings until the next week. The illegal merchants hawked their wares—copied disks that played foreign music and movies, cassette tapes of popular folksingers, special programs for computers—from collapsible wooden stands that could be dismantled with a kick of a foot and carried away when the police arrived.

The police would start at the far end of the market to give the illegal merchants a chance to close up shop and run away. The law was the law, but people needed to make a living. He had seen the police make a show of stopping to speak with merchants, slow down to light a cigarette, bend over to retie a shoe that was already tied, and like a wave swelling before their progress, men came running, their collapsible cases tucked under their arms. Within minutes, half the market would escape into the surrounding streets and the police would let them. The merchants that didn't run—the stupid or arrogant ones—were rounded up by the police and this made it seem that they were doing their job.

It was Sinan's third trip of the day. He was one block from the electronics store where he was to drop off the load. On the corner near the new mosque, a *döner* stand had just opened, and the owner had recently thrown water across the bricks, sweeping the water and the dirt that accumulated overnight into the gutter. Sinan's foot hurt, but he had found that if he stepped on the outside of the shoe the pain lessened and he could manage the load with little problem. The street was packed with jostling people and Sinan bounced from shoulder to shoulder in the flowing crowd.

He knew what was coming when he heard the men yell, "*Polis*," but the packed crowd bunched at the corner with the *döner* stand and he was sandwiched in the middle. Suddenly the people behind him were thrust against the television boxes. The crowd lunged forward, pushing him into the people ahead. Some people yelled and a group of merchants came wading through the crowd toward Sinan, their cases held above their heads. Something ahead of him broke loose and the pressure of the crowd burst like a dam giving way. He was knocked forward onto the wet bricks where his left foot slipped and twisted. His foot buckled with pain and he fell across the curb, the bungee cords snapping and tossing the televisions into the street.

One television tore through the top of its box and shattered glass into the street and he was sure the other two were broken inside. Lying on the ground, he watched the flashing of running legs, men dodging women carrying shopping bags, and soon two policemen appeared on the scene. One of the policemen noticed the crushed televisions and walked toward him. Sinan knew that nothing about this boded well for him, so when the crowd thickened once again, he managed to stand and disappear down a side street.

When he reached the ferry, he knew there was no going back to Aslan; going back meant losing the job and paying for the damages. There was little to do but escape and take the ferry back. There was little to do, period. He tried to remind himself that he was lucky—his family was alive. But a desperation was crowding in on him, as though strong hands were squeezing the air out of his chest, like the world was a fist grinding him to dust.

HE STOOD THERE AT the top of the hill, resting his weight on his right foot, cars whipping by him in a rage of gear changes and revving engines; he stared at his tent in the circle of grass. It was only thirty meters away, but the distance seemed impossible to cross. Smoke floated above the tent and just beyond the tent, where the grass flattened out, he watched Marcus pass a soccer ball to İsmail. His son tried to complete a fancy stop where he rolled the ball up his leg and kneed it into the air, but his feet got tangled. He rolled on the ground, laughing, and when Marcus took the boy's hand to lift him from the ground Sinan felt his son was being taken away from him.

A step of pain shot stars in his vision. He bit his lip and stared at the ground and watched his right foot fall against the dirt again and braced himself for another jolt. It felt like the ground was made of knives, each sharpened blade of grass slicing through his shoe. He listed with the next stab of pain before he felt a hand under his shoulders, lifting and steadying him.

"Hold on to me, Sinan Bey," Marcus said.

Marcus wrapped Sinan's left arm around his shoulder and the American bore half his weight down the hill until they made it to the tent. There, Marcus eased him down on a set of pillows Nilüfer frantically propped against the wooden frame.

Nilüfer stood over him, holding her hand to her mouth as Marcus removed Sinan's shoe. He didn't want the man to see his misshapen foot, but he was too tired to protest and he lay back on the pillows, feeling his foot expand as it was pulled free of the leather shoe. Nilüfer looked away, her hand still held against her mouth. The American's eyes were full of pity and Sinan wanted to slap it away.

But Marcus propped Sinan's foot on a stack of pillows and went back to the camp to get ice packs to bring down the swelling.

"You can't keep doing this," Nilüfer said, stroking his hair against his scalp. "Let them help us."

Marcus returned carrying a white briefcase with a red cross painted on the side. He had İrem bring him a bucket of water and a washcloth. İsmail stroked Sinan's hair.

"Tell me if this hurts," Marcus said.

The American took Sinan's stump in his hands and began to wash the cracked and bruised skin. Sinan looked away in embarrassment. For his whole life, since he was a boy and had to watch the other boys play soccer, he had hidden his foot from people, only letting his wife and children see the underdeveloped calf, and the square, misshapen fist that swallowed his toes.

"Not enough iron," Sinan explained. "The doctor said it happens mostly in third-world countries."

"Clubfoot is common," Marcus said. "Doctors in Ankara could have corrected it when you were a child." He poured alcohol onto a cotton swab. "Turkey is not third world."

Sinan laughed. "You haven't been to the Southeast."

"I have," Marcus said.

Sinan looked at the American, who was now holding the tip of his stump in his left hand and cleaning the ridges where his toes should have been. There was blood caked there and the swab grew scarlet.

"I worked in the refugee camps," Marcus said, not looking up from his work. "In 'ninety-one."

The Gulf War was raging then and Iraqi Kurds had streamed across the border into Turkey, afraid Saddam Hussein would launch gas attacks against them. Horrible things were said to have happened in the refugee camps—people starved, children died of diarrhea, and occasionally suspected Kurdistan Workers' Party members were taken away by the Special Teams in the middle of the night, right in front of the U.N. soldiers. Turkey belonged to the United Nations, after all, and the Kurds belonged to nothing. People said American spies were working the camps, helping the Turkish government crack down on the PKK in exchange for the use of air bases in Turkey.

"Sinan Bey," Marcus said. "You should come down to our camp. We have a tent ready for you, a real one that will keep the mosquitoes out at night. I know you're a good man, but—"

"My friend," Sinan said. "You know nothing about me at all. And I know nothing about you."

That seemed to throw the American off a little. He blinked and stopped washing the stump.

İrem brought a clean bucket of water.

"But I do, Sinan Bey. I know you prayed for days for İsmail. I know you'd give your life for your son."

İrem looked at the American and then shot a glance at Sinan. Sinan thought he knew what his daughter was thinking, that he had abandoned her, that he wouldn't give his life for her, and seeing that doubt surface across her face shamed him.

"I don't trust you Americans," Sinan said.

Marcus nodded and continued working on his foot. Nilüfer told İrem to move away from the men.

"I've noticed," Marcus said.

As Marcus continued to clean the blood away, Sinan saw the dark bruise discoloring the skin. It looked as if his flesh were rotting away. The circles around his father's eyes had looked that way the day Sinan had cleaned the body for burial. You could see where the bullet had cracked open his skull—a tiny, insignificant hole, like what a drill leaves in wood. He and his aunt had washed the body, smearing away dried blood where his left eye should have been. The bullet had finally lodged in his cheek, a gold spike puncturing bone. They pulled the bullet out with pliers, pressed the bone back in place, and sewed the skin together with sock-mending yarn. They poured warm water through his father's matted hair and smoothed it down against his scalp with a comb, just as he would have groomed it before leaving the house in the morning. But no cleaning could get rid of the bruise. It looked as though the force of the bullet had sent everything inside his skull bashing up against his eye sockets.

"Leave us," Sinan said to İsmail.

When the boy was gone, Sinan said, "My father was murdered."

Marcus snapped two plastic packages in half. He took gauze from the first-aid kit, surrounded the foot with the ice packs, and wrapped them tightly with tape.

Sinan sucked air through his teeth. "Yes, that hurts."

Marcus was careful not to push too much with the tips of his fingers, but instead cradled the foot in his palm, and Sinan felt a strange, involuntary gratitude, like a man who has had his shame exposed and hidden once again.

"I, myself, had to pull the bullet out of his cheek. It was an M-16."

Marcus hesitated, then finished wrapping his foot, and finally looked at Sinan.

"I'm a teacher, Sinan."

"Your government sold those weapons to—"

"I've lived in this country for nineteen years." He snapped shut the first-aid kit. "It's not *my* government."

He stood to leave.

"We have good tents," he said, "ones that will keep the water out when it rains, ones that will give your family some privacy. We're setting up a school, we've got toilets, we have food. It's not good for the children," Marcus added. "The exhaust fumes, the—"

"Please . . ." Sinan took a deep breath and waited until he could control his voice. "My friend, do not tell me what's good for my children as if I do not know."

"You cannot stay here and you know it."

"I know many things, Marcus Bey."

Marcus nodded as though he were giving up. "Many horrible things happen in the world," he said. "I, too, wish I had someone to blame for them."

He briefly placed his hand on Sinan's shoulder, and Sinan thought it was to remind him of a debt. Then he left the tent.

Nilüfer watched the American go.

"We have to go to the camp," she said softly when he was gone.

"I know," he said.

"We cannot stay here," she went on, as though she didn't hear him.

"I know!" he said, kicking the floor with his good foot. He was tired, so tired, and he was sick of fighting a war—a long, old, futile war that was over now anyway. "I know."

Part Two

Chapter 22

OUTSIDE INTO THE SUN, AND NOT TO BUY VEGETABLES OR to pick up shirts at the tailors! Outside without her mother dragging her by the hand and without eyes watching to make sure she didn't look at the boys smoking on the corner. She couldn't deny that she was happier since the earthquake—she felt a little guilty for it, but she couldn't help it; for a few hours a day, between meals at the soup kitchen, she was free in a way she hadn't been since she was a child.

It was a hot day and she passed the men playing backgammon and smoking near the soup kitchen. She passed one of the Americans playing a guitar on a red folding chair near a fire pit. He wore shorts and she could see the thick muscles of his legs where they disappeared into the darkness of the fabric. A few of the other workers sat on a blanket and sang with the man, happy-sounding songs they occasionally clapped to. She looked for Dylan at the soup kitchen. She looked for him at the school tent and at the soccer field, where the American men and even some of the women kicked up clouds of dust with orphan boys of the camp.

Down one of the rows, she found Dilek and Ayşe swinging a rope in the street, a game the American women had been teaching the girls. A little girl she didn't know jumped in the middle, her black hair slapping against her back as her feet hit the ground.

"İrem, *canım*," Dilek said when she saw her coming. She dropped the rope and the little girl got tangled up.

"Dilek!" the girl yelled.

Ayşe laughed and helped untangle the girl, while Dilek and İrem greeted each other with kisses on each cheek. Smiling, Dilek took İrem's arm and they walked together back toward the jump rope.

"How's your mother?" İrem asked.

Dilek's smile disappeared and she jerked her head in an uncomfortable way, as though İrem's question had reminded her of something she had forgotten. In front of the tent, Ayşe and the little girl uncoiled the rope. İrem said hello and kissed Ayşe on both cheeks.

"She won't come out of the tent," Dilek said. She scratched her elbow and looked away. Her arms were sunburned and blistered in a few places. Dilek was İrem's age, but she wore short-sleeve shirts and sometimes even shorts. To İrem, Dilek's clothing made her look like a little girl instead of a woman, and she fought back disdain for her friend's lack of modesty. But when İrem remembered the freedom of her childhood—the warmth of the sun on her legs, the coolness of the evening sea breeze on her bare arms, she found herself wishing her father was a secularist, too. No one expected modesty from a secularist.

İrem noticed crying coming from the tent.

"She always complained about him when he was alive, but now all she does is cry."

The girls swung the rope again, and it arched in the sky before slapping the ground and swinging around again. The sound of the rope and the girls jumping disguised the crying, but she could still hear it, and, for a moment, everything that had happened—the collapsed buildings, her dead cousins, her brother buried alive—crowded in on her.

"Have you seen him today?" Dilek asked, smiling now.

"Shh," İrem said.

"I have," she said.

"Where?" İrem grabbed her friend's elbow, but Dilek pulled away and jumped into the rope and skipped above it as it hit the ground; a puff of dust jumped from the ground where the rope struck it. İrem hadn't talked to Dylan for two days. He was too busy working in the camp with his father. Dilek just smiled back, her hair flying up and down in the air, her thin body skipping above the ground as though she were still a child.

"Jump in," she said.

İrem rolled her eyes at Dilek. She knew İrem couldn't jump rope, yet she asked. İrem loved Dilek, but she had a way of reminding İrem that her parents were the backward conservatives.

"I'm leaving," İrem said.

She checked the soccer field again and stuck her head inside the school tent. She walked down a couple rows of tents and began to stroll down the third, when she saw Dylan and his father ducking out of one of the tents. Dylan carried a white case with a red cross painted on the side. He smiled when he saw her and she stopped in the middle of the street. Then, turning away in surprise, she saw an old man watching her, his wrinkled hand resting on a wooden cane. She pretended to be lost and did a circle in the middle of the dirt path, acting as though she were trying to find her way while watching Dylan. He followed his father, but he looked over his shoulder toward her, that smile of his flashing down the aisle.

"Have you lost your way?" the old man asked.

"Efendim?"

With a shaky hand, he pointed his cane, the tip of it bouncing around in the air.

"Tents down there, tents down here. Everything's gone," he said.

He was crazy, she could tell, but he scared her and she walked quickly down one of the aisles, out past the soccer field, down a short path that took her downhill to the beach.

It was a small beach, barely a beach at all, really, just a strip of pebbles and the foamy edge of the sea. She felt the sun through her long-sleeve blouse and she wanted that warmth on her bare skin. There were so many things she hadn't noticed since she was a child and she hadn't paid attention to them then because they had always been there: the layers of blue sky, the yellow sun like a circle of fabric pasted in the sky, the water glittering like sequined dresses she'd seen in the magazines Dilek showed her. The wet pebbles on the beach and the sound of the waves shushing against them. The white sails of a ship unfurling on four masts. The pungent salt breeze taste on her tongue. The landscape had been lost to her, replaced by square windows and walls and doors and triangled rooftops eclipsing the sky, and she found herself hoping that they would never move back into an apartment in some concrete neighborhood. She would live in a tent forever if she could have this.

Crouching near the water's edge, she watched the waves turn white pebbles gray. A group of transparent fish swam in the shallows. She saw the skeletons through their skin and the little round shadow-like things that were their organs. She wanted to say, "Look, Dylan. A school of fish." And he would say something like, "Yeah, İrem, I've seen fish before." But that didn't matter. She sort of liked the way he was bored with everything. It made him seem more sophisticated, like he had seen something in the world, like, if she was lucky, he would show her those things, too.

She laughed at herself and slapped the water, scattering the fish. So stupid! *Aptal!* Why would an American boy be interested in her?

She filled her palms with water and splashed it against her face and the cool drops ran down her neck.

She looked around now. No one was on the beach, so she took off her shoes, looked behind her again, and then took off her socks, too. She pulled up her skirt bottom to reveal her white legs and felt the sun beat upon her skin. She liked her calves. They were thin at the ankles and curved into perfect ovals at the muscle. She tried to imagine them in high heels, and flexed her toes and unflexed her toes to admire the way the muscle moved. Smiling, she tilted her head back and let the sun beat down on her skin. Little beads of perspiration gathered along her calves, and when her skin began to turn pink she stood and dipped her legs in the water, so cool and oily feeling.

She heard a shuffling behind her and snapped her head around, her heart beating with panic.

It was Dylan.

She smiled and dropped her skirt to cover her calves; she even sat down and pulled her feet inside and stretched the fabric down to cover her toes. The pink fabric blossomed red around her feet. She watched the water, acting as though she didn't see him. She knew, though, that he knew she was playacting. Out of the corner of her eye she saw him strutting down the beach. A bubble gathered in her throat, threatening to burst into a giggle. When he sat down next to her, she could hear the music coming from his headphones, but she still looked away, her hand pressed against her mouth to squelch the laugh.

"You know," he said, pulling the headphones from his ears. "German women down in Bodrum lie around on the beach topless."

She blushed and crossed her arms over her chest.

"Stupid women," she said. "They'll make the men do terrible things." She could just imagine the Turkish men hovering around those women, their tongues hanging out of their mouths like feral dogs.

"Nobody gives a damn, really."

"Why do you always curse?" She looked at him now.

"They're just words," he said. "They're only offensive if you let them be."

"Turkish men see a woman's body and they think they own it."

"Maybe because you guys make such a big deal about it." He lit a cigarette and let the wind carry the smoke above his head. "You hide your toes," he said pointing with the cigarette, "and they become the sexiest thing alive."

He was making fun of her!

"You show it all off and it becomes nothing," she said.

He just shrugged and looked out at the water. Ah, he could be so frustrating! They sat like that for a minute, in silence looking at the cool water. It was hot; she could feel herself sweating beneath the fabric of her blouse. He was wearing dark jeans, and a black T-shirt that showed off the tattoos on his arms and the leather bands around his wrists. İrem wondered why he would wear such hot clothes in this heat, if he didn't have to.

She inched her toes out from beneath the skirt, just little crescents of toenails poking out.

He glanced at them and smiled.

"You know," he said, "my mom and dad and I took a trip down to the Sinai once, in Egypt. We were at this beach—Sharm el-Sheikh, I think—and I saw this woman swimming in her *abaya*. Man, it was the craziest thing—dressed head to toe in black, all the fabric billowing out like a parachute. Something happened, she slipped, a wave hit her, something, but she fell down and the wet fabric got so heavy she almost drowned. Her husband had to jump in and pull her to shore. He slapped her when he got her to the beach." He blew smoke away from his face.

Was he comparing her to this woman? A fundamentalist in an *abaya*? At least she got to wear pretty skirts and nice blouses. Her parents were conservative, but they weren't fundamentalists.

She remembered a trip to Büyükada Island years before, back when her father still took her swimming. She was floating in the water next to a man with a thick black beard. He kept paddling like a dog does, his head held just above the water, his eyes squinting against the splashes he inflicted upon himself. He kept splashing her, too, and she wanted to tell him to go swim somewhere else, but she would never do such a thing. Suddenly, he stopped thrashing around and stood up, his head and shoulders above the water. It surprised her because she couldn't see the bottom and her toes didn't touch anything. She had assumed she'd swum out into deep water, and she had been proud of herself for not being scared. He waved toward the beach and a woman in full *abaya*—a rare sight then—waved back. He kept waving, like a stupid child, but the woman—his wife, she guessed—had put her hand down and stared out at her husband with an absolutely blank expression, as though she were dead, a black ghost on a white beach.

"That's what used to piss my mom off the most about being here," Dylan said. "The way some men think they own women."

She thought about telling Dylan her memory, but she realized he'd compare her to the poor woman on the beach, and, even worse, he'd think her stupid for not recognizing the irony in her own memory.

"But that didn't happen here," she said. "Egypt is different. The Arabs are barbaric."

He looked at her, smiled, and glanced at her toes again.

"You won't even show your ankles," he said.

"It's immodest," she said. "Besides, men cannot control themselves. It's better this way."

"You really believe that?" He looked at her as though she were the stupidest girl in the world and she felt a hot embarrassment flood her body.

"Women here don't have to cover themselves," she said. "It's a choice."

"Is that what your dad said?"

She clenched her jaw. "Yes," she said. "I don't have to do this."

He handed her the cigarette, but she was too mad to smoke it. She just held it away from her face while he untied his shoes.

"What're you doing?" she said.

"It's hot."

He pulled off his shoes and stripped away his socks.

"What're you doing?" she said again, looking around.

He rolled up his pants to his knees, revealing dark curly hair poking out of white calves. He sat down and dropped his legs in the water. Goose pimples speckled his skin.

"Ahh," he said. "Shit, that feels good."

"Stop cussing," she said.

"Too bad you gotta protect me from myself."

The water distorted the shape of his legs, making him look short.

"You look like a midget," she said. It was a silly thing to say, but she felt like being mean.

"*Cüce?*" he said. "What?"

"A small person, a mini—like people in the circus, like a Roma."

"Hey," he said, laughing. "Come over here and say that to my face."

She laughed and looked around the beach again. There was a hill to the right, and behind them a rise separated the beach from the camp. From the camp, all you saw was the sea. You only knew a beach was there once you were practically standing on top of it.

She scooted over to him and slowly, timidly, rolled up her skirt. With each roll, a strange fluttering beat in her stomach; it was like being a little sick, but in a good way.

"Be careful," he said, holding his hands in front of his face. "I might lose control of myself."

Sometimes she wished he would shut up.

She stopped rolling the skirt when she reached her knees, and when she set her legs in the water, a sudden and pleasant chill shot through her body.

"*Cüce*," she said, jerking her face his way.

"American guys don't like to be called short," he said, with more seriousness in his voice than she expected.

"I'm sorry. I didn't mean it."

She watched their legs—so close she thought she could feel the heat from his skin, even beneath the water. He stared out at the sea and didn't seem to be paying attention, so she flexed her toes to make the muscle come up on her calf. Nothing. She was naked in front of him, and he didn't even notice! She thought about brushing her leg against his, but that was too much, and the silence thickened until the air felt as heavy as honey and she thought she couldn't stand it anymore.

He flicked the cigarette out into the water and she watched it bob on a wave.

"You know," he said. "I really don't care if you want to cover yourself." He dug a hole in the sand with his heel. "You make me nervous, so I tease you."

"I make *you* nervous?"

"Yeah," he said. "You're different than other girls."

Different how? she wanted to ask, but she was afraid to know, so she said nothing and they sat there in silence watching the tiny waves break and ebb against the shore.

"Hey, listen," he said, pulling his earphones from his neck. "I want you to hear this."

Before she knew what he was doing, he pulled the edge of her head scarf back to reveal her ear.

"Stop," she said, grabbing his hand.

"It's only so you can hear this."

She stared at him, still holding his hand.

"There's no one here," he said. "Don't worry."

She dropped her hand and let him push back the scarf from her other ear. His fingers touched her hair as he positioned the headphones, and when the music started—sad, beautiful music, like gray birds flying in a foggy sky—the sound swept over her in a way she couldn't explain except to say that she could feel it inside of her, as though the instruments were playing in her chest.

"What's this?"

"Radiohead," he said. "They're incredible."

She had never heard anything like this before. It was sad music, music like crying, music like a beautiful death and she felt he was letting her inside of him, into his own sadness.

He watched her as she listened, his eyes intent on her face as though he were hearing the music that was inside of her now. As she listened the world receded. There was no İstanbul, no destroyed town, no camp, just the two of them on the beach—a tiny warm bubble of music and their naked legs together in the cool water.

"It's good," she said. "Really good."

"You can have it."

"I don't have the right machine."

"No," he said. "I mean you can have the player, too."

She looked at him, stunned by the present.

"Don't worry about it," he said. "I've got another one."

Something moved behind them on the hill.

"Someone's coming," Dylan said.

Chapter 23

SINAN SLEPT FOR EIGHTEEN HOURS, A BLACK SLEEP FREE of nightmares of collapsing buildings and bodies wrapped in burlap, an uninterrupted sleep without startling awake and the late-night bouts of insomnia. He slept like he hadn't since he was a child, and for those precious few hours he had been free of the burdens of a man.

When he finally woke, he found himself staring at the blank whiteness of the tent's top. It took his conscious mind a moment to catch up to his eyes, so at first he thought the world had been erased, that he was with God in a paradise that was not green at all, but instead as clean as mid-winter snow. And in his exhaustion, before logical thoughts told him that this was ridiculous, before he remembered his wife and his children, before the memory of the earthquake jolted loose in his brain, he was glad for that emptiness. It demanded nothing, it did not ask to be interpreted or understood. It suggested that God was nothing more than a benign force; a mind could be at ease in such a world.

He moved his left leg and a stinging pain shot up his back. His heart throbbed with disappointment. First because pain still existed in Heaven, and then a half moment later—like a collision of realizations—because this was not Heaven at all but the inside of one of the American's tents. Through the white fabric, he saw a whiter splotch of light where the sun beat down. He was zipped inside a sleeping bag that smelled of detergent, and he threw it off himself and tried to sit up but his back hurt and his ribs felt like they had been stretched to the breaking point only to be pressed back together around his lungs. Nilüfer and the children were gone, but their unzipped bags lay next to him.

He couldn't find his shoes, so he crawled out of the tent in his socks and bandaged left foot. A family, sitting in the sun drinking tea and eating bread with honey, stared back at him as though he had landed uninvited in their living room. He was embarrassed. He had not combed his hair, his armpits smelled, and he stood in the dirt in plain socks.

"Excuse me," he said. "Good morning."

"Good afternoon," the woman said and smiled as though he were crazy.

That sent his heart racing; half the day gone and he hadn't found his family even a bite of food to eat or searched out a job. Still half-asleep and disoriented, he found his shoes beside the tent entrance, only because he kicked them over. He slipped his right foot in and carefully fitted his left into the special shoe, but because it was wrapped in the bandage it wouldn't fit inside comfortably. Out ahead of him stretched a sea of tents, like white sails rolled to points and fixed to the ground. He stumbled through the street as though he were trudging through oil, and he wanted to sit down, he wanted to go back to the tent and sleep again.

He found Nilüfer coming toward him, two paper plates of piled scrambled eggs in her hands.

"You stubborn man," she said. "You shouldn't be on that foot. You don't listen to me."

"Listen to you?"

"I told you to stay asleep," she said.

"I don't remember," he said.

"You're exhausted." She balanced the two plates of eggs in one hand and used the other to buttress his left shoulder, and they walked like that back to the tent.

"Where are the children?" he said.

"Around here somewhere."

"Where?" he said.

"Sinan, *canım*, they're safe. A doctor saw İsmail yesterday and said he is fine. Don't worry about them." She used her fingers to caress the fabric of his shirt where it was pulled tight around his shoulders. "Don't worry now."

When they reached the tent, she helped him inside. Sitting next to him, she crossed her legs like a child and revealed a sliver of skin between the elastic of the pantaloon leggings and her socks.

"İsmail and İrem have eaten," she said. "This is for you."

The skin of the paper plate was warm and soaked with grease.

"You should have seen it," she said. "They had eggs and fried potatoes and even orange slices. There were little flat cakes with sweet syrup, but the children ate all those and there weren't any left for you. I'm sorry." She smiled. "They were so happy to eat them that I couldn't say no. Also there was juice for the children, Kool-Aid, they call it." She picked at her eggs. "A real American breakfast."

Sinan scooped up the eggs with the plastic fork and placed a biteful on the tip of his tongue. They were watery and oversalted, but they tasted like Heaven.

"The children have eaten?"

"Yes," she said. "They'll serve dinner at five."

He nodded and felt a weight of responsibility drop from his shoulders. He took another bite of the eggs and the buttery yolks melted on his tongue. And before he could stop it, a welling rose in his throat and he nearly choked on the food. The water gathered in the back of his eyes, and exhaustion, like heavy blankets being folded around his limbs, took possession of his body.

He dropped the eggs on the floor of the tent and placed his fingers on the exposed skin of his wife's leg. He pushed the pantaloons up her calf, enough so that the whole palm of his hand could touch her skin. He dropped his head and kissed the skin there, rested his cheek against the ridge of her shinbone, and collapsed in her lap.

"Shh," she said. "Shh. Everything will be all right."

Chapter 24

SHE STRIPPED THE HEADPHONES FROM HER EARS AND JUMPED out of the water, shaking the skirt back down around her ankles.

She glanced up at the beach and saw a man carrying a fishing pole and cresting the hill. She recognized the man from her father's store, but she couldn't remember his name. He was looking the other way on the beach, his hand shaded against the sun and it seemed he had not seen them.

Dylan went left and she went right, hoping she didn't run into anyone else with her shoes in her hands. When she was out of sight of the fisherman, she sat down on the beach and scraped the black pebbles from her wet toes. She started to put her shoes back on, but suddenly felt stupid. She hadn't done anything wrong—just listened to some music and talked with a boy. Women were lying naked on beaches somewhere. Turkish women in İstanbul went dancing in clubs, drank and smoked with men they slept with. She had only had a conversation.

The ground was rough beneath her feet, but she carried her shoes, swaying from her fingers like two trophies to defiance. She walked up the path where bushes crowded the sand and thorns stuck between her toes, but she bit her lip and walked on anyway. The sun was lower than she expected and she thought she might have missed dinner, but she didn't care. She walked through the camp barefoot, watching to see if anyone noticed her bare toes, trying to get another look at Dylan but he was nowhere to be found and no one seemed to care about her feet. She found Dilek and Ayşe still swinging the rope for the little girl. People sat around outside, smoking and drinking and watching the girls jump, but she didn't care about that, either.

"I've found him," she said to Dilek and jumped into the rope.

The rope came around and she jumped just as she heard it hit the ground.

"Faster," Ayşe said to Dilek, and İrem watched the rope circle overhead.

She jumped and felt the rope pick up speed. She jumped and pebbles pressed into the raw skin of her heels and the soft balls of her feet. She jumped and jumped again, her heart beating faster, the blood rushing through her veins, her head spinning with the speed of the arc.

Chapter 25

THAT EVENING AFTER DINNER, MARCUS ARRIVED AT THE TENT
with bandages and antiseptic. Nilüfer and the children were out in
the camp, doing what he didn't know, but, for once, their where-
abouts did not worry him. Sinan had felt, for much of his adult life, as
though he were the last barrier at the edge of town, a wall between the
soldiers and his family, and should he fall asleep or look the other
way, however briefly, the hostile forces would carry his family away.
Even after moving to Gölcük, where there was no fear of attacks from
the Special Teams, he couldn't shake himself loose of this fear. Now,
though, the military was gone. Even the tanks that rumbled down the
streets of Gölcük each day were crushed under the cement of collapsed barracks, and the relief he felt was palpable in the leaden
weight of his body. He thought about refusing Marcus's help, but he
was exhausted, and, besides, he liked the idea of an American doing
something as base as washing his foot.

Marcus removed the sock and Sinan could smell the stench of
sweat and blood and dirt. The discolored skin had stretched and separated like a seam and bled from chapped tears in the skin. He
watched the American, thinking he would cringe or hold his nose or
put on latex gloves, but the American did none of those things. He

held Sinan's foot in his hand and washed the blood away with a cotton swab—his blood staining the man's skin.

"Do you know what your government did to us in the South?" Sinan said.

"I know what the American government allows the Turkish military to do," Marcus said, never removing his eyes from the foot.

"The village next to mine was burned to the ground," Sinan continued. "Women and children were killed."

"I know."

"And for what?" Sinan said. "Because—"

"Because you want to speak your own language, because you want your land, because the U.S. and NATO want Russia out of the Mediterranean."

"Oil," Sinan said.

There was silence for a moment while Marcus wrapped Sinan's foot and pressed a metal hook into the fabric to keep it in place.

"There will never be a Kurdistan," Sinan said, "because the Americans want the oil in Kirkuk."

"And the British and the Dutch and the Iraqis, the Iranians," Marcus said.

"The Turks," Sinan added, feeling, strangely, like he was agreeing with the man.

"Try to keep it elevated," Marcus said. "I'll check on you tomorrow."

And the next night he returned to perform the operation again. Sinan was happy for the American's return because a loneliness was setting in, and the darkness of the tent in the evening and the absence of his family only deepened the feeling.

"Do you know," Sinan said this time, "that this place used to be a prison?"

"No."

His foot was covered in less blood this time and when the American touched the gauze with the alcohol to the cuts, it didn't hurt so badly.

"When the military depopulated the South and rounded up boys they said were terrorists, they took them here. That tower near the soup kitchen is where the soldiers stood with their machine guns."

Marcus remained focused on his work—pressing gauze on the cuts, dabbing away dried blood between the toes.

"There was a room with wires attached to a car battery."

Marcus spread petroleum jelly on the split skin and taped a bandage there to keep the wounds from sticking to the wrapping material.

"There was another room without windows. They left them in there for days—left them sitting in their own piss, in their own feces."

"I've heard the same horrible stories, Sinan."

Marcus stretched the fabric over the stump—one time around, two times around . . .

"You Americans knew about this, but you never forced the government to shut it down," Sinan said.

"I was living here, Sinan."

He felt like kicking the American, but he controlled his foot if not his mouth. "You never made the Turks stop destroying villages, forcing people to move west. Did you actually believe, like the idiots in Ankara, that making people homeless would stop the war?"

. . . three times and then the metal clip.

"No. The Americans think, Just keep sending Ankara money, just keep selling them weapons, their war is our profit."

"The PKK killed teachers," Marcus said. "Because they had to teach in Turkish."

What he said was true. Kurdish teachers were killed by the PKK for no fault of their own; the state wouldn't allow them to teach in Kurdish. The Kurdistan Workers' Party killed whole Kurdish families, Sinan could have added, because they were suspected of collaborating with the Turkish military. But Sinan said nothing, because those disgusting facts embarrassed him.

"Depopulation was a bad policy," Marcus said, as though to appease Sinan. "An immoral one."

"The Europeans," Sinan said, his voice calming now, "got them to shut the prison down—the French and the Germans—not the Americans."

"Keep the foot elevated, Sinan. I think it's getting better." He stood to leave. "I'll see you tomorrow evening."

The next night, Sinan had Nilüfer make tea before she left for the evening. She said she was doing laundry, but he saw no laundry. What are the children doing? They spend time in the school tent, Sinan. İsmail plays soccer. İrem talks with Dilek and Ayşe. Don't worry about them. Rest.

The tea was bitter and tasted of metal and he was embarrassed to serve it, but Marcus drank it and, for a few moments, the simple act of pouring tea for a guest tricked his mind into believing everything was normal. Then, after the first cup of small talk, as though all the events of the last two weeks had been waiting to break loose from him, Marcus told Sinan about his wife's funeral—the long flight to New Hampshire, the knowledge that her body lay beneath them in the cargo hold, the way Sarah Hanım's sisters accused him of keeping her from them all the years they spent in Turkey, and how the next morning he and Dylan flew back immediately to İstanbul, and he delivered his resignation to Bağlarbaşi American School and organized the relief effort with people from Texas.

"I couldn't stay in America," he said, "knowing what you all were suffering here." He paused and rubbed the heel of his hand with his thumb. "Sarah's gone. Staying in the States doesn't make that any better."

"You must hate me," Sinan said.

Marcus looked as though he had been slapped in the face.

"Your wife is dead because of my son," Sinan said.

"My wife is dead because it was her time," he said. He shook his head. "I don't hate you or your son."

They sat silent for a few moments, sipping bitter tea and listening to the sounds outside the tent—a guitar being strummed somewhere and voices singing strange songs, the murmur of intimate conversations escaping nearby tents, the excited screaming of boys playing a soccer game. The silence lasted, and Sinan couldn't think of one thing to say to the man. The American's life—the job at the rich school, the flights back and forth from America, the simple ability to make the choice to quit your job—was so outside his realm of experience that he said nothing at all for fear of sounding stupid.

Marcus took a sip of the tea and made a face.

"It's terrible, I know," Sinan said.

"No, it's fine."

"You're very polite."

He took another sip.

"You're right," Marcus said, laughing. "It really is terrible."

They laughed, and Marcus tossed the tea out the door.

SINAN SOON REALIZED THAT here, in the camp, he wasn't needed at all. The Americans served three meals a day and donated clothes for his children. There was no rent to pay or grocery to run or even any chores to make his children do. İrem and İsmail escaped to the school tent each day, and he was glad to see them go, glad for the freedom of their absence but sad for it, too, and he wished they would return to the tent if only so he could hear their feet shuffle the fabric.

In the mornings after breakfast, Nilüfer and İrem would help him outside the tent, where he sat most of the day like some paralyzed idiot, on dusty pillows, and watched the people of the camp. The men spent hours sitting in the sun playing backgammon—the dice clattering against the wooden edges of the boards, the players roaring as the numbers fell. Children chased one another, their bodies threading between tents and kicking up dust, which mothers waved away as though swatting at offending flies. Uğur, the Gypsy boy who lost his whole family in the quake, dropped discarded fruit peels, husks of eggplant, and other refuse into a plastic bag he dragged behind him. Sinan didn't know if he was eating the leftovers, and he didn't want to know. A woman two tents down lay curled inside her tent. He could see the soles of her sunlit feet through the opening. Except for the occasional wiggling of toes, those feet never moved. An elderly man wearing a motorcycle helmet walked up and down the tent aisle each morning. "Another earthquake is coming," he said to everyone he passed. "God is punishing us." Ziya Bey, Sinan's next-door neighbor, tried to take the helmet off the man's head one day. "You're scaring the children," he said to the man. But the man screamed and kicked at him until he gave up. The next morning he was shuffling his feet through the dust again.

Some of the men drank *rakı* and beer all day and into the evenings as though they had given up on a future, and although Sinan despised these drunken men, a small part of him wanted their company. Ahmet would be drinking with them were he here, and sometimes he found himself closing his eyes and listening to their conversation— their Nasreddin Hoja jokes, their rude gossip about the women (their breast size, their hip size, which wife did this and which wife did that in bed)—and tried to imagine Ahmet's voice among them. Sometimes he did imagine his brother-in-law's voice and, briefly, the real world and the world in his mind combined to make one lost life exist again.

Nilüfer kept her normal motherly duties—comforting İrem when she arrived back at the tent angry about something one of her friends had said, hugging İsmail when he scraped his knee in a soccer game. She maintained her domestic chores, even within this small tent— brewing tea, shaking out dirty carpets, washing clothes in the buckets behind the food tent.

But for Sinan there was nothing to do. Maybe it was because of his foot, but he had never felt half the man his father was until he ran the *bakkal*; his father had died, after all, defending his rights against the government, while Sinan couldn't even make himself stand on a swollen foot. Ahmet had been a bad businessman and Sinan had been the one that turned the failing store into a profit-earning affair— albeit a very-little-profit-earning affair. Without the grocery to keep him busy and a household to keep in order, as he sat in the camp like a child being taken care of by Americans, he began to hate himself. Even after his foot had stopped throbbing and the swelling was down, he sat around the tent all day torturing himself over decisions and indecisions that had plagued his life—letting İsmail sleep by the open window the night of the quake, leaving İrem and Nilüfer alone for four days, leaving his village of Yeşilli, obeying his father the night of the Nowruz festival instead of kicking and screaming until his father came home with him—and dozens of other mistakes that seemed to lead him to this exact moment. When his wife returned from doing laundry, he was glad to have her near but he barely spoke to her. When İrem failed to return when told, he ignored it. When Marcus visited, he shook his hand and held polite conversation but forgot what was said as soon as the man left. So inward were his thoughts that he seemed to be separated from the world around him, as though curled into himself behind a glass wall.

One night early in the second week, while they lay together inside the tent, listening to the sounds of their children sleeping, Nilüfer said, "I thought I was going to lose you. You slept so long, I thought you might die."

Earlier that night, at dinner, between mouthfuls of watery spaghetti, Nilüfer had decided to voice all her fears openly in front of the children and the other people sitting nearby in the food tent. It had rained that afternoon, sheets of it blown by swirling wind and accompanied by strikes of lightning that set Sinan's teeth on edge. Their tent flooded, but worse, one of the portable toilets tipped over and spilled into the lake left by the rain. In the broiling heat that followed, some of the children splashed into the lake before their parents and the Americans could get them out. In half an hour, acrid steam rose off the lake and filled the camp with a mean stench. *Now we'll wallow in our own waste? How will we ever get another apartment? There's no work around here! This tent will be useless in wintertime. Have the Americans thought about that? What if the children get sick? How will we ever find İrem a husband? What if the Americans leave? What will the government do for us then? What will we do?* And Sinan had eaten an extra plate of spaghetti just to keep his mouth full so he wouldn't scream at her. What was he to do? How was he to fix such things?

Now his stomach was too full and it pressed uncomfortably against the waist of his pants.

"And what would you do without me?" he said, his voice strained with frustration.

"I don't know, *canım.*"

"There're a lot of people here to take care of you," he said.

She was silent a moment before she leaned over and whispered in his ear in a way that made him wish they were alone.

"They can't take care of me the way you can, my husband."

Yet he couldn't even be a man in that way, either. His children, though asleep, lay near, the canvas drapes of the tent were too thin to disguise the sound of such an act. A moment later, Nilüfer rolled over and before long he could hear her quiet snoring.

Chapter 26

HE LED HER UP THE HILL THAT ROSE ABOVE THE BEACH. Before they had only come here at night, but after the rains yesterday the stink of the camp was too much to bear in the afternoon heat, and now they walked the ridge between the sea and the camp. This precipice of land made her dizzy: to the right the sea lay like an opaque plate of glass and on her left the tents spread like tombstones in a distant cemetery. Their shadows fell across the ridge and seemed to double their size, and she thought she saw people below looking up at them as they moved together on the hill.

"Hurry," she said. "We should have waited until dark."

"They can't tell it's us," he said. "Just two shapes on a hill. We could be anyone."

No we couldn't, she wanted to tell him, but she wanted to believe he was right. They sat beneath a ridge that blocked them off from the camp. Before them was nothing but water, blindingly brilliant in the evening sun. He tried to kiss her but she made him wait. They watched the sun fall into the sea and as darkness dropped, her fear changed into excitement, as though at night she were not İrem Başioğlu but a woman in one of Dilek's stories. His hands moved over her shoulders and slipped occasionally to brush across her sternum. His tongue wrestled with hers, as though trying to pin it down, and then searched out her teeth, jumped across the roof of her mouth, and pushed against the thick skin of her cheeks. Each time his mouth moved, a spot in her chest tingled in just the right way to make her forget that what they were doing was wrong.

Then they'd stop to come up for air and the blackness of the sea stared back at her and the stars shined down like a billion eyes and she remembered her father sitting alone in the tent, his foot propped up on an empty apple box. Then she wanted Dylan to kiss her again, because when he kissed her she forgot her family and the camp and the earthquake and that she should not be here doing what she was doing.

"Oh, God," Dylan said. "Your lips are incredible." He shook his head, his hair whipping around his face, as though he were trying to get control of himself. "For someone who's never done this before, you've got serious skills."

She laughed an embarrassed laugh.

"What?" he said.

She laughed again, wanting to tell him the secret she remembered because she had never told anyone before and she was sick of keeping secrets to make herself seem innocent.

"You're laughing at me," he said.

"No, no."

"You are. What'd I do?" he said, acting genuinely upset now.

"No," she said. "I'm not laughing at you. It's just . . ."

"What?"

"I've done it before."

"Kissing?" he said. "Like in the shower, on the tiles?"

"No," she laughed again, this time at him because she briefly imagined him alone, kissing wet shower tiles with his thick, wandering lips. "No. Me and my best friend practiced."

"What?" he said, laughing.

"Just to see what it was like," she said, hitting him on the knee. "What are we supposed to do? Husbands want us to be good at it, but we can't get near any boys. A lot of the girls do it."

"It's freaky," he said, "but kind of cool."

"It didn't mean anything," she said. "I thought of Tarkan when I did it."

"Tarkan's gay."

"No, he's not."

"Have you watched him dance in his videos?" He laughed and while still sitting, rolled his body in an awkward belly-dancing move. "You're the only person in Turkey who doesn't know that. But I guess thinking about a gay, male pop star—I know, I know, you didn't know he's gay—while kissing your best girlfriend makes it all right."

"It makes it all right for you," she said.

"That's for sure."

Then they were kissing again, the self-consciousness and the guilt receding along with the dark hole of the sea. The spinning stars turned pinwheels in her vision before she closed her eyes and against that black canvas of her mind there was only the feeling and only the feeling mattered.

SHE DIDN'T KNOW WHAT time it was when she left him, but the dipper had moved from the fringe of the horizon to just off center in the sky. They had a routine: she scrambled down the hill toward the beach and he took the goat trail down to the edge of town where he waited behind the fence to the camp until he saw her climb into her tent.

Now she was stepping delicately from rock to rock down a dirt path, the sea on her left and the dull lights of the camp on her right. The white crescent strip of beach lay far below, resting against the sea tide like a huge rib bone. This part of the walk scared her because at night she thought one misstep would send her flying into the air to a landing, her neck broken, on the pebbles below. During the day, she knew this wasn't so. She would simply roll into the weeds—a few thorns poking her skin through her clothes—get up, and continue down.

An old tanker clunked its way up the coast. The call to prayer rang from the new mosque, the sound of the muezzin echoing off the hillside to the beach and coming back again in louder reverberations, and she knew it was near eleven and much too late to be out.

Because the cacophony of sound was so loud and because she was watching the beach and not the rocks beneath her feet, she tripped and, for a moment, she thought she was tumbling toward the beach. But a hand suddenly grasped her arm, crushing her muscle in its grip, as it steadied her against falling.

"Dylan," she said.

"No," a voice said, its arm pulling her toward it. "It's not your boyfriend."

It took her eyes a moment to adjust to the dim light, but she recognized the man. She had seen him many times in her father's store buying cartons of lightbulbs. She smelled onions on his breath and the damp stench of cigarette smoke.

"Thank you," she said.

"It's no problem," he said. His fingers gripped the skin near her armpit too tightly.

"I'm fine now," she said.

"Your father know where you are?"

She didn't say anything.

"Of course not," he said. She caught his teeth, shining gray through his black mouth, in the light from the camp. "What would a father do if he knew his daughter was out kissing a boy? Especially a father like yours?"

He still hadn't let go of her arm and now he was moving closer, his other hand floating toward her in the dark.

"He knows about it all," she said.

"Of course he doesn't. But don't worry, I won't say anything."

He pulled her toward him and then he was kissing her, his tongue slashing away inside her mouth like a sharpened knife. She tried to pull away, tried to grab the shard of glass in her pocket, but his arms locked around her. She tried to kick him in the groin, but he was too close. His tongue grazed her teeth, and, without thinking, she bit down as hard as she could. He groaned and his arms went weak.

Then she was running down the hill, jumping from rock to rock as though she had the placement of each one memorized.

OUT OF BREATH, SHE stumbled into the tent and accidentally kicked her father's leg.

"Sorry, Baba," she said. She braced herself for his attack, sure it would be vicious this time, and she knew she deserved it. She wanted him to attack her so she could admit to everything, so she could lie in his arms and be protected, but he simply moved his leg and curled up inside his sleeping bag.

She let her eyes adjust to the light, the taste of blood still in her mouth, and found her sleeping bag next to her mother. She slipped inside and wiped the blood from her tongue, cleaning her fingers on the inside fabric of the bag. Her mother raised herself up on her elbow and looked away from her toward her father. Nilüfer sat there for a minute, like a dark cloud hovering above her, and İrem thought she saw her start to shake. She lay back down and İrem felt an emptiness crowd her body, as though a stale air pressed everything good out of her and left her only with the taste of this man's blood.

Her mother's sleeping bag rustled again, and the shadow of Nilüfer's face hung near her cheek.

"You can't stay out so late," she said, loud enough that it hurt İrem's ear.

"Yes, *Anne*," she said.

Her mother lay back down and turned her back. Her father didn't move. İrem cried into the fabric of the bag, amazed that she could do it so silently.

Chapter 27

"ALLAHU AKBAR!" THE MUEZZIN CALLED IN A VOICE THAT WAS like a knife splitting the morning silence. "I bear witness that there is no god but the One God."

Nilüfer touched his hip and rested her hand there a minute, as though waiting.

His foot was healed and he could have gotten up to go to morning prayer, but he drew his head down into the sleeping bag and tried to ignore the wavering voice and his wife's insistent fingers.

I bear witness that Muhammad is the messenger of God.

The sun was not up yet but the lightening sky was turning the inside of the tent blue.

Come fast to prayer.

Her hand remained on his hip, and now one of her fingers tapped against his bone.

Nilüfer had told him about the wooden mosque the Americans had built, at the request of İmam Ali, to replace the one destroyed in the quake, but he had not gone.

Come to success.

If it had been İsmail's fate to survive the quake, then God had known his fate all along and had planned his fate as such. If that outcome was predetermined, he wouldn't have needed to leave his wife and daughter alone, unprotected for four terrible days. It seemed a cruel trick now, to keep İsmail trapped in that hell—a test no man could pass.

Prayer is better than sleep.

Nilüfer's finger stopped tapping. She pulled her hand away and turned her back to him.

God is the Greatest. There is no god but the One True God.

And then the call ended and silence filled the space left by the muezzin's voice, but the echo seemed to linger in the air.

Later, Nilüfer brought him breakfast. Again, watery eggs and an oily garlic sausage that was burned on one side.

"Your foot is better?"

"Almost," he said.

"I think it's better," she said.

"Is it your foot? Have you been dragging it around all your life?"

She set the eggs in front of him, but he was not hungry. He hadn't been hungry for days.

"You should eat," she said.

"I'm no child, Nilüfer."

"Then stop acting like one!"

He sat up. Her eyes were brilliantly angry. He took a bite from the sausage and chewed while looking out through the tent opening at the yellow ground.

"We can't stay here," she said, her voice calm now.

"You begged me to come."

"To get food, to get you better, to make sure İsmail was not bleeding."

"What do you want me to do?" He pushed the plate of eggs away and she pushed them back.

"Eat!"

He bit off another piece of the sausage and rolled it around in his mouth.

"We can go into the city," she said. "There are jobs there."

"Jobs," he said. "What do you know about jobs?"

"Yes, jobs," she said, as though just saying the word would make it all happen.

"And stay where?" he said, shaking his head at her now. "We have ten million to our name."

Her eyes widened as though she were surprised at how little it was, as though she had not thought of that.

"Don't be stupid, Nilüfer."

"This is the man I married?" she said, standing now. Her head hit the top of the tent and she tried to slap the fabric away with her hand. "You've never called me such things before. You were a good man, Sinan, but now you sit here like a stupid donkey. You still have a family."

"Don't tell me what I already know." He hesitated, trying to calm himself down. "I'm only one man, Nilüfer."

She clucked her tongue at him.

"If this is you, you're not even that," she said, and then she left the tent.

İREM STAYED AROUND THE tent that morning, serving Sinan tea and shaking out the sleeping bags. She asked him about his foot. It was getting better, he said. She asked him if he was tired, if he was sleeping well. I'm sorry if I disturbed you last night. He was sleeping fine. I love you, Baba. I love you, too.

That afternoon, after İrem and Nilüfer left to do the laundry, Sinan lay staring up at the ceiling when İsmail burst into the tent with an envelope in his hand.

"Baba," İsmail said. "Baba, a letter for you."

The boy handed the envelope to him. It was postmarked Diyarbakır, but there was no return address—a trick, he knew, in case the government thought the letter was a coded message for terrorists.

"Where did you get this?"

"A postman came to the school carrying a big bag over his shoulder. He poured them out on the floor."

He pulled the knife out of the breast pocket of his coat and cut open the envelope. It was from his aunt, written in awkward Kurdish.

Dear Sinan—

Oh, God, I hope you and your family are alive. The pictures on the television are horrible. May God, His mercifulness, keep you safe. If this finds you well, I want to tell you that the soldiers left last week. The PKK stopped fighting after Öcalan's capture. The men have hung flags in their shop windows and no paramilitaries have come to take them away. The war is over, Sinan. We've built a house for you and your family. It's a simple home, but it will keep the snow out and the chickens in! Come home. I want to see my brother's son again.

Love—

Aunt Melike

He read the letter again to make sure he had not misunderstood it. *The war is over.* It was impossible to believe, but how he'd hoped for it. *Come home.* Hoped for it forever, it seemed.

"İsmail," he said. "Come here."

The boy did and sat down next to him on his sleeping bag. He drew the boy to his side and placed the letter in his hands.

"You don't remember the woman who wrote this," he said. "But you'll meet her soon, God willing."

"Who is it, Baba?"

"It's your *dede*'s sister, my aunt. Someone who loves you very much."

"How can she love me, if she doesn't know me?"

"She knew you when you were very young." He kissed İsmail on the cheek. "You used to bring her handfuls of pebbles. She washed them and kept every single one of them on the windowsill." He laughed. "Once you brought her a dried-out goat turd."

İsmail wrinkled his nose in disgust.

"She washed your hands and put that one on the windowsill, too!"

İsmail ran his fingers over the words on the paper. "What does it say?" The boy could not read the Kurdish, a fact that saddened him. When they got back to Yeşilli he would teach the boy his language, even if the government still forbade it.

"It says 'Come home and tell İsmail to bring me gold nuggets this time.' "

HE FOUND NILÜFER AND İrem at the washing bins, hanging clothes on the line.

"Take a walk with me," he said.

"Leave me alone." Nilüfer hid behind a freshly laundered shirt, but through the white fabric he could see her angry face.

"Take a walk with me." He pulled the shirt off the line and was presented with her olive-black eyes. "I have something to tell you."

"Tell me now."

"No," he said. "Take a walk with me."

He grabbed her by the waist and dragged her away from the clothes.

"They're wet, Sinan. I can't leave them like that."

"Leave them."

"Finish hanging the laundry, İrem," Nilüfer said. "Hide the underclothes behind the blouses. I'll be back."

They walked beneath the old guard tower, where a man aimed a long camera lens toward the rows of tents. A man next to him scribbled notes on a small notepad and then spoke into a tiny microphone he held in the palm of his hand.

"I received a letter today," he said.

"A letter?" she said. "The government can't bring us food, but they can find us to deliver letters?"

They passed the soup kitchen and the wooden benches set out for eating. Beyond the benches, a crowd had gathered to listen to a Gypsy family playing music in the open field. Sitting on the tailgate of his dented Lada station wagon, the Gypsy father ran his fingers across an electronic keyboard powered by a gas generator.

"Who sent it?" She tugged on his arm now. "Stop playing these games."

But he wasn't playing a game. He was afraid it wasn't true. He didn't want to say it, for fear he'd wake up and have it all be a dream.

He handed Nilüfer the letter.

The blind daughter of the Gypsy family sang Roma songs with a twirling voice as though her tongue were a spindle, her white eyes staring blankly at the crowd. A single finger tapped against the microphone.

"Aunt Melike?!" Nilüfer said.

"Yes."

The Gypsy mother stood holding a tin cup in her hand, tipped just so to reveal nothing inside. On another day, in the old life before the earthquake, that cup would have been filled with coins before the song was finished.

"The soldiers have left Yeşilli?"

"Yes," he said. "That's what her letter says."

It was true then. He hadn't imagined it.

The Gypsy woman's skirt was filthy, her feet covered only in blackened socks. They had nowhere to go. Being a Gypsy was worse than being a Kurd.

"We can go home!" Nilüfer said.

THE MOSQUE THE AMERICANS had built was a sturdy A-frame with no walls; it looked nothing like a mosque, but it managed to keep the men sheltered from the weather. The Americans had placed a water truck near the entrance and it was here that Sinan washed himself before prayer, trying to keep the mud from splashing on the cuffs of his pants. Inside, the open floor was covered in worn prayer rugs and frayed blankets. A framed tile of God's name glazed in Arabic sat propped on a metal chair and acted as the prayer niche. Facing this, a couple of dozen men, mostly elderly, prostrated themselves in submission.

He decided to attend evening prayers, ashamed by his anger with God. God had a reason for everything, and a man who doubted His wisdom was arrogant, selfish, and sure to be damned. With each prostration, each recitation, he tried to become nothing, but his humbleness was clouded by the clear vision of his old home in Yeşilli: the jagged white teeth of the mountains, the crystalline blue sky, the snow-white steppes like blankets of bleached wool. His chest vibrated with the possibility of return, and while he bowed his head before the mihrab he remembered a day when he was eleven and his father took him to Ensar Bey's field on the edge of town.

His father didn't allow him to come here, and for that exact reason Sinan had been to this field before with the other boys of Yeşilli. He had seen the Turkish soldiers behind the cement barricades and knew not to pass them. He knew, also, that occasionally they came into town and took someone away and that that someone, whoever it might be, never came back.

The sun was low on the horizon. Two soldiers sitting in a car without a roof on the rise above the field were silhouetted against the sky.

"Here," his father said and turned his back to the men. "Face me."

Sinan did and they bent together among the tomato vines and removed the red fruit from the stem.

"See that car?" he said.

"Yes, Baba."

"That's a jeep." He carefully dropped the tomato in his bag and removed another from the stem. "They make them in America."

Sinan didn't understand, but he could tell it was a bad thing.

"See the soldier leaning against the fender and smoking?"

"Yes, Baba."

"See the rifle hanging from his shoulder?"

He did, but the rifle was no longer dangling from his shoulder. He held it now in both hands.

"Yes."

"That's an M-16," he said, carefully removing a worm from the center of the fruit with a penknife. The worm wrapped around his father's finger, and he gently rolled it off his thumbnail into the mud. "They make those in America, too, and the Turkish soldiers use them against us."

The next morning, instead of going off to the fields and leaving Sinan to sleep, his father woke him as the sun was just sprinkling the sky with light and piled him into an old Chevy that Celal Bey had bought cheap from a taxi driver in Diyarbakır. It was the only regularly working car in town and Sinan knew it was a Chevy because when all the men saw it pass in the street they nodded their heads approvingly and said, "Hmm, a Chevy." The one good thing Americans make, his father had once said.

As the sky turned the color of a bruise, his father piloted the car along a row of trees that shaded Haluk Bey's strawberry fields, down a dirt path through Emre Bey's olive orchards, and then into a dry riverbed scarred with so many tire tracks it created a sort of rail line for cars. His father didn't say anything, but he leaned over the steering wheel and turned his head left and right, watching the embankments.

They drove like that for a while until the riverbed came to a bridge and he followed a track up the embankment that led to the pavement above. When they were on the road, his father leaned back in the seat and lit a cigarette and then Sinan relaxed and nodded off to sleep.

His father tapped him on the shoulder and when he opened his eyes, the land stretched beneath him in a series of ridges and river washes and parched desert. They were parked on the edge of a mountain, the nose of the huge Chevy pointed into oblivion.

"See all this land?" his father said. "It's ours. It's been the Kurds' since before the Arabs, since before the Turks even came here from Central Asia." He pointed into the deep distance, to a triangular shadow capped with a cloud shaped like a winter hat. "From Ararat, where Noah set foot on ground again," he ran his hand across the panorama before them, "to Van to Babylonia. Ours."

The land was immense, pocked with mountain faces and dry steppes that looked purple in the shadows of morning.

"See that mountain there?" he said.

"Yes, Baba."

"The other side is ours too, but it's called Iraq. A man named Hussein gasses our people and America gives him money because they don't like Iran."

He was silent a moment and they watched together this land that was theirs but not theirs.

"Do you remember Rifat Bey?"

"The *yufka* maker?" Sinan said. "He died, didn't he?"

"No. He was killed," his father said. "Because he let his cousin, a PKK soldier being chased by the Turks, sleep in his home one night. His body is somewhere out there."

He pointed to the part of the panorama that was Turkey.

"Do you remember Altan Bey?"

"The saddle maker?"

"Yes," he said. "You've got a good memory. Him, too."

"Why?"

"There are many reasons, Sinan *canım*," his father said. "Many complicated reasons that make no sense. People are afraid to lose things—power, land, oil, money—and all these people—the Turks, the Iraqis, the Iranians—think we'll take those things away from them."

"I don't understand."

"You will," he said. "But for now, before it becomes confusing, remember one thing. None of these people are your friends—not the Arabs, not the Turks, and not the Americans."

"I don't understand. The Americans are far away, across the ocean."

"No, they're not. They're in the guns the Turkish paramilitaries fire, they're in the money they give to dictators like Saddam Hussein, they're even in the ground, pumping out the oil."

A jet screeched overhead. They both looked up and saw a white stream split the sky.

His father smiled, but not a happy one. "The Americans are never far away."

He wondered what his father would say if he knew the war was finished now. No, he would say. Not until our land is ours again. Not until we can speak our language and fly our own flag.

The war is over, Baba, Sinan imagined saying to him. They will leave us alone now.

And suddenly he felt God's presence and he understood His plan for his life. Without the earthquake he would not have returned to his village in the mountains. Without God he would not have honored his father's sacrifice.

"God is great," he said, cupping his palms around his ears to concentrate on Him and only Him.

Chapter 28

"No, Dylan," İrem said. Her parents had walked away together just a minute before. The other women at the laundry were watching them. They were folding men's shirts and hanging wet pants on the line but their eyes were fixed on the two of them. "I have to take care of these clothes."

"Where've you been?"

He pushed a hanging sheet out of the way, and it fell behind him like a screen to a puppet show. She wondered what their shadows would look like to the women, how their movements could be misconstrued.

He took her by the shoulder.

"Stop."

He let go and angrily fixed his jaw.

"Those women are watching."

"So what," he said.

"Something happened the other night," she said. "It scared me."

She told him what she hadn't told anyone, and her body shuddered again when she remembered the taste of that man's mouth.

"I'll kill him," Dylan said.

She was glad he said it, but Kemal Bey was a man with many friends, a man who ran a store before the quake and kept a loaded gun behind the counter, a man with a wife and ruthless eyes that seemed more powerful than any boyish strength.

He grabbed her hand and walked her through the center of the camp, and her body buzzed with electricity—an unsettling combination of fear and excitement. She saw Kemal Bey halfway down the row, his back turned, smoking with two other men. Before they reached him, one of the men nodded his head in their direction and Kemal turned around, threw his cigarette to the ground, and put both hands in his pockets, very deliberately, she thought, as though he clasped something in his fists.

Dylan must have thought the same thing, because his pace slowed and his body became rigid. He pulled her behind him with one hand, and as he did the other two men stood next to Kemal, their shoulders thrown back, their feet planted.

"Foreigner," one man spat.

The hand Dylan held her with shook, but he stared at them as they passed. İrem shielded herself behind his shoulders, one eye watching the black eyes of Kemal Bey watching Dylan's.

Chapter 29

OUTSIDE THE MOSQUE, HE PLACED HIS SHOES ON THE CARDboard that was laid across the mud and slipped them on his feet. A group of men stood smoking beneath a withered plane tree. He hadn't seen any of them in the mosque praying.

"Sinan Bey," Kemal said. He was leaning against the tree, but came to meet Sinan as he came down the path.

Sinan leaned in to kiss his cheek, but Kemal cringed and turned his face away.

"I'm sorry to be rude, Sinan, my brother."

"What happened to your lip?" Sinan asked. The cut looked painful.

"Playing soccer with the boys," he said. "It's nothing, but it hurts a little."

They left the mosque and Kemal guided Sinan by the elbow, through the rows of tents and toward the beach. In the distance, a line of oil tankers sat moored in the water, their shapes like jutting rocks in the evening sky.

"My friend," Kemal said. "How's the job?"

How could he tell him what had happened? He had cheated the man's cousin.

"Fine," Sinan said.

Kemal stared at him a second before smiling. "That's what I hear," Kemal said. "My cousin says you're a good worker. The foot doesn't bother you, then?" He fingered a bracelet of brown prayer beads in his left hand, his thumb working one bead nervously before his fingers threaded the next one into his grasp. Kemal was never without his beads, but Sinan had not once seen him praying at mosque. Before the quake, Sinan assumed he attended *Çicek Camii*, the mosque in the next neighborhood over from his.

"No."

Kemal asked after his family and Sinan did the same. Kemal asked about Sinan's health and Sinan returned the platitude. But Kemal had something else on his mind; Sinan could tell by the absent nods, the vacant way in which he said, "That's good" and "God willing." And it wasn't until they descended the hill that separated the beach from the tent city that Kemal said what he was thinking.

"Watch your daughter, Sinan."

"What are you talking about?"

"That boy," Kemal said, "they say he's a Satanist. People have seen him in Kadiköy, down in the basement music shops, drinking beer and smoking." He leaned in to whisper. "Some dead cats were found by the water. Their necks had been cut."

"Dead cats? I haven't heard anything about that." Before the earthquake, a child had been killed in İstanbul by two teenage boys. The police said it was a ritualistic killing, and the rumor spread that the boys were Satanists. They wore black, it was said, and colored their nails black and listened to certain American rock bands who hid dark messages in their music.

Kemal licked his lip and the scab glistened.

"You haven't been out in the camp, *abi*. People are talking."

"My daughter's a good girl."

"I know. That's why I'm telling you about it. They say they've seen her with that American boy, and you know, Sinan, what happens to some men when they think a young girl is doing things. Men get ideas they shouldn't get. I'm only telling you because she's a good girl and you're a good man. But some of these people don't know her so well."

"What are they saying?"

"Nothing, Sinan. I'm telling you so that it stays that way, so that your name remains honorable."

Chapter 30

SHE FORGOT ABOUT THE LAUNDRY, FORGOT SHE HAD LEFT it sitting in a wet pile. She forgot that people could look up on the hill and see them, and she ignored the fact that a girl like her, a village girl, didn't allow a boy—especially a *yabanci*!—to touch her in public. She felt powerful. She had seen the cut on Kemal Bey's lip. She had felt the strength of Dylan's hand and the safety behind his shoulders. He had defended her and her head spun with an amazing euphoria.

So she let Dylan hold her waist as they passed the soup kitchen. She let him whisper into her ear as they strolled down a row of tents. She said something, something funny that made him laugh, but forgot it as soon as it left her lips because she saw the rock coming—a black disc no bigger than a small bird—a second before it struck her above her left eye.

And as she fell, her mind flashed with the image of the old covered woman who threw it.

Chapter 31

FOR A MOMENT SINAN THOUGHT İREM HAD BEEN SHOT.

He had been sitting outside, sipping a cup of tea, trying to think what to say to her about the rumors when he saw her leaning against the American boy. From a distance, they seemed to be sharing a romantic moment and, at first, much to his surprise, he thought there was something beautiful about it—the way his daughter's cheek rested against his shoulder, the way he held her head as though it were his most important possession; it was exactly how he'd want a husband to hold his daughter's head.

But as they got closer he could see that she wasn't resting, but leaning on him heavily. Suddenly there was something grotesque about the scene, the way her left foot dragged, the way he struggled a bit to hold her up, and then the blood: running bright from a bullet-sized wound above her eye.

"Oh, God," he thought. "They've killed my daughter. Stupid girl."

He ran to her and placed her arm over his shoulder and he and the boy laid her down inside the tent.

"Oh, *canım*," Nilüfer said. "My daughter, you're bleeding."

"İsmail," Sinan said. "Go get Marcus Bey and tell him to bring a doctor."

İsmail burst out of the tent, and Sinan could hear his footsteps slapping against the dirt as he ran.

He touched the wound, pressed his fingers around it, trying to discern its depth, trying to find the shard of bullet.

"Is she okay?" the American boy said.

Nilüfer brought Sinan a wet towel and he dabbed the blood away.

"Jesus, is she all right?" Dylan said.

And Sinan realized it was just a scratch, a nick of skin shaved off above her eyebrow.

"She's all right," Sinan said.

"Jesus."

"Thank God, His mercifulness," Nilüfer said.

"That stings, Baba," İrem said, pushing his hand away. Nilüfer placed a pillow beneath İrem's head. "I'm all right," she said, and sat up, but her eyes looked glassy and unfocused.

"What happened?"

"That bastard," the boy said.

"A woman threw a rock," İrem said, glancing at the American boy before looking at Sinan. She looked down at the ground. "We were talking and she threw a rock."

Sinan looked at Nilüfer and he could see her concern turning to anger—she was grinding her teeth, her eyes were growing blacker.

"Please leave," Sinan said, standing to face the boy.

The boy's eyes darted around the room and settled on İrem's. Sinan saw the muscles in his jaw working and he thought that if that muscle flexed a third time he would have to push the boy out of the tent, but the boy dropped his eyes and ducked outside.

"What were you doing with that boy?" Nilüfer said after Dylan was gone.

İrem didn't answer.

"Answer your mother."

"Talking."

"And what else?" Nilüfer said.

"Walking."

"Don't play games with me," Nilüfer said.

İrem hadn't been crying, but now the tears began to run down her cheeks. She wiped them away with the heel of her hand as though she were embarrassed to have them be seen.

"We were walking and talking," İrem said, her voice growing frustrated. "What don't you understand, Anne?" She turned her back and faced the fabric of the tent. "Allah, Allah, I have a conversation in broad daylight and you two act like I've killed someone."

Light burst into the tent and İsmail stepped in. "I got them," he said, glancing at his sister. "Is she okay?"

"Yes, son," Sinan said. He was moved by İsmail's concern and touched his head to reassure him.

"You leave me alone for four days, praying for him," İrem said, motioning toward İsmail. She spat the words out. "I'm struck with a rock, and you attack me."

He was about to tell her what she already knew: you brought it on yourself, but her words stabbed him with guilt.

"*Canım*," Nilüfer said, softening. She sat down next to her daughter. "You have to be careful with boys." She stroked İrem's hair and İrem jumped under the touch. "Besides, it's not appropriate."

İrem rolled her eyes and blew air out of her mouth.

"He's nice," İrem said. "He's just sad about his mother."

"No," Nilüfer said. "Boys are dangerous—more dangerous than a tiny rock. They always want something."

"Like what?" İrem had a strange smile on her face; a dangerous smile that scared Sinan.

He told İsmail to wait outside.

"Things," Nilüfer said. "You don't want to give them."

The cut had started to bleed again and Nilüfer dabbed at it with the cloth.

İrem laughed. "Sex, mother. You mean sex?"

Nilüfer stood up immediately.

"What did you say?" Sinan said, more with shock than anger, though anger came on its heels.

Nilüfer touched his shoulder, and motioned her head toward the door. "*You* should leave now."

Outside the tent, he found the foreigners and İsmail waiting, as though for the coming of a newborn.

"Sinan Bey," Dylan said, grabbing Sinan's forearm, his eyes wide with childhood fear. "She's fine, right?"

"It's just a cut."

"Jesus, she like passed out. She was bleeding all over and I thought—"

Sinan placed his palm on the boy's hand and looked him in the eye. This was no Satanist. "She's okay."

The doctor said he should see her. Sinan gave him permission to enter the tent, and İsmail showed him in. Marcus told Dylan to leave and the boy did, occasionally turning around, though, to glance back at the tent as he walked away.

"It was a rock," Sinan said.

"Who?" Marcus said. "Do you know?"

"It doesn't matter. You must keep your son away from my daughter."

"It's innocent."

So he knew about them.

"You know what happened here," Sinan said.

"That's the village, Sinan. Not İstanbul."

"The village has moved here. You've been in this country long enough to know that."

"It's wrong."

"Your son has to leave my daughter alone."

"She makes him happy." Marcus looked at him, pleading with him, but also reminding Sinan of the boy's loss. Did the man really think he'd give up his daughter? But Sinan remembered the way the boy held her head, the way she fell so completely against him. Happiness in this world was no small thing to give up. İrem must have felt something, too, to risk what she had.

"We must live in the world we live in," Sinan said.

IF HE HAD BEEN a good father, the rock would never have been thrown.

This was the thought that kept him up all night.

The doctor thought İrem had a minor concussion, and they were to wake her every two hours. Early in the evening, he and Nilüfer traded shifts but Sinan couldn't calm his mind, and he finally told Nilüfer to go to sleep. He stayed up all night, listening to the sound of his daughter's breath, touching her forehead briefly when he thought two hours had passed, just long enough to see her eyes flash with accusation.

Yet by morning he wanted to find this woman who struck his daughter and slap her. He left early for prayer, seething with anger. He almost asked people if they had seen the woman who threw the rock, but asking would be an admission of his daughter's improper behavior and he was too embarrassed to acknowledge it in public. Instead, he stared at every woman he saw in hijab, his anger flaring when he saw a fundamentalist, dressed in black from head to toe, as if she were already dead. It was one thing to be humble and modest, but it seemed to Sinan that the *abaya* revealed men's disgust with women, as though men thought God had made a mistake and they needed to hide it. Sinan would never make his wife and daughter wear such a thing; he would never allow them to be so blotted out of existence.

When he was a child in the village, a beautiful teenage girl all the boys had crushes on disappeared one day. Her father and her brother disappeared, too, and the town became unusually silent, as though everyone knew something they were trying to ignore. Before this, people had been gossiping about the girl, saying she and a young married man were having an affair, saying finally that she was pregnant with his child. But during these three days, quiet pressed down on the village like an oppressive pall. The girl's mother was silent and she could be seen going nervously about her business in town—buying eggs at the egg seller's, stopping by the *yufka* maker, getting lamb legs at the butcher's. Even Sinan had trouble sleeping at night, not because he understood what was happening, but because the village felt different, as though some dangerous stranger had wandered into town and taken up residence.

On the third day, the girl's brother and father returned to town without the daughter. No one ever saw her again. When the government police came asking questions, no one told them what they all knew: that the brother and the father had taken her out into the mountains and killed her. They were justified in their actions to protect the family name from shame, but Sinan never looked at them the same again. Even as an adult, he never set foot in their electrical light shop—the only one in town.

The problem was that he was not the man he had been in Yeşilli. In Yeşilli he never would have ignored İrem's comings and goings. He would have stopped it the moment he saw her hugging the boy in the makeshift camp. But he'd yielded to his sympathy and despair and exhaustion and the guilt he harbored over the boy's loss. He was ashamed now of his weakness, of himself—no job, no way to take care of his family, no control over his daughter and he was angry that İrem had exposed it publicly.

After morning prayer, he returned to the tent and looked at İrem's forehead.

"It's looking better," he said, holding her by the chin. He couldn't look in her eyes, but he saw them anyway—big, black, angry: her mother's eyes.

"Does it hurt?"

"People are trying to teach you what's right," Nilüfer said before İrem could answer. "Sometimes what's right is painful."

"You'll rest for a few days," he said. "Then we'll talk."

—

HE ASKED AROUND CAMP to see if anybody knew of any jobs. If they did, they jealously guarded the information. The Turks said, "No, *abi*," and diverted their eyes, the Armenians hedged, perhaps out of a bit of minority sympathy, and said they had heard of something on the other side of the city, or that there *was* a job but someone else got to it first.

By the end of the third day he was furious, sure there were jobs but no one would tell a Kurd about them. He sulkily took dinner with his family under the shade of a leaning plane tree where fewer eyes could watch them, and listened to the blind Gypsy singer and her father on his keyboard. He watched the Armenian, Nazar—the only "Turk" serving food—a gold cross swaying from his neck as he leaned over to hand plates to people. A few of the Americans on break from serving food had gathered to listen to the Gypsy music, and sitting on the lap of one American woman was Uğur, the Gypsy child, his hair combed, his face a single color rather than mottled with dirt. The boy stared at the performers, his eyes heavy with a sagging loneliness that filled Sinan with his own, and he began to think he'd never see his home again. The house his aunt and uncle had built for him would stand empty, a waste.

As they walked back from dinner, a young man dressed in blue pants and a yellow Carrefour shirt strode past them on the dusty path. His clothes looked brand-new, all shiny and crisp—except for the dust on the pants cuffs—as though they had been recently pressed.

Sinan stopped him in the street.

"You're working at Carrefour?"

"Yes," the man said. He was a child, no more than twenty with hair barely growing on his face. "I spray water on the vegetables to keep them clean."

"They pay you for that?"

"Yes." He smiled. "They pay my friend to sign delivery forms when the trucks arrive. All he has to do is make sure all the stuff comes in, sign his name on a paper, then he sits around in the air-conditioning drinking tea all day."

Later that evening Sinan walked the three kilometers to the huge Carrefour. It sat on the other side of the freeway, in the middle of a sea of asphalt and parked cars that used to be a goat field. It was a monstrous building, larger than the big mosque with the broken minaret that stood next to it.

In Yeşilli, nothing was larger than the mosque. It towered over the mud buildings and its silver dome shone in the afternoon light. When the government came to town and tried to build a six-story apartment building to house workers building a dam for the Great Anatolian Project, İmam Khalid led a revolt against the contractors because the building's sixth floor was to be two feet taller than the tip of the mosque's minaret. Women on their way to market and children playing in the street threw stones at the contractors as they balanced on the scaffolding, and men, under cover of night, sledgehammered newly laid cinder blocks, reducing them to broken pieces and piles of dust. The contractor pulled out of the project and the government moved their workers to another town, but only after the paramilitaries burned a few stores to make their point. The apartment complex, only three stories high when abandoned, stood an empty shell and protected sheep from snowdrifts in winter.

Inside Carrefour now, the store felt cavernous, stacked to the ceiling with boxes of stereos and televisions and car supplies and even furniture. Sinan had forgotten how big the building was. There were at least thirty rows of shelves lined with food and the produce section alone was ten times the size of his old *bakkal*. Seeing so much food in one place after the earthquake was shocking beyond belief. He first wondered how they could sell so many things, wondered if there were really enough people in İstanbul to purchase all these products. But the store was packed with men wearing pleated pants and women draped in Vakko blouses. They pushed shiny metal carts around while they spoke on cell phones, and filled those shopping carts to the brim with amazing, useless things. For these people, it seemed, the earthquake was simply an unpleasant, passing sadness.

He found the employment office and was seated at a desk in a booth in front of a piece of paper covered in tiny typed words. The man asked him to fill out the form and left. Sinan wrote his name on the appropriate line and jotted down the numbers of the phone that didn't exist anymore, and then waited for twenty minutes before the man returned. He felt ashamed when the man picked up the blank paper and shook his head.

"Can't write?" the man said.

He could write, but in Kurdish. In Turkish, he could write the words for every product he needed in the grocery, but not to answer long questions on an application. He wanted to tell the man so he wouldn't think him an idiot, but he was afraid he wouldn't get the job.

"I used to own a grocery," Sinan said. "I have experience."

"You don't need experience for this job," the man said. "You just need to fill out the application. The home office has to have your information on file—for insurance and payroll."

"It was Brothers' Grocery. Maybe you know it? Just down Nation Street, near the water seller's?"

"I don't live around here, *abi.*"

"Oh." Sinan rubbed his hands together.

"It doesn't matter," the man said, picking up the pen Sinan had left on the table. He was middle-aged with a belly that hung over his pants, but his face was handsome and his skin glowed as if it were fashioned out of glazed ceramic. He didn't seem to be a Turk. He looked like the people Sinan used to see on television—the ones in the commercials with the unlined, happy faces, the ones who seemed to belong to a special television race who looked nothing like the people he saw in real life.

The man explained that the store had a problem. Since all the markets nearby were destroyed, more people than ever were shopping at Carrefour. Business was good, but so many employees were killed in the earthquake that they didn't have enough staff to keep up with the demand.

"Can you start tomorrow?" he said.

"I can begin right now."

"Can you work tomorrow, double shift?"

"Yes," Sinan said. "I can work triple shift."

The man flashed him a strange look and scratched his head.

"Tell me your name," the man said, leaning over the application in preparation to write.

"Sinan Başioğlu," he said. "Thank you, thank you very much."

"Your address?"

Sinan just stared at him.

"That one's not important," the man said.

Chapter 32

NILÜFER TOOK THE CARREFOUR SHIRT OUT OF THE PLASTIC packet, laid it out on one of the rugs, and used the bottom of the hot tea kettle to iron out the creases.

"There," she said. "Put it on." She was smiling—the first time since he could remember—and even though it was a little stupid, he put the shirt on and modeled it in the tent.

"We'll be home soon," he said. "I'll earn the money for those tickets."

"Baba," İsmail said. "Do they sell Galatasaray shirts there?"

IN THE MORNINGS AT the store, he set out newspapers in the metal stands by the registers. The pages were still filled with pictures of destroyed buildings, but the half-naked women began to appear again in the corners of the front pages, some of them with wet T-shirts pressed against their skin and others without the shirt altogether. After that, he moved huge boxes filled with smaller boxes of food or drinks or silly outdoor furniture for people who had patios. He had to match the boxes of products with the price tags and when there was a special sale on, he had to mark the item's tag with a red sticker that looked like a bomb exploding with the new price inside. All the prices were less than what he and Ahmet had charged at their grocery, and he thought they must have been stealing the merchandise to be selling it so cheaply.

He pushed a silver dolly stacked high with boxes of food through the shining aisles, cut open the plastic packing tape with the knife they gave him, and stacked the smaller boxes on top of one another beneath hanging lights that made all the boxes shine with brilliant colors. After stacking the products, he returned to the warehouse where he stacked new products, and returned to the aisles to stack those. There were no windows to see outside and a few hours into his work it was easy to believe the world outside the walls of the store was completely intact. He created pyramids of German beer cans, and the higher he stacked them the prouder he became of his work. He set out displays of wine and used a feather duster to brush away the patina of dust on the curves of the bottles. The lights above the wooden wine shelves glittered little stars in the liquid so that they looked like bottled jewels, and he wanted to taste the wine just to know what it was like, just to feel another world on the tip of his tongue.

That evening, as she had for the last three days, İrem made tea for him without complaint, although she wouldn't talk to him other than to say, too formally, "Here's your tea, Baba." Each request he or Nilüfer made was met with polite obedience—a docility that, while wished for by Sinan many times in the past, was more unsettling to him now than her flashes of anger. She played cards with İsmail, but didn't argue when he tried to cheat. She helped her mother wash the teapot and picked the ants out of the sugar tin one by one, their wriggling black bodies pinched between forefinger and thumb. When they went to bed, she even kissed him on both cheeks—coldly, though, her lips barely brushing his skin.

Later, as they took tea outside the tent, the children behind them safely in their sleeping bags, he asked, "Did the American boy come around?"

"You don't think I'd tell you?" Nilüfer said. She took his hand. "Don't worry. I spoke with her and reminded her that it's a question of honor, that she cannot ruin our name in front of so many people. People talk, innocent or not."

"She understood?"

"Yes," she said. "She cried and I held her a while, but she understood. She's just a child, Sinan." She laughed. "Sometimes I forget. Children are so foolish. They don't understand things. They can hurt you so easily, but really it's them who get hurt."

Sinan thought it was just the opposite. Children recovered from their wounds, they had the energy to do so, but adults carried them around like rocks in a grain sack.

"Yes, she's just a child," Sinan said. "Marcus Bey gave me his word, but that boy will come around again."

They sat silent together. A flare burst above the water and colored the camp red.

"Remember how it was for us?" he said, squeezing her hand.

"We were to be married, Sinan. That was different."

"Mohammed Bey's shop?"

They were just teenagers and her father had just recently set the date for the wedding. He had watched her through the painted advertisements of the egg seller's shop window while she ordered a dozen eggs. Lucky for him, to fill the orders Mohammed Bey had to go out to the back of the building where he kept the chickens in small wooden cages. That's when Sinan entered the shop and found Nilüfer waiting for him. Her shoulders were open to him and he could see her breasts poking against her blouse. She had a sly smile on her face that scared him.

"I'm to be yours, Sinan*can*," she said, her eyes dilated with a power that drew him in.

"Yes, you're to be mine," he said. He tried to make his eyes as powerful as hers, but he had little practice with such looks and it felt like he got it wrong.

In the corner where the cobwebs clung to their clothes, he stood just inches from her body, so close he felt her heat radiating through the folds of her skirt. Her fingers tickled his palm and he pressed his cheek to hers, his lips almost brushing her skin. When the back-door screen banged shut, Sinan darted out the front, composing himself as he came into the light of the street.

"I broke three eggs on the way home," she said now. Her father had hit her for her carelessness, a minor beating that didn't leave a bruise. "If my father had known what broke those eggs, who knows what he would have done!"

Sinan remembered the smell of her hidden hair, like a wet field of oregano under the scarf, filling his head.

"We were stupid children," she said. "Thank God my mother didn't know." The flare disappeared behind the tents and the red faded. "She was a good woman."

SOMETIME IN THE MIDDLE of the night, İsmail let out a scream. Nilüfer got to him first and pulled the still-sleeping boy to her chest and rocked him. The boy whimpered, but soon he was calm and his breathing became regular and heavy and both of them were asleep again, Nilüfer's arms locked around the boy's chest. Sinan was nearly asleep again, too, when he noticed a strange, hushed sound coming from just outside the tent—a tinny, rhythmic beat that sounded like tiny metal cans crashing together. He raised himself up on his elbow to look across the tent floor, past sleeping İsmail and Nilüfer, to find İrem's sleeping bag empty.

Outside the tent, he discovered her slouching in the plastic chair, her hands held up to her ears, her head rocking back and forth as though she were dancing in her seat. He came around to face her, but her eyes were closed, and she didn't notice him standing so close he could have stroked her cheek. He might have done so, too, if he thought she would allow it. Two black wires hung from her ears and were plugged into a small metal device that sat balanced on the chair next to her hips—a compact disc player, he realized.

He could take it from her, but what would that do? Start a fight in the middle of the night. Wake up his neighbors. He hadn't been a patient man with her, and he realized now, in the stillness of the night, that he could either push her away—away toward this American boy—or he could wait her out, offer her his love and bring her back to him.

So he sat in the chair next to her and listened to the muffled beats and bleeps of the strange music coming from the headphones. Above him, stars blinked down through millions of miles of space, and the camp was still except for a couple of cats pawing the bones of a half-eaten fish. And he thought this was all right; he could sit here calmly for a while next to his daughter and pretend she was not becoming a stranger.

But İrem startled. "Baba!" She immediately brushed the headphones from her ears and tried stuffing them inside her coat.

"İrem, don't treat me like I'm stupid."

She pulled the headphones from her jacket, quietly laid them on top of the player, and gripped the device tightly in her hands. He waited a moment, both of them sitting there quiet and still, the silence growing in his ears.

"I'm sorry," he said. "You were hurt and I became angry with you."

"It didn't hurt," İrem said, sitting rigid in the chair. Even in the darkness he could see her grinding her teeth against him. He tried to think how best to tell her what he wanted to say.

He looked out at the water and the lights blurred in the currents. "I didn't mean to hurt you, *canım*."

"I said you didn't hurt me."

"İrem, I'm tired of arguing with you."

She looked at him. Her eyes catching the light from the soup kitchen blazed the way they did the day he returned from the German hospital: scared, angry—betrayed eyes, he suddenly realized. She turned away, presenting him with the side of her face. He wondered what it was like for her those four days after the earthquake, and a memory of her begging him to help her flashed in his mind. İsmail was buried, he was panicked with fear, he had a concussion, but that didn't matter: he had chosen İsmail over his daughter. It was not a conscious choice; it was forced upon him by circumstance, but he had made it all the same and İrem knew it. His stomach seized in a cramp.

"I haven't been a good father to you," he said, pressing three fingers into his belly.

İrem lifted her head a little, but she kept her face hidden.

He wanted to apologize to her—being loved less was a burden a child shouldn't bear—but he couldn't bring himself to admit such a thing to her face.

"I just want you to live a good life, to be happy," he said.

"Which do you want more, Baba?" She looked at him now, her chin raised against him. Her eyes, reflecting the light, shone like polished steel. "Me living a good life or me happy?"

"I want both."

She looked away again.

"I will try harder, *canım*, to be a good father."

She offered nothing—no thank-yous, no apologies for her actions, no "I love you"s—just silence and the defiance of the side of her face.

"Hear how quiet it is now?" They listened together for a few seconds and it *was* truly silent, except for the distant drone of dock cranes lifting containers from the backs of Chinese cargo ships. "Back home—did I tell you this? Did I ever tell you how quiet it is?"

"Yes, a hundred times," she said.

"You don't remember. You were too young."

"I remember. I wasn't *that* young."

"It's so quiet at night it's like the earth has stopped spinning. Like everything terrible in the world has just fallen away." He looked up at the sky. "Someday we'll go back there and you'll hear it and you'll understand."

"I don't want to go back there."

He almost ripped the compact disc player out of her hands.

"It's your home, İrem."

"It's not my home. There's nothing there."

He felt the anger rise in him, a flood of blood pumping into his chest.

"Come inside and go to bed, please."

She blew air out her mouth and tossed her head in annoyance, but she got up and ducked inside the tent. He listened to her rustle around inside the bag—her frustrated kicks and sighs, her tosses and turns—until it was silent again, and he was left alone with the grinding echo of dock cranes and the two cats fighting over the scales left clinging to bones.

HE WAS SUPPOSED TO work a double shift the next day. He slept little that night and spent the early shift sipping tea at every break to get him through his duties. At lunch he was still thinking about İrem, and during his break he found himself in the electronics section of Carrefour, the headphones to a portable CD player cupped inside his ears. The music was a crashing of noise, like a band of carpenters had gotten together to record the banging of their tools. Things screeched and screamed, other things clanged like controlled explosions, yet there was a moment—one beautiful moment—where the music fell to a dramatic rumble, the banging notes dropped to a sustained chord, and a singer whispered something in English that sounded like a pleading, like a man begging for help. The sound of that desperate voice touched something in him; comforted him in a way he couldn't explain. He pressed rewind and listened to that moment again, and then pressed rewind and listened once more, until the voice faded out with the noise at the end of the song.

In the afternoon, as his back began to ache and his foot burned, he let his mind grow numb with the monotonous work. He was lulled by the rush of air-conditioner vents and the soft strains of pop music echoing in the metal rafters. He was grateful for the thoughtlessness of it, thankful for the relief, however brief, from the responsibilities of fatherhood. The customers in the store looked like foreigners; he was dressed like a foreigner—his khaki pleated pants, the brown belt, the polo-style shirt with the Carrefour logo on the chest—and for a few hours he was able to pretend that he was someone else, someone with money, a man living in one of the big *yalı* perched above the Bosporus, a man who could hop on a plane and go wherever he pleased. Pouring black olives into a silver bin, he was an olive farmer with rows of green trees rising above the sparkling Mediterranean. Stacking boxes of frozen seafood in the walk-in freezer, he was a Black Sea fisherman setting out with the tide to haul lines full of sea bass; he was a famous soccer star, an author of romance novels, a bank teller. He was a farmer in a small eastern village, his family growing with the years—children, grandchildren, great-grandchildren.

Toward the end of his shift, he was hanging a T-shirt on a rack in the clothing aisle, imagining himself a tailor of fine suits like Serdar Bey in the Yeşilli of his childhood, when he watched a man press a dress against his young wife's chest. One hand held the dress to the woman's shoulder and the other one draped it across her hip. The woman smiled, her red lips shining in the fluorescent lights, her hand posed on her hip. "Beautiful," the man said. "*Çok güzel.*" Then he pressed his body against hers, crushed the dress between them, and kissed her right there in the aisle. Sinan looked away, but looked again, and when he looked a third time, he was thinking of İrem and the American boy.

Chapter 33

IT WASN'T SAFE FOR THEM IN THE CAMP ANYMORE, SO AFTER five days, when her father left for his new job and her mother went to smoke cigarettes with the women at the laundry bins, İrem and Dylan took the bus into İstanbul.

She wanted to go to Beyoğlu district, where on television she had seen crowds of beautiful-looking people jamming İstiklal Avenue. She wanted to cross the bridge into Europe, and hold Dylan's hand in the alleyways of the old Jewish and Greek business district. She wanted to go to the fancy restaurants and clubs she had seen on the television gossip shows—the places where Tarkan drank beer, the clubs where women shone in camera flashbulbs, where the most exciting things happened at night, well after her parents had gone to bed.

But instead he took her to Kadiköy, still on the Asian side and full of more college students than stars. They stopped at a café in the bottom floor of an old house, and Dylan drank whiskey out of a small glass while she sipped tea. She watched the gold liquid slide like cooking oil down the glass, his Adam's apple jumping up and down as he swallowed. His fingers stroked the lip of the glass as though he were playing a silent instrument. He ordered a second whiskey while she picked at the fennel seeds and candied hazelnuts, and watched his eyes get glassy and distant.

"It doesn't look so bad," he said, taking İrem's chin in his hand and turning it toward the morning sunlight.

İrem brushed his hand away, and pulled her head scarf a little lower to hide it.

"Does it hurt?" he asked.

"A little."

"People are crazy," he said. "My father always said that some people would spit in Atatürk's face if they could. He thinks if he talks to them about God that'll change things. I'd just like to kill them."

"Can we talk about something else?"

He looked hurt.

"Let's go away," he said.

"We can't."

He took her hand.

"Germany," he said, looking past her now at a couple coming through the patio door into the courtyard. "You'll fit in there and I speak a little German."

"No. We can't."

He rolled the glass in his hand and drank the rest of the whiskey. He squinched up his face as though it tasted terrible.

"Just imagine it for a minute," he said, letting go of her hand. "Just forget about everything else for sixty seconds, would you?"

She felt stupid for ruining it.

"If my mom was still here," he said, "she wouldn't have a problem with this. But my dad—"

"And my father," she said.

"Yeah," he said. He lit a cigarette and stared at the couple who were now sipping coffee with foam and sprinkles on top. The woman wore big, black-rimmed glasses and red jeans and her black-booted toes kept creeping up the opening of her boyfriend's pant leg.

Dylan laughed and rubbed his palm across his forehead.

"What?" she said.

"Our parents don't love us," he said. "And you still want to make them happy." He threw a few bills on the table and stubbed out his cigarette. "Let's go."

He walked her through the book bazaar and showed her the tattoo rooms underground where the passageway was warm and muggy and smelled like sweat and where some of the corners glistened wet. He took her to a record shop full of posters of men with guitars and eyes like lizards. The man behind the counter had spiked hair and a nose ring and he stared at her the whole time. The passage scared her a little. Last year two boys killed a child, and all the papers said the boys were Satanists who hung out in underground passages just like this one. Outside the shop, the passageway was filled with slouching kids, their clothes hanging off their bodies as though the fabric concealed nothing but skeletons. Girls leaned on boys and shared cigarettes. She even saw one blowing smoke rings above her head so that she seemed ringed with halos. She wondered if any of these kids knew those boys.

He led her back into the light, between the stands of men selling DVDs in wooden cases, past the kebab restaurants and *gözleme* shops where, behind steaming windows, Kurdish women kneaded dough into pancakes, their hands white with flour, and spread the pancakes on the circular pan. The smell of brine and guts announced the fish sellers' street. Many of the men here wore beards and she noticed one man fingering prayer beads while taking a break with a *simit* and tea. Dylan wrapped his arm around her waist and pulled her tight. His fingers rested on her hip, right where her stomach met her pelvis. A rush of heat flooded her skin. The open lightbulbs dangling above the baskets of fish reflected light against the wet cement and the men stared at them. Their hands slit open bellies of fish, they called out prices, they wrapped fillets in white oil paper and smiled as they took customers' money, but they were watching, excitement and anger in their eyes, as though a fantasy about her had bled into hatred.

"Please, Dylan," she said. "Stop."

"Jesus," he said, and let go. He shoved his hands in his pockets and looked at the ground and they walked like that until they reached Tibbiye Road and the roar of buses and taxis.

"You can't do that in public," she said.

"Your father isn't here, İrem."

"We have to be married," she said. "How can you live here for so long and not know that?"

"I know it," he said. "It's just stupid. The other girls don't have to be married."

"I'm not those other girls," she said. "And it's not stupid!"

He spun around once with frustration. "You thought it was stupid until the other day."

People were watching them, but they were near the shoe and clothing stores now and it was a different kind of crowd, a crowd that would agree with Dylan about how stupid it all was. A crowd that would wonder what such a boy was doing with a stupid covered girl.

"I just want to touch you," he said, shaking his head. "You're all I've got."

They stood there for a moment in the middle of the street, saying nothing. Women with shopping bags rustled past. Children kicked bare feet in the fountain. With stained fingers, a shoeshine boy picked up the pieces of a broken shine jar. The boy reminded her of İsmail.

"Come with me," Dylan said. He was smiling now. He had this way of being upset then suddenly fine. It confused her.

"Where?"

"Don't worry," he said, turning now to walk back through the fish bazaar. "I won't lay a finger on you."

Chapter 34

THAT AFTERNOON THE MANAGER SAID HE DIDN'T NEED SINAN for the evening shift. Yilmaz Bey had just arrived at the store, and Sinan followed him to his office, where he watched him hang his coat on the hook behind his desk, take his wallet from his pants pocket, and slip it into the pocket of his hanging coat.

"Please Yilmaz Bey, I need to work."

"Sinan," the manager said, sprinkling lemon cologne on his hands and slapping his palms together. "There are no trucks coming in today. It would be a waste of your time."

"It wouldn't be a waste of my time."

"It'd be a waste of company time." The man combed his clean fingers through his hair and pressed his eyebrows in place. "I'm sorry, Sinan. They check on these things."

"Oh," Yilmaz Bey said, reaching into his desk drawer. "This should help. Payday." He handed Sinan an envelope. "It's only for the few days you worked last pay period. Next one will be better." The manager smiled and then started moving papers around on his desk and ignored him and Sinan knew it was time to leave.

36,732,045TL. He read the printed numbers again and rubbed his finger over their raised shape. It was the most money he had seen since his grocery. Nilüfer and the children wouldn't expect him for another eight hours, so he took the ferries to Kadiköy, cashed the check, and went to see about train-ticket prices to Diyarbakır.

Haydarpaşa train station echoed with the voices of passengers, merchants, and men loitering in corners. Well-dressed businessmen sat on a row of leather stools along one wall of the station, their feet pressed against wooden horns of copper shoeshine boxes. These men read papers or absentmindedly smoked cigarettes while snapping rags made their shoes sparkle. When the old shoeshine men bent to apply black to the shoe heels, it looked as though they were kissing their customers' feet. A group of boys, unable to compete with the old-timers and their fancy punched-copper boxes, squatted in the dirty corner near the washrooms next to their wooden boxes, their hands permanently stained black, their skin as dirty and rough as the cement floor. They were Kurdish boys, their eyes a reflective black, their faces etched with anger.

As he crossed the huge open floor, incandescent fans of sunlight streamed through the high windows and cast light across the steel tracks. The railings shone like strings of gold necklaces through the darkness of the station, out past the rusting freight trains, and on into the heart of Anatolia. Sinan felt the possibility of that distant horizon, then, and he imagined the mountains his train would climb, the valleys it would descend through, and finally the gray cement station in Diyarbakır where it would squeal to a stop.

A poster listing destination and price hung next to the ticket counter window. There were hundreds of destinations and their times, and Sinan had difficulty finding the listing because the words were so small and crammed together. He found it and ran his finger along the box until he discovered the price: thirty-five million lira per ticket. He had five million plus the check money in his pocket and four million more tucked away in a pillow back in the camp.

One hundred and forty million lira! The number seemed impossibly huge. He knew about inflation the last few years, but ticket prices seemed to be inflated above even that ridiculous number. He would be paid in two weeks, but who knew if the check would be enough to cover such a price.

He stopped and rested on a bench near a café and tried to decide whether he could afford to spend the two hundred and fifty thousand for a glass of tea. He finally decided he couldn't, although he was tired and his throat was dry and the taste of something sweet would have given him at least a moment's pleasure. He changed his mind— his life was too short on pleasures—ordered a tea, and sat and watched passengers board the trains. The doors to the cabins were just a few feet away and he smelled the pungent burn of smoke and leather and oiled steel. Nothing stopped him from boarding the train—no gates, no chains, no conductors or policemen, just a few steps of empty space, an open door, and then the tracks shining out ahead of him into the land, into the heart of another life.

In a sleeper car, a beautiful woman dressed in jeans and a white T-shirt reached to place her luggage above her seat. Usually he would have looked away, but now, here in this station where no one knew him, he watched her. Her thin exposed arms poked out of a shirt that clung to her torso. He admired the shape of her body—the curve of her breasts, the arc of each individual rib. He imagined kissing her in the compartment, pulling her tightly to him while the wheels of the train clicked beneath them. He imagined traveling with her to Sofia, Bucharest, maybe even Vienna, holding her tight in the middle of the European streets, caressing the knuckles of her thin fingers in smoke-filled cafés without anyone paying attention. He imagined sharing a room, watching her undress before bed. But in his imagination he didn't see her body; he simply saw the blurry impression of nakedness, a light in her brown eyes, and her hair brushing against her neck.

Then the train lurched forward and the woman dropped into her seat. A whistle sounded, the engine spat a dash of black smoke into the sky, and the train pulled away. He watched her face through the window, its reflection pressed against the glass, until, as the train snaked out of the station, her face was nothing but a memory.

Once the train was gone, Sinan found himself facing a wall papered with advertisements. A beautiful woman laughed into a cell phone. He hated the woman—her white teeth, her perfect clothes, her skin like the finest silk. No one was that happy. People were only happy on television or commercials, but not in real life. He finished his tea and fought off the guilt of his fantasy. By the time he left the station and stumbled out into the sharp morning light, he was arguing with himself in his head, explaining why his fantasy was not a sin and then explaining again why it was.

"Malatya," an elderly man called out. The man stood in the flow of foot traffic, travelers swerving around him as though he were a rock in a stream. "One ticket to Malatya just ten million."

Malatya was not Diyarbakır but it was close. So close that if he got there and didn't have the money for another ticket, someone would give him a ride.

"One ticket leaving tonight, third class."

By tomorrow morning he could be there, standing beneath that desert blue sky, sucking in the sumac dry air.

"This ticket is good?" Sinan said.

"Yes," the man said. One eye was clouded white but the other shone with sight. "My wife and I were to go together, but she was killed."

He could go tonight and bring his family later.

"I'll take it," Sinan said.

Sinan gave him the ten-million note and the man handed him the ticket. Holding the ticket, his hands shook with excitement. By tomorrow morning—just one more sunset and sunrise—he would be gone from this city. It would be like going back in time, as though he never got on the train at all, had never come to this place.

The old man hobbled toward the station, heaving a trash bag of belongings onto his shoulder. He looked like a hunchback, his thin body a cracking of bones, and Sinan felt an extreme loneliness that broke him out of his passion. His heart sank because he knew he could not take that train.

"*Efendim?*" Sinan called after the old man. "Sir?" The man turned around, his back bent into a hook by the bag of possessions, his good eye sharp and distrustful.

"I'm sorry, I can't take this ticket."

"Try selling it yourself then," the man said.

"No, no, you don't understand. I have a family. It was a mistake."

"Be glad you have a family. We all need the money."

The man turned and crossed the street between two speeding buses.

Sinan stood there and watched him go, a ticket he would not use pressed into his hand. God punishes us for our sins. Somehow this fact comforted him. A small sin, a small price. What he almost did was much, much worse. What price God would have exacted for that sin he did not know.

Chapter 35

She tried to catch up to him, but he purposely skipped two steps ahead of her. The men watched them again, this time, she thought, with approving eyes: a woman should always walk behind her man.

It was easy to miss the church; a whitewashed wall, twelve feet high, surrounded it, and from the street you wouldn't notice the bell tower unless you craned your neck to see it. He led her down an alleyway, past an arbor hung with wisteria, to a small metal door cracked enough to let a single person through.

They squeezed inside and suddenly all the street sounds were muffled. The city, just beyond the walls, seemed very far away. Three cats lay stretched in the sun on the steps to the church and a fountain dribbled water into a marble basin slimed with algae. Three orange trees stood in the courtyard, their branches dotted with overripe fruit.

She had never been in a church before and its beauty surprised her. It was a small building, crowded with rows of benches that made it feel populated even though no one was inside. The dome was painted with pink clouds, and a man, the prophet Jesus, she guessed, was frescoed on the wall above the front of the church. He held a black book in one hand. His other hand was held aloft, almost as though he were gesturing to touch her. One finger touched his thumb, while the others—three long, white, elegant fingers—dangled in the air in a sign she didn't recognize. Jesus' face was very calm-looking, very kind and thoughtful, almost sleepy-eyed, and she remembered the stories her father had told her about him—the miracles he performed, his admonishments of the Jews, the way the Jews betrayed him and the Romans nailed him to a cross. Hanging there in dazzling gold on the wall in front of her, he did look like a prophet.

She followed Dylan to the front of the church, where tea candles flickered in a metal box. He climbed the steps, and she stopped to watch him, feeling like an intruder on some sacred quiet.

"Come here," he said, looking down at her.

"Are we supposed to be here?" She glanced toward the rear of the church, looking for the screens that hid the women's prayer section, looking for anything that would tell her what to do. "The door was almost closed. Maybe they don't want people inside."

"Nah," he said. "Some Greeks were killed here, like back in 1922 or something. Right before the exchange of populations. They don't want everyone to know how to get in."

"Come on," he said again. "I want to show you something."

He lifted a candle from the metal box and took her hand. They passed beneath Jesus and his outstretched hands, his eyes following them across the marble floor. Dylan's candle flickered against the wall like light undulating through water. Then, in a darkened corner of the church, the light caught the slender body of a woman in full hijab. It was a strange *abaya*, though, one that wasn't black but a beautiful sky blue that matched Jesus' eyes. The candlelight exposed her feet first and then the curve of her hips beneath the fabric and the shape of her breasts and then her face. Her eyes were cast downward, her long eyelashes touching her cheeks. Her face was absolutely white, like snow freshly fallen on the street before the cars turn it black. A tear hung on her left cheek, suspended there as though it would never fall, and it wouldn't—it would rest there forever in this darkened corner of a church. The woman was beautiful, sad like all women, but beautiful in her sadness.

"My mom used to take me here when I was little," Dylan said.

She was covered, but she was different. İrem couldn't say in what way she was different—strands of her hair showed, the *abaya* was blue—but that wasn't it.

"You know the story of the Virgin Mary, right?"

For a moment she thought he was going to make a crude joke, but the candlelight illuminated the seriousness of his face.

"Yes," she said. "A little."

"Mom always said that Mary was the strong one. It was easy for Jesus, she said, because he knew he was God's son, he knew the pain would end. But Mary had to watch her son die, had to be left behind. I think that's why she couldn't buy the story the way my father can."

Then suddenly, as if that was all he wanted to say, he snatched the candle away and left the woman in darkness again.

"Stop," İrem said. She grabbed Dylan's hand and moved the candle beneath her again, a ghost rising from the mortar of the wall.

She watched the form flicker in the light. Her body seemed to move, just barely, under the spell of the single flame, as though the woman took shallow breaths to remain still.

"She's always been my favorite," Dylan said. "Out of all of them."

She looked proud, İrem decided. That's what was different about her. She was sad, but proud, as though she kept her sadness like a prize.

Dylan walked her to a podium now and took her hands and Jesus Bey still stared down at them.

"Marry me," he said.

"Marry you?"

"Yeah," he said. "We're in a church."

"No," she said.

"Yes," he said. "Do you, oh-so-beautiful İrem Başioğlu"—and here he smiled his best smile, the crooked one that was devious and inno-

cent at the same time—"take Dylan Roberts to be your lawfully wed-
ded husband?"

"You know this doesn't count," she said.

"For better or for worse, in sickness and in health . . ."

"You're crazy."

"If we want this," he said, "we've got to make up our own rules."

He untied a black leather bracelet from his wrist, took her left arm
and pulled her close to him so he could tie it around her wrist. His
shoulder was against hers and she watched his face, his downcast eyes,
their long eyelashes, as he tied the knot in the bracelet.

"My mother gave this to me," he said.

"No. I can't," she said, but she wanted it and she wanted him to
protest her protest.

"Yes," he said and turned the bracelet around on her pale wrist so
the knot wouldn't show. He ran his fingers across the blue veins that
showed just beneath her skin. Electricity shot up her arm and tickled
her side.

"Until death do you part?"

She laughed.

"I do," he said. "Say, 'I do.' "

"No."

"C'mon."

"All right," she said. "Now leave me alone."

"You may kiss the bride."

"Not in a church," she said.

When they were outside again, thunderclouds blackened the sky,
and the bricks were slick with smatterings of raindrops. It was getting
late and the express ferry had already blown its horn, but she couldn't
make herself care too much. She slipped and nearly fell and he
grabbed her by the waist and held her close and she let him. They
weren't married and maybe they never would be, but it was fun to
pretend, so fun it almost seemed real.

Chapter 36

LATER THAT EVENING, AS SINAN RODE THE BUS PAST THE crowded Kadiköy market, through the traffic and past the people standing in front of the fish stalls, their faces lit up by the exposed electric lights, he thought, for a brief moment, he saw İrem walking down a dark alley away from the brightly lit stalls, her arm around a man's waist. A storm had just blown through and the cobblestone was wet and shiny and the man held her close to him. But then the bus passed by the gray walls of the Orthodox Church and turned onto the long ramp to the TEM freeway and he was gone, the bus swerving into the evening traffic, the shoulders of the tired passengers bumping together like corpses forced to sit up straight.

After taxes, they needed nearly 140 million lira to escape. He'd written the exact number on a piece of paper he folded into his coat pocket and now, before the sun set over the Marmara, he unfolded the paper and read the number again. *Inşallah*, he could have it in three weeks. Twenty-one mornings, and on the twenty-second they would see the sun rise on Kurdistan.

Chapter 37

"THIS IS THAT BOY'S," NILÜFER SAID, HOLDING THE CD PLAYER out to him. "I found it under her sleeping bag."

Nilüfer attacked him as soon as he got home from Kadiköy, after he had sat for hours in traffic, sweating in the wet heat and brown exhaust. Now she held the device in her hand as though it were a murder weapon.

İrem sat in the corner of the tent with her arms crossed over her body. Her face was flushed and she scowled so that through her parted lips he saw her white teeth. İsmail was rubbing his sister's back, trying to calm her.

"It's not his," İrem yelled. She shrugged off her brother's touch and the boy went and huddled on his sleeping bag.

"Keep your voice down," Nilüfer said. "People are already saying enough. You lied to me and you're still lying to me!"

"He gave it to me," İrem said with a smug smile. "It's mine now. Baba knows about it."

Nilüfer faced him, her head cocked to the side, her pupils narrowing for an attack.

"You knew about this?"

"It's just music," he said.

Nilüfer smashed the CD player to the ground, the top to the device cracking off and rocketing across the tent.

"There," she said. "There's *your* music player."

"*Anne!*" İrem cried, diving across the sleeping bags to pick up the broken machine. "You ruined it! You ruined it, Anne. What will he do?" Her anguish was shocking.

"Yours, huh?" Nilüfer said. She stood over İrem and spoke down at her. "I will not have you ruin our name! Do you know what people are saying, Sinan?"

She turned to face him, her arm extended toward her daughter. "Do you know what people are saying? I was at the laundry today and they're saying terrible things, right in front of me. They saw them get on the ferry together. No one spoke to me, but they said things so I could hear."

"I don't care what they're saying," İrem said.

"Are they true?" Nilüfer said, pulling İrem to her feet with one swift jerk of her arm. "And where'd you get this," she said, tugging on a black bracelet hanging from İrem's wrist.

"Enough," Sinan said. He jumped between them, but they argued through him as though he were not there.

"Which rumors, Anne?" İrem said, looking directly into her mother's eyes. "You tell me which ones and I'll tell you if they're true."

Nilüfer stared at İrem a moment before she seemed to lose her will and turned away. She spun around again, though, pointed a finger at İrem, and whispered through her teeth. "I will not have you ruin our name, İrem!" She stabbed her finger in the air as though it were a weapon. "You will not ruin our name. You selfish child!"

İrem burst into tears and ran out of the tent.

Nilüfer watched after her. "She's running around like a wild animal." She put her hands to her mouth and began chewing her fingernails. "They're saying terrible things, Sinan. People have seen them. And where was she today? Where did they take that ferry? Marcus Bey didn't even know where his son was. You tell me if these rumors are true, since you seem to know all about this." She took a step toward him and poked her finger into his chest. "I've spent too many years sweating at hard work, too many years stuck in a hot kitchen. I've kept my mouth shut too many times so I could be called a good woman, and for this girl—for you—to ruin my name!"

"Nilüfer," Sinan said. "Calm down, Nilüfer. Like you said, she's just a child." He tried to put his arms around her.

"Don't tell me to calm down," she said. "A child, yes. Your child! You don't care about her. If you loved her, you wouldn't let this happen."

"I'll talk to her," Sinan said.

"Talk to her? I've already talked to her and she's lied to me. You should hear the things people are saying."

"People spread rumors about others to keep eyes off themselves."

"You should lock her up in this tent until she learns her place. Thinks she knows what it is to be a woman!" She ripped a piece of nail from her thumb and spat it on the floor. "If you loved her that's what you'd do, lock her up in here until that boy is back in America."

"Nilüfer, do you want to go to work sixteen hours a day?" Sinan said, raising his voice. İsmail cowered on the bag, hiding as best he could from all of them. "Do you want to worry about taking care of all of us? Do you want the burden of trying to make you all happy? Do you know what that's like? Don't tell me what to do, unless you want all that."

"Yes, you're the only one who works," she said under her breath. "Of course." She sat down and pulled İsmail into her lap.

"Nilüfer," Sinan said, coming to sit down next to her. "A hundred and forty million will get us to Diyarbakır. I'll have the money in three weeks. Just three weeks. We have a house there, family. The American boy won't matter then."

She didn't look up. Her palms remained pressed against her eyes and her wrists glistened with water.

"I never thought you were a weak man," she said quietly.

He stood up and looked down at her. "We're in a tent, Nilüfer," he said, spitting the words at her as though she had no sense at all, as though she were the stupidest woman in the world. He heard the tone in his voice, but he didn't care. "How do you lock a girl up in a tent?!"

She said something he couldn't hear and he let it go.

"In three weeks I'll have the money. Just twenty-one days more, Nilüfer."

"But everything can change in one day, my husband."

IT TOOK A WHILE, but he found his daughter on the bare hillside between the city and the camp where the sea spread below like a hole in the earth, just a dark pool of emptiness that was darker than the moonless sky. He had trouble seeing her at first, but soon he caught her shape hunched in the darkness.

"You scare me when you run away," he said.

She was silent, but he heard a sniffle and he sat down next to her. It was pitch-black on the hill between the fires of the tent city and the bulldozer floodlights in town, and he couldn't make out her face, only the outline of her head and shoulders.

"You don't know what it's like to be a parent," he said. "I'm always afraid something will happen to you. Every day I worry life will be mean to you."

Out of the corner of his eye, he saw a dark shape prowl the ridge of the hill. He turned to see what it was, but what he thought he saw was gone, replaced by the luminous rising moon.

"There are things in the world, İrem, that will try to hurt you. They don't care about you. They just want something. Everyone wants something. Your mother and I love you and we're trying to protect you."

"Yeah, I felt so protected after the quake, Baba. You disappeared."

Only his guilt kept him from slapping her. He suddenly felt the steepness of the hill. The land in front of him fell toward the sea, and when he moved his foot little landslides of rock tumbled silently into the dark.

"I kissed him, Baba. That's the 'terrible' thing people saw."

An image of his daughter kissing the American boy turned his stomach.

"What they're saying, though, I don't know," İrem continued. "What people say is always worse than what you've done. That's what Dylan says."

He tried to control his anger, but it boiled to the surface and he remained quiet for a minute, trying to get the burn to subside. "This is not how I raised you," he said finally. "It's a sin."

İrem blew air out of her mouth. "Baba, you raised me to be like mother." She scraped her heel into the dirt and loosened some rocks. "You told me you wanted me to be happy."

"And that I want you to live a good life, a moral one."

"Baba, I can't be unhappy and be moral, too. I cannot be like mother—unhappy, stuck cooking food all day long, cleaning floors that are dirty again by the end of the day. I can't keep my mouth shut like I have no thoughts, like I have no brain."

"Your mother is a good woman, she's happy with her life. And I don't treat her like she has no brain."

İrem said nothing in response to that. Sinan tried to see the expression on her face through the darkness, but he only saw the indefinite oval shape and the slope of her nose catching the light of the moon.

"I don't want to be like mother. Dylan told me women do whatever they want in America, they can be anything, they don't even have to act like women."

"You don't understand what you're doing, İrem. It's dangerous."

"Do you know how long it's been since I felt good, Baba? I didn't know what feeling good was like. Always cleaning İsmail's clothes, feeding him lunch, stirring sugar into your tea, doing all the jobs mother doesn't want to do—mopping the floor, scrubbing the toilet, hanging out the windows to wash the grime off the glass. It's like being born a slave. Is that what daughters are for?"

"What do you expect from life, İrem? Life is hard. Life is a test. Do you think I'm any less a slave at work each day?"

"I expect to wake up in the morning and think that something"—she shook her head—"just one thing will make me happy that day. I listened to his music through the ceiling, saw him in the halls, but I didn't know he was that one thing."

Sinan was confused, his head spinning with anger and sadness and understanding and resentment and, most of all, fear. He was going to lose her.

"That boy does *not* care about you, İrem."

"He loves me."

"A kiss is not love. It may feel like it, but it's not."

"He said he'd kill that woman for me, the one who threw the rock, if we knew who she was. Would you do that?"

"That's an easy thing to say," Sinan said. How could he argue he would? It was the argument of a hypocrite. He had left her, he had loved her less than İsmail, but he didn't want to be a hypocrite in her eyes, too. "He cares about nothing, believes nothing. A man who believes in nothing cannot love anything. I love you, *canım*, but he doesn't."

"You used to talk to me, Baba," she said. "You used to take walks with me."

He took a deep, tired breath. He did, it was true, but she was trying to change the subject. "You will not see him again."

"Baba, don't you understand?"

"It doesn't matter what I understand. It matters what's right. You won't see him again, İrem. If you do"—he hesitated—"then you're no longer my daughter."

He could not see her face but he could tell she was staring at him, shocked.

"I won't let you throw your life away." That's love, he wanted to say to her. Love was doing the painful things because they were right. "If you see him again, you no longer have a family."

She buckled at her waist and he could see that her face was in her hands. Tears pooled in his eyes and he was glad for the darkness. He tried to keep his voice calm, tried to make sure it did not waver. "Do you understand me?"

She began rocking back and forth.

"Do you understand?"

"Yes," she said, stifling her words with the palms of her hands.

Remembering the bracelet, he pulled up the sleeve of her blouse and found the leather still there, tied around her wrist. He tried to untie it, her arm hanging limp in his hand, but the knot was too tight. Holding her arm steady, he yanked at the loop and ripped it loose. It was then that she began to sob.

When he returned to the tent, dragging İrem by the arm through the camp, he handed her to Nilüfer.

"You're right," he said. "She stays here."

Nilüfer grabbed İrem by the arm, but İrem threw herself down on her sleeping bag and buried her face in the fabric. İsmail woke on the bag next to her and rubbed his hand across her back, his face gazing up at the two of them in confusion. For a moment, it felt to Sinan as if his children were conspiring against him, as if he were the enemy.

"One who does not slap his children will slap his knees, Sinan."

"Yes, yes," he said, hearing the doubt in her voice when he needed to hear her certainty.

YILMAZ BEY SHOOK HIS HEAD. "It's policy," he said. "I cannot give you the money before payday."

Sinan had left the tent and run to the store before closing time, catching the manager just as he was loosening his tie in his office.

"But I've worked. I've earned the money and I need it."

"I'm sorry," Yilmaz Bey said. "It's Carrefour's policy not to give advances."

"It's not an advance. I only want what I've already worked for."

The manager looked at the clock above Sinan's head and blew out a frustrated breath. Sinan knew the man had a family he wanted to get home to. "It doesn't matter, Sinan. Payroll is handled by the central office in Levent and they don't pay anyone until payday. They have to wait for the Paris office to give them the okay. I can't even get an advance. It's only a little more than a week away."

"It's almost two weeks away."

Yilmaz Bey shrugged, told Sinan he was sorry again, and walked into the bathroom to wash himself before leaving for the night. That was it; Sinan was supposed to leave now, but he stayed standing in the office until the manager returned. It was a shameful thing to do, and Sinan was embarrassed when Yilmaz Bey plopped himself down in his swivel chair.

"It's been hard for many people since the quake, I know," the manager said, pulling his coat from a hanger above his desk. He lifted a wallet from the coat pocket, and pulled a ten-million-lira note from a ribbon of bills.

"Here, Sinan," the man said. "I wish I could do more."

Sinan stared at the bill hanging limply from the manager's palm, the stern face of Atatürk staring back at him.

"Please," the manager said. "A gift. You're a good worker, Sinan."

Shame rose inside Sinan like an unfurling red flag, but he grabbed the bill and folded it into his shirt pocket. He was so disgusted with himself that it wasn't until later, as he passed through the shining foreign cars of the parking lot and down into the broken streets, that he realized he hadn't thanked the man. Then before he reached the tent he was angry again, spitting silent obscenities at the manager, cursing him and the money he could give away so easily.

Chapter 38

THE NEXT DAY, WHEN HER FATHER WAS AT WORK, HER MOTHER wouldn't let her out of her sight. She kept İrem inside the tent washing glasses that were already clean. She made her pull the sleeping bags out of the tent and beat them clean with a stick. She forced her to sweep the tent floor and use a broom to wipe away the spiders' webs spread like lace in the corners of the tent. And when İrem was done, her mother decided it was not clean enough and made her do it again.

"Stupid girl," she said, while İrem dragged the sleeping bags out of the tent again.

"Look," she said to İrem.

She held the bag in one hand and took the stick and hit it with amazing violence. "You will not hurt the bag. Hit it," she said, and gave it back to İrem.

"Stupid girl," her mother said again, standing in the sun watching her. "The rumors better not be true."

İrem slapped the stick against the bag that was already clean.

"Harder," her mother said.

The bag was heavy and her arm began to hurt, but she slapped the stick against the material as hard as she could, imagining she was hitting her mother.

The next day they did the laundry, hauling all their clothes to the wash bins near the bathrooms. Her mother handed her each article of clothing and made her do the hard work of rubbing them over the ribbed metal washer.

Two women were hanging clothes on a line and they watched Nilüfer and İrem.

"See," her mother said. "See what you've caused."

İrem ran one of her father's shirts over the metal washer and stared back at the women until they looked away.

"It doesn't matter if the rumors are true," her mother said. "Once they start they never go away."

She drowned the shirt in the rinse-water bin, wrung the water out, and dropped it in the dry bucket.

"I didn't do anything," İrem said.

"Didn't do anything, pah! It doesn't matter, anyway," her mother said. "Everyone thinks you have."

Nilüfer handed her a blouse. It was her mother's and İrem ground this one extra hard against the metal, so hard she stripped skin from her knuckles.

"That's why it's better to stay in the house and say nothing to the men."

She couldn't make the fabric rip and her arms were getting tired and there was a whole bucket of clothes left.

"But that's wrong, *Anne.*"

"It doesn't matter. It's how the world is."

"It's wrong."

"You're nothing now," her mother said. "You understand?" Her mother handed her another shirt. "They don't care. You make fun of all these women. You make fun of me!"

"I don't," İrem said. "I just want to be happy."

"Happy, happy!" She took İrem by the arm. "You think you cannot be happy like me? You think because I cover my hair and take care of the house that I cannot be happy."

Her mother's eyes bounced back and forth, her teeth bit off the words. It scared İrem and she looked away.

"Look at me," Nilüfer said. "Do you think my life is nothing?"

İrem wanted to say yes, if for no other reason than to hurt her, but she couldn't do it.

Nilüfer let go of her arm.

"Wash," she said. "Wash, wash, wash!" She pushed İrem out of the way. "Like this," she said, taking the shirt out of her hands and pressing it to the metal washer. "Can't even wash a shirt!"

On the third day there was nothing left to clean and that was worse, because her mother wouldn't let her leave the tent at all. They sat together all morning in the tent, İsmail coming and going as he pleased. When he was there, her mother smiled and touched his hair and played games with him, but when he was gone, she was silent, morose, and occasionally let into her.

"Stupid girl. You think men love loose women? They leave such women in the streets and come home to the ones that cook their meals."

Clouds pressed low to the ground and the tent was dark and İrem was beginning to think her mother would never stop. She was beginning to think she would never see Dylan again, never see sunlight again except to hang laundry and buy vegetables.

"Such women end up in the whorehouses in Beyoğlu, or worse."

Dilek came by the tent and Nilüfer wouldn't let İrem see her. "She's sleeping," she heard her mother say, and İrem almost yelled out to her friend but she knew that would make it worse and she didn't know if she could handle worse in this tiny space. When her mother came back in she complained about atheists and İrem's secular friends that made her act this way.

After three days her mother's words were sinking in. She was nothing. Her father didn't love her. Her mother hated her now. She was stained with rumors because of a kiss. But it wasn't a stupid kiss; it was everything; it was what she wanted most, the only thing that made her happy. And the walls of the tent were crowding in and her mother wouldn't shut up and she thought she would explode.

"I need to go to the W.C.," she said.

And her mother, just as she had for three days, walked with her to the toilets and stood outside and waited. But this time İrem didn't need to go. This time, she pulled the triangle of glass she kept hidden in her skirt pocket. She pulled her blouse sleeves up so that her wrists were exposed. She grasped the glass with her right fist and ran it across her left wrist. She slashed enough to bleed, but not enough to cut the veins there, just enough to feel the pain, to see her blood rise to the surface; just enough to keep her mind from spilling over the edge.

"İrem," her mother said. "What's taking so long?"

She slashed again and she felt the sting and her head started to clear and she felt strong again.

"İrem? Are you okay?" Her mother tapped on the door, but İrem had engaged the latch and she couldn't get in.

She dabbed away the blood with toilet paper and buttoned up the cuffs of her blouse. She thought, now, she could endure another three days of her mother's brutality.

Chapter 39

MARCUS BEY SHOWED UP AT CARREFOUR TEN MINUTES before Sinan's break.

"Can I buy you tea?"

The American's shoulders stooped as though something had been broken in him. The bags beneath his eyes were coal black.

"I won't change my mind," Sinan said. "My daughter won't see your son."

Marcus smiled wearily and rubbed his forehead. "I've kept my word on that," Marcus said. "But it seems we hold similar sway over our children. There's something else I want to talk with you about."

Marcus read a magazine off the racks while Sinan finished his shift, and afterward they sat at a patio table at Divan, the expensive *pastanesi* Sinan had never thought of drinking at. Marcus sat down, but his shoulders still sloped and he stared at the ground.

"A boy died," Marcus said. "Yesterday, in Row B. Although we didn't find out until this morning."

"Who?"

Marcus took a very small sip and then held the cup in the palm of his hand. The cup shook and a little tea spilled out.

"Derin Anbar."

A Kurdish name, though Sinan didn't know the child or his family.

"He was a friend of İsmail's," Marcus said. "One of the boys he played soccer with. Did İsmail say anything to you?"

"No," Sinan said. İsmail was quiet last night, he remembered, but nothing out of the ordinary. "He cried in his sleep."

"I thought you should know. I think he's upset, but he won't talk about it."

Sinan was again moved by this American's care for his child.

"The boy was sick, but they wouldn't let us see him," Marcus continued. "Diarrhea. He was one of those kids who jumped in the puddle after the storm." He took another sip and grimaced as though the tea tasted terrible.

"Are you all right?" Sinan asked.

"My stomach is bothering me." He shook his head with frustration. "We should have pushed into that tent anyway."

"God's will," Sinan said. "It was *his* time."

Marcus looked at him for the first time, recognizing, Sinan thought, his own logic about the loss of his wife being used against him. It didn't seem to comfort him.

"I knew a boy," Marcus said. "Not much older than İsmail. In the camp near Güzelsu." He stopped and sipped his tea again. He made a face as he swallowed.

"In 'ninety-one?"

"Yes," he said. "I used to buy these soccer jerseys to give to the boys. They loved them. Such a silly thing as an Arsenal jersey but they made them happy." He paused as though he had not told this story before, as though it was very painful. "This boy, Haluk, and I became friends. His parents were still in Iraq and his uncle had gotten him across the border. Someone brought a beach ball to the camp, so we'd kick it around between the tents. He always wanted to know about America, wanted to know if I knew Michael Jordan." He smiled as though remembering. "You know who Michael Jordan is?"

"Everyone knows Michael Jordan."

"I left for İstanbul to take care of school business and when I was there I bought a bunch of jerseys in a store in Beyoğlu. I don't know why I didn't think to buy a Bulls jersey, but I didn't. When I got back to the camp, I gave Haluk an FC Barcelona jersey. Red and blue with yellow trim."

"Blue?"

"Blue," Marcus said, nodding his head. "I know the Kurdish colors, Sinan, it wasn't green. I swear it wasn't green." He sipped his tea and then added more sugar. "Haluk put that jersey on and paraded around the camp like he had won the lottery." He laughed. "I'd never seen him smile like that. The other boys came around and touched the fabric and pulled on the numbers. They asked me if I had any more. I did, but I lied because I wanted Haluk to feel special, at least for one day.

"The next morning his uncle found me at my tent, and asked if Haluk was with me. He wasn't and we searched the camp all morning. We asked the U.N. workers if they'd seen him but they hadn't. We asked everyone, I think, on every single row of that camp—and it was huge at that point, a small city of war refugees—and no one had seen him. He just disappeared."

"The paramilitary?" Sinan asked, although he knew the answer already.

"How do they do that? Right under the U.N.'s nose and no one sees them?"

Sinan thought about telling Marcus who trained the Special Teams, but this story was not what he expected from the American.

"The next day, when we knew Haluk was gone, his uncle screamed at me. How could you let him wear that shirt? he yelled. Didn't I know? he said. Didn't I know those colors were illegal? I did, I told him, but the shirt was blue, not the forbidden green."

"It was blue," Marcus said, looking at Sinan now. "I swear it. FC Barcelona's colors are red, yellow, and blue. Not green."

"It's too close," Sinan said. "It's close enough."

"He was a boy, Sinan. A twelve-year-old boy, not a terrorist."

"He knew he shouldn't wear those colors, Marcus Bey. Every

twelve-year-old boy in Kurdistan knows not to wear the Kurdish colors. Or anything close to them."

"It was blue, Sinan," Marcus said. "Not green."

"I know, but it doesn't matter."

They were silent again and Sinan watched Marcus stare out the opening of the tent where the sun cast shadows across the dirt.

"The war is over now," Sinan said. "Öcalan is rotting on Dog Island, the PKK is dead, and the Kurds are sick of fighting."

In the evening light Marcus's face looked drawn, the bags under his eyes heavy and resting on the bone beneath.

"The boy who just died—Derin—was ten," Marcus said. "You can't tell me it was his time. We had medicine. It was treatable. Those people—"

"They don't trust you Americans."

Marcus slumped back into his chair as though he had run into this problem before, as though he thought his time spent in Turkey should earn him absolute trust. He raked his fingers through his hair.

"When I was twelve," Sinan said, trying to explain, "I buried my father. But seven others, some of them my friends, buried empty caskets. The village men said those seven had been bound and dragged behind jeeps out into the desert, but no one ever found the bodies. A few days later a goatherd found three ears, but no bodies. One of the nice things the paramilitaries liked to do to suspected PKK men—cut off their ears, among other things."

"Sinan—"

"Where do they make those jeeps, Marcus Bey? Detroit, is it? Is that the name?"

Marcus shifted his weight, and let out a frustrated breath.

"The army waited outside the cemetery," Sinan continued, "in American-made M-60 tanks and when a son of one of the dead men tried to drape a Kurdish flag over the casket—a flag with those three stupid colors that was to be buried in the ground—they ripped it out of his hands."

He paused a moment, remembering the scene—the little cemetery on the edge of town, the dry, frozen ground, the treeless hill
above the village where the government had written out the slogan
HAPPY IS HE WHO CALLS HIMSELF A TURK in huge painted rocks.

"The mountains were covered in fresh snow," he continued, "and
the sun was so bright it hurt your eyes. I couldn't watch when they
shoveled the dirt, so I looked out at the peaks of Hakkâri and every
rock looked like a body to me and all I could think was that somewhere out there were my father's killers and those killers had my
friends' fathers' bodies."

"I'm not responsible for every tank and gun that makes it into the
hands of terrible governments," Marcus said.

"That gets *sold* to those terrible governments."

Marcus leaned back in his chair and pushed his fingers against his
stomach.

"*Those* people that wouldn't let you see their son," Sinan said,
pointedly, "are Kurdish. Mine is not an uncommon experience."

"You don't trust me, either."

"I'm indebted to you," he said. "I don't trust your son."

"Or your daughter."

Sinan said nothing.

"A pill, Sinan. The boy that just died, just hours before this, simply
needed a pill."

"They were protesting the closing of a school, my father and those
men," Sinan said, leaning across the table. "That's why they were
killed. They wanted their children to go to school."

THE MOSQUE WAS PACKED with people for the *janazah* prayer. In
the back, behind the scrim separating the females' section from the
males', women cried quietly, trying not to disrupt the men's prayers.
Near the mihrab, just in front of his son's wrapped body and the
İmam saying prayers over it, Derin Anbar's father stood with his hands

cupped around his ears. He wore the deep Kurdish skullcap Sinan had not seen since Yeşilli. Instinctively, Sinan glanced around the room, expecting a soldier to rip it off his head, but there were no soldiers at the service—just the people of the camp, their faces drawn and tired, their skin ashen in the evening light.

"O Allah!" İmam Ali said. "Make him a cause of recompense for us and make him a treasure for us on the day of Resurrection and an intercessor and the one whose intercession is accepted."

The father swooned backward after the *takbir* and the man next to him, his brother, Sinan guessed, steadied him with a palm to his back.

İsmail, who was standing next to Sinan, leaned to see into the space left by the swaying father to where the boy's small body lay wrapped like a cocoon on a collapsible table. Sinan laid his hand on İsmail's shoulder and gently pushed him back, the boy pressing against his hand to get a last glance before the father was righted again. He should have been angry with İsmail, but the brief force of his resistance reminded Sinan how close he came to losing his son and he was grateful for that little push of curiosity.

Outside the mosque a group of Americans waited. Sinan had seen them when he and İsmail arrived for the funeral. Standing to the side of the dirt path leading to the water trucks, some of the women wore head scarves and all the men wore pants, and Sinan was relieved to see them covered. Marcus was among them, and Sinan had nodded to him as they passed into the mosque. They seemed respectful—not trying to enter the mosque, keeping their distance, covering themselves, but displaying their pain over the loss.

After the ceremony, the father and his family left first, filing out as quietly as they should, the mother covering her wet face in her shawl so as not to embarrass anyone. The mourners waited silently as they passed, the quiet enveloping the mosque as though death itself was settling into the carpet. Sinan had just taken İsmail's hand when an eruption of voices in front of the mosque shattered the cold calm. Through the crowd, Sinan saw the awkward jostling of middle-aged men pushing against one another—a broad back falling into an un-suspecting woman, thick hands shoving away a bulging belly, and the interlocking arms of men holding back the father.

"Stay away from my family!" the father was yelling. "Get away from here!"

As they passed, Sinan shielded İsmail from the barrage of limbs and the boy held on to his coat with both fists. Sinan could see the boy's father's face now—his eyes bulging with anger, his cheeks red from struggling against the men that held him—and the person his anger was directed toward. The young American held his hands in the air as if to calm the father, and in one outstretched fist he clutched a small black book. Marcus and a woman tried to pull the young man from the crowd and as they did he stumbled, dropping the book to the ground. He lunged to pick it up, but the father surged forward, pulling the men that held him nearly five feet until their rushing feet stomped the book into the dirt. Sinan, letting go of İsmail's hand, jumped in to help. He placed his hand on the man's stomach and felt the muscles working to rip loose from their restraints.

"It's time to honor your son," Sinan said in Kurdish. The man's eyes suddenly focused and a bit of the rage receded. "Will you send your son to Paradise soaked in anger?"

Then the man broke down; he simply dropped into his brother's arms as though he had turned to water.

Sinan found İsmail. The boy's eyes were wide, his mouth hanging open in fear, and Sinan picked up his son and carried him away from the crowd. As they walked down the hill, Kemal caught up with them and took Sinan by the elbow.

"Have the Americans come into your tent yet?"

"What?"

"They read the Bible to his wife and kids before the boy got sick." He lit a cigarette, took a puff, and pulled a thread of tobacco from be-tween his teeth. "He says they tried to convert them. He thinks they made the boy ill."

Sinan looked back at the man who was now being helped to walk to the old cemetery. He remembered the stories in the villages—the government poisoned the water, the Coca-Cola was laced with pesticides, nerve gas was encased in mortar shells.

"Have they—the Americans—visited your family when you're at work, when your wife and children are alone?"

"No," Sinan said.

"They will, Sinan Bey. They will."

When Kemal left, Sinan sat the boy down on a rock and looked him in the eyes.

"It's okay," Sinan said. "The man is upset. He lost his son and he doesn't understand why. Sometimes people need someone to blame. Do you understand?"

"No, Baba."

He said nothing and simply hugged his son because there was nothing to say. He didn't understand it, either.

SINAN WAS EXHAUSTED WHEN they returned to the tent. The sun fell behind a wall of fog sitting just off the coast, and the light inside the tent was gray and diffuse like light caught beneath the suffocating weight of dirt.

He sat on one of the pillows and watched his family—İsmail sitting in the corner of the tent and drawing pictures on a pad of paper, Nilüfer mending one of his Carrefour shirts where he caught it on a sharp box edge, and İrem stirring sugar into his tea. She put the cup to her lips and sipped the tea, checking it, he knew, to make sure it wasn't too hot.

The gesture brought tears to his eyes. He had never asked her to do that. She began testing the water years before, after he burned his tongue on a cup she had served him, and the kindness stuck, became a habit she wouldn't break despite blistering her own lips many times. Even now, when she was angry with him, she couldn't quash this bit of care she had learned out of love for him.

He watched her as she brought him his tea and thought how beautiful she was and what a wife she would one day make a husband, how proud he would be of her when he gave her away knowing the man would be blessed with such a woman. He wanted to tell her this as she knelt to hand him the cup, but, as always, the words he thought to say sounded nothing like the feeling. So, he simply took her hand and held it in his. She tugged at her blouse cuff, pulling it down so that the lace fell over the heel of her palm. He smiled at her, surprised and encouraged by her sudden modesty.

"I do love you, *canım.*"

She smiled but pulled her hand away and held it to her waist as she walked away.

He took a sip of the tea. It was perfect.

THE NEXT DAY, AFTER his morning shift, Sinan visited Derin Anbar's family. There was a line of people to see the family, and he had to wait behind the mayor, who had placed a flowered wreath on a tripod in front of the tent. The wreath read, IN LOVING MEMORY OF DERIN ANBAR, A BEAUTIFUL SON. Like bank sponsors at special events, the mayor had his name printed at the bottom of the wreath as a representative of the Faith and Justice Party. It was a tasteless political advertisement on a wreath that should have arrived the day before at the funeral. The mayor probably didn't even know where the grave was and would have to carry it over there later.

Sinan hadn't seen the mayor since the day of the mass burial and he wondered what the man had been doing in the month and a half that had passed. The man wore a pressed suit, and he kept rocking forward on the balls of his feet while he smoothed away a cowlick on the back of his head, and when he entered the tent—the tails of his coat still sticking out of the entrance—his voice boomed as though he wanted everyone to know that he was there.

The tent smelled of ripe fruit and rank sweat. It was clear to Sinan that Malik, the boy's father, hadn't taken a shower in a couple of days—the neck of his shirt was wet with sweat and blood, from what, Sinan didn't know, until he saw the man's neck and the scratch marks raised on the skin. Either the man had done it himself or the wife— who lay curled in the corner of the tent—had torn at his skin in her anguish. She was dressed in the colorful pantaloons of village women, her lined face turned toward the door so that her moans, like strange, rhythmic music, could be plainly heard.

"May your pain pass quickly," Sinan said, taking the man's hand and touching it to his chest and forehead. Sinan gave him the pastries he had purchased at the Carrefour bakery. The man didn't look at them and set them aside with the other food.

"You're Kurdish," the man said. "What village?"

"Yeşilli."

He nodded, but Sinan thought he hadn't heard of the village.

"He was my last son," the man said. "My other two, twins, were taken in Diyarbakır. The government said they were spies for the PKK, but they were just students."

"I'm very sorry for your loss."

"It's shit," the man said. "This world. It's shit."

Sinan didn't know what to say. There was nothing to say to some-one grieving. You just had to listen and accept what they said as truth.

"I might have killed that man," Malik said. He looked at Sinan with a strange expression, his head cocked as though he were memo-rizing his face. "If you hadn't stopped me." Sinan couldn't tell if he was being thanked or criticized.

"I'm out shoveling manure at a goat farm near Yalova. I think my son is playing soccer, kicking a ball around, but these people are talk-ing to him, telling him fantasies, lying to him."

"My brother," Sinan said. "Wait a few days, mourn your son."

"I'm not a very religious person," he said. He began to scratch at his neck, and Sinan had the answer to his question. "I believe in God, I say my prayers at weddings and funerals, sometimes at night when I feel things are bad. I drink *rakı*. But these people, they want to wipe

Muhammad out of history. They want us to think he was some insane goatherd, a crazy idiot scribbling worthless shit on goatskins. Have you noticed that they won't let any Turks serve the food here?"

Sinan hadn't.

"I asked once, and they refused my help. They only let that Armenian."

"You're hurting yourself, my brother," Sinan said, but the man kept scratching and Sinan could see the skin break.

"The man with the pills wouldn't put the book down. He had the pills but he wouldn't put the book down. My son is at peace now, he's in Paradise."

"I'm sorry, my brother," Sinan said. "But please stop."

"I'll see him soon. It's better this way. I know he's safe."

Sinan reached across the space between them and laid his hand over the top of Malik's to stop him.

"You're hurting yourself," he said.

Chapter 40

THE DAYS FOLLOWING THE FUNERAL, İSMAIL STAYED CLOSE to the tent. İrem's mother was easier on her, but only because she was too busy combing İsmail's hair, hugging him, making him dishes of food he only barely touched. He had been quiet since the funeral, and spent hours in the corner, drawing with colored crayons given to him by the teacher at the school.

"I'm worried," her mother said, watching İsmail as he scraped the crayons across the paper, his brow furrowed, his bare toes flexing and unflexing beneath his raised knees. "That boy was his friend."

When Nilüfer tried to see İsmail's drawings, he closed the pad and pushed it beneath his sleeping bag or he told her he wasn't done yet.

"Something's wrong with him," she said to İrem, and then she began biting her nails, the slivers of which İrem had to clean up before her father got home.

The next day Nilüfer sent İrem to do the laundry alone so she could stay with İsmail. İrem was glad for the freedom, glad for the sunlight on her face, glad for the simple work of washing and the cool water on her hands, but how quickly her mother's passion had passed disturbed her. Suddenly, she wasn't worthy of concern. It was almost as though she were invisible except when a chore needed to be done. She thought briefly about leaving the laundry and finding Dylan—

her blood raced with the thought of it—but three women stood watching her while wringing out clothes and hanging them on the line. She ignored the women, but she heard them whispering like a pack of crickets.

"A shame to her mother," she heard one woman say, while the others clicked their tongues in agreement.

She wanted to slap the woman, wanted to rip her tongue out, but instead she ground the shirt she was washing into the ribs of the rack until her hand slipped and she ripped open the wounds on her wrist. The blood swirled in the water, and she stood pressing a tissue against the wound to stanch the bleeding as she watched. She would have to pour the water out and wash the shirt again.

"She can't even do a simple chore," she heard one woman say.

She changed her mind and hung the shirt on the line despite the taint of blood, just three feet away from the women who said nothing now, who closed their stupid mouths when she was so close. In three quick steps, she grabbed her wash tub, spun around, and tossed the dirty water at the women's feet. The mud splashed against their pantaloons, and when she turned to leave she was so satisfied that she didn't even care when she caught one of them, out of the corner of her eye, ripping İrem's freshly cleaned clothes from the line.

"THERE YOU ARE," NILÜFER said. "I need to go to the W.C."

"Go then," İrem answered back, throwing her hand in the direction of the porta-potties.

"Don't start with me, daughter. Your brother's not well. You better not have seen that boy."

"Ask the women at the laundry."

Nilüfer stared at her a moment and then rushed off to the restroom.

Inside the tent, İsmail sat working on another drawing. The rice she had made earlier for him was untouched. Now *she* was getting worried.

"You have to eat something," she said.

He glanced at her and then began drawing again.

From the first-aid kit Marcus Bey had brought for her father's foot, she pulled out a length of gauze and some tape. She turned her back on her brother and began to cover her wound.

"Why is mother so mean to you?" İsmail asked.

She knew exactly why. She was jealous, jealous İrem might have freedoms she did not. The tape got folded up and she had to cut another length while holding the gauze in place with one hand.

"Maybe you should stop doing the bad things that make her mad," İsmail said.

"How can I do anything bad, İsmail!" She turned toward him more than she would have liked and she saw him look at her wrist. She turned her back again. "How can I?" she said, calm this time. "I'm locked in this tent."

"I don't like it when she's mean to you."

She finished with the wrist and pulled down the blouse cuff.

"I don't like it, either."

The rice was sticky and cold, but she carried it over to him anyway and sat down on the sleeping bag next to him.

"Eat this," she said, holding a spoonful up to his mouth. "For me." He opened his mouth and she placed the spoonful on his tongue.

"If it was me," she said, "they'd let me starve."

"I'm sorry," he said.

She ran her hand through his hair. It wasn't his fault, even though she sometimes wanted it to be. She crossed her eyes and stuck out her tongue. He laughed.

"Eat some more." He did and it was just like it was when he was a toddler and he wouldn't eat for her mother. He would always eat for her, though. Back then he might scream and cry with her mother, throw the food on the floor, but İrem would make a face and he would eat anything she put in his mouth.

"What are you drawing over here?"

He turned the page to show her. A boy with wings hovered above the soccer field. His wings were yellow and he flew toward a big yellow sun.

"It's pretty," she said. "That's your friend?"

He nodded, closed the book, and put it underneath his sleeping bag.

"Why do people die?" İsmail said.

"They just do," she said, looking up at the ceiling of the tent, surprised by the question. "Sometimes they're old, accidents happen."

"The earthquake?"

"The earthquake," she said, but she wondered how such a thing could be an accident. She shrugged. "Sometimes they're sad."

"And they get sick?"

"Yeah, sometimes."

İsmail played with his shoelaces, and she watched him, hoping he was okay and that he wouldn't ask her any more questions, because she didn't really know how to answer them. She could make it worse when she wanted to make it better.

"Or they stop eating."

He laughed again and opened his mouth for the spoon. When she laid her hand in her lap, he touched the wrist where the gauze was. She pulled her hand away, stood and dropped the rice in the makeshift sink.

"Don't you tell anyone," she said, pointing the dirty spoon at him.

He shook his head. "I won't."

She dropped the spoon in the saucepan and began boiling water for the evening tea.

"You're scaring me," İsmail said.

Striking the match against the edge of the propane stove, she lit the broiler and a blue flame flared up before settling to orange. She blew out a frustrated breath; she was scared, too.

"Everything will be all right, İsmail. Don't worry."

Chapter 41

ACOUPLE OF DAYS LATER THE SUMMER HEAT HAD BROKEN.
The brown haze lifted, the hills across the water returned, and Sinan
could feel the cool October air brush across his neck as he prayed.
Behind the prayer niche, beyond the two-by-fours that supported the
flimsy roof of the mosque, the sky shone like polished glass, the kind
of Anatolian sky that blinded you, bleached color out of carpets, and
sucked the water out of the ground.

He had stopped to pray before going to the tent, stopped to gather
his head before being confronted with an angry daughter, a frightened
son, and a panicked wife. He needed a break: the double shifts at
work, the upheaval in a home that wasn't a home, and the fear that he
would be stuck here in this city was more than he could bear. A resentment was growing inside of him like a thorn bush, and he found
himself acting out a fantasy in his head in which he broke down and
screamed at his family. He would imagine Nilüfer pleading with him
to do something and, in his mind, he would turn on her, saying, "I'm
only a man, Nilüfer. I cannot do everything." And suddenly she
would understand and embrace him and he would be relieved of responsibility. He imagined such scenes with his daughter while unloading boxes of cleaning supplies. He imagined them with his son,
though he never yelled at the boy, and İsmail would suddenly eat, he

would again be the happy child he'd been before the earthquake and Sinan could then sleep. He could then stop working sixteen hours a day. He could eat a meal of lamb kebabs in peace and know his family was safe.

Closing his eyes, he sucked in the air and the dryness chapped his lungs. He recited the prayers and his heart quit thumping in his ears; he bent his head to the prayer rug and the static in his brain receded to a quiet hum. He could breathe again, and when he sat up he could feel the sore muscles in his stomach, and he noticed the stiffness in his jaw where, for weeks it seemed, he had been clenching his teeth. And it was at times like this—these infrequent calm moments that washed over him like warm spring water—that he almost wished for death, that even though it was a sin to desire such a thing, he wished God would deliver him to Paradise this moment, because this temporary peace would break too soon. He said the prayers twice to extend the moment and allow the world to recede even further along his conscience horizon.

It was nearly sunset when he left the tent and it only took until he maneuvered his left foot into his shoe for the world to crowd in on him again.

"Sinan Bey," Dylan said, standing above him in the growing dark, smoking a cigarette. "Can I please speak with you?"

Sinan said nothing and felt the blood rush to the surface of his skin as he tied the shoelace.

"Please, sir."

"I know what you want," Sinan said. "There's nothing to talk about."

"You don't know everything I want."

Sinan stared up at the boy. He was dressed in black pants and a gray shirt. His arms were covered and he seemed to be growing a faint beard, one with patches of baldness where the hair wouldn't sprout yet.

"I'm tired," Sinan said.

"I know," Dylan said. "You work like crazy."

"And you know all the hours to my shifts, don't you?"

"I don't mean any disrespect," the boy said. "You just make it hard."

"You may not mean it." Sinan stood and started to walk away. "But you're selfish enough to cause it anyway."

Other men who had arrived early to prayer filed out of the mosque and some of them passed in a hurry to get to dinner. Fires were beginning to fill the tent aisles with orange smoke and the smell of barbecued mutton wafted in the air.

"Please, Sinan Bey. I'm trying to do the right thing, but maybe the right thing doesn't matter to you."

Sinan spun around, pressed his fist into the boy's chest. A few men stopped to watch what was happening.

"In your case, you might be right."

The boy's eyes filled with water, and he suddenly seemed younger than his seventeen years, as though his manhood were still some distant, unrealized possibility.

Sinan removed his fist from the boy's chest. "You're still a child and you don't understand." He looked the boy in the eyes. "Stay away from my daughter . . . please."

"I love her," he said.

"I know what boys think," Sinan said. "My daughter's thinking about love, but you're thinking about something else."

"No, you're wrong."

"I'm not wrong. Boys think you feel love with the lips. You think you feel it with your hands."

"Sinan Bey," Dylan said. "Would it be different if I was Muslim?"

Sinan looked at the boy, taken aback by the suggestion.

"It's something I've been thinking about," the boy said.

At that moment Kemal came up behind Sinan.

"Good evening, Sinan Bey." He laid his hand on Sinan's shoulder. "Is everything all right?"

The boy glared at Kemal.

"Yes, Kemal Bey. We're just having a discussion."

"Okay," Kemal said, lighting a cigarette now. "Okay, my brother.

I'm having dinner with friends over here. If you need anything, just let me know."

"He's your friend?" Dylan said. The boy's eyes were furious.

"Yes."

Dylan watched Kemal walk away, the muscles in his jaw working.

"Why?" asked Sinan.

The boy looked him in the face, his eyes full of anger, his teeth grinding now. "Nothing," he said. He looked away. "No reason. Forget it."

Creeping out from the cuffs of the boy's shirt were tattoos that blossomed across the tops of his hands—a dragon's tail, two points of a star, an ornamented leaf. He wore necklaces that fell beneath his buttoned collar. His eyes were blue, as foreign to Sinan as icebergs and freezing northern seas. His lips, those lips—red and chapped now— had kissed his daughter. Who knew what his hands had done.

"You don't become Muslim just by buttoning up your shirt," Sinan said. "Or by growing a beard." He tugged lightly on the scraggly hair of the boy's chin and Dylan pulled away, his eyes once again filling with water.

"Five prayers a day," the boy said. "Fasting during Ramadan. The pilgrimage to Mecca. Alms." Dylan shot him a self-satisfied look.

"Profession of faith."

The boy rolled his eyes, and Sinan knew he was cursing himself for his silly mistake. Sinan, though, was glad he had forgotten that one pillar of faith. It was too fundamental to be a nervous oversight, and the boy had lived in the country long enough to understand that.

"And modesty," Sinan added. "You must have modesty."

The boy was looking at the ground now.

"No," Sinan said, flatly. "It wouldn't matter."

Dylan looked up and Sinan saw the switch in his eyes. One moment he was pleading, his eyes soft and watering with what looked like desperate love, and then in the next second darkness flooded them.

"You just hate me," the boy said.

Sinan turned his back and walked away.

"Nothing I do is right."

Sinan didn't look over his shoulder, but he could tell Dylan was following him.

"You can't stop us."

"*Yabanci.*" Sinan heard Kemal's voice. "Foreigner, leave the man alone."

"My mom saved your son."

There was a scuffling of feet and then Kemal and Dylan were yelling, but Sinan didn't turn around; he just kept walking and let someone else take care of the boy.

AND THEN, AS IF God were angry with him, as though he was to be tested further, he found Nilüfer walking toward him through the row of tents.

"Can you not come home first, Sinan?" She held İsmail's pad of paper in her left hand, panic gathering in her face. "Even the muezzin is still finishing his tea."

"What's wrong?"

She grabbed his hand without stopping and tugged him in the direction he had just come.

"What's wrong, Nilüfer?"

She shook her head and squeezed his hand and they rushed together back toward their tent, Sinan trying to read her face. An image of his dead son flashed in his head, and he was angry with her for keeping this from him, for even a minute. No, he wasn't dead. She'd be on the ground weeping if he was. He was sick. He had caught the sickness from that boy.

At the tent, she shut the canvas flap and threw the pad on the sleeping bags.

"Look at this, Sinan," she said, flipping the pages.

Nilüfer stood back and bit her nails as he sat on his knees, bent over the paper.

In the bottom half of the picture, a boy stood among broken buildings and bodies drawn in red. He gazed into the sky at the floating body of another boy, his skin a bright yellow, his eyes two black holes in his head. The boy in the sky had something that looked like wings attached to his back.

"Look at this one." She flipped the pages to a sheet covered in black crayon. "This was before the boy died."

The crayon marks were violently stitched together as if İsmail had been trying to rip the paper. But in the left-hand corner, surrounded by a sickly yellow light, he had drawn the body of a boy, his legs curled up to his head in an unnatural fashion, his hands twisted behind his back, the elbows breaking at odd angles. But what was most disturbing was the boy's face—the eyes were drawn with X's and the mouth was a gaping red hole. Next to the boy, İsmail had written "Me."

"I think he's sick," Nilüfer said, whispering. "But not sick like bleeding inside, but sick here." She pointed to her head.

"He's not crazy, Nilüfer." Although he thought the same thing when he saw the picture. "He's just scared."

The boy used to draw pictures of birds he saw down at the waterfront. Beautiful, if childish, renderings of storks with their long, black plumes, terns with the bright orange arrows on their beaks, and wild flamingos, sketched in bright streaks of pink, that he spied last spring crossing the sea on their way to the southern coast.

"Oh, Sinan," she said. "What was it like? Our baby! He shouldn't have to go through such a thing."

"I know, *canım*," Sinan said. He held her hand. "I know."

"Talk to him, Sinan. He's saying things today that scare me."

"What things?"

"Asking strange questions he's too young to ask. Speak to him."

"Where is he?"

"The soccer field."

"You left him alone?"

"No, he's with İrem."

—

THE SOCCER FIELD WAS illuminated with floodlights nailed to wooden poles, and, against the darkness of the camp, it seemed to glow as if it were the center of the world. A few boys played a half-hearted game at the opposite end of the field, their voices echoing in the cooling night air like muffled screams. He found the two of them at the edge of the field, İrem sitting in the grass and İsmail juggling a soccer ball. For a moment it seemed they existed wholly separate from him, as though he had nothing to do with their presence in the world. He watched them as though he were dead, a ghost watching his children from the other side, hoping they reflected back some essence that said he had lived in the world. İsmail kicked the ball in the air. İrem smiled and clapped as he tried a fancy kick.

"İrem," he said when he reached them. She stood up immediately, stopped smiling, and brushed off her skirt. "Your mother is expecting you back at the tent."

"Of course, Baba." She brushed past him, her skirt rustling together, her feet scuffing up clouds of dirt, and he could feel her anger in all of her movements.

"Watch, Baba," İsmail said. "Watch." The boy bounced the ball on his left knee three times before kicking it into the air and heading it awkwardly to his left side where it rolled into the darkness beyond the field. İsmail ran to get the ball and came back.

"Where'd you learn that?"

"Wait, Baba, wait. I didn't do it right." He tried again and this time missed the ball when he kicked. He smacked the ball with his fist and tried again.

"Football's hard," Sinan said. "It's okay."

"Wait."

This time he headed the ball and it dropped right in front of him. He stuck his chest out in an attempt to control the fall, but he missed it and the ball hit the hard ground and rolled away.

He let out a little cry of frustration and kicked the ground, sending up a cloud of dust.

"That's good, İsmail. I'm very impressed."

"I'm not doing it right." He stared at the ground.

"No, no. It's good. You're just like Alpay." Sinan put his arm around the boy. "I couldn't do that, and I'm a thousand years older than you."

"Not a thousand," İsmail said, smiling faintly.

"Okay, okay," Sinan said. "Only a hundred and one years older."

İsmail laughed. "You can't do it because of your leg, not because you're old, Baba." İsmail playfully pushed him in the stomach.

"Yes," Sinan said, hurt by his son's innocent statement. "You're right. Where'd you learn to do that?"

"Marcus Bey taught me. But I'm supposed to bump it with my chest and then stop it with my foot. That's the hardest part," he said. "Stopping it."

"What else did he teach you?"

"Nothing," İsmail said. "Just that. He's nice."

"Get the ball and let's play."

"You can't play."

"What, you think I'm too old?"

"Yes, a thousand years too old." But he was running into the darkness toward the ball. He vanished for a minute and then reappeared, running full speed into the light, his skinny legs like little matchsticks pushing the ball ahead of him.

Then İsmail suddenly stopped and did a fancy behind-the-back kick that sent the ball rocketing toward Sinan. He stopped it with his good foot and bounced awkwardly on his bad one until he was able to return the ball. It was a soft kick that only made it halfway to the boy. İsmail ran to it and kicked it back, and without saying a word remained standing closer to his father.

They kicked the ball back and forth a few times, and the simplicity of the action—he and his son tapping a ball to each other—flooded Sinan with love. It was such a pure feeling that he wished he had spent more time doing this. It struck him that perhaps it was not his

leg that kept him from playing football with his son, but his seriousness, his obsession with work, and the way he had let everyday burdens become more important than simple joys. İsmail kicked the ball
a few feet to the right of Sinan, and he tried to run to get it but he
stumbled and fell.

"Are you hurt, Baba?"

"No, shoot it again."

"It's okay."

"Shoot again, İsmail."

İsmail kicked the ball softly, but Sinan's foot hurt now and when
he put weight on it he tripped and fell again.

"Kick it again, İsmail." He felt, for some reason, that if they could
just keep kicking the ball to each other in the lights everything would
be fine.

"It's all right, Baba."

"No. Again."

But İsmail was already at his side. "I'm tired."

They sat in the grass together and watched the boys flit and dodge
toward the water-jug goalposts. They pushed one another, all elbows
and flailing hands, and dashed across the field like insects fluttering
in lamplight. İsmail, tired though he said he was, bounced the ball
between his outstretched feet. Sinan waited; the boy was working
himself up to a big question, and Sinan didn't want to scare him out
of it.

"Baba," he said. "How come God gave you that foot?"

"I can't speak for God, İsmail." It wasn't the question Sinan expected.

"But if God can do anything, why wouldn't he give you a perfect
foot?"

"Sometimes God has reasons we can't understand, and we have to
accept them."

"Seems mean," İsmail said.

"God is not mean, İsmail." He made sure his son was looking at
him. "God is love and He is merciful and He is kind."

"If I was God, I would have given you a perfect foot."

"Son, look at my face." The boy did. "Look at my nose. It's crooked, but it can still smell the salt in the air. My teeth are brown, but they still chew my food. I may need glasses, but I have two eyes and they can see you—even if you are a little blurry." He smiled and İsmail smiled back. He reached down and pulled off his shoe and his sock. "This foot, İsmail, is part of God's world just like everything else. It's part of me, and without it I wouldn't be Sinan Başioğlu. You remember the Gypsy girl who sang so beautifully, the blind one?"

"Yes, Baba."

"God didn't give her the gift of sight, but he gave her a beautiful voice. That's her gift and it makes up for what she lacks. No man is made perfect, İsmail. Some have weak lungs, some have weak eyes, and some have weak hearts. I have this. If we were perfect, we wouldn't need God. He understood that when he made us, so he made us imperfect because he wants to keep us close to him."

"So what did God give you to make up for your foot?"

The question caught him off guard for just a second, before he jumped to tickle İsmail. "You, my son. You!" The boy laughed and giggled and squirmed out of his grasp.

Sinan sat back down and drew İsmail close to him.

"You can't change what God has given you. If a man has one good eye, he doesn't curse God for not giving him two. He thanks him for sight." Sinan held the boy's cheeks and kissed him on the forehead. "It's all a gift. All of life is a gift."

The two of them sat silent for a while and watched the boys chase the soccer ball around the field. Sinan could feel his son working on another question and he waited quietly for him to ask it.

"Baba?"

"Yes."

"What's Heaven like?"

"It's hard to explain, İsmail." How could he explain this to the boy? "The Qur'an says that Heaven includes what no eye has ever seen, no ear has ever heard of, and no human mind has ever thought of."

"Is it beautiful? Do you hurt in Heaven?"

"You *do not* hurt in Heaven," Sinan said. "No, there's no pain. And it's more beautiful than I can imagine, so I can't tell you what it looks like. God will reveal that on Judgment Day."

"How do you know it's beautiful if you can't imagine it?"

"Because the Qur'an says so and the Qur'an is the word of God and I trust God."

İsmail stared at the ground and ran his tongue over his lips in concentration. Sinan wished he could see inside his son, wished he could understand every turbulent thing that was happening inside his body and calm it.

"If you're a good Muslim, do you live forever? Because someone told me that if you're a Christian you'll live forever and ever."

"Who told you that?"

"Someone."

Sinan thought about forcing the name out of him, but it was the wrong time.

"Your spirit will live forever, İsmail, but not your body. Your body must die first, but your spirit will live in Heaven with God."

"But why do Christians live forever?"

"That's not what it means. A Christian has to die, too."

"That's not what he said."

"It's the same, İsmail. We all die, but our spirits live on."

"So is Dylan's mother in Heaven?" The boy looked up at him, his eyebrows knitted together. Sinan didn't know. Christians were people of the Book, but they worshipped God imperfectly.

"I'm sorry about your friend," Sinan said. "He was a good boy and now he's in Paradise with God."

"He wasn't my friend," İsmail said. "Just a boy I played soccer with. He was kind of mean."

It was silent a moment. They watched the soccer game break up and the field became nothing but a bleached plot of dirt.

"If Derin's in Heaven, then Sarah Hanım must be, right?"

"Yes, İsmail. Sarah Hanım is in Heaven."

"Good," İsmail said. "Good."

"Baba?"

"Yes."

"I don't want to die." He kicked the ball once and it rolled to a stop a couple of feet away. "Sometimes when I sleep, I feel like I'm stuck under the broken houses again and I think I'm going to die. I'm curled up and the space keeps getting smaller and my legs and arms get squeezed tighter and tighter and I can't breathe. It feels heavy and dark and lonely, and my bones hurt. I don't want to die."

He wanted to lie to his son, he wanted to tell him that he wouldn't die, but the boy already knew the truth and there was no comforting him about this fact.

"I don't want you to die, either," Sinan said. "But we all die some-day and then we get our reward."

İsmail rubbed his knuckles across his eyes, and Sinan ignored the tears so that he wouldn't embarrass his son.

"Let me tell you, İsmail, about Heaven." This, though, was a lie he could tell. One lie, especially a hopeful one, was okay. "Heaven is very green, the brightest green of the most beautiful trees. There are gardens of water with rivers and lakes and tall waterfalls that sparkle like a million cascading diamonds. When you peer into the water, thousands of brightly colored fish stare back at you. The mountains are tall and covered in snow, but it's not cold. You can slide down the face of the mountains, but the snow is as warm as bathwater. The sun always shines, but it never hurts your eyes and the sky is so blue it looks like it's been painted with hundreds of coats of paint. There is every kind of fruit you can imagine to eat, and even more you haven't imagined yet, and all of them, every single one of them, tastes like candy."

The boy was smiling now, looking out toward the cool white of the floodlit field, but his eyes looked distant, Sinan thought, distant as though he were looking beyond the field, out into the blackness of the nighttime sea, and imagining the perfect Heaven, building it in his mind out of the ugliness of this earth.

Chapter 42

IREM SAT IN THE DARKNESS FOR A WHILE, JUST OUTSIDE THE glare of the floodlights and watched her brother and her father. They kicked the ball to each other, and she felt a pang of sadness for her father—his foot made him so awkward and she suddenly felt embarrassed for him. But İsmail was beautiful—the way he moved with the ball was so elegant for a young boy, the way he balanced on one foot and popped the ball back in the air with the perfect arc to land on his knee, the way he danced above the ball when dribbling. He was beautiful and she could, at this moment, understand her parents' love for him because she felt it, too.

They played for a while and she tried to remember what it was like to play with her father. He had taken her fishing as a girl, in the stream that ran down from the mountains. She didn't remember ever catching anything, but both of their lines dangled together in the rushing water, and the snowcapped mountains shone above them like white teeth in the sun. They took naps in the afternoon sun and he held her hand as he snored on the riverbank, and even though the soldiers were just on the other embankment and jets occasionally passed overhead, she felt safe and happy, as though these terrible forces had no power over her crippled father.

"İrem," she heard a voice say.

She turned around and found Dilek rushing toward her. They hugged and kissed and held each other for a few moments.

"People said you were out," Dilek said.

"Not for long," İrem said. "What are they saying?"

"You don't want to know."

"I know anyway," İrem said.

"Ignore them. It's mostly the *şişman teyzeler* with missing teeth and breasts down to here." She held her hands like she were supporting heavy bags of water near her waist. "You weren't asleep the other day, right?"

"I almost called to you, but it would have made my mother furious."

"Dylan wants to see you."

"I know. I want to see him, too."

"No," Dilek said. "He wants to see you tonight. He said you'd know where."

İrem watched her father and brother. They were sitting now, two small figures in a pool of blinding light, looking out at the dusty field. Her father placed his hand on İsmail's back and something about that made her want to cry. She should have been excited about Dylan, but all she could think was that she wanted that touch from her father, that public display of affection.

"My father wants to go back to the village," İrem said. Saying it out loud for the first time made a lump rise in her throat. "He thinks there will be a Kurdistan or something stupid like that."

"It's no good here now," Dilek said.

İrem stared at her. "Do you know what it's like there?" she said, anger in her voice. "There's nothing there, Dilek. It's desert and mountains and in the winter you've got to sleep next to goats because they'll die outside in the cold. It smells like shit—all the time!"

Dilek laughed. İrem had never cussed before and it made her feel good in a guilty way.

"I didn't mean go *there*." Dilek smiled a knowing smile. "Allah,

Allah," she said. "He's so cute. I like his eyes. They have those flecks of brown in them."

"They're nice, aren't they?" She leaned into Dilek and Dilek wrapped her arms around her.

"You're so lucky," Dilek said. "I'm jealous. My mother's driving me so crazy, I think I'd run off with him if he wanted me to."

"Your mother wouldn't hate him. Your mother would be happy for you; she'd help you plan the wedding."

They were silent a moment. İrem knew she would have to make a decision tonight, and she didn't know what that decision would be.

"These two women came to our tent yesterday," Dilek said. "One of them was beautiful, İrem, and she wore this amazing diamond ring. I couldn't stop looking at it." Dilek showed her with her own bare finger. "Little ones all the way around and then one big one in the middle."

"What'd they want?" İrem said. She watched her father press the tip of his nose against his face and she laughed silently.

"We just talked about stupid stuff, mostly. I asked the beautiful woman about her house in Texas and she told me that it had a pond in the backyard and a barn for horses. She has four kids, she said, and my mother asked her how she stayed so skinny."

"How?" İrem really wanted to know. Turkish women had kids and their hips grew three sizes overnight, like a flower blossoming in the moonlight.

"She works out at a gym, she said. But I bet she had someone have the kids for her."

İrem laughed.

"It's true. I heard something about it on television."

"Shut up."

"No, the rich women don't want to get ugly for their husbands so they hire someone to give birth," Dilek said. "They use test tubes or something."

"Dilek," İrem said. "I love you but sometimes I think you're crazy."

"It's different in America. The husbands let you do what you want, but you have to stay pretty for them. If you're not pretty, they divorce you for a younger, prettier woman."

"Sounds like a dumb conversation."

"You're pretty, İrem. You could be like that woman. You might even get to skip all that pain of childbirth and still have the kids."

"Shut up, Dilek," but she playfully shoved her friend, enjoying her fantasy and weighing the possibilities.

"Well, they were nice. At least the pretty woman was. The ugly one handed my mother something on a piece of paper and when my mother read it she crumpled it up in her fist. They left after that. The other woman was mad, but the pretty one just smiled and wished us well."

"My father wouldn't have even let them in the tent."

"Yeah, well, your parents are backward, İrem."

İrem looked at her, surprised to hear her friend say it openly. It was understood between them that her parents were the "village parents," but Dilek had never been so rude as to say it out loud.

"I'm sorry, İrem. I love you, but you know it's true."

Chapter 43

IREM WAS NOT AT THE TENT WHEN HE DROPPED OFF İSMAIL. It made him angry, but he was thinking about his son now.

"Find İrem," Nilüfer said, as he walked back out into the night. "And tell her to come home before I swat her behind."

"I will," he said, but a man can worry about many things at once—his body stiff with concern, his head cramped with ache from it—and he can only take care of one thing at a time.

Now he stood outside Marcus's tent, a faint yellow light glowing through the skin of the material, and tried to keep himself calm. He was about to invite himself rudely into the man's tent at a late hour. He was about to accuse the people who had helped them. He called to Marcus. He heard a shuffling of papers, scratching of feet across the floor, and then the American pulled back the tent flap. He wore wire-rimmed glasses that magnified the blue eyes behind the lenses.

"Why are they preaching to my son?" Sinan said, losing control of his mouth.

Marcus removed the glasses from the bridge of his nose and rubbed his eyes. He looked like he had been sleeping or studying very seriously.

"Sinan," he said. "Come in." He held open the door flap to the tent and Sinan entered into the weak light within. Next to a turned-down sleeping bag, a large black book with gold-leafed pages lay open. A propane lamp hissed light over the book, and in the harsh white glow Sinan could see handwritten notes scrawled in blue across the pages.

"I'm sorry for disturbing you," Sinan said, suddenly feeling self-conscious as he entered the man's living space.

"No problem," Marcus said.

Marcus sat on the sleeping bag, placed a ribbon in the crease between pages, and closed the black book. He set his glasses aside and grabbed another pair, these causing his eyes to recede back into his face. Through the lenses and in the sharp tent light, his eyes looked like two blue crystals. Sinan was reminded of Atatürk and the power of blue eyes.

"Sit down, Sinan, please."

But Sinan didn't sit. "Who's preaching to my son? Is it you?"

"What are you talking about?" Marcus rubbed his eyes beneath his glasses. "Please, sit down, my friend."

Sinan suddenly felt foolish standing bent over in the middle of the tent and sat at the foot of Marcus's sleeping bag.

"I'm sorry we have no tea to offer."

"I didn't come for tea. I simply want an answer to my question."

At that moment, Dylan bent through the opening to the tent. Marcus looked up at him and then glanced down at his wristwatch.

"Is this about that stupid young man at the funeral?" Marcus said. "You tell me."

Marcus said something to Dylan in English. The boy was wearing headphones, and even here, some five feet away, Sinan could hear the beating of drums and hissing sounds coming from those earpieces. Dylan held his hands in the air, palms up, and said something that seemed to indicate that he didn't hear his father. He saw Sinan then and froze momentarily.

"*İyi akşamlar,*" Dylan said, an undisguised strain in his voice.

"Good evening."

Marcus pointed at his wristwatch and spoke sharply in English.

Sinan looked away until they were done, embarrassed to be present for the scolding. Dylan flopped down on his own sleeping bag, turned his back to the two of them, and flipped the pages of a magazine. Marcus slid his glasses off his nose and rubbed the lenses with the end of his shirt. "Explain to me what happened," he said, looking at Sinan now.

Sinan told him about the drawings, Nilüfer's concern, and the discussion at the soccer field.

"The boy simply misunderstood," Marcus said. "Whoever it was meant no harm."

Dylan laughed sarcastically. Marcus snapped his head in the direction of his son, but the boy continued turning the pages of his magazine.

"Children ask questions," Marcus elaborated. "Maybe the answer was a little misguided, but I'm sure it was meant only to comfort İsmail."

"They're trying to convert you, you know?" Dylan said suddenly, his voice sounding impatient, his back still turned. His Turkish was precise, better than his father's.

"Dylan," Marcus said, a violence in his voice Sinan had not heard before. Then to Sinan: "Dylan believes everything is a conspiracy."

"They think you're not good enough as you are," the boy said, turning around now to face his father. "They think they've got the way to Heaven all figured out and if you don't do it their way you're out of luck."

Marcus spoke very loudly and quickly in English to Dylan and Dylan spoke calmly and with authority back to his father. The boy turned around to face Sinan, but he stared at his father as he spoke.

"See, that's what these people do," Dylan said. "They come in after some bad shit happens, start feeding people and telling them they love them, and then they hit them over the head with the love of Christ and how *he'll* save all the poor, misguided Muslims from judgment. You know—the millennium's coming, Armageddon and all that. The earthquake is just the beginning, so get ready!"

"Dylan," Marcus said. "Stop being rude."

"Right," he said. "Rude." He laughed and his eyes lit up with bitterness. "The truth's always rude. They want to win your soul for Christ, promise you white clouds to sit on, some lame harp music playing in the background. They can't just let you be what you are. The whole fucking world has to be like them."

"Dylan, stop."

"You know, you trust the wrong damn people, Sinan Bey."

Marcus reached across and grabbed his son's wrist and said something in English. Dylan tried to pull away, but Marcus held his son's arm tightly and didn't let go. The boy tried to laugh it off, but his face was red.

Dylan quieted, looked at the ground, and said something in whispered English. Marcus let go of his hand and composed himself.

"Is this true?" Sinan said to Marcus.

Marcus spoke to Dylan in English. The boy snatched up his earphones and stomped out of the tent without looking back. Sinan wondered where İrem was.

"Forgive my son," Marcus said. "He's still angry, as you can see."

"Is it true?"

Marcus blew air out of his nose and Sinan could see that he was very tired.

"Sinan, my son's on medication. The doctors say he's bipolar. They try this drug and then that drug and then three or four drugs together, but they never get it right. Sometimes he doesn't know what he's saying. It's the medication talking, not him." He paused. "And since the earthquake he's been . . ." He shook his head. "He's been worse."

So the boy is crazy. He felt immensely sorry for Marcus, and secure that he had done the right thing by İrem.

"You've got to understand, Sinan, that these were the only people willing to come here on such short notice."

"So it's true?" Sinan said.

"Some people might talk about Jesus."

"They're trying to convert people?"

"Sinan," Marcus said, his voice growing more sharp and weary at the same time. "Listen, without these people, you'd still be sitting in that little circle of grass by the freeway waiting for the government to figure out which way is up." He pointed his finger in the general direction of the freeway. "Your kids would be starving. If a few of them want to talk about Jesus, that's a small price to pay, isn't it?"

"Is it them or is it you?"

Marcus ran his hand through his hair.

"Sinan Bey," Marcus said. "İsmail's been asking me questions. I answer them."

"You're not really here to help, then," Sinan said. "You're here taking advantage of our weakness."

"Not me, Sinan." He waved a finger at him. "I'm not with these people. I just got them through my school connections."

"Your missionary school connections," Sinan said. "You brought them here."

"I found someone who could help, and that's all I did. Some of them are Baptists and some of them don't believe the same thing I do. They were ready with people and supplies." He threw his head back and looked at the point of the tent top. "Lord! C'mon, Sinan, when the body can be saved you worry about the soul later."

"No," Sinan said. "I think you're thinking food and tents are a small price to pay to win some Muslims." Sinan stood. "You're all rich. What's a few tents and some bags of food to you? You smile in my face and stab me in the back. You Americans are all the same."

"No," Marcus said.

"At first it seems like you're helping, but really you're taking what you want and the helping stops after you take it."

"Please, my friend, calm down."

Marcus held out his hand to try to calm him, but Sinan was too angry to be calmed.

"That's not me," Marcus said. "I used to be like them, but that's not me anymore."

Sinan stopped pacing.

"Sinan," he said. "That's not me. When I first came here with my wife I was very young and I used to believe the things they told you in church. I used to believe it was only people who accepted Christ that went to Heaven, and that seemed like such a sad thing—that billions of people would die without a chance at salvation. That thought depressed me in a way I can't explain." He rubbed his hand across his forehead and Sinan could hear the passion in his voice. "It made me black with guilt—and mad. Why was I one of the lucky few when so many people were damned to Hell? I decided the only explanation was that they had not heard the good news of Christ, and I thought it was my moral obligation to share it. Now I think . . . I don't know, I think what any of us knows about God is like one drop of water in the ocean."

Sinan wasn't sure what to say. He wasn't sure if he should believe this man. His heart was telling him he should, but his mind was wary.

"And Sarah just confused me even more." He pulled his glasses from his nose and rubbed his temples. "When I met her she was as strong in her belief as I, but later she changed. She was so much better than I am—selfless, loving, thoughtful, not full of the egoistic passions I suffer from. When she died, she was more of a Buddhist than anything."

Sinan thought about what he told his son, and he was afraid he had actually told a lie. He thought people of the Book could be saved, but he didn't know about ones who rejected it completely.

"Sinan," Marcus said. "I should be happy for her now, but I don't know if she's—God, it sounds so stupid to say out loud—I don't know if she's in Heaven."

"She was a good woman."

"I know."

Sinan waited a moment, but he didn't want to be drawn away into Marcus's problems.

"If my son has questions," Sinan said, "I'll answer them."

"Yes," Marcus said. "Yes, you're right."

"There will be trouble if this continues," Sinan said. "If these people keep going into the tents."

Marcus nodded. "I'll talk to Peter."

"You'll get them to stop?"

"They're helping."

"You'll stop them?"

Marcus cocked his head to the side in an expression of doubt. "I'll try, Sinan."

Chapter 44

WHEN SHE REACHED THE TOP OF THE HILL, DYLAN WASN'T there. Fog stretched toward the beach, a wall of clouds reflecting orange from the dock lights that lumbered like the massive body of an approaching sea animal, and when the first wet tentacles surrounded her she shuddered and crouched on the hillside. The sea suddenly disappeared and she was surrounded by darkness, the orange light gone, the sky and its stars blotted out, leaving her lost on this small patch of dust at her feet.

She was alone and the fog blew the sound of her breath back at her. Her heart beat inside her head so hard that she thought it would convulse and shudder to a stop. Something touched her shoulder and she swung at it, her open hand hitting something solid and then something soft, cartilaginous, that gave away under the pressure.

"Ah, shit, İrem."

When she turned she found Dylan fallen over on the ground, on the little patch of earth that was hers. He held his hand to his nose. She pulled his hand away and there was a little blood, but she kissed him hard on the lips anyway. He kissed her back and she could feel the warm blood on her lips. She surprised herself by kissing his neck, his collarbone beneath his shirt, the curls of hair on his chest.

"Let's leave," he said. "Tonight."

"No," she said. "I can't do that."

But she couldn't stop kissing him.

He blew out a frustrated breath and pushed her away. The fog swirled around them and his head and shoulders seemed to fade in the mist.

"You want me to give up my family?" she said.

"Yeah. Haven't they already given you up?"

"No," she said. "They're holding on as tightly as they can."

"What's this then?" He threw his hand at her. "What's this we're doing?"

She said nothing and the silence enveloped them. She tasted blood and salt. A foghorn bellowed and she felt dizzy for a moment, remembering the steep fall to the water.

"I've been here every day and night waiting for you."

Her chest burst with love and anger and frustration.

"I thought I lost you," he said.

"No," she said. "You knew I couldn't leave."

"But you could," he said.

"Look at this," she said, holding out her wrist to him now. "Look. You think I've enjoyed being locked up in that tent? How stupid are you?"

He gazed at her wrist now, his eyes growing wider with realization. He took her hand and ran his thumb across her palm.

"You'd rather hurt yourself than hurt them?"

"I don't know," she said. "I—no, I want to be happy."

"Then come with me. This place is terrible now. Fuck our parents."

"Please don't say that."

"Jesus!"

He let go of her wrist, stood, and kicked dirt, and she could hear the pebbles launch into the air.

"What do you want, İrem?"

Allah, Allah! She stomped her foot.

"I want you to come to my parents' home for dinner. I want you to bring a box of chocolates and take your shoes off at our door. I want my father to kiss you on each cheek and invite you into the living room. I want my mother to serve you her terrible chocolate-and-pistachio cake and for you to eat every dry bite of it and tell her how wonderful it is." She was yelling now, screaming into the stifling fog. "I want to watch you and my father sipping tea as you ask his permission to marry me, and have my mother whisper into my ear what a handsome and good man I have chosen. I want my father to walk me down the aisle and deliver me to your arms. I want fireworks at the reception. I want to dance with İsmail in my wedding dress."

Dylan sat back down in the dirt, his head bowed between his knees. She stood for a moment, feeling empty and relieved somehow, and then sat down next to him, the heat between their legs a little fire of warmth in the icy fog.

"I went to see your father today." He lit a cigarette and the smoke flew away from his mouth to join the clouds. "I told him I wanted to convert."

A pang of hopefulness hit her, even though she knew that sitting here meant the meeting didn't go well.

"You'd do that for me?" She was moved, but the gesture bothered her, too. If he could so easily give up his religion, couldn't he easily give her up, too—for a more beautiful woman, for boredom, for almost anything?

"It doesn't matter," he said. "He hates me and it doesn't matter what I do."

"His father was killed by Americans."

"Jesus, I've spent my whole fucking life in this country. I'm about as American as you are." He blew smoke and the warmth hit her cheek. "He says it doesn't matter, it doesn't change anything, but he's over at my dad's tent bitching him out because 'someone's' been talking to İsmail about Jesus. It changes things for his precious son but not for me, not for you."

She pulled the cigarette from his fingertips and took a drag.

"Have you thought about that?" He took the cigarette back. "He's ready to tear my dad apart for trying to convert his son, but he's not willing to budge an inch for a guy about to come over to his side because he loves his daughter. Damn hypocrite."

"Is it true?"

"What, my dad trying to convert your brother?"

She nodded.

"Yeah, it's true. He loves the kid. Thinks İsmail's some sort of miracle or something." He laughed a sad laugh. "You should see the way he looks at him."

She envisioned her father looking at İsmail. When İsmail wasn't looking, she'd catch her father staring at him, a look on his face that betrayed all his pride, his love—a look that was glowing but full of pain at the same time.

"It's like he thinks he's perfect or something."

She touched his back. An intense desire to kiss him blurred into a need to comfort him. She thought, for the first time, she understood him completely.

"It's you, İrem," he said. "I've got you and that's it."

She put her arm around him and he fell against her, his face pressing into her shoulder.

"Jesus," he said, lifting his head now. "I think you broke my nose."

He pressed the end of it to the left and then he laughed and she laughed with him.

IF HER FATHER HAD hit her for defying him, she might have stayed. If he had left the tent in anger to attack Dylan or scream at Marcus Bey, she might have known that he loved her as much as Dylan did.

But when she stumbled in to the tent, well after dark, he didn't even look up from his tea. Her mother glared at her and waited for her father to do something. İrem waited, too, suspended in hope that he would take some decisive action that spared her decision.

"Your daughter is back," Nilüfer said.

"I see that."

He finished his tea and set it aside on a saucer next to his sleeping bag. He took off his shirt, his undershirt barely covering his strong shoulders, the muscles in his arms flexing as he laid himself down inside the sleeping bag.

"Your daughter is back."

"Nilüfer, I have a double shift tomorrow." He turned his back. "I can't do this tonight."

İrem walked over to her father and picked up his tea glass. He didn't even open his eyes, and she briefly thought about dropping the glass simply to get him to startle.

Her mother stood in the corner of the tent, the harsh white of the propane lamp casting a desolate glow over her skin.

When İrem dropped the glass in the sink, her mother grabbed her by the arm. "Get in bed," she said, her nails digging through her blouse. "I don't know what's wrong with your father, but get in bed and stay there."

İrem took off her head scarf and folded it next to her sleeping bag. Her mother watched her as she unpinned her hair and combed out the tangles.

"A man would love that hair," she whispered across the tent as she turned out the light. "But not now. Not anymore."

In the darkness and inside the sleeping bag, İrem slipped out of her clothes and into her pajamas—the scratchy material of the bag briefly touching her bare skin before being covered again.

Her brother lay asleep next to her—one bare arm slipped outside the sleeping bag. In the half-light of fire and floodlight cast through the skin of the tent, she watched İsmail's sides expand with each breath; she listened to the tiny whistling sound he made when he was deep in sleep, the same sound she had fallen asleep to thousands of nights before. She slid next to him, wrapped her left arm around his chest, and lay awake for hours. She hoped he wasn't having bad dreams.

Chapter 45

THE NEXT DAY İREM WAS GONE.

That morning, before his shift, before his wife arrived at work in a panic to tell him that İrem had left, Sinan stood on the edge of the school tent, partly hidden behind one of the poles, and watched the teacher. She was one of the American relief workers who he had been told was an elementary school teacher at an expensive private school in İzmir. She sat on a chair, a group of children crowded at her feet, and read a picture book in Turkish. Her accents were wrong, but she had the words right and the children watched her with wide eyes and upturned faces. One little girl, a poor child who had lost both her parents, held on to the woman's leg and occasionally thrust a finger into her own dirty nose. She rolled the snot between her fingers while staring at illustrations directly in front of her face.

He finally found İsmail in the back of the crowd, crouched over a piece of paper, furiously drawing with colored wax pencils. He occasionally looked up from his drawing to listen to the story before returning to his artwork. Sinan noticed no crosses in the tent and saw no signs of Bibles. The teacher, while her head was uncovered, was dressed modestly and did not show any unnecessary skin. After watching for twenty minutes—long enough to see a game in which one child ran around a circle of kids and slapped the tops of their heads—

he heard no mention of the prophet Jesus. The children seemed content, and to be content here was no small thing.

He watched a pickup soccer game, and while some of the Americans played with the boys, there were Turkish men also, and no one was standing around talking. They were too busy passing the ball, tripping over their own feet, and falling down to let the boys beat them to the goal.

For breakfast, he stood in the line that led to the Armenian. The man leaned over the table to serve the woman in front of Sinan, and the gold cross he wore around his neck fell over his shirt collar and dangled there just above the yellowish fluff.

"Peace be with you," Sinan said when he took the eggs.

"May the Lord bless you, my brother."

Sinan threw the eggs in the nearest trash bin before walking to work.

In the middle of his first shift, Nilüfer, dragging İsmail in tow, found Sinan bent over boxes of goods he couldn't buy to earn money he couldn't get.

"She's left with that boy," Nilüfer said. Her eyes were so dark and angry they looked solid, as though two rocks had been dropped inside her head.

"What do you mean she's left?"

"She left, she's gone," Nilüfer said, her body shuddering with anger. "I go to the W.C. and when I come out she's gone. I need to relieve myself, what do you expect me to do? The boy," she motioned to İsmail. "The boy can't stop her."

İsmail, who a moment before was marveling at the wall of televisions broadcasting two dozen images of a Manchester United match, hung his head.

"You can't even stop her," Nilüfer said, waving a hand at Sinan.

"No, because I'm here lifting boxes all day!"

A handsome couple dressed in black and wafting with perfume and cologne turned to look at Sinan when he raised his voice. The man looked away as soon as he saw him, a disregard that was infuriating, but the woman stared Nilüfer up and down, taking in her dirty pantaloons, the cheap scarf wrapped around her head, the scuffed leather shoes with the soles tearing off. Sinan saw what she saw and he was disgusted with his wife and with himself, disgusted with his children, disgusted with everything.

"This is because you let her watch those American shows," he said to Nilüfer. "You let ideas into her head."

Trying to calm himself, he thrust the packing knife into the seam of a box and sliced it open.

"Who hid the earphones from me?"

He stabbed the next box open and shredded the seam apart.

"Don't accuse me, Sinan."

He slit open yet another box. Now three boxes full of goods lay open, and he began to recognize the stupidity of his actions.

"Why didn't you tell me?" she said again, tears of betrayal threatening her eyes. "What else have you hidden from me?"

"Leave me alone," he said. "I have work to do."

"What are you going to do?"

"Leave me," he said, raising his voice again.

İsmail started crying and Nilüfer ignored him. He stood there holding his mother's hand, tears running down his face, and it was as though Nilüfer couldn't hear him at all.

"No. What are you going to do?"

"I'm going to work! I'm going to finish my shift."

Nilüfer blinked with shock. She finally seemed to notice İsmail and pressed his head up against her hip, patting his head in a gesture that was more like hitting than stroking.

"I wouldn't have taken your name, Sinan Başioğlu, if I knew it meant so little to you."

He stabbed the knife into another box so that the handle stood straight in the air before pointing his finger at his wife.

"You didn't have a choice," he said.

She stood completely still, her mouth hanging open so that he saw her rotten teeth, nubs as black as spoiled grape stems.

She stepped up to him and grabbed his arm.

"I found bloodstains in her sleeping bag," she whispered loudly.

Her eyes filled with water, and she waited until he felt the words lodge in his gut before she turned and dragged İsmail by the hand through the aisles of the store. Even as she strode through the sliding glass doors, he could hear İsmail's cries echoing off the linoleum floor and rattling around in the aluminum roof.

AFTER WORK, HE STOOD at the bus stop along the edge of the highway and watched six buses unload and load up again. He searched the destroyed town, in the empty façades of buildings where men crouched in corners, hidden from the midday sun to drink cans of beer and smoke cigarettes; he checked the waterfront where the old men squatted on chunks of cement, their fishing poles dangling above the water like wilted antennas; he even climbed the hilltop where he and İrem had talked the other night, where the earth seemed to fall away into the sea, where she had told him that she had kissed the boy. And the whole time he tried to come to some conclusion in his mind about what he would do when he found her.

That night he attended mosque and prayed, but the words meant nothing to him. He didn't even hear his voice, they were empty recitations, ritualized motion, full of as much meaning as the loudspeaker announcements of product specials at Carrefour. Maybe she would never come back. If she did, was he to be understanding and welcome her? He couldn't bear losing her, but he couldn't bear her rejections anymore, either. Her willingness to disobey him pierced him with an impotence he had never felt. The ease with which she gave up her family tore him with betrayal, but mostly—more than all of this—he was desperately hurt that his daughter didn't love him as much as she loved this boy.

When he left mosque, men were gathered outside, smoking cigarettes and listening to the mayor.

"The government has forgotten about you," the mayor was saying, "because they only care about the rich Kemalists, the liberals who want to destroy religion, turn themselves into little Frenchmen."

"And what have you done?" It was Malik, and he spat on the ground in front of the mayor. "You weren't here when my son was ill. Talk, talk, talk. That's all it is."

"Malik Bey," the mayor said. "I'm very grieved over the loss of your son. Had I been here and not in Ankara pushing the Kemalists to send supplies I would've done everything in my power to save him."

"Talk, promises, but you do nothing." Malik left the crowd and the men watched after him.

"Where's the military, where's the Red Crescent? I'm here, but where are they?"

A few men started a backgammon game, but they were still listening.

"The Kemalist generals are free with their tanks," the mayor continued, "when an Islamist party gets elected into parliament, but when you're suffering . . ." He threw his hand over his shoulder, as though casting seed into the wind. "Paah." He spoke more loudly and turned his face toward the soup kitchen. "They leave you to have Jesus shoved down your throat."

Kemal Aras, squeezing through the crowd, approached Sinan in the gathering darkness. At first Sinan didn't recognize him, but as his eyes adjusted he saw the newly grown beard and the white skullcap pressed on top of his head.

"Good evening Sinan Bey. Peace."

"Peace to you," Sinan said, feeling tired and unwilling to talk.

But Kemal took his arm and they walked toward the rows of tents, through the rank-smelling clouds of propane stove smoke and the groups of children playing in the street.

"I'm sorry about your daughter, my friend."

"Why are you sorry?" Sinan said. How did this man know, after only half a day, that his daughter was gone?

"You're a good man, Sinan," Kemal said. "It's not your fault. Our women are going bad. It follows that our daughters would, too."

"My daughter is just sad. This earthquake has made her act strange."

"Yes, yes, of course," Kemal said. "It's been hard on all of us, but people forget the cause, Sinan, and only see the effect. They're afraid if you let loose of your daughter, theirs will try to follow. And when our women go bad, the men will be next. Believe me, I hear this every day from people."

The men drinking tea and smoking at the card table watched them come, only to turn and resume their conversation as they passed, as if they hadn't been watching them at all.

"I've been thinking that this earthquake is punishment from God," Kemal said. "We've forgotten the straight path."

He stopped and lit a cigarette before taking Sinan's arm again.

"I've been an immoral man," he continued. "I've cheated people, as you know. I've been tempted and succumbed to it." He turned his lips up as though disgusted with himself. Sinan noticed that the scab was gone and only a faint pink mark remained. "There's something evil in us all, and God is reminding us that he sees it."

They passed a group of women who were beating rugs with sticks. One woman shook her head and clicked her tongue as though something horrible had happened right in front of her.

Kemal waved his hand at her. "Bite your tongue, woman."

She turned away and slapped the rug. A cloud of dust burst from the pile.

"People are speaking ill of you," Kemal said. "It's the first time I've heard such comments. Before, people respected you. A bit quiet, yes, too quiet perhaps, but they didn't doubt your good name."

Sinan's chest tightened.

"This is important, Sinan. People say she's pregnant."

Sinan untangled his arm from Kemal's and faced him in the street.

"What people say and what's the truth are often two different things."

"Does it matter, Sinan?" A few young men gathered to watch now that he and Kemal were face-to-face; theirs was no longer a quiet evening stroll between acquaintances. "She's running around with the American boy. He worships Satan, pierces his skin, carves up his arms with symbols. Do you want to give over your daughter, your only daughter to that?"

Sinan thought about hitting him, but you didn't attack a man for offering you the truth.

"These Americans," Kemal said, looking toward the relief workers' campfire, "they want to take everything from us." He touched Sinan on the shoulder. "Well, you, far more than I, know what Americans are like." He let go of Sinan's shoulder and fingered the prayer beads in his palm. "Your daughter is forgetting about God. As soon as she turned away from you, she turned away from God. You need to bring her back."

"No man should suggest to a father what you're suggesting," Sinan said. "No man outside the family."

"It's your name, Sinan. Your son's name. Your father's honor as well as yours."

Sinan began to speak and then stopped as Kemal's words cut through skin and muscle tissue and lodged, like a shard of broken glass, beneath his rib cage.

"Sometimes you need to slice away the cancer to preserve the body." Kemal rested his hand on Sinan's shoulder.

İrem was the cancer; his own daughter was what needed to be cut away and discarded.

"These people would understand, Sinan. We would understand."

Chapter 46

THAT AFTERNOON DYLAN'S ARM LAY DRAPED OVER İREM'S shoulder as they rode the *belediyesi* bus into İstanbul. It wasn't that she didn't like it, exactly, but people stared. A neatly dressed man with a little boy scolded the child for watching them and lifted him over his lap so that he faced the window instead of the aisle. The boy turned around in the seat, his brown eyes hovering above the backrest, until his father tapped him on the head and turned him around. She watched the backs of their heads, the child's cantaloupe-shaped, like his father's, each with a swirl of black hair spinning out of their scalps. She imagined the feel of İsmail's hair in her hands, so thick, so coarse like the clipped hair of a horse's mane, and everything she was leaving behind overwhelmed her and she had to look away.

Now, out the window, the sun was high in the sky and it shone down on the broken industrial buildings of İzmit and made them look horribly small, like the whole city was cast in miniature. Sunlight glanced off the water in blinding sparkles and the horizon stretched on into the sky until the two met and seemed to become one. It seemed to her that the sun was terribly large, as though it grew in force and size by the moment and would eventually burn everything to the ground. And riding high up on the freeway she couldn't escape it. Its heat beat onto her arms and shoulders no matter how many towns they passed, no matter how many kilometers they rolled away from Gölcük. Already she was farther away from her home and her family than she had ever been, and she suddenly felt hopeless. She wanted to go back, she wanted to turn the bus around, and when she heard the brakes squeal she thought, for a moment, the bus driver had read her mind.

But the bus stopped on the side of the highway and a *şişman teyze* climbed on, waddling like a flightless bird, pulling a cart full of rotten eggplant behind her. She sat in the empty seat in front of them and turned her head just enough to be heard as she tsk-tsked her tongue at them.

"She's my sister, *teyze*," Dylan said. "That man over there kept staring at her." He pointed his thumb toward the father. "I thought he might be dangerous."

İrem laughed into her hand. No one believed it, of course, but it shut the woman up. She calmed down immediately. She wasn't alone; Dylan would take care of her. His weight pressed on her shoulders, the heat of his body radiated through her skirt to tingle her skin. She imagined her father here on the bus, staring at them, and in her mind she said to him, "Look, Baba, this boy loves me! A boy—a man!—loves me." She imagined the look on his face, the hopeless pain in his eyes, the water pooling there as he realized he was losing her forever. "You didn't love me," she imagined saying to him. "But I do, *canım*," he said back. "I love you best, more than you can know, more than anything." She felt a brief imagined joy and realized, coming back to the world, that she was staring at the side of the father's face across the aisle. He had a hooked nose and a flap of skin that sagged from his jaw like a chicken's and he looked nothing like her father.

"Here," Dylan said. "You look nervous."

"I'm fine," she said.

"Listen to this."

He took his headphones, severed the wire down the middle, and pulled the earpieces apart.

"I understand," he said. "It's shitty the way your parents treated you."

But he didn't understand. It was her parents' right. She had defied them.

He placed one earphone in her right ear and the other in his left.

"Lean back," he said. "It'll be all right. Everything'll be just fine."

He pushed the button that started the music. It was Radiohead again—the music that was like floating, like dying, but dying beautifully. Dylan had told her the lyrics and she sang them in Turkish in her mind while the singer sang them in English in her head.

I'm not here. This isn't happening. I'm not here.

Below the raised highway, an apartment building lay accordioned in the street. A chair hung from a telephone pole.

In a little while, I'll be gone.

She wondered why he would play such sad music for her now. Why couldn't they listen to Tarkan or Cher? But she loved the music. She loved the sadness. It hurt so wonderfully, hurt in a way that made her realize she had never really felt anything before.

The bus turned inland and the sea receded into the sky so that soon it was just a distant streak of silver. The city replaced the sea on the horizon, all jumbled honeycomb blocks of apartment buildings. She had never in her life seen so many buildings in one place and it was difficult to imagine all the people squished together here. As far as she could see, red-tiled rooftops and satellite dishes spread before her like a sea of cement.

"Here it comes," Dylan said, his voice full of excitement. He jiggled his knees up and down. "These are just the suburbs."

They drove on for another twenty minutes and the traffic got heavier and the sun began to drop in the sky and an orange haze settled over the city. *Dolmuşes* stopped to pick up passengers on the side of the highway and then swung back out into traffic. Men sold fruit from wooden stands propped up by the highway guardrails, and dust smattered their faces as the buses passed. She saw a man carrying three silver birdcages, the beaks of doves poking between the bars like living thorns. She saw a turned-over donkey cart and a dented taxi. A Gypsy woman screamed at the taxi driver, her open palm gesturing toward the dead animal, his hooves resting in a puddle of his own blood. And behind the accident, the cars piled up like a river had been dammed. They went on forever, their headlights glowing a trail into the city.

"It's too big," she said.

"Don't worry."

What she had known was her neighborhood—Dr. Özferendenci Sokak, Atatürk Caddesi, İmam Ali Sokak, Deniz Caddesi—and the walls of her apartment.

"It's so big. You won't leave me?"

"No," he said and he pulled her closer, his hand wrapped around her waist now, her shoulder pushing up against his chest, the smell of his cologne, the pressure of his fingers against her hip bone.

The sun dropped into the haze and spread like butter in a pan. Lights began to come up on the city—millions and billions of lights in millions and billions of windows—and the city, for the first time, replaced the sky with its own brightness. Towering antennas sparkled on a hill, their red lights twinkling in the bruised sky. The road curved and dropped into a path between hills and in the distance she saw the gray towers of the bridge and the cascading wires that held the road in midair. A wonderful fear shuddered across her skin: she was *in* the world! Right now, she was in the world, a part of it, not watching it from behind a dirty windowpane or on the tiny square face of the television.

The traffic was heavy at the bridge and after a few minutes of idling in one place, the bus driver got out and disappeared on foot into the jammed traffic. Two police cars whipped past the bus, their blue lights reflecting off the glass windows. A few moments later the driver returned, lit a cigarette while standing on the roadway, and climbed back onto the bus as the traffic began to inch forward again.

They crossed the bridge over the Bosporus, swerving around a police van and the two police cars blocking the right lane. Three policemen peered over the edge.

"Whoa," Dylan said, twisting around in his seat to get a view. "Someone must have just jumped."

But as he said it, the bus changed lanes into the far left and she was presented with a full view of the city: the last of the sunlight caught the water and set it alight, as though the streak of sea was made of gold. Edging the water, the lights of the city were brilliant jewels tossed across the hillsides. It took her breath away and she was angry such a place had been kept from her.

They passed beneath the second tower and followed the stream of red lights into the city. Dylan tapped her on the shoulder and pointed to a sign.

"Welcome to Europe."

Beneath the bridge stood a palace lit up white like a wedding cake.

And something broke loose in her and she started to cry because it was too beautiful and she didn't know it would be so and because her mother would never see it and because she and her father would never look at it together.

"Hey," Dylan said. "Calm down, now. It's just a city."

Chapter 47

"SLICE AWAY THE CANCER." TO HEAR SUCH A SUGGESTION spoken out loud made bile rise in his throat. On the surface it seemed like evil—as though Kemal were Satan whispering in his ear—and because it was so disgusting it seemed entirely impossible. No one could ever think about killing his own child; it was a genetic impossibility, the very thing that set man apart from the lower beasts. Yet it happened. He himself had already had the thought. He hadn't considered the act directly—that would be like stabbing yourself in the eye. But the thought came to him obliquely, rising from some dark recess of his mind that would have otherwise remained unchurned if İrem had not placed him in this position. No, he had not thought of actually killing İrem, my God! But why then would he remember the killing of the young adulterer in the village, a memory he had not had for years? Why then had he not killed Kemal for even making the suggestion?

"Your son needs washing," Nilüfer said to him, taking his untouched cup of cold evening tea and leaving a towel and a bar of soap in its place.

At the solar showers, Sinan helped İsmail undress.

"I can do it, Baba," the boy said.

İsmail stripped off his shirt and pulled down his pants and left them crumpled in the dirt. His nakedness was not an offense since the boy had not yet hit puberty, but Sinan tried to shield him anyway with a small towel.

"Pick up your clothes, İsmail." The boy did and set them on the wooden bench.

He pulled the orange curtain closed so that Sinan could only see the boy's calves and ankles and feet. The soapy water ran in little bubbles of froth over his toes and drained through a pipe into the grass nearby.

"Baba, will İrem come back?"

"She'll come back, İsmail."

"She's been doing bad things hasn't she?"

"Wash between your toes."

He lifted one foot and ran his fingers between the toes, a frothy knot of knuckles and joints.

She had kissed him, he realized, and the thought of the boy's tongue searching around inside his daughter's mouth stabbed him with pain. His heart flipped like a fish on land, fluttering then seizing for a moment before flipping again.

"She's with Dylan Bey, right, Baba?"

"Clean behind your ears, İsmail, and wash your mouth out, too."

He heard İsmail gurgling water.

"You don't need to call him mister," he said. "He's just a boy."

That boy was stealing his daughter away from him and he was letting it happen.

"İrem shouldn't do those things, Baba." İsmail's feet did a little dance on the wet cement floor as he turned to let the water fall on his back. "She makes you yell at Anne, and God won't like it, either. She doesn't want God to be mad at her."

He couldn't speak to what made God angry, but he knew what people would do. They would ruin his name, his father's name, and his father's father's name. Did she get to dishonor the whole family? Did she get to dishonor İsmail's name and that of his children, simply because she wanted her own freedom?

"Let's wash your back."

Sinan pulled the curtain back just enough to let his hands inside. Taking the soap, he lathered it up in his palms, and scrubbed down İsmail's shoulders before moving to his back. The boy's skin was so soft, clean, and without blemish. His shoulders were broad, especially for someone so young. His spine was perfectly straight and both legs were the same length, the calves of each perfectly formed and connected to tendons that allowed him to walk with a grace Sinan could only dream of. If each man was the image of God, then God was a malformed thing, given to weakness and petty selfishness. Yet his son, this boy, seemed the perfection man was supposed to reflect.

He was a Kurd and the world would tell him he was nothing. He was poor and the world would give him nothing. He was a Muslim and the world would ignore him, and being ignored was like being dead. The boy had his name and his name was everything. Take away his name and the boy had no future, no honor, no respect, no reason to look in a mirror and see his own perfection.

"Ouch, Baba! You're doing it too hard."

İsmail's skin was red from the scrubbing. He stopped and told the boy to rinse off.

What if İrem did something that denied her entry to Heaven? Skin was only the container of the soul, but the soul was a fragile membrane—it could easily be ripped and once it was, there was no sewing it back together. To kill her before she destroyed that, she would remain innocent, she would enter Paradise as a child, as clean as the day she was born.

And İsmail wouldn't have to feel less than anyone in this world, ever.

"We're done, İsmail." He handed the boy a towel. "Dry off."

When they got back to the tent, Marcus was waiting for him.

"She's with Dylan, isn't she?" Marcus said.

Sinan simply nodded because if he spoke it would be to attack the man.

"Go inside, İsmail," Sinan said.

"He hasn't been back in two days." Marcus thrust his hands into his jeans pockets. "I think I know where they are."

"Then you'll take me there tonight," Sinan said.

"Too late for the buses."

"Don't you have a car?"

"No."

Sinan thought he might be lying, but, then again, why would he?

"Tomorrow then."

Chapter 48

SHE SHOULDN'T HAVE BEEN ALONE WITH HIM IN THE APART-
ment. No, she could do anything she wanted now! Her father wasn't
here. Her mother wasn't watching her every move. Like Dilek had
said, another quake could hit tomorrow. Besides, what was she thinking when she ran off with him? That they would sleep in the street
like Romas? But she couldn't help the feeling; it was wrong for her to
be here.

He was in the bathroom, taking a shower. She sat petrified on the
couch in the front room, listening to the water running and watching
the steam tumble through the cracked open door. She wished he
would close the door. Was he expecting her to come in there? Did he
simply forget? She thought about closing it herself, but as much as
she had dreamed about his body, she was afraid to see it now.

Pictures of Dylan's mother hung on the walls. Not just his
mother—the whole family, too—but it was his mother that caught her
attention most. It was like sitting in the room with a ghost, her green
eyes shining down from every wall. She wondered what Sarah Hanım
would think about this. Would she accept her as her daughter? Did
she realize—somewhere in Heaven or Hell—that none of this would
have happened if she were still alive? There was a picture of her on a
beach—young, blond, her hair blowing into her eyes. She wore a two-

piece red bathing suit, and her stomach was flat as unleavened bread. The curve of her breasts peeked beneath the bathing-suit top and she looked very happy despite being nearly naked in public. There was another picture of Sarah Hanım hiking a canyon in shorts and carrying a huge pack on her back. A black-and-white photo of her smiling, her head thrown back laughing, as though she were a star in an old movie. In all these pictures, it was obvious the person with the camera was in love with her, not just in love but in love with her beauty—the way her hair caught the light, her bright green eyes, her perfect lips. There were other pictures, though, and in these photographs Sarah Hanım stood on the periphery, hiding behind a tree at a terrace dining table, holding her hand up against the camera eye. At a certain point, the pictures of her stopped and were replaced with pictures of Dylan. Then one last picture sat above a small desk in the corner of the room: Sarah Hanım much older, on a beach again, her body covered in long pants, her arms hidden in long sleeves, her thinness gone. Her weight was apparent even beneath the billowing clothes, and İrem thought she was trying to disguise the fact that she had grown ugly. In the center of the picture, Dylan and his father smiled at the camera, their teeth very white, their naked chests red with sunburn, their arms wrapped around each other. She suddenly felt sad for this dead woman; a woman, it seemed, was always forgotten eventually.

The water stopped running in the bathroom and she dug her nails into the couch. She tried not to look, but the door was open and she couldn't make herself ignore it. His movements disturbed the light, bouncing shadows around the small room. Through the crack in the door she watched the steamed-up mirror and the blurry image of his slender body—a white hip, a dark spot beneath the smear of his belly, the curve of his back as he bent to dry his feet. He suddenly swiped the towel across the mirror and she looked away, back at the picture of Dylan's once-beautiful mother half-naked on a beach.

When he came out, he was dressed and his wet hair dripped onto his tight black shirt. She could see the plates of his chest beneath the fabric.

"Won't they find us here?" she said.

"My father doesn't give a shit," he said. He scraped his fingers through his scalp. "He's too busy saving people."

"My father will come after us."

He would find them. She couldn't imagine what he would do to Dylan, but he would take her back to the camp, lock her up inside that horrible tent all day, and she would sit there sweating, listening to the people outside in the sun, lie there as the laughter of children echoed from the soccer field. They would move somewhere else and she'd be locked up inside another gray apartment. Eventually, he'd find her a husband, some kind traditionalist that would treat her like a jewel box, like some prized possession that cooked and cleaned and gave birth and changed diapers and did it all again whenever he wanted, and she would wake up one morning and realize she had become her mother. And that every day from that day forward would be like the day before it and the one before that until day and night didn't matter anymore and life would feel like one long hour of work with death at the end.

"He'll find us," she said.

Dylan smiled, a strange smile full of disregard.

"We won't be here," he said. "C'mon, we're going out. But you've got to change."

He took her hand and led her into the bathroom. The steam had cleared, except for a few streaks on the mirror. He stood behind her. They both stared into the mirror, and his blurry nakedness flashed in her mind. She smiled with the memory until she really looked at them together. He was head and shoulders taller than she. Dressed in black, with his hair slicked, with his leather bracelets and tattoos, he looked like someone from a television show, and she the poor peasant girl, the ones the television shows always made fun of, the ones people thought were stupid and passive and ugly.

"If you want to fit in where we're going," he said, "you've gotta get rid of this."

He placed his hands on either side of her head. They were big hands and she thought he could crush her head if he wanted. "I mean, I don't care," he said. "But people here will."

"For months," he said, "I've wanted to see your hair. It's got to be beautiful."

She wanted to believe he thought her beautiful, but it sounded forced; somehow she didn't believe him. She looked away.

"Hey," he said, grabbing her chin. "Look at yourself."

She did. Her big, hooked nose, the pimples on her chin, the shadow of hair above her lip. She looked Kurdish and Kurds weren't known for their beautiful women. Macedonians were beautiful. Armenians. The light-skinned Turks with their blue eyes and blond hair.

His hands pulled at the scarf now.

"No," she said, and placed her hands on his. This was dangerous. She thought if she let this happen, then there was no stopping anymore. That's what her mother always said. Let a man see your hair, your neck, and you'll soon be pregnant. But no boy had ever spoken to her like this.

"I love the way your lips always pout."

He pulled on the scarf again, despite her hands.

"Makes me want to kiss them."

And she found her hands moving to help him. How stupid her mother was—as if exposed skin could get you pregnant, as if it took nothing more than that! As if a woman's self-control was contained in a sleeve of cheap fabric!

"I've been dying to do this," he said.

Together they pushed it off her head and her hair, all pinned up like a bird's nest, shined in the bathroom light.

"You're so beautiful," he said as he pulled the first pin from her hair, his hands so soft, his fingers combing out the tangles one by one.

THEY MET HIS FRIENDS in front of the French *lisesi*, a colonnaded building locked behind a huge wrought-iron fence. Dylan slapped hands with one of the boys before kissing him and the others—another boy and a girl—on each cheek. Dylan's friends were Turks, but rich Turks, she could tell, just from the cut of their jeans and the easy arrogance of their movements. Nothing about them suggested they had suffered or sacrificed anything, and it was only rich Turks who could seem this purely unburdened. It took Dylan a while to introduce her and she stood behind him, wishing she could disappear.

The boys ignored her, but the girl kept glancing at her between interjections in the conversation. İrem looked away and pretended to be listening to the boys' conversation, but when the girl joined the conversation, İrem watched *her*. Baggy jeans rested on the girl's hips, and she wore big, black shoes with silver studs on them. The strap of a black canvas bag hung between her breasts so that the material of her tank top pressed closely against her chest and İrem could see the points of her nipples. The girl was Turkish, but not even Dilek would dress like this. What shocked her most was the way the girl seemed to be trying to look like a boy. If İrem could show as much skin as this girl, she'd try to look as beautiful, as feminine as possible, so that she could enjoy boys' eyes watching her.

"Who's this?" the girl said, pointing at İrem with her burning cigarette.

Everyone stopped and looked at her. She felt her face go red.

"My girlfriend," Dylan said, grabbing her by the waist and pulling her against his thigh.

Girlfriend! He had never called her that before. The girl looked her up and down and İrem was embarrassed by her long skirt, the silly flowers on her blouse bought for a million lira at the Gölcük outdoor market.

One of the boys, the one with a hoop pierced through his eyebrow, leaned forward and offered her his hand. "Serkan," he said, and she took his hand even though she shouldn't.

"This is Attila," Serkan said.

Attila jumped forward. In a flourish, he grabbed her hand, bowed, and gave her knuckles a very ceremonious kiss.

"Hey, lay off," Dylan said.

Attila came up smiling, and Serkan playfully pushed him.

"Sorry about your mom," Serkan said to Dylan.

"Yeah," Dylan said. He took his hands from her waist and shoved them into his pockets. "Thanks." He nodded his head and looked down at the ground.

"May your pain pass quickly."

"Yeah."

The girl flicked her cigarette on the ground and hugged him, her breasts pressed against his stomach. He returned the hug, the tips of his fingers pressing into her back.

"What're we doing?" Dylan finally said, pulling away from the girl.

"Not much's happening," Attila said. "Because of the quake."

"People are dead," Dylan said. "Staying at home's not going to change that."

"They're just being respectful," Serkan said.

"Seventh House is shut down for who knows how long," Attila said, lighting a cigarette now and dramatically blowing the smoke into the sky. "Club 2019 is closed tonight."

"Secret Garden's got something going on," the girl said. "There's a guy spinning there tonight who used to work with Murat Uncuoğlu. Produced one of his records or something. Some guy from his London days."

İrem had no idea what they were talking about, but the way they spoke made her feel stupid.

Down an alleyway—past darkly lit cafés with empty tables set out on the cobblestone street, past a church gate and a statue of Mary with her eyes downcast and yellow sun rays shooting out from her head—stood a blue door with trash set on the steps for collection. From the outside, the building looked abandoned—the stonework stained with centuries of lipid coal smoke, the windows darkened and reflecting the violet sky. She wondered what they were doing here, but then Dylan opened the door and inside, placed on the steps of the circular stairway, stood flickering candles lighting the way to the top.

As they neared the fifth-floor entrance, the stairway shook and her heart jumped before she realized that it was just the thumping of the music.

Inside, the walls glowed green as though lit from inside and every corner of the room was filled with plants—ferns, tall ficus trees, others that looked like short palm trees, their leaves like huge wings spread above tables of candles. They had to brush greenery aside to sit at a table, and behind them, through the leaves of a fern bush, a man pressed his lips against the soft part of a woman's neck. Dylan nodded to a bartender, held up five fingers, and said, "Efes." In a moment, five bottles arrived, held between the fingers of a woman with dyed orange hair.

"Şerefe," Dylan said. He and everyone else held the bottles up and clinked the glasses together. She didn't touch hers.

"How cute," the girl said. "She's not going to drink."

Dylan shot a glance at the girl, but didn't say anything.

"Sorry," Dylan said, turning to İrem now. "I don't know what I was thinking." He took the bottle and placed it in front of him. "I'll drink it."

"To being back in the city," Attila said. They took sips.

"It's too damn depressing down there," Dylan said. "My dad's trying to convert everyone."

"Your dad's like the crazy fundamentalists in the Fazilat party," Serkan said. He had his arm wrapped around Attila, who smoked a cigarette—he seemed always to be smoking a cigarette—and nervously jerked his knee up and down. "Those stupid people'll turn this country into Iran."

"My dad's just an asshole."

The girl laughed. İrem still didn't know her name, and she wondered if this was on purpose.

"He thinks he's always right. Thinks if I spend enough time down in the camps I'll 'feel the spirit of God' or some stupid shit like that. Thinks it's more important than keeping me in school my senior year."

"School's still out," the girl said. "They've got to check all the schools for damage. Education Ministry says two weeks, but you know how that goes."

"Yeah, three or four, probably."

"My parents have me going to *dershane* already," Attila said.

"Shit, Attila," the girl said. "Fucking University Exam already?"

"Yeah, two hours a day after school, studying math problem after math problem," Attila said. "My parents'll disown me if I don't get into Boğaziçi."

"My parents'll murder me if I don't get into Harvard," Serkan said.

"Serkan, you're not going to America," Attila said, suddenly passionate. "I'll kidnap you on the day of exams if I have to. We can be male belly dancers or something crazy like that."

Serkan gave him a pathetic look.

"Boston's too cold," Attila said. "You hate the cold."

"You been going?" the girl asked.

"To *dershane*? No. I keep ending up at Akmerkez, trying on shoes." He touched Serkan's cheek and smiled. "My parents are in Vienna. My dad might be taking over Coca-Cola Europe."

"Shit," the girl said, and turned to watch a man near the bar with headphones clasped over his ears.

"You going with them?" Dylan asked.

"No," he said. "Not unless Serkan comes. They don't want me there anyway. My father says I'll embarrass him."

The music stopped briefly and then rose with a whirling sound of oud strings that sounded like the traditional songs her father sometimes played on old cassette tapes. Then the strings were overtaken by a thumping beat again. She felt the floor shake beneath her feet.

"This guy," the girl explained, "started mixing Sufi music with Jamaican beats."

"It works," Serkan said. "It's like dub but more Middle Eastern, more mystical-sounding."

"Yeah," Attila said. "It's like religion stoned on hashish."

Everybody laughed and İrem pretended to understand.

"So," the girl said, turning to İrem. "Where's your chaperone?"

"Stop it, Berna," Dylan said.

"Seriously, aren't you supposed to be chaperoned until your wedding night?"

Dylan spoke sharply to Berna in English, and stabbed the table with an index finger. Berna yelled back at him in English and he turned his face away from her. İrem could see the muscles working in his jaw.

"Your father probably wants you to be some kind of slave," Berna said to her now. "Washing, cleaning, cooking."

"No. He just doesn't want me to be like you," İrem said, wanting to slap this girl. ·

"Oh, okay, I get it now," Berna said.

"Stop it," Dylan said.

"So an American boy." She lit a cigarette, nodding. This girl was mean like a man—meaner than a man. "I get it, of course, meet an American guy, go to America, get your freedom."

"This is boring," Attila said. "Leave her alone, Berna."

"Oh God," Berna said. "You think he's taking you to America and turning you into some fairy-tale princess, don't you?"

"Shut the hell up, Berna," Dylan said. "I swear, just because your father wanted a son."

"Allah, Allah," Attila said. "If I knew I was going to be hanging out with a bunch of Arabs I would have brought a gun to shoot you all with."

Berna was taking a sip of her beer when he said it and she burst out laughing, spraying the beer out of the corners of her mouth.

"Forget about it," Dylan said. "C'mon."

He grabbed İrem's hand and he took her into the crowd of people dancing in front of the man pushing records on the player. She loved him at that moment, as he took her hand, having defended her against his friends. He found a table on the terrace, behind a huge vine lacing up a trellis. Through the vine a few stars shone weakly in the city sky. Beyond the rooftops, the Bosporus was streaked with reflected city lights.

"I don't get it," he said, his brow creased, his hands combing through his hair. "I don't get it, shit!" He kicked the table. "Everyone wants you to be someone."

"Shh," she said and touched his wrist.

He sat back in his chair and looked at her, water in his eyes, and she felt her heart would break for him. He was so fragile, so easily hurt.

"Everyone wants you to be something," he said. "Except my mom. She never wanted me to be anything. I was fine as I was."

"Shh," she said again. "I don't want you to be anything."

"Sure you do," he said. "Berna's right."

"Berna's jealous," she said. "Any woman can see that."

He laughed and pressed his palms against his eyes. "Yeah," he said. "I guess you're right."

A flare burst in the sky, drenching the rooftops red as it arced toward the water.

Berna *was* jealous. Jealous of her!

The flare disappeared beneath the rooflines of Beyoğlu, but a streak of smoke remained as a pink smudge in the sky. She smiled. It was the greatest feeling she had ever experienced in her life. She was someone. She could make a woman jealous!

Hollow explosions echoed from the water and soon fireworks bloomed purple and blue and silver in the sky.

Dylan turned to watch.

"A wedding," he said.

"A wedding."

The fireworks fell in arcs above their heads and burned out.

Dylan turned around, suddenly excited. He pulled his chair in close and touched her cheek. "It's just you and me now," he said, his blue eyes bouncing back and forth, as though searching her out, as though she were the most important thing in the world to him.

A waiter slid two small glasses between them. They were filled with a deep crimson liquid.

"What's this?" Dylan said.

The waiter pointed back toward the bar, toward Attila, who was holding up his own red glass. "*Şerefe*," he yelled. "To young love!"

Serkan burst out laughing, as though this was the funniest thing in the world, but Berna just turned her back.

Dylan laughed and held up his glass in a long-distance toast. "Asshole!" he said, and took a sip.

İrem looked at the glass; the liquid was a beautiful red, as though it were a newly polished jewel.

"Tastes like red licorice," Dylan said. "You'll like it."

She put her mouth to the glass and let the liquid seep through her lips. She half expected it to burn her lips or strip the skin from her throat. Her father had suggested such a thing. Alcohol was poison, he had said to her once. But Dylan was right; it tasted like candy, like the gumdrops she used to steal from the bins at her father's store.

SOMETIME IN THE NIGHT everyone must have made up, because she found herself wedged into a corner in the backseat of Attila's sports car. The car raced through a cavern of apartment buildings and squares of window light melted into streams of color. Attila had the radio turned up and the backseat rattled with the beating bass. Dylan, his arm wrapped around her, took a drag from a cigarette and blew the smoke out the open window. He kept the beat with his other hand and between songs his fingers fell below her shoulder where the slight curve of her breast began and she was aware of his fingers but she didn't mind.

She didn't know where they were going and each turn Attila made was like going deeper into a maze until she saw the bridge appear above the hills of the city. Everything else was a blur, her head swimming in what felt like a warm, lazy sea, but the bridge anchored her focus and as long as she stared at it she could remember flashes from the night—she and Dylan dancing, his mouth on her neck; more little red drinks; a brief and tender kiss between Attila and Serkan; Berna lighting a cigarette for her and, smiling, telling her Dylan was "a shit." These moments of clarity, though, were lost in fragmented images of colored lights and bodies and laughing faces and the thumping of music and the flash of matchsticks and bottles shining on shelves and the remembered feeling that this was freedom, that this, because it seemed to have no rules, was perfect and she had felt light and warm and lost and she liked being lost.

The car now sped around a corner and Dylan's body pressed against hers.

"Take it easy," Dylan said to Attilà. "You're drunk."

"You're a genius," Attila said, and she could feel him shift gears and the car raced up a hill, past the darkness of a cemetery on one side and the brilliant brightness of hanging open bulbs on a row of *kokoreç* shops.

They came to a house on a steep hillside, the glimmering water of the Bosporus below, the arc of the bridge, like a hovering cement shadow, above. Dylan helped her out and she could hear the roar of cars above. They entered a dark courtyard through a gate and were met by a man with a German shepherd. The dog barked and she jumped. Dylan laughed and gripped the back of her neck.

"It's me, Yusef," Attila said.

"Attila Bey," the man said. "Good morning."

"*Günaydın.*"

"Your father doesn't like friends, Attila Bey."

"My father doesn't like Serkan and I don't care."

"I'll have to tell him. He likes to know."

"Your girlfriend visiting tonight?"

The man said nothing, but cleared his throat and moved out of the way.

The courtyard was dark, but she heard water running somewhere and she could tell it was filled with plants and trees.

"That man's got a wife and kids in Üsküdar."

"A new dog?" Serkan said.

"Yeah, the last one was poisoned. Someone threw a beefsteak over the fence with rat poison inside."

"Your father's still getting threats?"

"Yeah, he's on some terrorist's list. When he's here there's like ten men with wires hanging from their ears and guns strapped inside their jackets, but when he's gone it's just the dog and Yusef."

"And Yusef's girlfriend," Serkan said.

"Yeah. Stupid little Ukrainian girl. He's probably told her he owns the place."

She had never seen a house like this. Inside, the marble was polished so that she could see their reflections as they walked toward the terrace in the back. It was cool inside, air-conditioned, and round lights were embedded in the ceiling and shone down brightly on beautifully framed paintings of shapes and color that seemed to represent nothing.

Attila drew open sliding-glass doors that revealed the water and the curve of the bridge above. She heard the rushing of the cars again, a distant honk, a foghorn on a ship. They lounged on leather couches near the open windows, and Berna fell asleep with her arms hanging off the couch and her breasts pressed together to reveal her bra.

Attila laughed. "Night-night, Berna."

She didn't move or make a noise.

With her head against Dylan's shoulder, İrem was suddenly exhausted. She had a headache and when she moved her head it took a moment for her vision to catch up, rendering everything a blur before each thing fell back into its place. Out the window, the sky began to lighten, a shade of blue casting the hills as paper cutouts. She wondered if her father was up yet, if he had even slept. She wondered if her mother was snoring now, her arm clasped around İsmail.

Serkan passed around a small white cigarette that wasn't a cigarette. It smelled different and when Dylan inhaled, he kept the smoke inside his lungs for a long time before passing it back. Then Attila and Serkan got up and she and Dylan watched them climb a white marble staircase, Serkan holding on to the belt loop of Attila's jeans.

"Goodnight, sweeties," Dylan said.

"Get in your coffin before the sun comes up," Attila said in an ominous voice, making Serkan laugh and press his forehead against his back.

"Let's go out on the terrace," Dylan said.

"I'm tired," she said. "Let's stay here and sleep."

"C'mon," he said, standing up and pulling her by the arm. "You've gotta see this."

She blacked out a moment as he lifted her and he held her and walked her outside as the city opened up beneath them—the water, a blue mirror for the brightening sky, two oil tankers crossing beneath the bridge, the lights of the city on either side of the water, glittering like fallen constellations.

"Attila's rich—like *rich*, rich," Dylan said.

"It's beautiful," she said, but the pain was growing at her temples, a throbbing pain that was like her heart banging inside her head.

"I'm tired," she said again. "My head hurts."

"Let's sleep out here," he said, and led her to an outdoor couch next to a pool.

He laid her down and settled next to her, stroking her hair.

"Where does it hurt?"

"Here," she said.

He stroked her temples and the pain worsened.

"Try this," he said, and took her hand and pressed his fingers into the meat of her palm. He found a sore spot and pressed against it.

"Ow," she said.

"Pressure point," he said. "It's supposed to hurt."

He rubbed it some more and then his hands were on her back, stroking below her shoulder blades, pushing the edge of her shirt up her back.

"I love you," he said.

She opened her eyes and looked at him. The sky was growing lighter now and she could see the red veins in his eyes.

"I love you," he said again. "I do."

She felt her heart jump, and with the excitement her vision blurred again.

He kissed her on the lips and she kissed him back and let his hands explore her bare shoulder blades. His palms were warm against her skin and she felt each finger pressing into the muscle there. He kissed her on the neck and somehow turned her over so that his leg was across her lap. His hands moved up her belly and the feeling on her skin was electric.

"God, I love you," he said.

His thumb grazed her breast and she knew she would have to stop this soon. But her head was spinning now and her skin felt willing and the sky was growing a perfect blue and he loved her and that was all she had wanted for months, for a lifetime it seemed.

Then he was moving quickly, his hands here and then there and suddenly her bra was falling off her shoulders. Her head pounded and his hands were strong and she heard a siren screeching across the highway above her head. He was on top of her now and he said I love you and she heard him crying and then it hurt, hurt like she hadn't imagined. Above her the siren moved away, and as she jerked her head with the pain she saw a man and a dog walking away from the pool, just two shadows beneath the morning shadow of the bridge.

Chapter 49

THE NEXT MORNING SINAN REPORTED SICK TO WORK, HID
the knife he had quartered the sheep with inside the pocket of his
coat, and rode the buses with Marcus into the city. They sat in
silence—the kind of painful silence that is full of angry things need-
ing to be said—and from the window Sinan watched the folded apartment blocks along the highway. Whole kilometers of buildings had
been tossed onto their sides, broken apart like children's blocks, until
there were only buildings with collapsed roofs and then simply buildings with little holes through the red shingles and then, when they
neared the city center, buildings that seemed completely untouched.

They passed beneath the gray towers rising into the blue sky, the
cables like steel spiders' webs trapping the thin road high above the
silver water. On either side of the bridge, the Bosporus slithered like a
snake's back between the wooded hills of Europe and the hills of Asia.
The bus drove in the far left lane and Sinan peered over the edge
toward the sea below where the hull of an oil tanker parted the water
in front of it. He had always been scared of heights, and the dizzying
emptiness between roadway and sea left his head reeling—they were
neither on land nor in the air, simply riding a blade of metal fixed
precariously between slopes of solid ground. He gripped the knife in-

side his coat pocket as though it would save him should the metal collapse.

Then the bus passed into the caverns of the city with roads swerving away like spokes on a wheel to meet hundreds of other roads. They would never find İrem in such a place. She would only be found if she wanted to be, and he suddenly felt the futility of everything.

They exited the bus, caught a taxi in front of the *kokoreç* restaurants, and rode the curving street up the hill to Taksim, where Marcus paid the driver five million lira while Sinan looked away and pretended not to see. Marcus led him down a side street, away from the crowds partying on İstiklal Avenue. They ducked into arcaded alleyways, cut between people drinking beer in the midday sun, dodged rickety tables full of tourists eating fish and *mezeler*. They squeezed through crowds in the Galatasaray fish market, the people gawking at tables of fresh meat sliced open at the bellies, the gills torn open like bloody jaws. Marcus moved so quickly through the crowd, sometimes pushing people out of his way, that faces became blurs; they could have passed İrem and he would never know it.

Then they were free of the crowds, standing at an L-shaped corner of a wide street that passed in front of the fortresslike British Consulate. They followed a tall stone wall capped with razor wire, past armed guards in white kiosks, their hats falling low over their eyes so it seemed they were machines meant only to pull triggers, until Marcus stopped at the door of an old apartment within sight of Galata Tower.

"Dylan still has his key," Marcus explained.

Sinan expected to climb the circular staircase all the way to the top, but instead Marcus led him to a basement apartment where in the corner of the hallway, near the front door, stood a puddle of water that was as black as blood in the dim light. Marcus had trouble sliding the key into the lock.

"Damn lock," he said. "Rusted inside."

Sinan stared at the door, wondering what he would find on the other side, wondering what he would do when he found it. He gripped the knife in his hand and managed to slip it out of the leather with his thumb and index finger without revealing it to Marcus. Sweat beaded on his forehead and a rush of heat passed through his body.

Marcus shoved the door open. A light was on inside.

"Dylan," Marcus yelled as he strode down the hallway.

Sinan's heart beat in his ears; it pumped so loud and fast that he thought he might have a heart attack.

The apartment was small—one room sparsely furnished with brown couches, an attached kitchen, and a long hallway down which Sinan could see a bedroom and a bed with the covers turned back as though someone had recently awakened and neglected to remake it.

"They've been here," Marcus said as he came back down the hall-way. "They're gone now."

Sinan eased his grip on the knife, relieved that his strength would not be tested, but he watched the bed as if it might reveal its secrets, and as they walked out into the sun, the image of that unmade bed, the sheets thrown aside with a mocking carelessness, stoked his anger, like İrem herself had fanned the white-hot embers inside him.

Then Marcus took Sinan into a world he could never imagine existed. They searched the underground markets where kids wore black and pierced their skin with ink-stained needles and threaded silver hoops through holes in their noses. The hot passageways smelled of spilled beer and smoke, and music hissed from the open doors of music stores.

They searched dark shops, the walls lined with glowing skull posters and pentagrams and naked women with fangs for teeth. They entered a club without any windows and it was so dark inside it seemed the sun had never shone on earth. Teenagers drank and smoked at tables lit by dying candles, their pale faces turned away as though the flickering light hurt their eyes. If they found İrem here, she was already lost and there was little he could do.

Marcus screamed over the music to a man behind the bar. The

man shook his head, lit a cigarette, and blew smoke in Marcus's face. Then Sinan followed Marcus down a black corridor to the bathrooms, where he knocked open the stall doors. In one they caught a woman on the toilet and in another they found a boy with a needle stuck in his arm, his eyelids heavy, his pupils as thick and watery as honey.

They climbed the circular staircase, a helix of steps lined with melting candles, out of the basement passageway and exited through an inconspicuous door to an apartment building on a residential street. A man wearing a beard passed them, his cane clicking along the cobblestone street. Two boys kicked a soccer ball against the stone wall of a small cemetery, the turbaned headstones peeking above the masonry as though to see what the living were doing. It was the most average of streets—women leaning elbows on windowsills, lines of laundry flapping in the late morning breeze, a *simit* seller balancing a tray of bread upon his head and calling out to the hungry. Shocked, Sinan turned to look at the door they had just exited through. There was nothing special about it, nothing to indicate what was beyond its threshold. It looked like every other door on the street—faded blue with strips of paint peeling off the wood, a copper knocker shaped like a woman's hand, a tiny window with bars pressed against blackened glass. On this street alone there were fifty doors just like it and he shuddered with the thought of where those doors might lead.

Marcus said something in English and kicked a heap of trash bags stacked in the street for garbage day. The bags ripped, spilling fish bones and chicken skin into the street, and three cats appeared to gnaw on the marrow. The bones cracked in the cats' jaws.

"I don't know where they are." Marcus rubbed his temples.

"What has your son done with my daughter?" Sinan said. "What have you let him do?"

"I'm not happy about this either, Sinan," Marcus said with surprising anger. "Besides, your daughter is as much to blame for this as Dylan."

"No," Sinan said. "She wouldn't have thought of doing such a thing if you hadn't been here."

"And you'd still be sleeping in that cardboard tent near the free-way, eating rotten tomatoes and stale bread if I hadn't been here." He stopped, took a deep breath, and ran his hand through his gray hair. "The problem with you, Sinan, is that you live in a world that doesn't exist anymore. You still think women don't think for themselves. You believe there are boundaries people shouldn't cross—Americans should stay in America, Brits in England, Kurds in Kurdistan, if such a place even exists. The world isn't like that anymore, and you can't escape the world. Your daughter knows that and you don't yet, that's why she's gone, Sinan, that's why she's running around with my son. She wants to get away from you, and she's *using* Dylan to do that. So don't you for one moment think I'm happy about this, that I've caused this to happen in some way."

More cats arrived and they climbed on top of the bags, swarmed around the spilled meat, and devoured it.

"You're trying to hold on to your daughter, Sinan. And I'm trying to hold on to my son."

Later, as they passed over the bridge once again, Marcus said, without taking his eyes from the window, "Our children are not ours. That's our mistake. We think they are. It seems so for a while—a few brief years—but they aren't. They never were."

Chapter 50

WHEN SHE WOKE—TWO HOURS, THREE HOURS LATER? — the city looked like an overexposed picture, as though a flash had just gone off and blew white holes out of the center of buildings, leaving only the sharpened silver water and the black bridge arching above. Whatever blurry beauty there was in the lights the night before was replaced now with a sickening flatness of light that penetrated her stomach with nausea.

And there was blood, not a lot, but it was there, a blossom on her skirt and marks like cabbage stains on her fingertips where she had, apparently, held herself in her sleep. It was real, it had happened, and after she cried silently so as not to wake up Dylan, she pried his fingers from her skirt and pushed away his hand. Somehow she hadn't thought there would be blood, as though it were a myth told by conservative mothers to scare their daughters, a fantasy to excite boys. Yet the truth was here, and, also, the finality of it, and no regret would turn back the clock and make her say, with confidence, "No."

Dylan's shirt was off and his chest looked pale, almost like translucent salamander skin against the ugly scarring of his tattoos. His hair was caught in his mouth, his pants turned sideways on his skinny hips, and she couldn't find any beauty in him now. He looked like a stranger, like some man passed out in the morning in front of a *mey-hane,* the pores of his skin reeking of cheap *rakı.*

She pulled the edges of her blouse together, and that's when she realized she had lost a button. She panicked and dropped to the patio and searched for the circle of plastic. She patted the ground beneath the chaise lounge and ran her fingers through the grass and checked the grooves between bricks. She plunged her hands into the pool, but the water was blue and the button was blue and the sun shot blinding sparkles across the surface. She couldn't catch her breath and she slapped the ground even where she could see it wasn't there. She needed that button. She had to have it. She would sew it back on her blouse, and she would wash the skirt—even though the blood had already dried and no cold water would wash it away now—and she would wash her mother's clothes and fold her father's shirts and she would kiss İsmail with all the love of a mother. If she did everything exactly as it was supposed to be done, she could turn back the clock, erase one day and one night from existence.

Chapter 51

I̶T WAS A COLD NIGHT, A FIST OF AUTUMN AIR PRESSING DOWN. Wrapped in wool blankets the Americans gave them, they ate in silence in the tent, hiding from the eyes of the people of the camp. Even İsmail joined the silence. He solemnly ate his bowl of chicken soup and stared at the ground. Silence, though, couldn't hide the shame and anger passing between Sinan and Nilüfer. It was as though they were live wires just waiting to be touched.

Shortly after they turned out the light for the night, the door to the tent ripped open and İrem came stumbling in.

"Anne, Anne," she said. She sounded out of breath and panicked.

Sinan turned on the lantern and the tent lit a brilliant white until his eyes adjusted to the light. İrem stumbled across the tent, tripping over İsmail's legs, and tried to find her mother's arms. Nilüfer, though, had already turned her back; she did it so quickly that it seemed she had practiced for this moment. She sat like stone, her head up, staring at the canvas of the tent.

"Anne," İrem said. "Please, Anne."

But Nilüfer did not move.

"Anne, please," İrem said. "I'm sorry, Anne!"

İrem pulled at her mother's blouse, stretching the fabric to reveal

Nilüfer's shoulder. She grabbed at her mother's arms, trying to lift them, trying to get them to hold her, but Nilüfer would not move.

İrem stopped then and a sound, like the wind being sucked out of a pipe, escaped her mouth.

"Baba, please. Please listen to me," she said crawling to him. She stared into his eyes and her teeth chattered. Streaks of tears ran down her face, but these were not the tears of juvenile frustration, these were a different kind of tears, the kind Sinan never wanted to see his daughter cry. And he never would have if she had only obeyed him.

Without hesitation he took her in his arms and held her.

"Oh, Baba."

He could feel her ribs expand against his arms as she gasped for air. Her heart beat against his chest and he could feel how alive she was with pain, so full of it like a terrible disease lodged in her muscle tissue.

"*Canım,*" he said. "Calm down."

"She can't stay here," Nilüfer said.

"Close your mouth," Sinan said to Nilüfer.

"*Canım,*" he said, stroking İrem's head now, feeling the fibers of her hair beneath the rough cotton head scarf. "*Canım,* calm down."

She took in a deep breath and shook letting it out.

He stroked her cheeks, smoothed the water away with his thumbs, and pinched the drops that hung from her earlobes.

"We'll take a walk, *canım,*" he said. "Okay?"

She sucked in another breath and nodded.

He put on his coat and wrapped his wool blanket around her shoulders.

Outside, people were burning fires—a bonfire in front of the soup kitchen where the Americans gathered, fires in metal trash cans where the men smoked, and smaller fires in propane grills where the women huddled. İrem leaned against him as they walked past the tents. He wrapped his arm around her thin shoulders, feeling the bone beneath the skin. People stared at them as they passed in the street. A family pressed together around a propane stove, blue flames lighting their cheeks and reflecting in their eyes. Sinan stared back at them, trying to stab them with his eyes, trying to get them to look away, but they wouldn't.

He took her to the beach, the spot where the sand ended and the hill that separated the camp from the ruined town rose into the dark sky. They sat together near the water, İrem still clinging to his chest, holding fistfuls of his shirt.

"I loved him, Baba," she said.

He was afraid to ask what happened, because he thought he already knew the answer, but it was important to be sure.

"What did he do?"

The flames reflected in the small waves as though fires burned beneath the surface.

"I wanted him to touch me." She looked at him, her chin pressed into his stomach. Her eyes were as black as soil, beautiful and glowing with water, fantastically her own, his daughter's. It was unbelievable to him that someone with his blood running through her could be so beautiful. "I'm sorry, Baba, but I did. I wanted him to touch me, but I didn't want him to do that. I swear I didn't. I didn't know he would do that!"

She buried her head in his stomach, the wet bleeding through his shirt, her sobs echoing off the hillside with amplified intensity. The firelight caught the edge of her neck, the skin exposed where it led to her chin, and he could see her larynx jump as she cried. Understanding what she meant, he looked up at the sky and saw a faint star, just one dim point of light through the orange smoke and fire reflections. She was ruined. She had tempted the boy and he had ruined her. The pain caught in his throat and he thought he was choking. She had ruined him, his name, everything. What is a man who cannot control his own daughter? What is such a man? Nothing.

He shoved her away and his hands grew minds of their own—his fingers desired to choke her, his knuckles were desperate to break her nose. She had soiled İsmail's name, too, and the only way he could make it clean again was to destroy her. She had forced him to this, given him no choice, and for that reason alone he wanted to rip the life out of her.

She tried to grab on to his legs but he kicked her away.

"You're not my daughter," he said.

She was on her knees, her arms outstretched to him.

"Please, Baba! I thought I wanted to leave you. I thought he would make me happier, but I was wrong."

He needed to rip her hair out, had to knock her teeth down her throat. He wanted to kiss her, rock her to sleep, lay a blanket over her tired body and let her rest.

"I love you," she said. "I want to be with you and Anne."

"You're not my daughter." It was the most horrible thing he could say, so horrible yet he still spat the words at her.

She lunged at him, but he slapped her to the sand.

"Leave," he said, his voice shaking. "I will *not* see you again."

"I can't," she said, getting to her feet again.

He reached into his pocket and held the knife in his hand. "Leave," he said, his voice growing weaker. "You *won't* go back with me."

She glanced at his hand in the pocket.

"Baba," she said, her voice as soft and as distant as though she were falling off to sleep. "Baba. You wouldn't."

He stared at her, grinding his teeth to stay strong, the handle of the knife gripped firmly in his palm.

She looked him up and down, as though he were a stranger just presented to her, and then she turned her back and stumbled through her first step. Recovering her balance, she walked down the beach, past the orange smudges of fire smoke, until very slowly, like a person becoming a ghost, she disappeared.

Chapter 52

BEACH PEBBLES ROLLED BENEATH HER FEET BEFORE WAVES sucked them out to sea. She watched the wet line where it met the dry beach, watched as the sea froth touched the outline of the previous wave and created a new line, one farther up the beach, one that crawled higher up her ankle with each swell. Water in her eyes blurred the dock lights and stars, but she didn't cry anymore. She was surprised by her silence, intrigued by her lack of pain—it was exactly like something had snapped inside her, some sinuous connection between mind and heart.

Behind her she heard footsteps, the quick landslide of rocks shoved aside by feet. She didn't turn around and she didn't speed up, she didn't even feel her shoulders rise, waiting for the blow to her head, and she smiled to herself with the recognition of this strange new freedom.

The feet drew closer, a splash followed by another.

"İrem."

A kicking of pebbles.

"İrem," and she recognized her brother's voice.

When she turned around, he was nearly to her, a full-out sprint as though he were chasing a ball passed behind a defender.

She bent to her knees and he flew into her like he was trying to tackle her.

"Come back," he said. He held on to her forearms as though bracing to tug her back to the tent.

"No," she said.

"Baba's crying," he said.

"I know."

"He'll forgive you," İsmail said. "He's just mad right now."

She touched his forehead, the way she used to when he was a baby to check his temperature. For a moment she imagined him years younger—the line of snot coming to a bubbling rest on his top lip, his hot head resting against her bare arm, his little boy fingers holding on to her pinky.

She wanted to tell him what was in their father's pocket, but he was a child and she wanted him to remain so as long as possible.

"They love you, İsmail," is all she said.

She kissed him on the forehead. His eyes were huge, two round planets hovering between eyelids.

"It's okay," she said. "I'm just going for a walk."

Chapter 53

THIS TIME HE WOULD USE THE KNIFE.

All that night he stood outside Marcus's tent and waited for Dylan to come out. He would catch him on his way to the toilets, stab him in the dark while everyone slept, slice open his throat so he would gasp and gasp and gasp until it was finished.

He stood there in the shadows and waited until the air was filled with snores and the Dipper slid behind the black mountains. He stood there in the cold, his heart still pumping hard, his hands sweating, until a ribbon of red, like an open wound, appeared in the sky.

But there was no movement in the tent and when the sun was well above the mountaintops and people had risen to eat their breakfast, he realized that neither Dylan nor Marcus was in the camp anymore. Even if they were, Sinan would have to kill the boy now in broad daylight, in front of people's children. He felt more than willing to do so, even savored the idea, but the American and his son were gone.

"WHERE IS SHE?" NILÜFER said when he returned.

İsmail was wrapped to the neck in his bag, but his eyes were open, watching Sinan.

"Gone."

"Where?"

"She's gone, Nilüfer."

She looked at him closely, checking his eyes to see if it were true. She turned and stared at the white wall of the tent a moment, holding a flute of tea to her lips but not drinking. Then with firm precision she slapped the glass against the floor of the tent so that it made a muffled pop. She sat for a moment with her flattened palm against the broken glass before picking every piece off the floor, placing them in the palm of her other hand like they were splinters of priceless jewels.

İsmail watched Sinan for a moment, his eyes unblinking, and then turned and tugged the bag over his head.

Chapter 54

S HE DIDN'T KNOW HOW FAR SHE WALKED, BUT SOMETIME IN the afternoon she made a decision and once that decision was made it was as though all her organs stopped pumping and her body felt quiet.

She climbed the hill that led to the highway and stood with the men who waited for the bus into the city. They smoked and talked while cars blurred by. She noticed one man watching her, his eyes falling on the spot of blood on her skirt. She untied her scarf and handed it to him.

"Here," she said. "This is yours."

He wouldn't take it. He turned away and smoked his cigarette.

She laughed and dropped it at his feet.

She didn't take the bus, but instead hailed a taxi.

"Beyoğlu," she said.

"Beyoğlu?" the taxi driver said.

"Yes, to meet my husband. Hurry, please, I'll be late and he'll be angry."

The man looked at her strangely, but threw the car in gear and sped down the highway.

She rolled down the window and felt the wind in her hair and watched the fractured buildings of the broken towns become the red roofs of the suburbs until the city exploded in yellow and pink high-rises, their glass windows shining in the sunlight.

The taxi followed the highway around Camlica coming into Üsküdar and she could see the water, a huge gash through the middle of the city. The strait glistened like a river of silver sparkles. It looked very beautiful to her suddenly, a distant, separate beauty, as though she were watching it on a movie screen.

The taxi came around a hill and in the distance, just poking out over a rise, she caught a glimpse of the bridge towers. Tomorrow was a military holiday and the span was draped with red flags, the banners furling in the wind. The tower disappeared again behind a hill, and her stomach turned. Her heart skipped strangely and she couldn't stop shaking her legs.

She noticed the cab fare, the yellow lights counting out thirty million now. The driver's eyes filled the rearview mirror. She didn't have even one lira on her.

She bit her fingernails and tried to calm down.

Then the taxi barreled down the grade that led to the bridge. Her view of the towers was unobscured now—gray and graceless, standing like cement gates. Cars rushed on either side of the taxi, just inches away, raced down the grade toward the bridge growing larger and uglier in the windshield. She bit through her nail to the skin on her thumb but the pain didn't matter.

She remembered the lyrics to the Radiohead song she had loved.

Ben burada değilim. Bunlar başıma gelmiyor. Ben burada değilim.

The music echoed in her head, the floating guitars, the undulating bass.

I'm not here. This isn't happening.

The music was like the soundtrack to a movie and that's how she began to imagine this. This was her movie. She had the lead role. The audience would cry when she did this. She imagined her mother and father in a plush theater, dabbing their eyes in front of the brightly lit screen.

Kısa bir süre içinde gitmiş olacağım.

The cut in the hill opened up to the mouth of the bridge. She could see the line of cars at the tollbooths on the east-side lanes and beyond that the Bosporus like a sheet of polished metal between hills.

"Stop here," she said.

The taxi driver looked at her through the mirror.

"You're meeting your husband here?" he said.

"Yes."

He looked at the road and then back at her. His eyebrows nearly poked him in the eyes.

"It's illegal," he said. "You have to wait until the other side."

And then the taxi was on the bridge and she thought it would be impossible. That's not how the movie ended. She sang the lyrics in her head again, the drifting bass, the levitating strings. She wanted to float; she wanted to be weightless.

They passed the first tower and she watched the water, blue now, ripe as a bruise, infinite as the sky, flow beneath the bridge. The desolation crept back into her. She couldn't do this. She had made a decision and now she wouldn't be able to do it.

Then up ahead red brake lights flashed and the traffic slowed.

The driver watched her through the rearview.

In a little while, I'll be gone.

Traffic was coming to a stop just on the other side of the rise in the middle of the bridge. The taxi slowed and the driver changed to the middle lane of traffic, right between an Ulas delivery truck and a *dolmuş* full of passengers.

The taxi stopped.

A motorcycle raced between the taxi and the delivery truck, nearly shearing off the driver's side-view mirror. The driver stuck his head out the window and screamed at the motorcycle.

At that moment, she threw open the door and jumped onto the road. The edge of the bridge was just a few meters away. She ran around the delivery truck and almost got hit by a moving bus. As she dodged the bumper, she glanced behind and saw the driver getting out of the taxi and running after her.

She had one lane left to cross. She could see the edge and the huge bolts that held the cables in place. She looked over her shoulder and the driver was closer now, gaining.

"Stop," she heard him say.

But she wasn't stopping now. He would hold her by the arm and drag her back to the taxi and take her to the other side.

She squeezed between the bumpers of two cars.

"Don't," the driver yelled.

She lifted herself over the short wall and held on to the cable. Beneath her was nothing but blue water, deep and formless. It looked like she might fall forever. She let go and for a few moments she was weightless, tumbling like a bird whose wings had been clipped. The only sound was the wind in her face.

Part Three

Chapter 55

THE NEXT DAY, SINAN MET THE POLICE AT THE BEŞIKTAŞ ferry landing. The sea was choppy with the wakes of ferries docking and disembarking, and the hull of the boat slapped against rubber pontoons. He fell dizzy, and a policeman held him beneath his right shoulder and helped him into the boat. As soon as they left the dock, speedboats filled with reporters and cameramen followed, their lenses sparkling in the sunlight like little round planets fallen to earth.

"We can't do anything about them," a policeman said. "They're vultures. I'm sorry."

Atop the cabin of the boat a rotating beacon slapped Sinan across the face.

"Can you turn that off?" he said, motioning to the emergency light.

"Yes, *abi*," the policeman said. "Of course."

The policeman called to the captain and the captain switched off the light. The policeman offered him a Maltepe, but Sinan refused the cigarette and stared at the water.

Everything was incredibly bright—the sunlight flashing off the water, the white of the boat's hull, the endless, ugly blue of the sky. The light burned a hole into his brain, but he watched the water, scanned the coastline, double-checked wood drifting on the surface, and every few seconds he had to cover his eyes to stop the burning.

A young policeman stood swaying with the wakes on the bow of the boat, holding a long silver pole with a hooked end. It looked like a gaffing hook, like something fishermen used to stab through the bellies of large fish they had to haul inside the boat. He wanted to tell the man to put that hook away, but his stomach was roiling now and he couldn't find his voice. The policeman who offered him a cigarette seemed to notice Sinan's staring and called out to the man with the hook. They argued for a moment, before the hook man fastened the instrument to a rack on the bow.

Birds gathered together on the surface of the water and formed the shape of a human body before becoming birds again; a pod of dolphins broke the surface, their gray backs like elbows piercing the skin of water; fish jumped and for a moment a head seemed to rise.

Soon—how long Sinan did not know—the boat bobbed into the shadow of the bridge. From here the bridge didn't look so tall. İrem could survive a fall from that height, he was sure of it. It was only water, after all. The captain cut the engine and scanned the water's surface with binoculars. With the engine off, Sinan heard the rush of cars on the bridge—a mechanical hum, like a river of metal parts flowing over steel rocks; that rushing had never stopped, not even as İrem jumped.

Jellyfish rose around the hull of the boat before sinking into the green darkness again, their bodies appearing and reappearing like pale, severed heads. Trash gathered in heaps of foamy bubbles where gulls foraged for scraps, sending up clouds of flies.

The powerboats circled the police boat. Men with huge cameras dangling from their shoulders crowded the decks and pointed lenses toward the water. Sinan saw two men pass a cigarette between them, one said something to the other, and they both laughed, their white teeth shining in the harsh light. If he could reach them across the hulls of the boats, he'd kill them, he'd stab them right now in front of the police.

"The current's stronger to the north," called the policeman standing on the bow. He motioned his hand downstream toward the shore.

"Beylerbeyi," the captain said. "Got it."

The engine growled to life and they crossed beneath the span, past the disgustingly ornate summer palace, moving up the waterway toward the Black Sea. They would never find her; there was too much water, too much darkness beneath the boat they couldn't search. She would not be buried in twenty-four hours; she would not be buried ever. And for a moment he panicked because he could not remember what his daughter looked like. An image flashed in his brain—her eyes, her nose, the shape of her head beneath the head scarf—but he could not remember her hair. Was it straight or curly? He couldn't remember her legs. Were they thin and brown, thick and pale? Did her belly button stick out the way it did when she was a child?

Then a huge oil tanker came plowing through the middle of the waterway, its faded red hull towering above the police boat, the bow sending up three-foot waves that swelled and broke into whitecaps. The ship was monstrous, as long as three soccer fields, as tall as a cliff, and the engine roared ahead of it, thundering out a warning. For a moment it seemed they would be run over by the ship and he was ready for it, hopeful even that the bow might rip through the middle of this boat and grind it into bits of wood and spilled fuel and drowning men. But the bow passed and the waves smacked the hull of the police boat, lifting it into the air and dropping it back down with a slap. He grasped the railing and closed his eyes to keep the sickness from rising.

When he opened his eyes, he saw something bobbing on the surface of a wake. The white shape was sucked into the vortex of the passing ship and then shot out on top of the next cresting wave, the red bow pushing it away as though it were driftwood. The first thing he recognized was a leg and in the thrust of the wave the leg seemed to kick. Then an arm broke the surface of the water and splashed back through as though swimming. And that's what he thought was happening—İrem was swimming toward the boat, her limbs stiffly rising and falling, breaking the water and sinking back through. She seemed utterly animated and he thought, for a brief horrible, hopeful moment, that he was once again witnessing the grace of God.

"We've got her," the policeman on the bow said, standing and pointing out toward the swimming body.

It *was* a miracle. There she was swimming toward the boat, her head turned to the side for air, her feet throwing up little splashes, her elbows bending and stretching in awkward strokes. Then the wake subsided as the tanker passed and she dove beneath the surface of the water, the bottoms of her feet waving at him as she disappeared.

"She's under, she's under," the young policeman yelled.

The captain cut the motor and yelled to the powerboats with the photographers to do the same. The water rippled and flattened and rippled again. The sea here was dark, deep in the center of the passageway, and in the placid places between ripples he could momentarily see his reflection before it was torn apart.

Then a few meters from the boat her pale head emerged, her mouth releasing a watery spit of air.

"İrem!" he called out, and flashbulbs burst from the powerboats, their sparks electrifying the water.

The policemen scrambled to the edge of the hull, the young one holding the gaffing hook out over the surface of the water.

"Oh, thank God!"

But then the rest of her body surfaced—her shoulders first, dragging her arms, one broken sideways like a piece of timber so that the palm of her hand rested between her shoulder blades—and the realization that she was dead blew a hole in his stomach and he retched into the sea.

The flashbulbs went off like handheld explosions, the clicking shutters like chattering insects.

Her flowery blouse still clung to her torso, but her hips emerged as white as whalebone. Her legs came last—so thin, so like a little girl's, and pink along her hips and knees as though they had been sunburned. He wanted to look away, wanted to tell the others to look away, but the cameras kept clicking and the policemen leaned out over the edge of the boat, reaching toward her body. The wakes caused by the powerboats jockeying for position spun her body around and pushed her right leg toward his hands. He reached to grab her ankle, but at that moment, the young policeman with the gaffing hook caught her around the waist and hauled her toward the boat.

"Don't," Sinan screamed. "Don't!"

The man shook with Sinan's voice and dropped the hook into the water, releasing her body.

Leaning out over the water, he took hold of his daughter's ankle. Her skin was slick with salt and spilled engine oil. When the young policeman reached for her hips—their nakedness shocking in the light, the hips of a woman, not his little girl—Sinan pushed him out of the way and, alone, lifted her body up.

Chapter 56

T HE SHROUD WAS GREEN, THE COLOR OF HEAVEN, BUT IT
didn't matter—İrem would not go to Paradise. *Whoever purposely
throws himself from a mountain and kills himself will be in the Fire
falling down into it and abiding therein perpetually forever.* This
phrase, locked in his brain for years—some learning in Arabic he had
kept secreted away from his childhood education at the madrassa—
repeated in his head. Since he pulled her from the water, all through
the paperwork he had to sign at the morgue, as he held Nilüfer while
she choked on her own disbelief, and now, as they lowered İrem's
pine casket into the hole in the ground, this phrase would not leave
him.

The men scrambled on either side of the box, releasing the ropes
through gloved palms to lower the casket. *God is great*, read the gold
lettering on the shroud. *God is great.* And terrible. And unforgiving.
The box was so tiny, so incredibly thin, like a jewel case, really, like
something you hid wedding gifts in.

The box settled into the hole and the men pulled their ropes loose
and coiled them around their shoulders before picking up the shovels.
He seemed to be watching this through a dirty pane of glass—a night-
mare from which he might awake. But he felt İsmail's hot hand holding his. He heard Nilüfer's wailings, a sound like someone pulling her

lungs through her mouth. He wanted to tell her to shut up, wanted to tell her she had no right to give up her daughter one minute and mourn her the next. But it is one thing to give up a child who lives and another to lose a child to death. In death she becomes more your child, more a limb of your own body, and her death is also your own.

Nothing made sense. The sky was a brilliant blue, gorgeous in its depth and absolute perfection of color. The birds sang in the trees. Roses, a garden of them, bloomed from the center of sarcophagi, and he imagined their roots grabbing the rib cages of the dead, their thin fingers shooting up through soil and blooming red to laugh at mourners, as if to say, "Look what's become of your loved ones." The sky should have been raging with clouds and rain, the flowers should have been nothing but knotted thorns.

Nothing made sense in this world—Nilüfer's crying, the numbness in his chest. He should have felt more. He had no heart, yet he could hear it beating in his head.

"Oh, it's the worst thing," he heard someone say. "The worst."

He killed her; that was certain. She jumped, but, really, he pushed her off. It would have been better had she died in the quake. It would have been better—though he would not have been able to live with himself—if he *had* killed her. She would enter Paradise then, but not this way, not now.

In love you try to kill a daughter to save her.

It didn't make sense. None of this.

The Americans, the ones who caused this, bought the tombstone, laid huge wreaths of flowers across the casket. They stood on the edge of the gathered crowd, dabbing their eyes with tissue, the women covering their heads as though they were Muslim.

The people of the camp stood with their heads bowed, mourning the death of a girl whose name they would not utter, today or ever again. Never speak the name of a suicide; treat them as though they never existed yet cry for them.

The sky above him began to spin and Nilüfer's screams became distant and he felt himself falling. The treetops toppled in on him and the world became a small circle surrounded by darkness until the circle disappeared and he could only hear the people around him gasping. Hands pushed into his back and propped up his shoulders, and in the darkness he felt himself lean against men's chests.

"Careful, careful," a voice said. "*Abi*, Sinan, can you hear me?"

He could, but he didn't want to. He wanted the darkness to overtake his ears.

"Sinan."

Leave me alone.

"Get some water."

Please. Leave me alone.

But the light came back into his eyes and all the shapes of the world filled his mind, and when he looked up at the faces looking back at him, there was the strangest thing of all, the thing that made the least sense: Marcus Bey bent toward him, pouring the coolness of water upon his lips.

FOR FIVE DAYS AFTER the funeral, people delivered food to the tent. And for five days the food sat in the tent rotting, filling up the space with a sickening smell, until Nilüfer finally carried each plate away to the trash. A line of people came to offer their condolences, not one of them mentioning Irem's name, simply saying sorry for your loss and leaving.

Sometime during the five days, two policemen came to question him, their hats in their hands. The younger policeman with a mustache that hung over his top lip asked the questions, and the older one, the one with the wrinkled shirt, ate from the plate of pastry that had been sitting in the corner gathering flies for days.

"Was there anything upsetting her?"

"She was sad because of the earthquake."

"People say she was with an American boy?"

"No."

"People say he was a Satanist? Ran around Kadiköy and Taksim in the bars and tattoo parlors. Someone said a half-dozen cats were found with their necks slit? They say—pardon me, *abi*—they say she might have been pregnant?"

Sinan looked at the man a long time and the man, embarrassed by his own question, looked at the ground.

"She was sad about the earthquake," he said. "She was scared another one would come."

The policeman nodded solemnly. "We all are."

On the sixth day, after everyone else had made their appearances, just when Sinan thought he wouldn't have to shake another hand or thank another person for their words, Marcus came to the tent carrying a loaf of bread. Sinan didn't have the energy to refuse him, and as soon as he entered, Nilüfer left, taking İsmail by the hand, and glancing daggers Sinan's way.

"I imagine you're not hungry," Marcus said, setting aside the bread.

Sinan said nothing. Marcus sat down and looked at the floor as though he were in great pain.

"I'm so sorry about İrem."

Sinan was thankful to hear someone utter her name, and, for a moment, it lightened him. He almost thanked the American.

"I want to help you," Marcus said. "We believe in the same God, but the way we think about Him matters." He wrung his hands together and bit at a thumbnail. "She was a child, Sinan. She didn't understand what she was giving up."

"Where's your son?"

Marcus lifted his hand and ran his fingers through his hair.

"New Hampshire. I sent him to his aunt's."

Sinan remembered the snow, the American wife's dream of going back for a dog.

"I know what the Qur'an says about suicide, Sinan. Christ was a man, too, so he understands a man's suffering. That's the difference. He'll forgive İrem."

"Your son raped my daughter."

"No, no," Marcus said, throwing his head and shoulders back, assuming the posture of certainty. "He wouldn't do that."

"He raped İrem and that's why she jumped. Does your Jesus forgive such things?"

"That's not what happened," he hesitated, "and you know it."

"Keep your son in America," Sinan said. "If I see him again, I *will* kill him."

Chapter 57

IN THE DAYS FOLLOWING İREM'S DEATH SINAN CONTEMPLATED his own. In his mind he replayed the look on her face when she realized what he held in his hand—the way her eyes blinked with shock and then froze on him as though she were already dead. Why was it easier—he asked himself countless times—to hold the knife instead of his daughter? He never intended to use the knife, or at least that's what he told himself. He wanted to believe it was İrem's fault, that she misunderstood his actions on the beach, but then he remembered the knife in his hand and he knew she had seen what she had seen. If he could take it back, those few seconds of blinding anguish, he would take her in his arms and parade her in the streets of the camp as his beautiful, worthy daughter. God could judge him, but not these people, not these people anymore.

It would have been easier to give up, to swim out into the sea and never swim back, to drain the blood from his wrists, but what saved Sinan was İsmail's silence. The boy would not speak. In fact, he barely opened his mouth at all except to eat a bite of food, push the plate away, and draw strange, dark scenes in his coloring book.

By the end of the sixth day after the funeral, Sinan was afraid the boy would waste away, and it wasn't until he began to worry about İsmail that he knew he would survive İrem's death. İsmail's arms—

already skinny—were as thin as ropes, his ribs pushed against the skin of his chest. His skin was pasty and occasionally his gums bled. Sinan tried talking to him. He tried kicking the soccer ball with him. He bought him a toy gun from a Gypsy merchant selling plastic wares, but nothing would get the boy to speak.

"Eat," Nilüfer said that night, forcing a spoonful of rice into his mouth only to watch him spit it out into the palm of his hand and place it on his plate. Since İrem's death, she wouldn't let the boy out of her sight for even a minute. He couldn't play soccer with the boys or visit the school tent. She held his hand when she walked him to the water closet and held his hand again when returning to the tent. She held his hand everywhere, even sometimes at night while the boy fell asleep.

"Eat," she tried again. He turned his cheek and Nilüfer smudged the rice into his skin and smeared it around his lips. But he would not take it. He simply wiped his face clean with his hands and rolled the remaining rice off his fingers.

Carrefour allowed Sinan two unpaid weeks off, but he refused to take the second week. He couldn't sit around this camp, replaying the memories in his head, trying to figure out the maze of mistakes he had made leading up to that day. He would go crazy.

The first day back Yilmaz Bey brought him tea on his breaks, patted him on the shoulder as he made his rounds of the store, and offered to have Sinan's family over to his house in Bebek for dinner. Even after a week, İrem's picture was on the front page of the papers, and when the manager realized this, he apologized to Sinan and had all the papers removed from the bins. When Sinan got home, he found İsmail buried deep in his sleeping bag, the fabric pulled over his head so that only a few strands of hair stuck out at the top.

"He'll kill himself, too," Nilüfer said, her eyes rimmed red from lack of sleep, her lips thin and chapped with worry.

"İsmail," Sinan said, patting the bulge beneath the fabric. "İsmail, sit up."

The boy pushed back the sleeping bag, revealing his head. He lay there looking up at Sinan, his eyes glassy and tired.

"Sit up," Sinan said.

İsmail did, but he let his head droop.

Sinan ran his hands through the boy's hair, but İsmail jerked his head away.

"Son," he said. "I miss İrem, too. She's gone, though, and nothing we can do will bring her back."

İsmail said nothing. He bit his bottom lip and looked at the floor.

"You loved her, I know. I loved her, too."

İsmail looked at him, his eyes full of a question, his lips parted as though ready to ask it. Please don't ask where she's gone, Sinan thought. Please don't ask that question.

İsmail knitted his brow as though something sharp had sliced at his stomach. The boy looked closely at Sinan's eyes—too close—and seemed to analyze his whole face before falling back into the bag and covering his head.

"It's okay to be sad," Sinan said. "But it will get better." But he felt like he was lying.

Later that night, after they had turned out the light, Sinan heard the rustling of İsmail's sleeping bag. It became quiet again, but he had the feeling he was being watched. He looked in his son's direction and found İsmail sitting up in the dark, the boy staring directly at him.

"What's wrong, İsmail?"

The boy didn't say anything but kept staring.

"İsmail?"

"Nothing, Baba," he said, and lay back down.

AT FAJR PRAYER THE next morning, Sinan found the ritual comforting, found that the prayers, spoken as easily as his own name, calmed him. There was nothing but God. God had a plan for everything. Nothing, no matter how horrible, was accidental—it just seemed so to us.

It was payday at Carrefour, but the check only came to fifty-six million. No one paid you to mourn your daughter. He needed nineteen million more, just nineteen, but he would have to wait another two weeks.

He went through the motions at evening prayer—the washings, the recitations, the prostrations—and he noticed how his back hurt, the way the muscles in the palms of his hands ached. He felt each tensed tendon, every tender strand in his body. The worst of it, though, was that while he recited the suras, when he was supposed to be focused on God, he kept seeing the American boy's face. He was out there somewhere, in some snowy American landscape, his face smug with the knowledge that he had taken İrem.

The men were gathered again in front of the mosque, and whatever quiet he was able to manage during prayer was ruined immediately. The crowd was larger this time, and Sinan sat and listened even after he had pulled on his shoes.

"The government lets these people stay here and preach to you," the mayor was saying, "because Ecevit and the others in Ankara don't want you thinking about how they've failed you. They want you mad at these Americans and not them."

The crowd grew louder, the men playing backgammon suspending their game, the ones quietly smoking under the plane tree standing up to hear.

"In Yalova—Do you know this?" the mayor continued. "Have you heard? The military is building houses for the people while you sit here in tents. I don't have to tell you that it's because the politicians have summer homes there."

Sinan saw Kemal light a cigarette and spit a leaf of tobacco on the ground. Kemal had not spoken to him since İrem's death. He hadn't even offered condolences. Sinan wasn't sure if it was because he was ashamed of himself for making the suggestion or ashamed of Sinan for being so weak as to allow his daughter to take her own life. It didn't matter. Sinan didn't want to speak to the man anyway.

"You just want our votes in the fall," Malik said. He had been hidden in the crowd, but he stepped forward when he spoke. "You have a summer home in Yalova."

"I do."

"And a mistress."

The mayor's face grew red and he played with his tie.

"Is that where you've been these two months?"

"I was in Ankara—"

"Ankara!" Malik threw his cigarette to the ground.

"Winter is coming," the mayor said. "Do you know what they have planned for you? Square cubicles made of particle board and aluminum."

"Shut up and do something," Malik said. "Get these people out of here."

"It's not that easy," the mayor said. "They're guests of the government."

Malik laughed, the bitter laugh Sinan remembered from the men in the village, the laugh that was like releasing steam from a boiling pot.

Finishing the loop on his laces, Sinan stood to go.

"You're just another stupid politician," Malik said. "Using God to get votes." Malik caught Sinan's eyes as he walked past the crowd. "My brother's lost his daughter."

A sharp pain stabbed Sinan's gut and his heart began to thump in his ear and he stopped to listen.

"I've lost my son, and you're just standing here talking. You'd be more useful if you were selling oranges."

"The Fazilat party will be here soon to help you, my friends. We'll kick the Americans out and *we'll* feed you."

İmam Ali came out of the mosque and the men quieted. He embraced the mayor and kissed him on both cheeks. The mayor accepted the greeting but his face was red and there was sweat on his brow. He pulled a scarf from his back pocket and wiped the beads of water away.

"Don't worry about the Americans," the İmam said. "They cannot change you unless you want to be changed."

"But *Efendi*," Malik said. "Already little Uğur has let them splash water over his head. He wears a cross around his neck now."

"Since when have you cared about Gypsy children," İmam Ali said, in a voice filled more with the deflated hiss of disappointment than the bite of condemnation. "The Qur'an is the truth," the İmam said. "The truth will win, because it is the truth and people will recognize it as such. Do you make these Americans out to be stronger than the truth?"

Some of the men looked at the ground in embarrassment, but Malik clicked his tongue in disgust.

"They take advantage of us," he said.

"Ignore them, Malik," the İmam said. "Your struggle is inside yourself. If these people scare you, then it's your own doubt that makes you weak."

But Sinan knew that wasn't true. A daughter cannot fight for herself, a son cannot defend himself against his innocence. İmam Ali looked small and fragile, his voice was strong but his words were weak. He dressed as an old cleric, his robes yellowed from years of use, his skullcap frayed at the edges. He seemed ancient and out of date, a man too lost in thought to understand action.

The men argued with one another until the mayor spoke again.

"Please," the mayor said. "Brothers, please." The men quieted. "İmam Ali is wise. He understands God better than I. But I understand men. When men make our own struggle more difficult, then those men interfere with our path to God. The straight path is difficult enough to follow."

The men erupted with anger and Sinan turned to leave. İmam Ali tried to quiet them, but even as Sinan turned the corner to his tent row he could hear the rumble of their voices.

FOR THE NEXT FEW days, rumors raced through the camp. The Christians had baptized four orphans, brainwashed them so badly that the children even forgot their names. They were given new names, Western names, and had been sent to America to be adopted by people in Texas. The Christians put pork in the soup-kitchen meals without telling anyone, a sabotage meant to soil the souls of the faithful. At one of their evening bonfires, three children had seen the Christians burn pages from the Qur'an, sending God's words rising into the night sky with the sparks.

The rumors, as ridiculous as they seemed at first, were difficult to ignore. Each time Sinan heard a new one—after prayer, while walking to work, stepping out of his tent to use the water closet—the rumor gathered the strength of the previous ones and was lifted upon a wave of anger that made him want to believe them, until, finally, they began to feel like the truth. Didn't the Americans kill his father? Didn't they kill his daughter? Didn't Marcus try to make him a Christian?

Then one night the whole camp was presented with evidence to prove the rumors. It was after dinner when everyone sat outside their tents, taking tea and smoking cigarettes before the evening cold set in. Sinan was outside with İsmail, trying to get the boy to kick the soccer ball, when the Armenian paraded Uğur, the Gypsy boy, down the street. The boy, who before the earthquake had worn nothing but dirty sweatpants with a funny-looking mouse sewn into the pocket and an equally dirty plaid button-down, now wore clean jeans and a red American basketball jersey with a bull's face on the chest. He had new white shoes on his feet and he walked as carefully as possible, avoiding all puddles and trying not to kick up any dust. And around his neck, hung a gold cross, just as Kemal Bey had said.

Sinan had never seen the boy smile, either before or after his parents' death. He was simply a thin brown thing that foraged in the trash, gathering cardboard and wood to fortify the walls of his squatter's house. Now, though, he smiled widely, his little boy cheeks pushing his eyes into creases. He looked back and forth at the people as he came down the street, flashing his wide grin at them as if to say, *Look what I've got. Look what you can have, too.*

"Stupid Roma," Ziya Bey, the man next door, said.

But everyone watched him—his brand-new clothes, his expensive shoes, his gold necklace—and in a way he didn't seem so stupid anymore. İsmail stopped to watch him, too. The sun hung low in the sky and the light glinted off the necklace. İsmail stared without blinking at the Gypsy boy until the Armenian led Uğur around the corner of the street and out of sight.

"Go inside," Sinan said.

İsmail ignored him.

"İsmail," he said. "Go inside."

The boy did, but not before he leaned on one foot to see around the corner.

Chapter 58

HE WOULD NOT LOSE HIS SON, TOO.

On Sunday, when he had the morning off, he and İsmail took the ferries into the city to visit Eyüp Camii, the holiest mosque in İstanbul. İsmail still wouldn't speak, nearly ten days now of silence. Sinan's stomach turned at the thought of traveling into that city again. So, the two of them sat silent together in the hull of the ferry, listening to the *clang* and *ping* of the engine. Outside, the fog was as thick as curdled milk and water droplets streaked across the window.

When they caught the last ferry from Yalova to İstanbul and he saw the opening to the Bosporus, Sinan lowered his head and stared at the floor and he didn't raise it again until the boat bumped the dock in Sirkeci. Even then, as he held on to İsmail's shoulders in the rushing crowd, he would not look over his shoulder toward the bridge.

In Sirkeci, men opened doors to groceries, splashing buckets of water on the cement sidewalks and sweeping away the grime before laying out the produce of the day. He remembered the simple pleasure of washing down his square of pavement in front of the *bakkal* and he swore if he could have that life back again he would never complain.

In the windows of a pastry shop, a woman placed colorful cakes under bright lights that made the glazed fruit shine like jewels. The *pastanesi* was famous in İstanbul and Sinan stopped to show the boy. The woman waved to İsmail and offered him a pistachio madeleine. İsmail took the sweet bread but he stood there in the shop, the bread between forefinger and thumb, his hand dangling at his side. The woman handed one to Sinan, but stared at the boy, apparently wondering what was wrong with him. Sinan bit into the madeleine and raved about the taste, but İsmail simply set the cookie on the silver tray next to the register and walked out.

The fog lifted and they walked the thin, twisting streets draped in the morning shadows of leaning Ottoman buildings, their ornamented balconies and cracked floral tiles radiating the morning sunlight. Here the sky above them was just a mean sliver of gray, and he wondered how people could live their whole lives in such a place. Living here was like being pressed between cement slabs. In Yeşilli the mud huts of the village sat low to the earth, the walls curving from the ground like something sculpted out of the soil. And the sky was towering, as though a million paper-thin layers of blue had been draped atop one another all the way up to Heaven. It made a man feel small and that was a good thing.

At Sobacılar Avenue, they had to wait to cross and when they did they could only make it to an island in the center of the street. There they were swallowed up by traffic, the blur of cars and taxis racing by on either side, the dark smoke of bus exhaust blowing into their hair, and pop music blaring from passing windows. When there was another break, Sinan lifted İsmail into his arms and ran, his body swaying awkwardly, to the other side before the next wave overtook the street.

They crowded into a bus packed with covered women heading to the open market in Fatih, and İsmail squeezed in among a crowd of soft hips and long skirts. Every few hundred feet the bus stopped to let someone off or take someone on or both. The broad street ran beside the Golden Horn where the waterfront was lined with hulls of rusting ships, and, this morning, even before the heat of the day, the water stank of rotting fish, leaking oil. It took the bus forty minutes to cover the four-kilometer trip, and by the time they reached Eyüp it was nearly eleven A.M.

They passed the wooden stands of trinket sellers and pushed through a large group of tourists standing in the middle of the street. And then, suddenly, there it was, the gleaming white marble of the mosque, the place where the Prophet's friend, Eyüp Ensari, was buried.

Since arriving in Gölcük from Yeşilli years ago, when İsmail was just barely walking, Sinan had wanted to visit Eyüp Camii, but it was a long way to come, and being at the store from seven in the morning until ten in the evening every day had not allowed it. He had decided it would wait until a day worthy of a sort of pilgrimage and this was that day. He wasn't sure if he would ever make it to Mecca; he would if he ever had the means to do so, and it would be a profound disappointment in his life if he didn't, but now such a trip seemed impossible. This was probably as close to the Prophet as he would ever come.

"Look at how tall the dome is, İsmail." He touched the back of İsmail's neck, right where the hair met the soft skin. "Do you know why they make it so tall?"

İsmail looked at him, but his lips didn't part and he didn't shake his head. He just looked and that was enough for now.

"So God can fit inside." He tickled the boy's neck, but İsmail stepped aside and looked back at the mosque, his eyes squinting against the yellow sun.

The white bricks of the mosque glowed in the midday light, rising above the courtyard in a series of domes and windows that was like light itself being created. The courtyard was busy with people—women dressed in full hijab, their bodies like black apparitions against the white building; men in skullcaps rolling up their sleeves to wash at the ablutions fountain; still other men seated at a café beneath the shade of a huge plane tree, smoking cigarettes and drinking tea from tulip-shaped glasses cupped in the palms of their hands. But for all the people, the place was quiet, and the din of car-laden streets, the horns of ships, and the yelling of merchants was lost in a distant hum that was like the murmur of rushing water.

Of all his failures as a father, not teaching İsmail the suras was among the worst. He should have taken him before the *sünnet*. He should have made him read the Qur'an at night before going to bed. But he hadn't, and now all he could do was make up for lost time and hope the beauty of this place touched İsmail in the same way it moved him.

In the center of the courtyard stood a marble ablutions fountain.

"Watch me," Sinan said to İsmail. "And do what I do."

The boy nodded. A small sign, a thread of hope in that nod.

Sinan found an empty spigot. "*Allahu Akbar*," he said. "God is great." He dipped his palms in the cold water, using his thumbs to clean the webbed skin between fingers. He drank from the spigot until his mouth was cold and fresh with the taste, and then spat the water into the drain at his feet. "God is great," he chanted in his head as he filled his palms again, and sniffed the water into his nostrils. He washed his face, starting at the top of his forehead down to the bottom of his bearded chin, leaning forward to keep his pants from getting wet. He splashed the water across his forearms and it was so cool on his skin, that he thanked God for it. Then he pulled off his shoes and laid them perfectly side by side. He folded his socks neatly atop his shoes and scrubbed the calluses on his right foot and massaged the sore stump of his left. All of this he did three times each, and when he was done his head felt clear and focused on God.

He lifted İsmail onto the worn marble stool in front of the spigot. Helping his son and explaining as they went, he cleansed his body for prayer. He helped İsmail get the spaces between his toes, removed the crust of sleep from his eyelashes, scrubbed the dirt from the cartilage of the boy's ears, and prayed to God that the water might wash away his fears, flush away everything dark inside him.

The tour group had gathered at the entrance of the mosque, a semicircle of exposed skin, gold jewelry, and sports shoes. Repeating "please" in English, Sinan was able to push through the crowd without touching anyone, and when they reached the front both he and İsmail pulled off their shoes and carried them inside. Through his socks the marble entrance felt hard and cold, but as soon as they entered the mosque the plush carpet cushioned his feet. Sinan raised his eyes to the ornamented dome with its painted arabesques and shields of Ottoman script. Above him rose an archway of honeycombed marble, and beneath that, on the wall of the mosque, hung rows of intricate floral tiles, so delicate they looked as if actual flowers had been pressed in amber.

"Look at this, İsmail," Sinan whispered.

In the Southeast there weren't any mosques as beautiful as this. In Gölcük, too, the mosque had been cheap, built of wood and plaster rather than marble. This is why he had brought İsmail. What did the boy know of being Muslim? Poverty. Poverty and ugliness. He had known the pain of the knife, the loss of his home, the loss of his sister. He knew that God was capable of punishing innocents. But here was beauty, a Heaven built to reflect God's mercy.

İsmail spun around, his head thrown back to see the very top, and Sinan did the same, astounded by the light, like threads of white silk, cascading toward the floor. They passed beneath wrought-iron chandeliers, the hush of their socks pressing into the carpet, the glow of the bulbs illuminating İsmail's face. The carpet glowed a brilliant green and Sinan was sure this green was the exact color of Heaven.

İsmail rubbed his eyes and swayed on his feet.

"Now is not the time to be tired," Sinan said.

Sinan placed his feet in the center of his prayer rug and motioned to İsmail to do the same. They stood together, İsmail half as tall as his father, and faced Mecca.

He closed his eyes and so did İsmail, but then Sinan opened his and watched his son stand there blind to the world. His face was intent, lines gathering between his eyes as if he were concentrating on a difficult problem in his homework.

"No, İsmail, watch me and follow."

Sinan then brought his palms to his ears as though listening out through the walls of the mosque, putting the world behind him, separating himself from all unimportant things. "*Allahu Akbar*," Sinan said.

"*Allahu Akbar,*" İsmail said. And Sinan felt a flood of relief at the sound of his son's unsteady voice.

He placed his left hand over his right just below his stomach, and stared at the flowers in the carpet.

Glory to You, O God, Yours is the praise.
And blessed is Your name, and exalted is Your Majesty.
And there is no deity to be worshipped but You.
I seek refuge in God from Satan, the accursed.

And for Sinan, the world, except for the sound of his son's voice, began to disappear. There were no toppled cement apartments, no tents filled with dusty blankets, no devastated wives, but his daughter was still there, hovering in his mind like a ghost. He was getting used to her being there, accepting the fact that she would stay.

In the name of God, the infinitely Compassionate and Merciful.
Ruler on the Day of Reckoning.
You alone do we worship, and You alone do we ask for help.
Guide us on the straight path,
the path of those who have received your grace;
not the path of those who have brought down wrath, nor of those
who wander astray.

İsmail got lost and stumbled through the words, quietly whispering out a gibberish that was an approximation of the prayer. Sinan repeated the lines until İsmail said each one correctly, and he thanked God for giving İsmail back his voice.

Repeating *God is great,* Sinan dropped his arms to his side as he bent at the waist. He tried to keep his back perfectly parallel to the ground, and to help this he rested his hands on his knees. *Holy is my Lord, the Magnificent.*

Suspecting something, he glanced at İsmail. The boy's arms dangled loosely and his back curved like a cat stretching after a long sleep.

He pressed his palm against İsmail's back, flattening it out. "There," he said. "It's not supposed to be easy."

Holy is my Lord, the Magnificent, the boy repeated, breathing dramatically hard.

Sinan raised his shoulders, letting his arms fall to his sides.

God listens to him who praises Him.

He heard a shuffling sound behind him, the movement of shopping bags against cotton shorts. He tried to put it out of his mind and concentrate, but his head filled with the exclamations of people spinning in place to take in the sight of the dome, the excited voices of women touching beautiful cold tiles.

Our Lord, to You is due all praise.

God is great.

He sat on his feet and İsmail did the same, both of them placing their palms on top of their knees. The voices grew louder and phrases in English bounced around the dome, echoed across the walls, hung in the cool air and settled in the carpet.

A deep breath and Sinan touched his forehead to the soft carpet, and held himself there for a moment with his palms next to his cheeks.

Glory to my Lord, the Most High.

A flash and the click of a camera shutter. Something was said in English followed by another flash.

Then Sinan briefly forgot what came next. When he opened his eyes he found İsmail staring back, waiting to follow. Being caught in this momentary lapse only extended it and he felt a pang of embarrassment; a good Muslim should be unaffected by such small things, his concentration focused only on God.

"Bend down," Sinan said too forcefully.

İsmail's eyes widened and he did it immediately.

Sinan again pressed his forehead to the carpet, the cool scent of the pile filling his nostrils.

More flashes burst from the tourists' cameras.

Allahu Akbar.

Sitting up, he leaned his weight on his twisted ankle and raised his right foot so that the top faced the mihrab. He paused, closed his eyes, and tried to get the quiet back, tried to open himself up like a door through which God could visit, but the anger had already risen in him and it was growing like sharp thorns in his stomach.

All greetings, blessings and
good acts are from You, my Lord.

The tour group shuffled around the mosque, gazing at columns, leaning down to rub their fingers through the carpet, even walking up to the minbar to gape at the carved staircase. Sinan, ready to explode, focused hard not on the voices of these strangers, not on his own voice, and not even on his thoughts of God or the Prophet, but on the voice of his son. İsmail's voice was like a young bird learning a song, missing certain notes, but trying and straining and trying again.

Peace be unto us, and unto
The righteous servants of
God.

Silence floated back to him.

O God, bless our Muhammad
and the people of Muhammad;
As you have blessed Abraham
and the people of Abraham.

He opened his eyes and the silence he had achieved retreated into the dome like pigeons startled into flight.

He glanced over his right shoulder, above the top of İsmail's black hair, toward an unseen angel recording his good deeds, and said, *Peace and blessings of God be unto you.* He looked over his left shoulder toward the unseen angel recording his wrongful deeds, but when he did he was presented with a man in a tank top, his exposed skin like blank paper, his hands lifting a camera with the lens pointed directly at him. Sinan forced himself to look straight into the lens, right through the focusing mechanics of that eye, and into the eye behind the lens, the one of a man as soft and vulnerable and full of sin as any man, as he himself even.

The click of the shutter echoed across the floor, a crack in the solace of still air.

Peace and blessings of God be upon you.

AFTER PRAYERS, SINAN SHOWED İsmail the hair of Muhammad pressed in sealed glass and gold leaf. He lifted İsmail up to see the embroidery on the green shroud draped across Eyüp Ensari's tomb, and he couldn't help but think of İrem's casket being lowered into the ground. They ran their hands across the cool tiles outside of the mosque, the floral designs rising on the walls like an untamed garden.

But none of it seemed to impress İsmail and they made the trip back to the ferry in silence. The boat arrived and Sinan held his son's hand as they pushed through the crowd to board. They descended the stairs into the ship and sat down in the very back where there were no windows and the rumble of the engine cut out the sounds of the world. Sinan slid İsmail against the wall and wrapped his arm around his shoulders and didn't let go of him until the ferry left the dock.

"I'm proud of you, İsmail," Sinan said. "You prayed very well. You're a good Muslim."

The boy said nothing.

"You're a man now," Sinan said, "and men have to control their feelings." He didn't really believe this—or he was unable to do it himself—but it seemed like the right thing to say. "You have to think of your mother. You have to be strong."

"Why'd you send İrem away?" İsmail said, watching his fingers pinch the end of his shirt.

"I thought it was the right thing to do."

İsmail was silent and rolled the end of his shirt into a little cigarette and unrolled it again.

"Did you love her?"

"Yes, I did."

They were quiet for a while, the clanking of the engine gears growing louder in his ears, and in their silence Sinan could feel his son's
accusation. He wanted to tell the boy that he did it for him, but the
truth was he simply wanted to share the burden of his guilt.

"She hurt me," Sinan said.

İsmail looked at him and he felt stupid for saying it.

"I was wrong."

"Where's she now?" İsmail said.

Sinan looked at his son—the ridge of his brow concealing his eyes,
the bridge of his nose, his eyelashes blinking like insect wings.

"She's in the cemetery, İsmail," Sinan said. "You know that."

"No," İsmail said. "That's not what I mean. Where *is* she?"

Sinan felt his throat tighten.

"Is she in Heaven?"

"I hope so, my son. I hope so."

Chapter 59

THE NEXT DAY AND THE ONE AFTER THAT, ISMAIL WAS SILENT again. He nodded or shook his head in response to questions. He drew pictures in his book, sitting in the darkest corner of the tent, the pad propped up on his knees. They let him play soccer again with the boys, but even after returning he sat in the tent, his jaw clamped tight, and refused to eat. Marcus sent a doctor to the tent, but Sinan wouldn't let him inside. The man stood outside for a few minutes, his shadow falling across the tent, appealing to Sinan in broken Turkish to let him see the boy, but Sinan wouldn't allow it. Nilüfer, if it bothered her, said nothing, even after the man had gone.

İsmail coughed in his sleep and tossed and turned until his mother pinned him in one place with an exhausted arm. But he never seemed to sleep, his breath never became steady and low, he never snored the small, child snores that calmed Sinan into his own sleep. So, by the third day Sinan was exhausted. All day he moved products and stacked them on shelves. All day he unloaded trucks and smiled at customers when they asked him for garden hoses or beach towels or California wine that cost as much as one ticket to Diyarbakır. And all day he wanted to sleep, but he knew he wouldn't. He would lay awake worrying again tonight, listening to the erratic rhythms of his son, hoping İsmail would go to sleep and wake up in the morning the child he had been just a few months before.

When he left Carrefour, an early evening fog had gathered over the sea, engulfed the evening sun, and spread to swallow the coast. By the time Sinan had crossed the bridge above the highway and reached the field where three plane trees poked into the sky, the clouds blew in shards across the treetops, pressing the sky downward upon his head.

In the gray, he noticed a group of men standing in a circle near the trees, and as he got closer he saw a skinned goat hanging from the limb of the largest tree. The head alone had its skin, and blood dripped from its extended tongue and made a thick puddle in the dirt. Its body was pink and sinewy with exposed muscle and marbled fat. In the middle of the circle of men stood a half-dozen more goats, their bleating and wailing being carried away on the wind; Sinan could see their mouths moving, a silent pantomime of terror. Standing away from the goats as though he were scared of the beasts was the mayor. Three other men dressed in suits stood near him and they directed two butchers to kill another animal.

One man took the hind legs and the other pulled the goat's head close to his belly. Before Sinan even noticed the knife, the man slit the goat's neck and blood streamed onto the ground and quickly faded to a trickle that ran down the animal's limp neck. They hoisted the goat from the next tree with a rope, cut the hide around the neck, and with gloved hands yanked the skin over the shoulders and down the back and soon the animal was stripped of its coat and no longer bore a resemblance to a living thing.

"These are for your families," the mayor said. "Share the meat with your neighbors, too. Remember *zakat*, my brothers. Remember charity."

The mayor came to him and handed him a piece of paper.

"The meat's a gift from the party, Sinan Bey," the mayor said. Sinan was surprised he knew his name. "You don't have to take their food anymore."

He looked at the paper in his hands. He couldn't read the Turkish, but "Allah" was written in Arabic and it was superimposed over the image of the Turkish flag.

"I'm very sorry about your daughter." The mayor patted Sinan on the shoulder. "It's a shame, a waste. But you must go on. You have a son to raise, a wife to take care of. A man's work is never done on earth, but his struggle is rewarded." He kissed Sinan on both cheeks. "I'll have some boys bring you the hindquarters, if we can get them past the gendarmes."

"Soldiers?"

"Yes, they showed up this morning. They wouldn't let me through earlier."

When Sinan reached the camp, a soldier stopped him and asked him his tent number. Sinan gave it to him and the soldier let him through. He passed the soup kitchen where two more soldiers stood on either side of the canopy, guns dangling from holsters. At the tent he was surprised to find Nilüfer alone.

"Where's İsmail?" he said.

"He finally spoke today," Nilüfer said. She touched him on his forearms. Relief flooded her eyes. "He ate, too. Not enough, but he ate some cheese and bread."

He was excited by the news and it seemed that a pall was lifting. The boy would be all right. He would go on and live, and, because of that, so too would Sinan and his wife—a family again, though a lesser one than before.

"Where is he?" he said. "I want to see him."

"Playing soccer."

Sinan took off for the soccer field. The sky was purple now, blown by a wet wind, and a circle of boys skipped around the field throwing up brown dust that mingled with the clouds. The ball escaped the circle and İsmail burst forward. He caught the ball, dribbled it into his control, and set off for the goal. It was beautiful to see, his son so alive with speed, his skinny legs throwing up dust as though he had real weight in the world.

İsmail had one last boy to beat. The boy tried to slide-tackle him, but İsmail, with amazing grace, kicked the ball over the defender's feet while flying into the air to avoid the tackle. He caught the ball again, made a fancy move to throw off the goalkeeper and took his shot.

"Goooaaall!" the boys yelled as though they were television announcers.

They tackled İsmail, one tall pile of legs and arms singing the Galatasaray fight song, and Sinan thought İsmail might get crushed. But he emerged smiling from the pile, his fist raised in the air in victory. He spun around in the field, glancing around the sidelines as though looking for someone.

Sinan limped across the field, through the middle of the boys who continued playing.

"İsmail," Sinan said.

The boy turned around.

"Baba," İsmail said, disappointment in his voice, Sinan thought, as though the boy was expecting someone other than his father.

"That was a beautiful shot." Sinan tousled the boy's hair. "You're very fast. Like lightning." He used his excited voice, the one that İsmail loved to hear, but the boy turned around and glanced across the field, to the other sideline.

"Come on," Sinan said. "We're going." He placed his hand on the boy's back.

"Wait," İsmail said.

"Let's go." Sinan took the boy's hand and pulled him back toward the camp.

"I'm good now," İsmail said. "Before I was bad and the boys laughed at me. Marcus Bey taught me a lot and now they don't laugh. Now they choose me first."

"You're good," Sinan said, squeezing the boy's fingers in his palm.

"It's because of Marcus Bey," İsmail said. "He taught me. Have you seen him?"

"Your grandfather was a great soccer player."

İsmail looked up at him. "You never told me," he said.

"He was great," Sinan said, passing now in front of the short line at the soup kitchen. "It's in your blood, İsmail. You're good because it's in your blood."

"I wish I had met him."

"You would have if people would leave us alone," he said. "You would have, son, if these people would just go away and leave us."

"But *Dede* died a long time ago."

"Time doesn't change anything."

Sinan was aware of the strange look his son was giving him, but he couldn't stop himself.

"*Dede* died because he was old," İsmail said, a question in his voice.

"No, İsmail," Sinan said. "He was young. These people killed him."

İsmail's brows pushed together, and his eyes shone with fear. "Not Marcus Bey. He's nice."

"No, İsmail. They seem nice, but they're not. They seem to love you, but they don't." He was walking fast now, his anger dragging İsmail along until the boy tripped.

"I'm sorry." He bent down and brushed the dirt from the boy's knees.

İsmail's eyes were wet and Sinan wished he had kept his mouth shut. The boy was innocent still, innocent even after all he had experienced, and he did not want to ruin that. "I'm sorry." He kissed İsmail on the forehead. "*Dede* would have loved you. He would have loved you very much. I wish you had met him, too."

"Maybe I'll meet him in Heaven."

"Someday, maybe."

They began walking again and for a few moments they were quiet.

"Too many people die, Baba."

"Yes," Sinan said. "Too many die."

THE MAYOR BROUGHT SINAN the hindquarters, and Sinan offered him tea until a soldier came.

"I'm causing a 'disruption,'" the mayor said to Sinan. He stood quietly when the gendarme touched his elbow, and he didn't fight as they led him by the arm out of the camp.

Nilüfer cooked the meat into a stew. It was tough, but it was meat, and it was meat slaughtered by a Muslim.

After dinner, Sinan was still angry. So angry it unsettled his stomach. He took a walk to calm down, and passed two men yelling at one of the soldiers. The soldier stood with his rifle by his side and stared straight ahead as though the men were not there. Even though it wasn't prayer time, he went to mosque. There he found İmam Ali alone, cleaning the mihrab with a wet towel.

"Good evening, Sinan Bey," the İmam said.

"*İyi akşamlar.*"

Sinan sat on the rugs and his body settled with a familiar weariness, as though his insides were made of wet dough. The İmam sat next to him.

"I'm tired," Sinan said.

İmam Ali touched Sinan's hand and held it. His palm was warm and callused and it reminded him of his father's. He had forgotten what it was like to be comforted by a man. A man understands what another man feels in a way a woman cannot. A woman's comfort can make you feel alone, but not a man's. Ahmet was the last man to understand, the last man who knew him.

"You'll kill yourself with anger, Sinan."

"I don't know what to do, *Efendi.*"

"Do nothing, Sinan. You must submit to God's will."

He looked at the İmam. The man's eyes were red-rimmed; one was clouded over and Sinan thought he might be blind in it.

"Life begins and ends when it should, even your daughter's." He touched Sinan's hand to his forehead and then to his heart. "God has a plan you cannot control. You must accept that, no matter how painful. Accept that and the pain will fade."

Submit, though, meant "do nothing" and when he left the mosque, just as the muezzin began the nighttime call to prayer, he was even angrier than before. Why would God give us a brain, why would he give us free will if we are only to submit? If we were only meant to submit then we might as well lie down in the dirt and die right now, we may as well let ourselves be killed.

When he got back to the tent, İsmail was tucked into his sleeping bag and drawing in his book. Nilüfer lay asleep with her hand resting on the boy's back, her exhausted snores ruffling the fabric of the tent.

Sinan sat next to İsmail and kissed him on the back of the neck. The boy squirmed.

Over the boy's shoulder, Sinan watched him draw. Every other picture his son had drawn was dark and full of nightmarish images, but this picture was bright with a shining yellow sun that sent bursts of color across the page. The sky was blue, and pink flowers sprouted from the green grass. There was a rock tomb, but it wasn't a scary place. The rock covering the tomb had been pushed aside, and a man dressed in white cloth stood in front of the tomb as though he had just emerged. People stood to the side of the tomb, their faces drawn with smiles, their hands held up to the sky. And near these people, drawn in glowing yellow light, was another man, a circle of gold floating around his head, a beard clinging to his face, his eyes as blue as water. He held his hands out to the man covered in cloth as though commanding him to rise. It was—though a child's drawing—a beautiful picture.

"What is this?" Sinan said.

"Prophet Jesus bringing Lazarus back to life."

Sinan sat up then and saw, for the first time, the small book from which İsmail was copying the picture. He reached over the boy's shoulder and grabbed it. Sinan turned the pages of the book—a flimsy pamphlet stapled together at the center—and his heart beat in his ears, the blood rushed to his face. He couldn't read the other words in the title, but he understood "İsa Bey." Jesus was a prophet, although not the son of God as the Christians told the story, and he recognized all the prophets' names. Inside were drawings of Jesus' life. Jesus walking on the surface of the sea. Jesus turning water into wine. Jesus fixing a blind man's eyes.

"He had been dead for four days, Baba!"

Turkish words were written in white squares in the style of comic strips. Sinan couldn't read the story, but the pictures told it all. They were beautiful pictures—the sky blue, Jesus' robe a clean white, the grass green with bright flowers growing in places, waterfalls in the background.

"Do we have miracles, too?"

Sinan didn't answer because he was so enthralled with the pictures; they were like stepping into the innocent world of a child, where everything was clean, all people were kind, and the most amazing things could happen simply because they could be imagined.

"Marcus Bey said it was Jesus who saved me. If Jesus was here, Baba, think of all the people he could have saved. Maybe he could've brought İrem back, too, even though she did a bad thing."

Sinan's head was spinning. Jesus—the Jesus in this little book— was so kind-looking, so unlike men he had known.

"To be a Christian all you have to do is let them pour water over your head. It's easy and it doesn't hurt."

But the pictures were lies, lies told to children to make them believe.

"Who gave this to you?" Sinan said. He controlled his voice this time, made it sound as though he were not angry.

"Marcus Bey." The boy kept coloring. "I told you he was nice."

HIS HEAD SPINNING, SINAN ran down the street, shouldering past the men returning from mosque. The late-night bonfires of the camps blew heat in the wind that burned his cheeks. He loosened the leather on the knife and pressed the blade to his thumb, the edge biting into his skin. When he reached the tent, the light was on inside and what he was about to do crowded in on him. But then he remembered the look on his daughter's face when she told him about Dylan; he remembered her white, dead face and the starker whiteness of her naked hips, and he felt free again to use the knife, felt an expansive rage surging in his muscles; it had been thrashing around inside him for too long now, ripping his insides apart.

He pulled the knife from his pocket and held it in the palm of his hand. He threw open the flap to the tent and pushed inside and he didn't stop when he saw Marcus throw up his hands to shove him away. The American slapped at his face and tried to knock away the knife, but the blade cut through the skin of his palms, stabbed into the tips of his fingers. Marcus yelled but Sinan couldn't understand what he said; the sound mixed with the rush of blood in his head. Then he was hit across the temple and sent tumbling sideways. It took a few seconds to get his vision back and when he did he was rolling across the tent floor, Marcus on top of him and then beneath him, a knee in his chest, a bloody hand in his eye, a rushing of breath in his ear, a slash of his own knife across his arm.

Then the labored breath of Marcus filled his left ear, and he realized that the American lay beneath him now. When the dizziness in his head cleared, he discovered his hand pressing his knife against the lump in Marcus's throat. He had planned this, but, still, he was surprised to find himself so close to murder. He had thought of murderers as monsters, as profoundly debased human creatures, but now he realized that he was as capable of murder as he was of love.

Marcus's fingers strangled Sinan's wrist, trying to push the knife away, but Sinan was stronger, and he was filled with the excitement of being stronger. Sinan lay across the man's body, his weight bearing down on the American, his own face so close to the man he could see specks of brown in the American's blue eyes. He pressed more of his weight against the knife. The American breathed hard and the lump rose and fell against the edge.

Then, without warning, Marcus's hands let go of Sinan's wrist, and before he knew what was happening, the knife blade sliced open the surface of the American's skin. The sudden blood shocked Sinan and he quickly jerked the knife away and held it just above the American's throat.

"You must understand, Sinan." The man was crying. "İsmail

needed hope," he said through labored breath. "I had to give it to him."

Marcus's whole body went slack, his arms now loosely wrapped around Sinan's back, leaving his throat exposed there, just an inch away from the edge of the knife. There was no fight left in the man and Sinan was so shocked by this fact that all he could do was lie there, holding on to the American as though caught in an embrace. He felt the soft weight of Marcus's palms resting on his shoulder blades and the pressing of the man's rib cage against his with each labored breath. The windpipe was right in front of him, right there, and all it would take was one cut and all of this would be over. The knife shook in his hand and it bit into the skin at Marcus's throat, streaking blood down the edge of his neck and into the collar of his shirt.

"She died to save your son, Sinan. She gave her life. Do you understand?" His eyes worked back and forth in a kind of impassioned pleading. "There must be a reason for it. I need there to be a reason."

İsmail was the reason, Sinan understood now, and as a Muslim he wasn't worth the American's wife's death. Sinan realized that if he, too, could have a reason for İrem's death, something tangible, something he was sure was true, he would take it. He would do anything for it. He would even steal it from another man.

He pulled the knife from Marcus's throat, and unwrapped himself from the man's limp arms. God, he wanted to kill him! He still wanted to slice open his neck. He wanted to shove that knife into his chest, stab all his anger into this man and leave it there, but he couldn't do it, and he was too weak to force his betraying hand.

Chapter 60

HE FOUND THE WATER TRUCK IN FRONT OF THE MOSQUE.
Prayers were done until morning and the darkened building stood
empty and silent as though it had been bombed. His bloody hand
slipped on the faucet handle before he was able to turn on the spigot.
The water, still heated inside the drum by the afternoon sun, felt like
blood rushing across his already bloody fingers. But he could see the
color come back to his hands as he scrubbed and after a few minutes
they seemed to be a part of his body again. He thought about throwing the knife into the sea, but God knew what he had done and He
would punish him if he were to be punished. So he wrapped the
blade back into the leather and placed it in the chest pocket of his
coat.

When he returned to the tent, he sat outside on the plastic chair
and waited for the military police. They would arrest him for trying to
kill a humanitarian worker, a friend of the Turkish state in its time of
need. They would lock him in a freezing cell until they discovered he
was Kurdish. Then the real policemen would show up, the ones
dressed in business suits. They would accuse him of terrorism, beat
him, ask him for PKK members' names. He almost felt ready for it,
proud, in a way, that it would happen to him, too.

But the soldiers never came. He sat all night, watching the cats, listening to the snores of men, and thinking of his father. The stars slid toward morning, a band of yellow appeared on the horizon, and the call to prayer announced the sun.

SINAN WOKE NILÜFER.

"Pack only what you need," he said. "We're leaving tonight."

She fingered the lapel of his jacket as though trying to rub something away, and Sinan saw the stain.

"Throw the jacket away," he said. "But keep the knife."

She watched him change into his Carrefour shirt, fear blazing in her eyes.

"I can't talk now," he said. "Just be ready."

She nodded and rolled the jacket into a ball.

He leaned over the sleeping İsmail, opened his coloring pad, and found the pamphlet. He slipped it into the pocket of his pants.

"Keep him here today."

HE SKIPPED MORNING PRAYER, but found Malik Bey and another man playing backgammon on a card table near the mosque. Three other men, including his neighbor Ziya Bey, sat on a rug in the dirt, smoking cigarettes and talking with one another through their smoke. A few men exited the mosque and slipped into their shoes, but they were elderly and waiting to die and they shuffled back to their tents to lie there until the next call.

Sinan dropped the Jesus book in the middle of the board, just as Malik rolled the dice.

"First my daughter," Sinan said. "Now my son."

"Sit down, brother," Malik said.

Malik set aside his cigarette, hanging the burning end over the edge of the card table. He flipped the pages of the book, shaking his head as the pictures passed before his face. He closed the cover and set his hands on top of it.

"Every night after the quake," Malik said, "I'd come home from the field, shoveling shit all day, to find my son eating candy. It made him happy, so I was happy." He picked up the cigarette and smoked it. "So one night I came back to the tent and Derin starts asking me about the end of the world. I tell my son the world's not ending. He tells me that the earthquake is a sign that everything's ending." He blew smoke. "I just looked at him and told him about the plates underneath the water, that it was nothing but the earth moving. But the next night he's asking again, and I tell him again about the plates, but this time I notice his eyes—they're scared in a way I've never seen, even after the quake, and I know he doesn't believe me. He doesn't sleep that night or the next and then he gets sick and then my wife tells me that the American kid with the Bible keeps coming around and telling my son things, asking him to accept this and to take that into his heart."

He finished the cigarette and lit another with the tip of the first. His hands were shaking. He blew the smoke out and watched the cloud fly away from his face.

"When he died, he was looking at me," Malik said, glancing away as though ashamed.

He turned back to Sinan. "I couldn't let that doctor in the tent."

Sinan took Malik's hand, but he couldn't stop thinking that Malik should have let him in.

"When we came here, I thought Derin would go to a good school, get rich with a good job. He'd never have to see all of that mess." He threw his hand in the general direction of Diyarbakır and the dry, empty South. "I never gave a damn about independence, anyway. All I really wanted to do was farm. Didn't care if the land was called Kurdistan or Turkey or Iraq. But the stupid PKK and the military won't leave you alone; you're everyone's enemy if you just want to be left alone. You've got to pick a side." He tossed his cigarette down in disgust. "Is there anywhere in the world you can just be left alone?"

"I don't know, my brother," Sinan said.

What Sinan was about to say was shameful and the shame would follow his name forever, but he knew what such a man as Malik would do when he heard it.

"That American boy raped my daughter," Sinan said. "That's why she jumped."

Malik stared at Sinan, his brows narrowing, his eyes welling with water.

"Now this boy's father is trying to take my son, too," Sinan said. "Just like they tried to take yours."

Malik slammed the table with the palm of his hand, the backgammon pieces jumping off the board.

"The fight's inside myself!" he said. "What does this İmam know?"

HE WORKED A DOUBLE shift, polishing the wine bottles, stacking pyramids of beer, lining up the boxes on the shelves perfectly so that no edge hung over another. He waxed the floors and swept beneath the metal racks. He wanted everything to be perfect, wanted to be a model employee so that no one would suspect him later.

After he had punched out, he said goodnight to the manager.

"I wanted to thank you for your kind offer of dinner."

"Yes, yes, it's nothing," Yilmaz Bey said. "Join us one day, please. No one should suffer what you've suffered." The manager placed his hand on his shoulder. "You're a good man, Sinan. My best employee."

"Thank you."

"May your pain pass quickly."

Then Yilmaz Bey was off to the bathroom, leaving the door wide open and his coat with the wallet in the chest pocket hanging on the wall just a few feet away. Sinan waited a couple of minutes, just long enough to make sure the manager had not forgotten his toothpaste or the comb he brushed his hair and mustache with, and stepped into the office.

When he opened the wallet there were at least a dozen ten-million-lira bills folded neatly inside. The manager wouldn't miss two

of them until later, if he missed them at all. He hung the coat back on
the wall, pulled the creases exactly as he remembered them being before, and pocketed the money inside his own coat, right next to the
knife wrapped in leather.

It was almost dark when he reached the camp and fires were already burning. Orange smoke rose into the sky and sparks flickered
and died like extinguishing stars. A produce truck was parked next to
the soup kitchen and a mob of people gathered and pushed against
one another to get to the open bed. Sinan was shoved forward by a
group of women, and he saw the mayor and another man standing in
the bed of the truck, dropping goat meat wrapped in bloody butcher
paper into the hands of the people. On the platform where the
Americans' stoves stood, Kemal and Malik pushed over steaming pots,
sending scalding soup splashing into the street. Already three silver
pots lay glowing in the bonfire, and when Kemal tried to toss this one
in, a soldier hit him across the face with a club.

"You're Turkish soldiers," Malik screamed, pointing his hand at the
man. "Attacking your own people! Your mother must be ashamed."

Sinan struggled through the crowd, looking for Marcus, wondering if he had been attacked in all of this, wondering if he had already
left, and wondering which he wanted more. Behind two soldiers, a
few of the Americans stood and watched with their hands hanging at
their sides. One woman sat in the dirt, her hand on her forehead, resigned, it seemed, to the chaos. Marcus wasn't among them.

The camp was nearly deserted and the few people left on the street
headed toward the commotion of the bonfire, their sad faces lit up
with the orange light. He passed İmam Ali as he rushed out of the
mosque, his face lined with worry, and Sinan wanted to say to him,
"You cannot stop it," but there was no point.

He found Nilüfer and İsmail huddled together in the corner of the
tent.

"We're leaving," Sinan said. "Come now."

But they didn't move. The fire was high enough now that the walls
of the tent glowed orange and İsmail's eyes were brilliant with fear.

"It's okay," Sinan said. "They won't hurt you."

Sinan hoisted the laundry bag of clothes over his shoulder and Nilüfer carried İsmail into the street. People ran in the street, some of them clutching packages of meat like bundles of wood to their chests, and the tents of the camp seemed to be on fire with the glow from the soup kitchen. As they walked out toward the freeway, three police cars sped by them, their blue and red lights flashing uselessly in the night.

They reached the highway and hopped on the first bus that stopped along the road. All the people inside stared out the window at the flames and when the three of them climbed the steps into the bus, people stared at them. The lights were bright inside and the glow of the fire out the window was partly obscured by the reflections of the passengers' faces. From here the flames looked very small and in-significant—a shepherd's campfire, an open barbecue on a beach, the dying embers of a Nowruz fire.

As the bus pulled onto the highway, İsmail took his hand and Sinan noticed the blood still clinging to his nails.

"Is Marcus Bey okay, Baba?" İsmail looked like he was afraid of the answer.

"He's all right," Sinan said.

İsmail looked closely at his father, looked deep into his eyes, and Sinan looked back at him. He grabbed the boy by the back of the neck and pulled his face close to him. "He *is* all right," he said. "I promise you."

İsmail smiled then, a small, sad smile, and looked out the window at the millions of lights that became the city.

Chapter 61

THE TRAIN LEFT AT MIDNIGHT. IT PASSED OUT OF HAYDAR-paşa station and rolled on a path of darkness through the lights of the city, millions of windows flashing back at Sinan, millions of people hidden away behind the concrete walls, all wondering if another quake would hit, all closing their eyes and hoping the walls of their apartments wouldn't come crushing in on them in their sleep.

İsmail fell asleep on his mother's lap and Nilüfer took Sinan's hand in hers. She wrapped each one of her fingers through his and clasped his palm tightly, and he was amazed at the perfection of a hand, the simplicity of a woman's hand held in his. Before the city disappeared, she fell asleep, her head jostling against his shoulder, and soon the lights faded away and the land became nothing but steady darkness and somewhere out there, somewhere back among those constellations of lights, lay his daughter's grave.

Sometime in the night he slept and when he woke the train was coming through a mountain pass. The trees stood high and green and above the train granite peaks held freshly fallen snow. Then the train came through the mountains, and the earth opened up beneath them, wide and bright and as expansive as sight itself. It was the steppes of Anatolia and his heart flooded with gratitude for the land.

He woke İsmail and sat him on his lap. The two of them pressed their noses against the window.

"Look at that, İsmail," Sinan said. "You don't remember this land, but it's ours. It's Paradise on earth."

He and İsmail watched the land grow closer and the horizon shorten as the train descended, and when they reached the valley floor it seemed there was nothing but blue sky.

He had nothing except his son and his wife, and if anyone tried to take them away from him again—anyone—he would kill them for it. He could feel this strength growing in him, like a fist strangling the last of his weakness. He would let nothing threaten that strength again.

The train came into a village and it slowed to let a shepherd pass his goats across the tracks, the wheels squealing to a shuddering crawl.

"Look, Baba."

İsmail pointed to an old man driving a donkey cart on a dirt road that ran beside the train tracks. The cart was loaded with apples and with each bump a few rolled out across the road. İsmail laughed at the apples as they tumbled out and split open into white-fleshed halves. The donkey was old, its hip bones poking against its graying hide, but for a brief moment, just a few wonderful seconds, the man and his cart sped along faster than the train.

Acknowledgments

I WISH TO THANK THE MANY DIVERSE PEOPLES OF TURKEY, whose kindness, generosity, and grace always made me feel welcome while I lived as a guest in their country. Thank you to my students and colleagues at Üsküdar American Academy, who taught me much more than I taught them.

Without the support of the teachers, students, and staff at the University of Iowa Writers' Workshop this book would never have been attempted much less finished and published. I am particularly indebted to Ethan Canin for his enthusiastic support for my less-than-polished writing, Marilynne Robinson for her wisdom, and Chris Offutt for his humor and advice. A great big belated thank God for everyone from the Workshop and Trinity Episcopal Church, who provided dinners for Mimi and me after the birth of our son. Thanks to Ben Caldwell for the cigs and drinks and good conversation. Connie Brothers provided support to me and my family in numerous ways that not only made our stay in Iowa more pleasant but also helped me to keep writing at a time when this book was in its infancy. Thanks to Jan Zenisek and Deb West for all the enjoyable wasted time hanging out in the Workshop office when I should have been writing.

Rex Honey's course on the Middle East at the University of Iowa was immensely important in spurring me to begin this book. Thanks to Dr. Honey for allowing me to write fiction for a term paper project.

Murat Ozay graciously provided the translation of the Radiohead lyrics.

Few people were more critical to the creation of this book than my wonderful agent, Dorian Karchmar. Her more than four years of patience, support, insightful criticism, and stubborn determination to make me work when I wanted to stop gave me confidence and hope when I had little.

I'm extremely grateful to Kate Medina at Random House, who showed so much enthusiasm and interest in this book. Publishing for the first time is an overwhelming experience, but Kate managed to make the process enjoyable. I couldn't have asked for a better editor. Thanks to Gina Centrello, publisher, for strongly backing this debut. A big thanks, also, to everyone at Random House who worked to get this book to as many readers as possible, particularly Tom Perry, Sanyu Dillon, Avideh Bashirrad, Sally Marvin, and Carol Schneider. And last but in no way least, a very grateful thanks to Robin Rolewicz and Abby Plesser, who made this whole publishing process as easy as possible.

I had essentially given up writing until I met Robert Rosenberg in İstanbul. He had the guts to begin a novel when I was scared to begin a short story, a fact that was both intimidating and inspiring. His kind but forceful encouragement for me to write, his trust in me to read the early drafts of his novel, and our shared mini-workshops over Efes beer on various rooftop terraces stoked my long-extinguished desire to be an author. He is a great friend, a fantastic critic, a wonderful writer, and a constant source of positive encouragement.

Janet Baker volunteered to read the manuscript at a critical time in its genesis and provided important objective critiques.

Cheers to Caren Streb for her incredible friendship, her sublime taste in food and wine, and her endless excitement and joy for life; to Adam Davis, whose talent in all the arts is a constant inspiration to me; and to Craig Rutter, for being one of my oldest and dearest compadres. Thanks to all of the above for helping me keep one foot always in California.

Thanks to my family and my wife's family for all their encouragement and support in countless ways.

Without my wife, Miriam Drew, I would not have had the confidence to write this book. Her faith in me got me through all the days I thought I was not smart, talented, or tough enough to write anything worth reading, and my love for her makes me want to impress her. And my son, Nathaniel, always reminded me that few things are more important than good macaroni and cheese, big trains, and slow bike rides in the sun.

BOOK SOURCES

Books that were indispensable to me in the production of this novel are as follows: *Atatürk*, by Andrew Mango, *Who Are the Turks?*, by Justin McCarthy and Carolyn McCarthy, and *Turkey Unveiled*, by Nicole and Hugh Pope; *The Kurds: A People in Search of Their Homeland*, by Kevin McKiernan, and *Kurdistan: In the Shadow of History*, by Susan Meiselas; *The Qur'an*, as translated by M.A.S. Abdel Haleem, and *The Qur'an*, as translated by M. H. Shakir; *Merriam-Webster's Encyclopedia of World Religions*, edited by Wendy Doniger, *Biblical Quotations for All Occasions*, by J. Stephen Lang, *The Koran: Selected Suras*, translated by Arthur Jeffrey, and *The Wisdom of the Prophet*, translated by Thomas Cleary; *Understanding Islam*, by Thomas W. Lippman, *Islam and the West*, by Bernard Lewis, *The Middle East*, by Dr. William Spencer, *Warriors of the Prophet*, by Mark Huband, and *Terrorism, Theirs and Ours*, by Eqbal Ahmed.

The New York Times, *The Economist*, *The International Herald Tribune*, and *The Turkish Daily News* kept me up-to-date on happenings within Turkey.

Gardens *of* Water

Alan Drew

A Reader's Guide

A Conversation with Alan Drew

Random House Reader's Circle: You were in Istanbul at the time of the devastating earthquake upon which the events of the novel are based. Can you tell us a little bit about that experience?

Alan Drew: My wife and I arrived in İstanbul four days before the 1999 Marmara quake. Even though I had grown up in Los Angeles and had lived in San Francisco for five years, I'd never felt a stronger or longer lasting earthquake. The quake hit at 3:00 in the morning. My wife felt the shaking first and woke me. I grabbed her and we stood in the doorway of our bedroom and we held each other as the apartment shook. I kept saying, "It'll be over in just a second," but the shaking wouldn't stop, and those forty-five seconds seemed to last forever.

Finally, it ended. We walked around the apartment, and were surprised that nothing had fallen off the walls or shelves—not the pictures we'd hung, not the wine bottle sitting on a glass shelf above the sink. We called our parents in the States and told them that we were okay. Then we went back to bed, not realizing the magnitude of the disaster. A couple hours later, we woke to the sound of people outside in the street, news reports blasting from car stereos. We realized then that something significant had happened. Our building was fine; it was a well constructed apartment built for a private school that had the funds for good building materials. The buildings that collapsed in İstanbul and nearer to the epicenter in İzmit were built on landfill, or built of poor materials. Those buildings were, of course, the apartments in which the poorer people of the city lived, and those people made up the greatest numbers of casualties—perhaps as many as 30,000 killed. For months after the quake, wanted signs were posted around the city for a general contractor who had mixed beach sand in the cement he used for cinder blocks. When the quake hit, those blocks turned back to sand with the shaking. I don't know if they ever caught him or not, or if this was simply a way for the government to take the attention off their inability to enforce building codes.

Many of the people who were killed were, like Sinan and his family, displaced from their Anatolian villages by the war in the south, by a simple lack of economic opportunity, etc. Many news reporters spoke of the quake as though it were a disaster that struck the rich and poor equally, but while some wealthy people were killed in their summer homes in Yalova, the vast majority of the people killed were the poor, the displaced and the disenfranchised. The earthquake revealed the great chasm between the experiences of the wealthy and that of people living in poverty. The earthquake was not only a natural disaster, but a political and social one as well.

RHRC: When did the idea for the novel come about? How long after the earthquake did you begin *Gardens of Water*?

AD: There were many experiences living in Istanbul that feed into the story, but the germ for the book came very shortly after the quake. School was cancelled and my wife and I found a relief agency that was feeding and providing shelter to victims of the quake. As we traveled to the epicenter, it became clear how horrible the quake really was. High-rise apartments lay pancaked in the street, roads were cracked into deep fissures, and people camped in the grassy centers of freeway on-ramps. We were shocked at the thousands of white tents laid out in rows along the coast, and the dozens of orphaned kids playing soccer in the dirt.

The Turkish government was completely overwhelmed by the tragedy, so many foreign relief organizations flooded the region to provide assistance. Since the school we worked for had missionary connections going back to the early nineteenth century, they had set us up with a southern Baptist church group from Texas that ran this particular tent city. They all wore blue shirts with doves on them and crosses on the chest pockets. The camp was organized and clean and we helped feed a few hundred people breakfast and lunch. While we were cleaning dishes after lunch a young man approached our group of teachers. He wore pleated shorts with the blue shirt tucked neatly into the waist. I remember his hair was neatly combed and he smelled of cologne or aftershave. He got down on his knees in a gesture of intimacy. "You're all Christians, right?" he said. Before anyone could answer him, he said: "Well, why don't you get out there and spread the Good News." He jumped up and ran off into the sea of tents with unbelievable energy and confidence.

Later, as winter approached and the Turkish government had recovered from the shock of its own ineptitude, this group was kicked out of Turkey for proselytizing to children in the camp.

If true, this struck me as such an abuse of the people they were caring for. It also struck me as such a wasted opportunity. Had these people simply cared for the Turkish Muslims who had lost everything, had offered them food and kindness, and had not tried to convert them, what a positive impression these Muslims would have had of Christian charity. Since this group was American, too, what a positive impression the people of the camp would have had of American kindness. Instead, this group used food and shelter as power over helpless people. To me, this seems like a sort of religious imperialism that is counterproductive to peaceful coexistence in a world that is religiously pluralistic. In the book, I wanted to explore the anger I imagined a devout Muslim, such as Sinan Basioglu, might feel in such a situation.

Another experience that fed into the book happened in our last year in Istanbul. A series of honor killings on the fringes of the city shocked people in this western leaning, cosmopolitan town. The press covered the killings in a most sensational way—shocking interviews with relatives, particularly a mother who while seeming bereaved suggested that her husband did the right thing and that her daughter had provoked the killing. There was courtroom drama, bloody details of the acts, etc. The killings exposed a deep divide in the country between east and west, fundamentalist Islam and more moderate, secular Muslims, the village and city, the ancient and modern.

Strangely enough, I didn't begin the book until I returned to the States and began working on my MFA at Iowa. For some reason, I found it difficult to write about Turkey while living there. Instead I stored up as much information as I could in pictures, notes, mementos, and sifted through these things later to find the right details to inform the narrative of the book.

RHRC: How much research did you do for the book? Did you know much about the plight of the Kurds beforehand, or the political situation in Turkey?

AD: Without knowing it, I was doing research for the book the whole three years I was living in Turkey. When I arrived in Turkey I knew very little about the country. My wife and I took jobs teaching there, simply because it seemed like it would be a great adventure. While there, I became completely fascinated by the country and the Middle East, in general. Everything about Istanbul defied my expectations. My wife and I travelled extensively throughout the country, and continued to be surprised by the complexity of the country as well. The region is so rich in history and so complex in its conflicts, and I read everything I could get my hands on about the history, the political situation, the culture to try to understand these complexities. The Kurdish situation was interesting to me from the beginning, since Ocalan, the leader of the Kurdistan Workers Party at the time, had just been captured in Africa by the Turkish secret police. Before I even thought about writing a book about a Kurdish character I read about and studied the Kurdish situation as much as I could. While at Iowa, I took a Middle-Eastern studies class and continued my studies on my own—reading translations of the Koran, various books about the Kurdish issue, and political websites. In general, there is no research substitute for living in a country, for learning the language, and for sitting down and talking with people. That research was the most valuable of all.

RHRC: You've created a fascinating cast of characters, all with such distinct and unique personalities. Do you have a favorite?

AD: It sounds strange to say, but, despite the horrible things he contemplates doing, I love Sinan. He feels like he really does exist to me, even though he only exists in my mind and on paper. His conflicted nature and his complexity are what I love most because I think we're all like that. No one is absolutely bad and no one is absolutely good. We all struggle with our conflicting natures, that struggle can be exacerbated by outside influences—war, poverty, loss, etc. I think, Sinan's honesty, or his desire to be honest is of utmost importance to me. Sinan wants to be a good man, he wants to love his children equally, he wants to understand people, but he is also powerless, angry, bitter, and above all, scared. It's difficult for me to talk about Sinan in a way that will shed any more light on his character than the book already does because he is confusing to me as well, just as he should be, I think. If I read the book today, I would still struggle with his character—I would love him, be disappointed in him, be repulsed by him, but in the end, I would still care about him because he does struggle, and there is nobility in that struggle

RHRC: You were a teacher in Istanbul for three years. Did you ever meet any girls like Irem? Is the character based on anyone in particular?

AD: The students I worked with were mostly from very wealthy families, and they tended to be Western leaning secularists. While Irem is not based on any particular person I met, there are two girls I kept in mind while writing the book. One was a girl my wife taught in one of her classes. She was a new student, and despite a strict ban on headscarves in schools and other public institutions at the time, she tried to attend classes wearing her headscarf. This caused a huge uproar in the school, which involved meetings between the American and Turkish principals and the girl's parents, a threat to expel her, and her family finally acquiescing. The girl remained at the school, but she had to take her headscarf off each day before she walked through the front gates. She was often ostracized by the other students as being backwards.

Another girl was a student of mine. In the winter of 2001, she committed suicide and the Istanbul media ran very sensational stories about her and her death. According to the media, she had fallen under the influence of "Satanist" leaning friends who took drugs and hung out in the tattoo parlors and music shops of Kadikoy. The media and the family accused the school of not caring enough to help her, and the people at school suggested that the parents hadn't done enough to save their daughter. It was a very sad and confusing time, and it seemed that the only way people could deal with the loss of such a young, intelligent girl was to lay blame on others. Irem, I think, grew out of my memory of these two girls and my own need to understand what would drive such a young girl to kill herself.

RHRC: This is your first book. Can you tell us a little bit about your writing process, and the journey to publication. Did you always want to be a writer?

AD: I wanted to be a painter or a musician, actually. It wasn't until I was in college that I realized I was not a great painter or a talented enough singer to try and make a living doing either. I graduated with a BA in English/Creative Writing and wrote off and on throughout my twenties, but it wasn't until I moved to Istanbul that I really began writing seriously. I wrote an article about the earthquake, which I published in a few newspapers. I colleague of mine, Robert Rosenberg, who was working on a novel at the time, read the article and suggested that I keep writing. We started exchanging our work and having mini-workshops together over beers once a month. Robert applied to and was accepted to the Iowa Writers' Workshop. I applied the following year and was accepted as well.

At Iowa, I wrote every day for the first time in my life and produced a ton of work, writing new pages in the morning and editing in the evening, a process I try to maintain today. I began *Gardens of Water* towards the end of my first year at the workshop just before I met my agent, Dorian Karchmar and signed on with her. I thought I would get the novel done in a year or so, but I didn't have a clue about how complicated writing a novel could be and it actually took me a little over four years to write. Dorian stuck with me throughout the process and provided me with excellent editorial feedback.

I had the arc of the story done about two years into the process, and the last two years I spent reworking the story, cutting whole sections, adding others, moving scenes from one part of the book to another, adding characters and even adding Irem's point of view which didn't exist in the early drafts. As far as publishing the book, I feel very lucky. While I was at Iowa, Ethan Canin had sent a novella of mine to Kate Medina at Random House. She liked the story, and four years later when Dorian sent the manuscript of *Gardens of Water* to her, she remembered me, and the story and she made an offer on the novel very quickly. I thought I'd have to go through months of tortuous rejections, and feared the book might not be published at all. Instead it happened very quickly, and for that I'm very grateful.

RHRC: What other books would you recommend for those who enjoyed *Gardens of Water*? What are some of your favorite novels?

I read a ton of nonfiction for some reason. Nonfiction is more relaxing to me than reading fiction, since when I read fiction, I often find myself thinking more about how the story is put together than simply enjoying it. I recently read Rory Stewart's *The Places in Between*, and thought it was fantastic nonfiction, but with a strong narrative thread. I've been working through Naomi Klein's *The Shock Doctrine*, which I find to be fascinating, scary, and disheartening.

As far as fiction goes, I love most anything by Graham Greene, especially *The Quiet American*, and *The Heart of the Matter*. I think *Gilead* by Marilynne Robinson is brilliant and beautiful. One of my all-time favorite books is *Angle of Repose* by Wallace Stegner. I just finished *The Beautiful Things that Heaven Bears* by Dinaw Mengestu, which I thought was a very powerful debut novel. I also love *Atonement* by Ian McEwan and *Disgrace* by J.M. Coatzee.

RHRC: What's next for you? Can we expect a book that's similar to *Gardens of Water*, or something different?

AD: I'm currently working on two different possible novels, one that is set in Istanbul and focuses on the art scene there, and another that is very different from *Gardens of Water*. For the moment, I'm focusing on the latter as that book is feeling more emotionally compelling to me. I hope to have one of them completed in the next two years.

Questions for Discussion

1. Sinan is a character that is full of contrasts. On one hand, he's indebted to Marcus, and grateful to his help. But on the other hand, he's resentful of Americans, and particularly Marcus's Christian values. How does this inner conflict affect his judgment? Do you think he should have acted differently with regards to Dylan and Irem's relationship? Do you think it would have mattered?

2. Dylan's mother, Sarah dies while saving Ismail from being crushed by the rubble from the earthquake. Do you think Nilufer would have made a similar sacrifice for Dylan?

3. The relationship between Dylan and Irem has been described as star-crossed. In what ways is this true? How is their situation similar to the one in *Romeo and Juliet*? Do you think there was another way their story could have ended?

4. The idea of honor plays a large role in the book. Dicuss the differing standards of honor in men and women, Muslims and Kurds, locals and foreigners.

5. In what ways do Sinan and Marcus represent the larger issues of East vs. West?

6. Music plays a large role in Dylan and Irem's relationship. Why do you think Drew chose Radiohead to be their favorite? Why do you think Irem identified so powerfully with the lyrics? Do you think music is the only thing universal enough to truly connect such different people?

7. In some ways, *Gardens of Water* could be seen as a commentary on the way Americans are often quick to come to the rescue in foreign countries, only to further complicate the situation. Do you think the story would have been different if Dylan and Marcus had been from a different country?

8. At one point in the book, Marcus says to Sinan: "Our children are not ours. That's our mistake. We think they are. It seems so for a while—a few brief years—but they aren't. They never were." Do you think this is true? How does this opinion influence the different ways in which Marcus and Sinan view their children?

9. The story has an almost claustrophobic feeling to it at times, as the world literally crumbles around the characters. Describe the ways in which the different characters feel trapped, and how this affects their actions.

10. What do you think defines a happy life? How do the characters' perceptions of this differ from one another?

11. There's a big contrast between Irem's family duties and her own interests and passions. Discuss the ways in which the story might have been different if it were about a Kurdish boy and an American girl, rather than the other way around?

Alan Drew was born and raised in Southern California and has traveled throughout Europe, Asia and the Middle East. He taught English literature for three years at a private high school in Istanbul, arriving just four days before the devastating 1999 Marmara earthquake. In 2004 he completed a master of fine arts degree at the Iowa Writers' Workshop, where he was awarded a Teaching/Writing Fellowship. He lives with his wife and two children in Philadelphia.